Praise for Libby Fischer Hellmann

A Bitter Veil

"The Iranian revolution provides the backdrop for this meticulously researched, fast-paced stand-alone ....A significant departure from the author's Chicago-based Ellie Foreman and Georgia Davis mystery series, this political thriller will please established fans and newcomers alike."
Publishers Weekly

"Hellmann crafts a tragically beautiful sto   er
sacrificing the quality of her storytellir   he
psychological and emotional conflict paintir   nat
will stick with the reader long after they finis.
Crimespree Magazine

"Readers will be drawn in through the well-researched inside look at Iran in the late 1970s and gain perspective on what the people in that time and place endured. *A Bitter Veil* is so thought-provoking that it especially would be a great title for book clubs to discuss. "
Book Reporter

"*A Bitter Veil...* is a social statement about what can happen when religious fundamentalism trumps human rights, but that's hardly a drawback in this suspenseful, well-researched book. It might even serve as a warning."
Mystery Scene Magazine

Set the Night on Fire

"A top-rate standalone thriller that taps into the antiwar protests of the 1960s and 70s...A jazzy fusion of past and present, Hellman's insightful, politically charged whodunit explores a fascinating period in American history."
Publishers Weekly

"Superior standalone novel...Hellmann creates a fully-realized world...complete with everyday details, passions and enthusiasms on how they yearned for connection, debated about ideology and came to belief in taking risks to stand up for what they believed."
Chicago Tribune

"Haunting...Rarely have history, mystery, and political philosophy blended so beautifully...could easily end up on the required reading list in college-level American History classes."
Mystery Scene

Also by Libby Fischer Hellmann

A Bitter Veil

Set the Night on Fire

THE GEORGIA DAVIS SERIES

ToxiCity

Doubleback

Easy Innocence

◆

THE ELLIE FOREMAN SERIES

A Shot to Die For

An Image of Death

A Picture of Guilt

An Eye for Murder

◆

Nice Girl Does Noir (short stories)

◆

Chicago Blues (editor)

HAVANA LOST

Libby Fischer Hellmann

The Red Herrings Press
Chicago

Cover design by Jeroen ten Berge
Interior design by Sue Trowbridge

ISBN: 978-1-938733-38-3
Library of Congress Control Number: 2013907027

The Red Herrings Press
Chicago, IL
libbyhellmann.com

To Robin and Angela, with fond memories of Regla

"If we open a quarrel between past and present,
we shall find that we have lost the future."
—Winston Churchill

PART ONE
1958 — CUBA

CHAPTER ONE

In the half-second between the explosion and his awareness of it, Federico Vasquez wasn't sure it was real. The flash of white light slicing through the tropical noontime sun could have been an illusion, something he might have missed if he'd blinked. The ear-splitting boom, oddly crunchy, was followed by a deep rumble and could have been a dream. Likewise the wave of hot noise that expanded until a deafening silence took its place. Even the shaky ground, rattling windows, and trembling leaves seemed unearthly and strange.

But the smells confirmed it. The chalky smell of overheated Havana pavement gave way to a gunpowder-y, flinty odor. With it came the scent of char, all of it tinged with a slight alcohol—or was it gasoline?—aroma.

This was no dream.

A scream pierced the silence. Then another. Flames erupted from the bank on the corner. Plumes of orange and yellow climbed the sides of the building, then rose as black smoke. Traffic on both sides of La Rampa skidded to a stop. Horrified pedestrians bolted in a frantic rush. Vasquez was safe, a hundred yards away in the jewelry store he owned, but the terror was contagious, and he started to shake uncontrollably. A sickly sweet odor, like fat sizzling on a grill, filtered through the air.

"*Aaayy Dios Mio!*" he cried out to the only customer in the store. "What is to come of us? It is one thing when the rebels are in the mountains, but when they come to Havana… on La Rampa…" He wrung his hands. "This will not end well."

The customer, Señorita Pacelli, joined him at the front of the store, and together they watched the scene unfold. Vasquez sensed she wasn't fearful, as most women would be. Just quiet.

Within minutes, La Rampa was blocked by police cars, sirens wailing. A platoon of fire trucks, ambulances, and military jeeps followed. The police set up barricades on both ends of the block. A cadre of soldiers tried to manage the crowd, which now that the initial horror had subsided, was huge.

Vasquez glanced over at the young woman. Her composure in the midst of mayhem was unsettling. Then again, she wasn't Cuban. She was an American. Of Italian descent. From a family that would as soon cut off your hand as shake it. But she and her ilk were his best customers these days. He ran his hands up the lapels of his jacket and cleared his throat.

"My apologies, Señorita." He made an effort to bring himself under control. "For my outburst. It was—inappropriate. Are you all right? May I bring you a glass of water to settle your nerves?"

The girl didn't appear as if she needed anything, and she shook her head. With her long black hair, high cheekbones, and slim but curvy figure, she was the kind of girl men stopped to look at. And when they saw her eyes, large and dark and luminous, they usually took a second look. Why, he could—Vasquez stopped himself. He was old enough to be her grandfather. "I will get your watch. It is ready."

"Oh, Señor Vasquez, I don't care about the watch." She looked through the shop's window. The blinding mid-day light offered no respite, and the scene at the bank looked bleak. "Do you think perhaps it was merely an accident? A gas explosion? Something overheated, maybe? That kind of thing has been known—"

"Not possible." He cut her off. "Banco Pacifico is a government bank. Favored by Batista…" he paused, "… and Americans."

The girl looked down. Vasquez couldn't tell if she was angry or ashamed. Señorita Pacelli's father was manager and part owner of La Perla, one of the newest and most luxurious resort casinos in Havana. Before that the man had managed the casino at the Oriental Park Racetrack for Meyer Lansky. Vasquez didn't particularly like Pacelli, but he depended on him. At Pacelli's recommendation, tourists flocked to his store, eager to buy a bracelet, ring, or bauble to remind them of their Havana vacation. Pacelli never asked for anything in return: no kickback, discount, nothing. Still, this girl and her family would always be outsiders. Tolerated, perhaps, because of their money, power, and connections, but like all colonialists, never truly accepted.

The girl craned her neck toward the bank. A sad look swept across her face. "When I was a little girl, my father used to take me with him when he went to the bank. I remember how cool the marble floor was, especially on hot days; how the ceiling fan blades made slow, lazy circles. How I could tell how much taller I'd grown since the last trip by measuring myself against those tall black counters." Her voice trailed off. Vasquez almost felt sorry for her. Then her face took on a determined expression, as if she'd made a decision.

"Señor Vasquez, I will come back for the watch. I want to go down to the bank."

He wagged a stern finger. "No, Señorita. It is not a good idea. Too dangerous. Stay here until the street reopens. I will call your father and tell him you are safe."

"But what if there are people who need help? I could—"

A long black Cadillac with enormous tail fins suddenly slid to the curb, and a man in black pants, white shirt, and black cap jumped out.

The chauffeur. How had he made it onto La Rampa? Vasquez opened the door of the shop. The chauffeur had driven the car onto the sidewalk, that's how. A few nearby shopkeepers and pedestrians who'd gathered to watch the carnage stared. They probably didn't know who the car belonged to, but their subtle hostility indicated they knew it was someone rich. And therefore not to be trusted.

"Too late." The girl squared her shoulders, and went through the door. "Enrico!"

The chauffeur spun around. When he spotted her, a relieved look swept over him. He hurried over. "Señorita Pacelli, you must come with me. Your father is crazy with worry."

"Tell him I'm fine. I want to stay."

"No, Miss Francesca." He gripped her arm. "Your father says you must come home. Now."

Her body seemed to deflate, and she allowed him to lead her to the car. Vasquez knew the chauffeur was, in fact, a bodyguard. Hired to protect her, especially in a situation such as this. Vasquez saw her take one last glance at the bank.

Water poured out of hoses and helped smother the flames. Several people on gurneys were wheeled toward ambulances. The crowd was still growing, and there didn't seem to be any order to it, but the screams and sirens had stopped, replaced by occasional shouts and commands. Two police officials emerged from the bank, carrying what looked to be a dead body. Vasquez turned away.

The chauffeur led the girl to the Cadillac. The engine was still running; Vasquez could see tiny puffs of white coming from the tail pipe. The chauffeur opened the back door, and the girl climbed in.

CHAPTER TWO

La Perla: The Night Before

The ostrich feathers didn't line up. Frankie could tell; she'd seen the show at La Perla at least a dozen times. The showgirls' headdresses were supposed to form a precise, level wave of pink and white that swayed as one when they danced.

"Is that too much to ask?" Marco the choreographer would have pouted in his high-pitched, nasal voice. "After all, you're not wearing much else."

But Marco was on vacation back in the States, and the feathers were a jagged, uneven line. Frankie sipped her daiquiri and tried to figure where the problem was. She peered at the stage.

There. The fourth girl on the left was at least two inches shorter than the others. The girls were supposed to be the same height, five-six, give or take an inch. One of them probably got sick—no surprise in this heat—and arranged for an understudy. The understudy knew the steps, but she wasn't in the right spot. She should have been on an end.

If her father knew, Frankie thought, he would be furious. Everything at La Perla was supposed to be perfect. Elegant. Classy. How often had he berated the staff for a slip that Frankie herself hadn't noticed? She gazed at the girls, mulling it over. Maybe he wouldn't have to know. His eye wasn't as discerning as hers—as far as the shows went—and he had other things on his mind, especially these days. She could drop backstage after this show, alert the stage manager, and everything would be fixed before the midnight show.

Then again, it might not matter. The audience probably hadn't noticed. They weren't watching the girls' headdresses anyway; they were ogling the girls' skimpy bikinis, adorned with glittering sequins. Staring at breasts and

4

legs as the girls sashayed across the stage in the series of sultry poses Marco called a number.

Frankie decided not to do anything. It wasn't that important. She sat back and tried to let the music sweep over her. Like the girls, the music was meant to be seductive—to bolster the sensual, anything-goes atmosphere of Havana. Tease the tourists enough, ply them with liquor, and they'd loosen their wallets at the casinos. That was the theory.

At the same time everyone knew that tourists, especially Americans, weren't ready for *real* Cuban music. They wouldn't understand. Wouldn't appreciate its "foreignness." The band played with energy, adding a Latin riff here and there, but it was controlled. Familiar. The conga drums of the cha-cha—or a more exotic rumba—were tempered by a cheerful sax or trumpet. Benny Goodman meets Santería. Even Frank Sinatra came to Havana to perform. She imagined him trying to perform a tribute to the Santería gods and grinned.

"What's so funny?" A male voice whispered in her ear.

She turned to Nicky and squeezed his hand. Nick Antonetti was in love with Frankie. Everyone knew it; her parents, the maitre d' who gave them the number one table, even the housekeeping staff, who, when they saw them together, were more obsequious than usual. Nick had come down from Chicago to see her during the hottest part of the year.

"No one does that unless they have a reason," her mother had said, smiling, as she fanned herself that afternoon.

"You're saying that because you know his family," Frankie said.

"What's wrong with that? They're good stock. Smart. Not showy." She peered at Frankie. "And you're not getting any younger, Francesca."

"Mama, I'm only eighteen."

"Like I said…" Her mother looked down her nose at her. "I don't know why you don't want to settle down. Nicky is crazy about you." When Frankie didn't reply, her mother added, "The world don't owe you any favors, you know."

Frankie sighed. How many times had she heard her parents say that? That and the "What grocery store does his father own?" refrain her father lobbed every time she dated someone he didn't know.

With Nick, though, her parents didn't have to make annoying comments. The Antonettis and the Pacellis had known each other forever, maybe as far back as the Old Country. Nick was two years older than Frankie; they used to play in the sandbox together when they were babies. Now he was going into his senior year at Penn, the first Antonetti to go to an Ivy League school, his father crowed. He was handsome, with thick blond hair—some Northern Italian in his lineage—green eyes fringed with thick lashes, and a tight, athletic build honed by three years of crew. After college Nick would be going to business school. She was a lucky girl, her mother never failed to remind her, to have hooked such a prize.

Now he draped an arm around her back. "You going to let me in on the joke?" he asked.

She swiveled and flashed him a smile. "It wasn't important."

He kissed her cheek. "As long as you're happy."

Frankie scanned the room. La Perla occupied a full block off the Malecón in Vedado, the up and coming neighborhood of Havana. The resort dripped luxury: a three-story lobby, mirrored walls and ceiling, plush upholstery, and elaborate chandeliers, which were never turned on full, but if they were, would scorch every shadow within a square mile. The casino was large and hired more dealers in Havana than any other place. In fact, La Perla was more lavish than the Riviera or the newly opened Hilton. Plus, it was fully air-conditioned, which helped profits during the off-season. Everyone knew gamblers spent more when they were cool.

"Look at this crowd," Frankie said. "It's the middle of August. Low tourist season. At least it's supposed to be. But the place is packed. Of course, it's not the same crowd you see in the winter—you know, the women who throw on their mink stoles at night after tanning by the pool all day."

Nick cocked his head, as if he was trying to figure out what she meant.

"These tourists are on the budget plan. They couldn't afford to be here otherwise. Still, here they are, in their fancy clothes, dropping all their hard-earned cash at the casino, convincing themselves they're having the time of their lives."

"No one forced them to come," Nick said.

"That's true." She waved her hand. "But then you go outside and see the boys diving off the cliffs over in Miramar—sometimes the Malecón to scrounge a few pennies or nickels. Or the girls in the streets selling themselves for a bowl of rice and beans. It doesn't seem fair that some have so much, and others so little."

Nick pulled her close. "That's what I love about you, Francesca. You have a big heart."

"Mine isn't so big. It's that others' are too small."

A waiter in a tuxedo approached with another round of drinks.

"*Gracias*, Ramon, but I think we're fine." She peered at Nick. "Unless you want another?"

Nick shook his head.

"May I bring you something else?" Ramon asked. "A sweet? Some *helado*?"

"No, *gracias*."

Ramon nodded and gave them his back. Frankie watched him retreat.

"Take Ramon, for instance. I overheard him talking to the maitre d' the other day. His mother is sick, and he had to take her to the hospital. He asked for extra shifts, so he can pay for her medicine. It's being flown in from New York, he says."

"That's a shame." Nick paused. "Look, I don't want to be insensitive, but there will always be the 'haves' and 'have nots.' Class structure depends on it."

"Is that what they teach you in Philadelphia? I doubt the rebels in the Sierra Maestra would agree."

"Ah, the rebels." His expression turned serious. "It always comes back to them." He dropped his arm. "You know what I think, Frankie? Fidel and Che can spend a century trying to change society, but in the final analysis, they will fail."

"How do you know?"

He smiled, but there was a slightly patronizing air to it. As if he was teaching a slow child. "The rebels want to topple the Batista regime, correct?"

She nodded.

"Let's say they succeed."

She crossed herself.

"Yes, I know. But imagine for a moment they do. What do you think will happen?"

She furrowed her brow. "They will create a new democratic state."

"Exactly. But who exactly will run that new state? Fidel, Che, Cienfuegos, Fidel's brother, and the others who've been hiding in the mountains. *They* will become the new ruling class. The privileged ones. And a new class of underlings will take *their* place. Probably those who profited under Batista but whose fortunes will have been confiscated by the rebels. And doled out to the *new* ruling class. So you see? It's simply a re-ordering of class structure. Not a new model."

Frankie thought about it. "I hope I'm not here when it happens."

"*If* it does. But I hope you're not, too. I don't want anything to happen to you. Or your family." Nicky leaned over and kissed her.

His lips were soft and accommodating. Frankie let her own linger on his. Then she pulled back. The walls felt like they were closing in. "Let's go for a walk."

Nick pulled back. "I'm not sure that's a good idea. Your parents told me not to take you out alone. The streets... they are—"

Frankie waved a dismissive hand. "Just along the Malecón. Nothing will happen to us."

"I don't know, Frankie." Nick's voice was uncertain.

"With you protecting me," she said with a smile, "No *mala gente* will come within twenty yards of us. Please."

He gazed at her for a long moment. Then he nodded, as she knew he would, got up from his chair, and guided her out.

***

They linked arms as they strolled east on Havana's boardwalk. A rocky seawall fortified by concrete separated the street from the bay, but in stormy weather, waves often crashed over the top, flooding the street. Tonight, though, the waves were puny. The trade winds, which usually cradled Havana with a gentle breeze, were dead calm, and the heavy air held a salty tang.

The Malecón was mostly a fishing spot by day but a gathering place at night. Frankie and Nick passed a couple locked in a passionate embrace; a young beggar who stared at them blankly; another with shifty eyes that indicated he had a plan. Still others congregated in small groups, singing and strumming guitars.

Beyond the seawall, the bay was inky black. They'd missed the sunset with its pink and orange streaks that dipped so low they seemed to touch the turquoise water. Cuba was the most beautiful place on earth, Cubans would tell you. "Christopher Columbus said there was no prettier place seen by human eyes," Frankie explained to Nick. "That's why they call it the 'Pearl of the Antilles.'"

"Which is why there was no other name for the resort," Nick replied.

She smiled. "Exactly."

They walked on. Frankie loved Cuba. She hadn't really known any other home. Now, though, her parents were pressuring her to go back to the States. If she was going to college, she wouldn't have minded. But she'd been entertaining thoughts of getting a job. Starting her own restaurant, perhaps. Unfortunately, her parents would never permit that. Not that they'd say no, but they'd make something else sound so much more attractive she couldn't afford to turn it down. Like marrying Nick. Becoming a wife and mother.

"You wanna own a restaurant?" she imagined her father saying in his flat Midwest accent with the Italian twist. "Fine, I'll buy you one. But I don't want you working long shifts where you come into contact with all dat—dat…"

"Cooking?" she imagined herself replying. "Kitchen work? Employees?"

Her father would shake his head. "Nah. You got it wrong. You wanna be a success, you gotta be the boss from the get go. You set up a company, get investors, become one of those—whadda they call 'em—entrepreneurs. You get other people to do the hiring, cooking, and all. But you get the profits."

"Once your children are in school," her mother would add coyly.

Frankie's thoughts were cut short by Nick. "Frankie…" He slowed as they rounded a curve on the Malecón. "Frankie…" his voice was soft and husky. "I think you know why I came down here."

She squeezed her eyes shut for an instant. She hoped he didn't see.

"I love you. I have from the first time I met you."

She giggled. "In the sandbox?"

"Well, you know…"

She tried to keep it light. "And when you tried to put a frog down my dress?"

He cracked a smile. "Puppy love."

She giggled again. "And now, I can expect what? Maybe since we're in the tropics, a lizard or scorpion?"

He placed both hands on her shoulders. "You can expect my love, trust and loyalty. Forever. Francesca, will you marry me?"

An uneasy feeling fluttered her stomach. "Oh, Nicky."

"Is that a yes?"

She gently ran her fingers down his cheeks to his jaw. Nick had a pointy chin. It jutted out too far, giving him an aggressive look, but it had a deep cleft in the center, which she loved. He covered her hands with his own.

"Well?"

"If I wanted to marry anyone, it would be you."

He let go of her hands. "But?"

She swallowed. "I'm not ready. There's so much I want to do. You know. Before."

"Like what?"

She looked around the Malecón as if it might hold the answer. "I'm not sure. But I—I've lived here since I was a little girl. It's paradise. But it's not real. I need a taste of the real world before I—I get married. I want to do something. Be someone."

"You are already. To me."

"Oh Nicky, you always say the right thing. You know what I mean. I want to be something besides Tony Pacelli's daughter. I want to travel. Contribute. Participate."

He didn't reply for a moment. Then, "Okay. Let's do it together. I don't have to go to business school."

"Of course you do. Your father—he's so proud of you."

"What about you, Frankie? Are you? Proud of me?"

She smiled up at him. "Oh, yes."

"And you love me?"

She took his cheeks in her hands again and nodded.

"But you don't want to marry me."

"That's not true. I do. But not yet."

He bit his lip, as if he wasn't sure what to say. Then he brightened. "I have an idea. They have this new—arrangement—in the States. They call it being pinned. I give you my fraternity pin. You wear it. It's like—a commitment. More than going steady, but not quite engaged."

"Engaged to be engaged," she said.

He nodded. "Exactly."

"I read about it in a magazine. Didn't Eddie Fisher and Debbie Reynolds do that?"

"I have no idea," Nick said. "But I want us to."

Frankie hesitated. Then she rose on her toes and kissed him. "Oh, *amore*... I think—"

The syncopated thumps of drums cut her off. Frankie pulled back. The drumbeats were coming from a spot nearby that Cubans called the Balcony of the Malecón because of the view. Across from the Hotel Nacional, the Balcony was filled with people. She turned toward the drums. By their sound, they could have been bongos, a *congas* or a *batá*—Cubans played a profusion of percussion instruments. The beats were overlaid with a sweet but mournful guitar. She gazed at the rocks. A muted glow threw irregular, flickering shadows their way. Candles. Someone was dancing in front of them. She took Nick's hand and urged him forward, but he resisted. She moved closer anyway, as if pushed by an unseen force.

A group of young, dark-skinned Cubans sat in a circle. Two men had the drums, another a shaker, yet another a guitar. All of them dipped their heads to the beat, watching a young woman in the middle of the circle. She was tall, with red lips, cinnamon skin, and dark hair. She wore a sleeveless top and a pair of shorts that showed off her legs. She swayed to the beat, arms over her head, sweeping them from side to side. At the same time she fluttered her hands at right angles to her wrists, as if pantomiming a story.

Her eyes were narrowed to slits, and she looked like she was in a trance. But her dreamy expression told Frankie it was a trance of joy, of sexuality, of knowing the men wanted her, but that she wanted the gods of Orisha, the most important god of the Santería religion. Santería, a mix of West African, Catholic, and Native American rites, was full of magic, trances, drums, and dance, and was practiced by many Cubans.

"Look, Nicky," she whispered. "Isn't she amazing?"

His expression was uncertain.

Frankie turned back. The persistent beat, the flicker of the candles, and the sheen of sweat on the woman's face were hypnotic. As the dancer whirled and turned, a primal urge surfaced in Frankie. She felt as if the trance was claiming her too, forcing her hips to move, pushing her forward. Then the dancer's eyes opened, and she looked straight at Frankie. Frankie felt a spark pass between them. The dancer stretched out her arms and beckoned. Frankie stole a glance at Nick. He was frozen.

Frankie crept to the edge of the circle. The men on the ground parted to make room for her. The candles threw shafts of orange and yellow across the group. The dancer continued to beckon and twist and sway. Frankie felt an overpowering urge to give herself up to the music, the glow of the candles, the beat. To fly with the Santería dancer. Pay homage to the god Orisha. All it would take was one step. One tiny step.

CHAPTER THREE

The Next Afternoon

"What were you thinking going out by yourself? You know you're supposed to take Enrico!" Frankie's father bellowed the day after the explosion. Shouting was unusual for Tony Pacelli. He was a bull of a man who made any room he entered seem small. Sturdy and round-faced, with an olive complexion and thick dark hair, he was handsome in a rugged, old-fashioned way, before men took to perfumed after-shave and manicured nails. He'd started out as a bodyguard for a Chicago Outfit boss but was promoted to manager of the Family's restaurant supply business. He did a good job, and didn't skim much off the top, so when Meyer Lansky offered him an opportunity to run a small venture in Havana, Tony jumped. A few years later, he was running La Perla and starting his own Family.

Tony was successful because he gave his employees and capos the impression he didn't care about power. Which, of course, was why it had been given to him. Another reason for his success was his calm demeanor. Pacelli was a soft-spoken man who rarely lost his temper. Over the years he earned the nickname "Silver-tongued Tony."

The only exception was his family. His wife and daughter could send him into fits of passion and anger more violent than a cockfight. And he was angry now. He picked up the morning paper and swatted it against his knee. "Where is your *buon senso*, Francesca?"

"I was there," Frankie replied evenly. "And if you'd seen the rubble, and the flames, and heard the screams, you would have stayed, too. People were trapped. They were dying. They needed help."

Her father snorted and peered at the paper. The bomb blast was front page news, and since the papers were controlled by Batista, the story was covered in lurid detail. Nine people had been killed, mostly bank employees. The police had rounded up several rebels and were "interrogating" them. Which, Frankie knew, was code for torture.

"It's a good thing Enrico showed up when he did," her father said, eyes flashing. "Did you ever stop to think that *you* could have been kidnapped, wounded, perhaps killed by those animals? Francesca, you must remember who you are."

He threw the paper down and stomped over to the balcony of their penthouse. Now that her father managed La Perla, they'd moved from the suburb of Miramar into the resort. The other penthouse was rented out to VIP celebrities who visited the island, and Frankie had spotted a showgirl or two sneaking out in the morning, hair mussed and make-up smeared.

Frankie knew what she was supposed to do. "I'm sorry. It won't happen again."

"You're right." Her father gazed down at the bay and the ocean beyond. "It won't." He turned around.

Frankie cocked her head.

"It's time for you to leave Cuba."

"No." It slipped out. "I can't. I mean, not yet."

Her father came back to the table where she, her mother, and Nick were seated. "You can, and you will." He turned to Frankie's mother. "Marlena, you help her pack. Nick can take her back when he goes."

"But I don't want to go." Frankie turned to her mother. "Mama, you don't want me to leave. I know you don't."

Marlena Pacelli, a small woman with soft features and a quiet manner, always deferred to her husband. But when he wasn't around, she had a wicked sense of humor and the heartiest laugh Frankie had ever heard.

"Mama," Frankie begged. "Please."

Pain shot across her mother's face. Frankie knew what she was thinking. She'd showered all her hopes and dreams on her daughter. She'd borne a son a few years before Frankie, but he died from scarlet fever when he was four. His portrait, painted from a family photo, hung on the wall of their living room. Separation from her only living child would be unbearable.

But her mother surprised her. "*Cara mia*, I want you to be safe, and Havana isn't safe any more." She glanced at her husband. "I'm sure this is only—temporary. Things will settle down. Then you can come back."

"But Mama—"

"*Silencio,*" her father ordered. "Don't you understand you are a target? There's nothing more the rebels would like than to kidnap one of their enemies." He paused. "And you'd better believe we are their enemy." He looked at Nick. "When do you fly back?"

"Tuesday."

Her father nodded. "That's plenty of time to pack, Francesca. Your mother will ship the rest of your things. You can stay with your Aunt Connie. I'll call her this afternoon."

Frankie stiffened. "I can't possibly get everything together in two days. I'll need at least a month."

Her father scowled. "Too long. I want you back in Chicago."

"A few weeks, at least," Frankie said.

"You have until the end of August."

Two weeks. She'd bought herself a little time. She nodded, fighting back tears.

"All right. That's settled." As far as Frankie's father was concerned, the conversation was over. He could take it off his to-do list. His expression turned pleasant; you might almost call it a smile. He shooed them out with his hand. "Now, I know you lovebirds have other things to do." He chuckled. "Don't do anything I wouldn't." Which was a cue for her mother to raise her eyebrows in mock horror. Which she did.

Frankie noted the flush that crept up Nick's neck. He was probably remembering what they did in his room after they came back from their walk on the Malecón last night. Frankie, full of the sensual Cuban music, had been hungry for his touch, and Nick had obliged in a way of which her father would definitely not have approved. Now they exchanged sly smiles.

If he treated her that way every night, maybe it wouldn't be so bad to be married to Nick. In fact, it might be the very thing she needed.

CHAPTER FOUR

That night Frankie and Nick stayed at the hotel. Although La Perla's casino was bigger than the Nacional's and air-conditioned, too many bodies in one space made for a distinctive blend of odors: perfume, hairspray, and smoke, all of it overlaid with losers' sweat. A trio played softly in a corner; her father was experimenting to see if people gambled more with live music. The alternative would be to pipe music in. Frankie didn't care one way or the other. Crooner Tony Martin was performing in the nightclub; she and Nicky would be going to the ten o'clock show.

Underneath the music she heard the chink of martini glasses, the jangle of the slots, the clack of dice on green felt tables, the shuffle of cards, the squeals from people with winning hands. It was barely nine, but already it was packed, and a thick haze of cigarette smoke hovered below the chandeliers. Cigars would be lit later, at which time Frankie would leave. Made from the finest tobacco, from Pinar del Rio and Havana, they were gifts to players from "management," but she couldn't stand the smell.

The women were dressed in low-cut gowns or cocktail dresses and most dripped plenty of pearls and diamonds that caught the light. One or two had mink stoles draped over their shoulders, although it was eighty degrees outside. Most of the men wore suits and ties, but the dealers and Tony Pacelli and Nick were in tuxedos. The more a gambler lost, the more formal and gracious the staff grew, as if elegance and good manners were the consolation prizes for going broke.

Still, the casinos were known for their honesty. Meyer Lansky, the overlord of Havana casinos, insisted on dealers and croupiers with the highest integrity. According to Frankie's father, the Little Man had worked out the probabilities of gambling, and realized the odds always favored the house. There was no need to stack the deck. If anyone was caught skimming, other than Lansky and Batista, of course, they could count on big trouble. With rigorous standards in place, you could almost forget that Havana was run by the largest criminal organization in the world.

Frankie made the rounds on Nicky's arm. She watched an elderly lady with white hair playing roulette. The woman's expression never changed as the marble clattered around the wheel. She moved her chips from one number to another after it settled. At the crap table a couple who couldn't keep their hands off each other whooped with every throw of the dice. A quartet of men at the blackjack table tossed back shots and either joked or swore at the dealer.

Frankie turned to Nick. "You want to play the slots?"

He slipped his arm around her. "I'm not much of a player. And I already have the best hand in the house." He squeezed her shoulder.

A waiter passed carrying a tray of champagne. Frankie lifted two glasses and turned around to hand Nick his, but he was staring at a dark, handsome man playing poker. The man was surrounded by a bevy of young blondes, one of whom lit his cigarette, while another handed him a drink.

"Is that who I think it is? The actor, what's his name?"

"You mean George Raft?"

Nick nodded.

Frankie smiled and handed him a glass of champagne. "It is. He owns part of a casino not far from here. He comes down between movies to say hi and check things out."

"Really? That's strange, you know?"

"What do you mean?" Frankie sipped her champagne.

"Well, he plays gangsters in the movies... and now..." Suddenly Nick cut himself off. "Oh no. I'm sorry. I didn't mean—"

Frankie's smile widened. "Don't worry. I know what you mean." She paused. "Maybe it's good that I'm going back to America."

"Really?"

Frankie looked around. "There's more to life than Havana. This is my father's world. Maybe it's time to discover my own."

"I'll help you every step of the way," Nick said eagerly.

Frankie kissed his cheek.

Nick gazed back at the women around Raft. "Well, at least the guy's in good company."

"Oh, he's small fry. You should see the place when the Rat Pack is here."

"I'll bet." Nick sipped his champagne.

She laughed. "They only come in winter, though."

They kept moving through the crowd. "So why do you want to have a restaurant, Frankie?"

She stopped. "When I was little, I was raised by a Cuban nanny. I was always at her apron strings. She taught me how to cook. Sang me Spanish songs and lullabies. Told me tales of Santería magic. I knew she wasn't my mother, but…" She turned pensive. "Anyway, when I was about six, she got sick. We didn't know what was wrong, but one day she didn't come to work. Or the next. Or the day after. My parents finally had to let her go."

"What happened?"

"I never found out. They wouldn't let me see her. But one day, not long afterwards, they told me she died. I cried for days." She paused. "I thought she was family, you know? And that we were deserting her. But Papa said she wasn't. She was just the help."

Nick brushed a lock of hair off her forehead. "You really do have a big heart."

She went on as if she hadn't heard. "So that's why I was thinking of starting a restaurant. Or maybe a coffee house. For all those Beatniks I keep hearing about."

Nick chuckled. "What if your husband doesn't want you to work? What if he wants you to raise three wonderful children instead?"

Frankie smiled back. "I could manage both. If not, I'm sure my 'husband' would let me know. After all, family is the most important thing."

"Speaking of which…" Nick pointed with his chin. Tony Pacelli stood at the entrance to the casino. Another man in a tuxedo—one of the croupiers, Frankie guessed—was motioning her father over to a corner where a couple of barrel-chested, bull-necked men had flanked two people. Frankie and Nick crept closer. Her father's back was to them.

The man in the center of the tiny group was middle-aged, fleshy, and American. Thinning blond hair fell across his forehead, and his suit, while expensive-looking, hadn't been tailored and bunched in all the wrong places. A young buxom brunette in a tight blue satin sheath and too much make-up was by his side. The man was red-faced and sweating, and the way he swayed back and forth made it clear he'd had a few.

The band went on break, but the noise in the room more than compensated. Despite that, his voice carried over it.

"If you really wanna help me," the man sounded belligerent, "you'll tell me where it is."

Her father replied in a low voice. "Not here, Mr. Whittier. Not now."

"What the hell you think I came to Havana for? The weather?"

Her father gently took the man's arm. "Why don't you and your lady friend come with me and we'll figure this out."

The man shook off her father's hand. "Bullshit. All I want is the fucking address of the sex house." He made a sloppy gesture toward the brunette and leered. "So I can watch her get fucked."

"Please, Mr. Whittier. Keep your voice down. I told you we don't furnish those recommendations to our guests."

"Then you better talk to your bellman, 'cause he sure as hell does." The man began to sway again. "How did I know I'd lose the damn card?"

"Mr. Whittier, I think it's time you came with us." Pacelli's voice was still quiet and relaxed, as if he had all the time in the world.

"Who do you think you are? The fucking pope? You're a stupid guinea. An asshole gangster. Get away from me!"

Her father nodded at the two muscle men, who gripped the man under his shoulders.

Whittier squinted at one goon, then the other. "Lemme go. Unless you're taking me where I wanna go."

"What is he talking about?" Nick whispered.

Frankie led him away from the group. "There are private homes in Havana where tourists can watch live sex shows. Even choose a woman or man who will have sex in front of them. We don't approve, of course. But the tourists... they think they can do whatever they want in Havana. Anything goes."

"No wonder your father wants you to go home."

"This city is no different than any other place. If you look, you will find it." She slipped her hand in his. "But we don't need to stay here. Come. Let's go see Tony Martin."

But Nick stayed her hand and watched as the men dragged Whittier, still shouting and cursing, out of the casino. His girlfriend was told to remain where she was. She looked frightened and alone.

"Where are they taking him?" Nick asked.

"Where do you think?"

Nick blinked. "Why not just kick him out?"

"Because he's not like us, Nicky. He's a pig."

"He wouldn't be the first pig to come to Havana."

"Yes, but my father thinks he needs to be taught a lesson."

CHAPTER FIVE

Two days later, Frankie took Nick to the airport; or rather, accompanied Enrico as he drove Nick in the Cadillac. Havana was home to thousands of Buicks, De Sotos, Oldsmobiles, and Packards with huge fins and lots of chrome. Their sheer size made traffic sluggish, although it wasn't as bad as rush hour in Chicago, Nick said. Still, the preponderance of American cars, casinos, entertainers, and businesses that migrated from the mainland helped fuel the notion that Havana was simply another American outpost.

Back at La Perla, Frankie went down to the storage area in the hotel's basement to get her suitcases. Her mother, a notorious pack rat, had kept all her childhood possessions: her roller skates, the hula hoop that she had to have after seeing it on Candid Camera, her books, her records. The furniture from the house in Miramar was here, too: a large floral couch and matching chair, not as elegant as the furnishings in the penthouse, and her old four-poster bed, the one with a pink and orange canopy that made her feel like a princess.

And there was the cabinet that held her collection of painted snails. Unique to Cuba, the snails weren't really painted, but their shells were so colorful and intricately designed that legend said they'd been painted by the sun. Over the years, they'd become highly sought after and quite valuable, so her parents, and then Frankie herself, made it a point to buy every snail they found. Her father had paid to have a glass-fronted display case made. It had hung on her bedroom wall.

She knelt beside a box packed with the snails and unwrapped one. It was bright yellow with a perfect white swirl around its middle, and another deep blue swirl near the top. She clasped it to her chest, unprepared for the wave of sadness that swept over her. Her entire life in Cuba was spread out on this floor. And she was going to leave it, probably forever. She lightly caressed everything in reach. Mama had to ship everything back to the States. Otherwise, what record would there be of her existence?

After a moment, she reluctantly rewrapped the snails and returned them to the box. She stood and pulled out two big suitcases. She *was* looking forward to going back. Rock and roll had become a huge phenomenon in the States. Nick kept telling her about Elvis Presley, who'd been inducted into the army a few months earlier, and there was Buddy Holly, Ricky Nelson, and Johnny Mathis. She couldn't wait to see them. Of course, they'd get front row tickets for any show or sporting event they wanted. It wouldn't be all bad.

She started to drag the suitcases out, but they were heavier than she expected so she decided to ask one of the hotel workers to bring them up to the penthouse. She took the stairs back up to the lobby and cut across to the pool, hoping to run into Ramon, Enrico, or one of the other men who worked at La Perla.

She blinked as she went outside. There was no breeze, and the heat was so ruthless that waves of hot air rose from the concrete. The kidney-shaped pool was enormous. A bar was built in at one end so that guests could sip a daiquiri or mojito while in the water. A kiddie pool was beside the big one, and dozens of lounge chairs sprawled on the patio. Everything—tiles, umbrellas, and chairs—was an artificial blue or yellow or white. The pool was filled mostly with women, and the hum of conversation was punctuated by children's laughs. Husbands and fathers were undoubtedly at the tables.

The waiters serving drinks and sandwiches poolside wore white jackets with long sleeves, bow ties, and pants. They had to be sweltering, Frankie thought as she scanned the scene. She didn't see any familiar faces, so she went back inside. When she pushed through the door, the contrast between the outside glare and the dim interior temporarily blinded her, but she could hear a conversation a few feet away. Men. Talking in Spanish. Almost whispering. As her eyes adjusted, she saw two men in a corner on chairs they'd pushed so close together their knees touched. Although Frankie had attended the American school, she was fluent in Spanish, and she picked up that one of the men needed something the other could supply. She looked over.

One of the men was Ramon, the waiter at the nightclub whose mother needed medicine. He must be working the day shift. Frankie had never seen the other man. She slowed to take a closer look, but as she did, he turned toward her, and their eyes met.

He wasn't that handsome. He had thick, dark, unruly hair that refused to lie straight and stuck out at all angles, and his Roman nose was too big for his face. His lips were full, his chin unimpressive. His skin was olive, and in the dim light, appeared sallow. But it was his eyes—dark and smoky—and the expression in them that made it impossible for her to look away. Insolent. Challenging. As if she had crossed a line by staring at him, and he would show her. She couldn't remember anyone looking at her that way. Then his expression softened. It was subtle, but she could tell he liked what he saw. Her pulse sped up.

A glint of amusement seemed to fly out from him and connected with her. She found herself firing it back. Communication received and returned. It couldn't have lasted longer than a second, but Frankie felt as if they'd shared an intense conversation. Then she had been released. But from what? Who was this man?

She turned toward Ramon, who had been watching their exchange. His tone changed, and he lowered his voice. He was telling his friend that she was the boss's daughter and not to mess with her. She expected the friend to show surprise, perhaps embarrassment, but he did something that flustered her. Instead of looking away or down at the floor, his amusement deepened. As if he'd seen straight into her soul.

Finally he broke eye contact and whispered to Ramon. Frankie couldn't hear what, but Ramon's reaction was to violently shake his head. His friend repeated whatever he'd said. Again Ramon shook his head, this time lifting his palms as if to ward off danger. Frankie knew she should leave. She stayed.

The man rose from his chair. He was about three inches taller than her, and his body didn't carry an ounce of fat. He walked—no—sauntered over.

"Señorita Pacelli," he said. His voice was deep but melodious.

Frankie cocked her head. "*Sí?*"

He took her hand, making sure he kept his eyes on her.

"I am Luis," he said in Spanish. "Luis Perez."

She replied in Spanish. "And what brings you to La Perla, Señor Perez?"

"I am visiting my friend, Ramon."

"I see." The words seemed inadequate. Insubstantial. She turned to Ramon. "How is your mother?"

"Better, Señorita. *Gracias.*" Was there a touch of disdain in his voice?

"*Bueno.*" She realized Luis was still holding her hand. She eyed it.

He let it go. "I am honored to make your acquaintance."

She raised her hand to her cheek. "I must go." She turned away, wondering why she'd come downstairs, and started toward the elevator. She remembered at the last minute and spun around. "Ramon, there are two suitcases in the storage area. They're too heavy for me. Could you please bring them upstairs?"

"Of course, Señorita."

"You are going on a trip?" Luis asked.

Flummoxed, Frankie ran a hand through her hair. She didn't know this man. It was none of his business. "I'm moving back to the States."

"Ahh…" Luis fell silent.

For some reason she felt compelled to explain. "It's my father. He insists." Now, why had she said that?

"I see." Another pause.

Frankie's stomach churned. She wanted to tell him more. But more of what? She stole another look at him. He was still watching her.

He took her cue. "It was a pleasure to meet you," he said and stepped back to let her pass. "Perhaps our paths will cross again."

***

Frankie wasn't hungry that night. Restless, she paced from the patio door to the other end of the apartment. Her father was at the casino, her mother visiting a friend. She turned on the television but snapped it off after a minute. She wasn't in the mood for "I Love Lucy" tonight. Ricky Ricardo wasn't your average Cuban. Hollywood had stripped away his Cuban *pasión*, except for the silly accent.

She took the phone into her room and closed the door. Nick was back in Chicago; he wouldn't be going back to Penn for a few more weeks. She dialed his number, made pleasantries with his mother, waited anxiously until he came on the line.

"Frankie? Is everything okay?" He sounded breathless, like she might have interrupted a game of basketball.

"Do you remember what we did the other night?" she said by way of introduction.

Nick's voice grew husky. "Oh yes."

"Can we do that again?"

"Oh yes."

"I want you to imagine we're together. Right now."

"Frankie…" His voice rose. "Our parents."

"Mine aren't here."

"Mine are."

"Then get on the upstairs extension and take the phone into your room. I want you, Nicky."

"Oh, Francesca. If only I could. Darling." His breathing grew heavy.

She smiled when she heard that and imagined what she would do to him if they were together. Then, suddenly, she caught herself. What kind of wanton creature was she becoming? "I'm sorry," she said softly.

"Are you kidding? I love this." Nick replied. "By the way, I left the pin in an envelope by your bed. Did you find it?"

She hadn't, but now she scrounged around the bedside table. There, in a corner held down by the lamp. "Yes. I found it." She reached for it and tore open the envelope.

"Put it on. And then tell your parents what it means."

"Oh Nicky, I miss you so much."

"I love you, Frankie."

"Me too, you."

She hung up and felt inside the envelope, withdrew a small lapel pin. Diamond-shaped, with three Greek letters embossed in gold on a black background. She turned it over. A tiny clasp on the back could be attached to the collar of her blouse. In addition, a delicate chain extended about two inches to a second, smaller clasp. She turned it over again and gazed at it. This pin was her future. She would go back to America, and in time, Nick Antonetti, a kind, handsome, intelligent man who was crazy about her, would be her husband. They would make love every night and have lots of children. She couldn't do better than that, could she?

CHAPTER SIX

Although the penthouse was air-conditioned, Frankie spent a restless night. She rose at dawn, sweaty and hot, with the sheets tangled between her legs. She showered, dressed, and decided to take a walk. A cup of strong Cuban coffee would set her right.

She crept out of the penthouse, taking care not to wake her parents. They would go crazy if they knew she was going out alone. Again. The day had dawned clear and surprisingly crisp, and it was an easy trek east on the Malecón. In the distance were the fortresses first built by the Spanish in the 1500's, but before she reached them she turned south towards Havana Vieja and threaded her way through cobblestone alleys that looked like they belonged in Europe.

She was drawn to the narrow streets crammed with apartment buildings, homes, monuments, and churches, most of which had elbowed each other for centuries. Every once in a while a small courtyard would appear, giving the illusion of space, but it was just that, an illusion. Havana Vieja was the most densely populated area of the city, but the swarm of people who usually packed the streets hadn't yet arrived.

Frankie made her way to the Plaza de la Catedral, dominated by the Cathedral of San Cristóbal and its baroque exterior and towers, one larger than the other. She slipped inside and lit a candle, asking the saints to bless her journey to America. A sign for a mass later that morning was posted, but she didn't wait. As she exited the church she saw three young people who looked like students milling around the broad stone plaza. The University of Havana was closed. Frankie wondered what they were doing up so early.

As she turned right down a narrow street, a sudden movement behind her made her spin around. No one was there. How strange. She'd been sure she'd felt a presence. She pulled her cardigan tight. Maybe it wasn't such a good idea to go out by herself. But she hadn't dressed up, and she wasn't wearing makeup. She should be able to pass. Just another Cuban woman shopping after morning mass.

The aroma of rich coffee from a small café drifted into the street. Frankie slowed, looked both ways, then went in. The café wasn't much more than a counter and four tables, but most Cuban restaurants were run by families who lived in the back or up the stairs. She sat at a table. A radio in the back spewed out anti-Batista blather. An elderly woman with gray hair and a thick waist emerged from the back.

"*Café, por favor.*"

The woman nodded and disappeared. The radio went silent. A moment later, a little boy—possibly her grandson—came out gripping the cup and saucer, as if dropping it would incur the eternal wrath of his *abuela.* Frankie thanked him, dug in her bag for a peso, and handed it over. The boy grinned. His two front teeth were missing.

She sipped her coffee and read today's *El Diario,* which she'd picked up in the lobby. The past year had been volatile, marked by sudden attacks like the bank bombing and brutal reprisals by the Batista regime. The rebels had torched sugar crops, set fire to an Esso refinery, and periodically blocked the roads outside Havana. The army mounted a campaign in the Sierra Maestra Mountains to wipe them out, but the rebels survived. Then last month the rebels had won a surprising victory at the battle of El Jigue. A story in today's paper reported that Fidel would broadcast a speech to the entire island on a rebel radio station. The entire island!

On the other hand, the police kept arresting rebels whose pleas of innocence usually changed to guilty after a few days. And through it all, the tourists kept coming, prompting her father and his associates to build more resorts and casinos. No one she knew thought the revolution would succeed, and people carried on as if the violence was simply a fly in the ointment of progress. Still, her father's increasingly grim expression—and the fact that he wanted her out of Cuba—told her he was worried.

He'd nagged her mother to leave too, but she announced she would never leave Cuba without him and that the conversation was over. Marlena Pacelli, an Italian-American of Sicilian descent, knew her place, and it was with her husband, no matter what.

It must be nice to have that clarity, Frankie thought. It wasn't that she *didn't* know her place, but why did they expect her to settle down right away? Why couldn't she do something else—at least for a while? If she got a job, her parents wouldn't have to know, and by the time they found out, she might even have been promoted. She smiled, warming to the thought, and raised her cup to her lips.

"And what does Señorita Pacelli find so amusing?"

Startled, she looked up and nearly dropped her cup. Luis Perez, the man who'd been talking to Ramon yesterday, stood by her table. It was all she could do not to let her mouth fall open. She slowly lowered the cup onto the saucer, hearing the clink of china on china. How did he know she was here?

"You've been following me."

He nodded.

"Where did you pick me up? At the Cathedral?"

"At the hotel."

She crossed her arms. The concept of kidnapping was no longer theoretical. Her parents were right. She steeled herself for what was surely coming. At the same time, she'd be damned if she'd reveal any fear. "Leave me alone or I'll have you arrested."

The old lady came out from behind the shop. Her eyebrow arched, and she eyed Luis. "Is there a problem?"

Luis raised his hands in a gesture of surrender. "No, Señora. There is no problem. I mean the Señorita no harm." He turned to Frankie. "I—I wanted to talk to you. Alone. Without Ramon."

Frankie looked into his eyes. For a moment her world tilted. Then it tilted back. She didn't know this man. He could be anyone. He was dangerous.

He pulled out a chair and sat down. "It is all right?"

This time her mouth did open. The nerve! The old woman planted her hands on her hips and cocked her head, as if to ask, "Should I call the police?"

Luis gazed at her, the smile more in his eyes than his lips. Frankie gazed back. "Thank you. It won't be necessary."

The woman hesitated, then turned and disappeared.

"Who are you? What do you want? Why were you at *La Perla* yesterday?"

"All questions I intend to answer. But first I clearly need to win your trust. I hope you will permit me to try."

Frankie hardly knew this man, but she'd known he'd say that. They sat across the table, a distance between them, but something was drawing them together. A Santería god working its magic?

He smiled, as if reading her mind. "You feel it too," he said. "You will deny it, but you have been struck by *el flechazo*. And wounded by its sweet poison."

She didn't answer. She sensed that this man was going to change her life. At the precise moment she knew where it was heading. She felt untethered, as if her body had become too light for earth's gravity. She searched for something to say. Nothing came out.

"*Te comieron la lengua los ratones?*" He laughed. Did the mice eat your tongue?

She made a last effort to assert control, but it was just for show. "How can you be so sure I want anything to do with you?"

"If I am wrong, you should get up, leave a few pesos for the coffee, and go back to your hotel."

Her unsettled feeling grew. He was right. She should leave. Retreat to familiar territory. To stay was madness.

She stayed.

"I am a law student," he finally said. "Or was. I left university before it closed. Ramon and I have known each other since we were boys and pulled the tails off lizards together."

"Why were you at La Perla?"

He hesitated, then leaned forward. As he did, his scent drifted toward her. Dark and male. With a touch of oil. So different than Nicky's.

"I have recruited Ramon to our cause," he said softly.

Frankie felt as if a steel blade had sliced through the table. "You are with the rebels."

Luis laced his hands together. Only then did she realize he was as nervous as she. He had taken a huge risk. She looked away.

"You're going to kidnap me, aren't you? Spirit me off to the mountains and use me for ransom."

"Look at me, Francesca."

A shiver ran up her spine as he called her name. Rolling it over his tongue like music. She looked back.

"I will never harm you. And I want nothing from you. " He paused. "No. That is not true. I want everything."

For the second time in a minute she couldn't catch her breath. He leaned forward and stretched his hand toward hers, palm up. Then, as if her hand had a mind of its own, it slid forward and covered his.

***

Tony Pacelli didn't particularly like Meyer Lansky. No one did. People respected him. And feared him, especially after his buddy Bugsy Siegel was whacked and people figured out Lansky himself was behind it. When it happened, more than a few were surprised, mostly because Lansky wasn't a *paisano*. He was a Jew from New York. A small man with small eyes, a big nose and ears. His hair was slicked back, he wore nice suits, and he kept himself well-groomed. But Tony rarely saw him smile, except when he was with his wife Teddy. He was all business. Still, Pacelli had to admit that Lansky had made him rich. Thanks to him, Pacelli owned a good chunk of La Perla, and had been invited to invest in other projects, most of them outside Cuba.

So when Lansky called for a meeting that afternoon, Pacelli made sure his office was stocked with fresh coffee, booze, and water. Whatever the Little Man wanted. He put on a fresh shirt.

As usual Lansky was punctual, arriving on the dot of four with two beefy bodyguards. Like him, the bodyguards were dressed in suits and ties despite the temperature, which had to be well into the nineties. Pacelli stuck out his hand. Lansky gave it a weak shake. Pacelli motioned him to a small circular table. "This is a rare honor," he said, smiling.

Lansky shot him a look that was half-simper, half-grimace. Pacelli was relieved. With people he didn't know or didn't like, Lansky remained stone-faced.

"What can I get you?"

Lansky lifted his palm. "Nothing." He settled in the chair across from Pacelli. "Our friend wants us to increase his cut."

"El Presidente?" It was well known Fulgencio Batista had practically begged Lansky to set up shop in Havana years ago. Lansky complied, emerging from the shadows of the U.S. Mafia to create a gambling mecca on the island, all of it legal. It was also well known that in return for allowing Lansky and his friends to control the casinos and racetracks, Batista took a healthy piece of the action.

"He's becoming insatiable," Lansky said.

"You think he's protecting himself in case—" Pacelli was reluctant to say the words "rebels" or "revolution" for fear it would lend them too much credibility.

"I can't answer that. I don't talk to him much."

Pacelli hid his surprise. He had assumed Lansky and Batista were joined at the hip.

"But our partners up north are worried. With Castro all over the New York Times, and the pullout of the Vegas operators, we're in a tough spot."

In a move designed to improve the struggling Vegas casino business, the Nevada Gaming Commission had decreed last April that anyone holding a license in Nevada would have to pull out of Cuba if they wanted to remain in Vegas. Several operators did.

"I hate to admit it," Pacelli said grimly, "but bookings at La Perla are down for the first time."

Lansky scowled. "How much?"

"Not much. Maybe eight per cent."

"I'm hearing that from Santo as well." Tony knew he was talking about mobster Santo Trafficante, who was also heavily invested in Havana. "Well, we'll drop our prices. The airlines will go along."

"What happened to the meeting in the Dominican Republic?"

It was an open secret that given the problems in Cuba, Lansky,

Trafficante and others were looking for opportunities elsewhere in the Caribbean.

Lansky leveled a strange look his way. "It didn't turn out the way we hoped."

Pacelli knew enough not to pursue it.

"I don't see a way around this," Lansky said. "For the time being, we'll have to cut a few corners. Cough up another twenty-five K to feed the beast."

"A month?"

"A week."

Pacelli rolled his eyes.

"Yeah, I know. Used to be all we hadda do was sell a few more shares to our friends. But now, with the Vegas situation, a lot of people are on the sidelines."

"They're waiting to see what happens."

"It's a goddammed shame. But don't worry, Tony. We're still the best investment this island has ever seen. Even if Castro deposes Batista, he'll never close the casinos. We make too much money. Think about it. We've brought stability and progress to Cuba. And not just us. The banks, the electric company, United Fruit. Esso. Castro is not a stupid man. We'll have a new partner. You'll see."

He smiled then, forcing Tony to respond with one of his own. But inside Pacelli was incredulous. Did Lansky really believe what he was saying? Tony's sources told him Batista's chances of surviving were two to one. Against. Hadn't Lansky been listening to Castro? Overthrow the regime. Nationalize. Reform. Share the wealth with Cubans, not foreigners. Was he nuts? Or had self-interest made him blind and deaf?

Lansky rose from his chair. "Sorry about this, Tony, but it's just temporary. Until this business is resolved."

"I understand."

Lansky went on. "My wife Teddy is in Florida for a while. You thinking about relocating your family?"

"My daughter's leaving next week. My wife... well," he said, "she won't go."

Lansky clapped him on the shoulder, not an easy thing since Pacelli towered over him. "You got a good one, Tony. Count your blessings."

Pacelli watched him go. Then he went back to his desk. He thought about what Lansky had said. The Little Man wasn't really interested in Pacelli's future, no matter what he claimed. No one would look out for Tony except Tony. He'd worked hard. He'd achieved. He wouldn't let it slip through his fingers without a fight. He picked up the phone. He hesitated, then dialed a number. This would change everything.

"You know that proposition we've been talking about?" he said in his quiet, silky voice. "Well, I'm in."

CHAPTER SEVEN

Frankie couldn't decide what to wear. Usually she threw on whatever was clean—she changed clothes several times a day during the hot season. This morning, though, she tried on at least three different outfits before settling on a pair of blue shorts, white blouse, and sandals. She paid special attention to her make-up, ensuring that her Maybelline mascara, eyeliner, and eye shadow were perfect. She swept her hair up in a twist, put on a hat and sunglasses, and sneaked out of La Perla before her mother was awake, a pattern she had followed every day this week.

Luis was waiting for her on the Malecón as usual, and when he saw her, his face brightened as if lit by a morning sunrise. He took her arm and steered her down the street.

"Where are we going today?" Frankie asked.

"You will see." He squeezed her arm. "It is a surprise."

Each day they had explored different neighborhoods of Havana. Frankie thought she knew the city, but Luis's knowledge of Havana's history and architecture was deep. Understanding the detail on a church gargoyle, or learning about the past through his eyes made her realize how little she knew about her adopted homeland. Except for her Cuban nanny, her parents had kept her sheltered from the "real" Cuba. Now that she was finally discovering it, she was losing it. She almost laughed at the irony.

When they weren't talking about Havana, Luis discussed subjects no one had before. He would lay out his views, about reason versus passion, for example, or whether God exists, then ask what she thought. For the first time she felt as if her opinion mattered. She felt adult. As she grew more comfortable with him, she told him things she'd never told anyone, even Nicky. How she felt about her father's business—she was ashamed, yet at the same time curious; how did it work? Who really made the decisions? How she was reluctant to settle down; how she wanted to do something worthwhile.

One day while they were sipping coffee at an outdoor café, he pulled out a pad of paper and charcoal.

"What are you doing?" she asked.

"The light is perfect. I want to sketch your face."

"You are an artist, too?"

"I enjoy drawing."

"Will you give it to me when it's done?"

He tilted his head. "No. I will keep it to remember you by."

Now they struck out toward the mouth of Havana Bay. Across the water in East Havana were the La Cabaña hills. "I thought I would be able to borrow a car, but it didn't work out."

"That's all right," she said. She preferred walking, where every once in a while their shoulders touched, or she caught a trace of his scent. Sitting in a car would keep them too far apart.

"So, we will take the ferry." A few minutes later they boarded the slip at the port outside Havana Vieja. As they walked past one of the crew, the man nodded at Luis. Luis nodded back.

"Who's that?" Frankie asked.

"I don't know," Luis said. "A friendly soul."

They stood side by side as the ferry chugged across the bay. A breeze lifted Luis's hair and left it disheveled. She wanted to reach out and run her fingers through it.

Luis had been a perfect gentleman. He hadn't made any advances, and when they parted for the day, he left her with only the lightest of kisses on both cheeks. In fact, Frankie was worried. Men made passes at her all the time. Was Luis less infatuated now that he knew her better? He was used to university women, women who challenged him intellectually, maybe sexually as well. With her high school education, she was no match for them. And while she was now discovering how much she liked sex, Nicky had been her only lover. She looked out over the water. How strange to feel inadequate, after feeling like a princess most of her life.

"Francesca..." His voice cut into her thoughts.

She turned. "I'm sorry."

"Where were you?" He gazed at her as if trying to see inside her mind.

"It was—nothing."

He pointed to the stone fortress on top of the hill they were passing. "You see El Morro?"

She nodded. You couldn't walk down the Malecón without seeing El Morro. The fortress and the lighthouse towering over it, guarding the mouth of the bay as it had for centuries. Over time it had become a famous landmark; the stuff of picture postcards and photos.

"It is the second oldest fort in all the Americas. It was designed and built by an Italian, you know."

"I didn't."

"You see? Your ancestors have deep roots in Cuba." He smiled. "It took eleven years to build."

Luis swept his arm up. "About a kilometer away—you can see it from here—is La Cabaña. It was built two hundred years after El Morro. At one time it was the largest colonial military installation in the New World. It's actually a miniature city."

"Are we going there?"

"No." His face darkened. "It is being used as a prison by Batista."

Frankie turned away. The waves sparkled, as if all the stars from heaven had dropped to earth. A few gulls swooped and wheeled. Luis was from Oriente, he'd told her the other day, a mostly rural province on the eastern end of the island. Fidel Castro was from nearby Biran, also in Oriente. Luis's father, like Fidel's, had cut sugar cane. But Fidel's father had become wealthy. Luis's had not.

"Did you know Fidel?" Frankie had asked.

"Not really," he replied. "We played baseball together." Later, though, like Fidel, Luis went to the university in Havana to study law, determined to bring himself and his family a better life. It was at university, he told her, that he began to see how wide was the disparity between rich and poor, the powerful and the powerless, and how it was all fueled by graft.

Now they disembarked from the ferry and climbed a series of steep stone steps. At the top of the steps they walked to the El Morro fortress. He faced La Cabaña with a grim expression.

"Why are we here?" she asked. "You must hate this place."

"It reminds me of the work we have yet to do."

She groped for a respectful way to say it, but the words wouldn't come. Finally she blurted it out. "Why do you fight? Why can't you go to another university? Maybe one in the States. Your English is good. I could—"

He cut her off. "You could what? Use your family's influence to get me into an American university?" He scoffed. "Then I become part of the problem, not the solution."

She felt stung. He led her to a nearby bench and sat down, patting the space beside him. She sat.

"Listen, Francesca. The more I see, the more I realize that Cuba today is simply a colony to America."

Is that so bad? she thought.

Reading her mind, he said, "Which might not be so bad—theoretically. There are American companies that treat Cubans well. The problem is that Batista treats U.S. corporations like mobsters. Yes. Like your father. No taxes, sweetheart deals all around, everything oiled by payoffs. Your country occupies ours, economically speaking."

"So let Fidel and Che take care of him. No one likes Batista, including my father. Why do you have to be involved?"

"Unless all of us work together, nothing will change. The system is broken. Cuba needs a new one."

"But why must violence be a part of it? I was there when the bomb exploded at the bank last week. People died. It was terrifying."

"No one will react otherwise. And…" he paused… "you can't deny there is violence in your life as well."

"How would you know?"

He gave her a smile. "If there is not, your life is too protected."

"I'm spending time with you."

"And for that I am thankful." He smiled for an instant. Then it faded. "The Cuba you know—or think you know—will disappear. The decadence, the corruption, is so pervasive it is like the last days of the Roman Empire. And it's not only the regime. The poison has spread through the culture. The tourists pour in, spend their money in a frenzy, determined to flout every norm of social behavior. For them Cuba is a playground where they can do what they want, no matter how obscene, and go home without accountability. That is not the homeland in which I want to live."

Frankie flashed back to the piggy man who wanted to see the sex show. She thought about the shows at La Perla. The girls were wearing less and gyrating more. But that's what customers wanted. And you had to give the customers what they wanted, her father said. "But how will you stop it? The people I know—"

"The people you know have a vested interest in maintaining the status quo." He paused. "You're right about one thing, though. Most Cubans despise Batista. It is sad, really. If he had shared with the people, improved conditions for the poorest of the poor, there would be no need for Fidel or Che. Or me."

She was quiet for a moment. "If you succeed, you will destroy my family."

He turned to her. "Francesca, I know the risks you are taking to be with me. I live in fear that any moment, you will wake up and realize how impossible it is for us to be together. But you will be leaving Cuba soon. And so it will end."

She blinked. "Then why continue to see me? Why delay what you know is coming?"

He hesitated, then tapped his chest. "I cannot stay away."

"Oh Luis." Frankie reached for his hand and squeezed. She felt like she might cry. But if she started, she didn't think she would stop.

***

"No more!" Frankie's mother thumped her hand on the dinner table that night. "You will not leave La Perla without my permission. Or your father's. And certainly not without Enrico."

Frankie, who had been picking at her veal and pasta—she had no appetite since meeting Luis—cringed. She'd only seen her mother this angry once before, the day Frankie beat up a boy at school after he called her a wop. Her mother's cheeks were flushed, her neck muscles taut. The only consolation was that her father was downstairs in the casino. If his fury had been part of the mix, there would have been an explosion.

"You were gone all day," her mother said. "No one knew where you were. I was terrified. If I had told your father, he would have called the police."

Relief washed over Frankie. "You didn't... tell him?"

Her mother arched her eyebrows. "Not yet."

"Please don't." It came out fast.

Her mother eyed her, her suspicion obvious. "Why? Where have you been?"

Frankie blinked. Whatever her mother knew, or thought she knew, had to be managed. She couldn't tell her about Luis.

"I—I went shopping at El Encanto. And then I went to La Cabaña." That, at least, was the truth.

"La Cabaña? What in the *Nome di Dio* were you doing there?"

"Mama, I'm leaving the only home I've ever really known." Frankie was surprised how easily the lie came. "And—well, I don't think I'll be back."

Her mother crossed herself. "Don't say that."

Frankie went on. "I want to revisit all the places I've come to love—you know, one last time."

Her mother's spine could have been a steel rod. "Places..." she spat out. "Or people? Someone saw you with a man. In Old Havana."

Think fast, Frankie thought. "It couldn't have been me. I wasn't there."

"You went to El Encanto." Her voice was sharp. "Where are the things you bought? Where are the packages?"

Frankie realized she was teetering on the edge of a trap. Better cut it off. "I didn't see anything I wanted. Who said they saw me?"

"That does not matter."

"Well, whoever it was is mistaken. I was alone." Did it sound as patently false to her mother as to her? Apparently.

"Francesca, are you carrying on with a local?"

Frankie drew herself up. "Of course not."

Her mother murmured something. Frankie couldn't quite catch it. It was probably a prayer, meant to ward off a hex. "When did you last talk to Nicky?"

Frankie was taken aback. She hadn't thought about Nicky in days. Luis filled her up. "It was—the other day."

Her mother's eyes narrowed. "Francesca, I don't know what you're doing, and I don't want to. But it must stop. Immediately. It is not seemly. Do you know what will happen if your father finds out?"

He'd keep her a prisoner until she boarded the plane for Chicago, Frankie thought. Her mother knew it too. She obviously knew more as well. Or suspected it. Frankie had underestimated her.

Now she sagged in her chair. "You're right, Mama," she said meekly.

"So, you will take care of—this situation?"

She understood what her mother was saying. She nodded.

Her mother's tone softened. "You must be careful, *Cara Mia*. There are only a few days left."

Frankie knew. She'd been counting the hours and minutes, willing time to stop. It didn't of course, and now there were only four days until she left Cuba. She hadn't told Luis.

CHAPTER EIGHT

They'd planned to meet the next day at the usual spot on the Malecón, but after the conversation with her mother, Frankie knew she had to cancel—or at least postpone—their date. She told her mother she was going down to the nightclub to help the girls put on their costumes. She'd done that when she was younger—thinking in an adolescent way that being around them, touching their outfits, would confer their glamour and sophistication on her.

Downstairs she searched for Ramon. He was a small, wiry man, with sandy hair, hooded eyes, and a weak chin. He wasn't bad looking, but his lack of height gave him a chip on his shoulder, Frankie thought. She'd rarely seen him smile. She found him in the nightclub with two other waiters, all in white jackets and black pants.

She went up to him, smiling prettily. "Ramon, I'm sorry to interrupt, but could I see you for a moment?"

"Of course, Señorita Pacelli." Ramon was always polite. She was the boss's daughter. Still, she felt the layer of contempt beneath the surface.

"Has your mother recovered?"

Ramon winced just a bit. "We thought she was better for a while, but she has fallen ill again."

"Has she seen a doctor?"

"We cannot afford it."

"Why don't I make an appointment for her with my doctor?" She realized she didn't know Ramon's surname. "What is your last name?"

"Señorita Pacelli, it's very kind of you, but I do not think so."

Frankie felt puzzled. "Why not? What's wrong with her?"

Ramon looked at the clock on the far wall. "I'm sorry. I must get back to the tables." He started to leave, but before he could Frankie grabbed his arm. He stared at her hand as if it was a repellent object.

"Ramon," she said softly. "Could you deliver a message to Luis? Tell him I can't meet him tomorrow. I—my mother and father—will not let me go out alone."

"Your parents are right. The streets are dangerous."

What did that mean? "Ramon, could you—could you tell him to come to the hotel tomorrow afternoon? I will meet him there. Three o'clock in the coffee shop. Could you give him that message for me?"

Her voice must have sounded desperate, because a shrewd look came over him. As if he realized he had the upper hand.

She dropped her hand as if touching his arm had singed her. "Please."

A small smile came over him, and he gave her a curt nod.

"Thank you." She was embarrassed at how grateful she felt.

***

Frankie spent the next morning packing, figuring out which things to wash, and making a list of everything she needed to do back in the States. By noon, she doubted she could wait three more hours, and by one o'clock she knew she couldn't. At two, she went downstairs to look for Ramon to make sure he'd given Luis the message. When she couldn't find him in the restaurant or the nightclub, panic flooded her stomach. He was her only link to Luis. He had to be there. She finally found him delivering lunch to guests at the pool. She hurried over. He was carrying a tray loaded with sandwiches and drinks.

She tapped him on the shoulder. "Well?"

He turned around. When he saw her, she saw a catch in his eyes. *"Momento, Señorita."*

She'd been rude. She took a step back and waited until he'd finished giving the food to a pudgy woman in a bikini she had no business wearing. Finally he headed back, deliberately slowing his pace. Frankie wanted to scream.

Once inside, Frankie struggled to keep her composure. "Ramon, did you talk to him?"

Ramon scowled. "I cannot do this, Señorita. It is not right."

Now what? She was frantic. Should she offer him money? No. He'd consider it an insult. But offering to help his mother hadn't worked. She hated being dependent on this man, a mere waiter. "I understand. I won't ask you again. Just this once. Please. I'm begging you."

Ramon gazed at her. "He cannot come today. He will meet you tomorrow morning at eight o'clock."

***

Frankie spent another sleepless night. Why didn't Luis meet her this afternoon? Had he decided she wasn't worth the risk of a secret tryst? She thrashed between the sheets, then rose at the first blush of dawn, torn and confused. On the one hand, she would see Luis in a few hours. On the other, there were now only two days until she left Cuba. She dressed, applied her make-up, and at seven forty-five left a note for her mother saying she'd gone to the coffee shop for breakfast.

Done up in blue and tropical greens, the coffee shop was empty, except for two disheveled, bleary-eyed men at the counter who'd clearly been at the tables all night. She looked past them to the row of booths. Luis's back was to her, but she knew his hair and the set of his shoulders. She slid into the booth across from him.

"*Buenos dias*, Francesca." He smiled.

"Where were you yesterday?" she asked.

His smile faded. "Yesterday?"

"You were supposed to meet me at three."

"I didn't know."

"Ramon didn't tell you?"

He shook his head.

"But I asked him—" She cut herself off. "Oh well, you're here now. Luis, my mother suspects. She won't let me go out alone. She said Enrico, my bodyguard and chauffeur, must be with me. That's why I couldn't meet you yesterday morning. I am so sorry."

He looked slightly annoyed.

"You look like something is bothering you."

He nodded. "I saw Ramon yesterday, but he said nothing about a three o'clock meeting. I thought you didn't want to see me. When I told Ramon last night, that's when he told me about this morning."

Frankie felt her eyes narrow. Was Ramon playing her? He didn't seem that calculating. She pushed the thought away. He wasn't around, and every moment with Luis was precious.

"Like I said, what's important is that we're together now. And I won't let you out of my sight."

His smile was warm and sweet. A sudden achy feeling tightened her throat. She looked down.

"What is wrong?" Luis said.

"If I'm not back in an hour, my mother will probably call out the army."

He looked crestfallen. "Oh. I had a surprise for you."

Her interest was piqued. "What kind of surprise?"

He stole a look at her. "If I show it to you, you will not be back in an hour."

She ran her tongue around her lips. Why shouldn't she do what she wanted? She was leaving Cuba in two days. Her parents might keep her a prisoner until she boarded the plane, but being with Luis a few more hours was worth it.

"Well then," she said in a husky voice. "I guess we better get started."

***

"This is this where you live?"

They'd walked from La Perla south through Vedado, winding through upscale streets lined with hotels, businesses, and elegant mansions. When they crossed La Rampa, Frankie remembered the bomb blast at the bank. They continued to the University of Havana. Three blocks further on was a beautiful 19th century French-style home.

"I live on the third floor. The attic."

"But—it's so—?" Frankie said.

"Luxurious?" He smiled. "It belongs to the cousin of my cousins. A successful doctor and his family. I pay rent."

Frankie gazed at the neat yellow stucco with white trim, the front porch supported by columns, the balconies festooned with flower boxes. "Do they know who you are? I mean, what you're doing?"

"I am sure they suspect. The university has been closed over a year, and I am still here." He looked at the house. "But they've never said anything. I think they are—how do you say it in English—hedging their bets."

"I don't understand."

"If Fidel does succeed, they're probably hoping we will go easy on them because I know them."

"And will you?"

"I cannot make any promises."

The air was heavy, almost sulfurous in the absence of a breeze.

"Come, Francesca, let's go."

"But I want to see your room."

"We do not have time." He led her around the corner and stopped at a blue and white Chevrolet. He fished out the keys from his pocket.

"I didn't know you had a car."

"It belongs to a friend." He opened the passenger door. "Get in."

She hopped in, briefly wondering if she was making a mistake. Maybe this was the moment he planned to kidnap her. She brushed the thought away. *She'd* made the decision to go with him. Then again, maybe he expected her to. Maybe his absence the day before was intended to fuel her desire. Make her want him more. Maybe it was all a ploy leading up to this. She decided she didn't care.

"I need to be back by five," she said, closing the door.

"I will bring you back."

Before they left the coffee shop she'd called upstairs and told her

40

mother she was going to the movies with Theresa, a friend from the American school. She was seeing a double feature and wouldn't be home until dinnertime. She hung up before her mother could say no.

Luis started the engine, pulled out carefully, and drove east past the outskirts of Havana. An hour after they left the city behind, the clouds lifted. A lazy sun broke through, its rays seeming to home in on the Chevy.

They rolled the windows down, and the breeze whistled through the car, making it difficult to talk. Frankie didn't mind. Luis drove with his left elbow on the window frame. She stole a glance at his skin, covered with delicate dark hair all going in the same direction. Sensing her gaze, he turned to her and reached for her hand. She grasped it and scooted across the front seat to sit closer. She brought their clasped hands to her lap. A wave of sorrow flooded through her. How could she tell him she was leaving?

"You are quiet," he said.

Her eyes welled.

"And sad."

A tear rolled down her cheek.

He pulled to the side of the road. "What is it, Francesca?"

"I—I leave Cuba day after tomorrow."

He straightened. "So soon."

"I couldn't tell you."

He stared through the windshield.

"Oh Luis…" Her voice trailed off, and the tears started to flow. He gathered her in his arms, and stroked her hair until she calmed down. Then he released her, smiled, and kissed her softly on the lips. They parted, then kissed again, not so gently. By the time they broke apart, both of them were breathless. Without another word he put the car in gear and started driving.

An hour later they turned into Varadero, one of the most beautiful beach resorts in Cuba. They drove from the beachhead onto a skinny peninsula, with white sand and turquoise water on both sides of the road. Luis parked near a secluded area, not far from a nature preserve. He pulled a blanket out of the trunk, and they headed hand in hand to the sand. They found a grove of leafy palm trees that provided both shade and privacy.

He shook out the blanket, and they sat. Luis cupped her cheeks and kissed her again. Frankie wrapped her arms around his neck and pulled him down. The weight of his body on hers felt right. When they came up for air, his hair was tousled, but any thought of her smoothing it vanished when she saw his expression. He grabbed her fingers and brought them to his mouth. She let out a whimper.

He helped her take off her clothes.

CHAPTER NINE

"You lied to me, Francesca." Her mother was smoking a cigarette in the living room when Frankie returned. Her mother never smoked.

Frankie thought about lying again, but she was tired of the pretense. She would be leaving soon, anyway.

"Yes. I did," she said.

Her mother took a drag of her cigarette. "Well? Who is he?" Smoke streamed out of her nostrils, like one of those dragons in comic books. "I demand you tell me."

Frankie refused. "You don't know him. And it doesn't matter. I'll never see him again."

Her mother continued, undeterred. "Ramon? A friend of Ramon's?"

Frankie stayed quiet.

Her mother took another drag. "As you say, it doesn't matter. Ramon has been let go."

"That's not fair. He didn't do anything."

"If you are not involved with him, why do you care? He is a waiter."

"But I wasn't—he wasn't—his mother is sick," she said miserably. "He needs money to get medicine for her."

"That's what he told you."

"You don't believe him?"

"Who knows?" Her mother waved a dismissive hand. "If it's the truth, that should spur him to find another job quickly." Her mother crushed the cigarette stub in an ashtray. "He is—was—not family, Francesca." She sniffed. "It does not matter."

Frankie crept to her bedroom. Her mother was not a cruel person, and Frankie knew she was worried. Attacks on police stations and other places were a daily event. Her mother was probably afraid she'd been kidnapped. Frankie couldn't blame her. The thought had crossed Frankie's mind, hadn't it?

But her mother didn't know Luis. She wanted to tell her about him. How intelligent he was. How principled. How he made her feel like a graceful, sensual woman with a fully functioning brain.

She couldn't. She hugged her pillow and stared at her clock radio. Each passing second marked the grim reality. She'd never see Luis again. She'd tried to soak up every moment, every sensation, every inch of his body. But those memories were already slipping away, and she knew they would fade more until only a few fragile wisps remained. And those would eventually disappear into the dead, shriveled realm of the past.

***

There was always a short dry period at the end of August, but the autumn currents of September brought in a heavy rain, as if all of Cuba were crying at Frankie's departure. She spent most of her last day in bed, feeling sorry for herself. At six she put on her underwear, her garter belt and stockings, and dressed in a sapphire blue evening gown. She applied her make-up and went down to La Perla's nightclub for the farewell party her parents were throwing.

Her friends from the American school were there, at least the ones who hadn't yet left for college. Her parents' friends, too, dressed in expensive clothes with expensive jewelry. The decorations were festive, the food abundant, and the band played Frankie's favorite music—including rock and roll. There was a huge cake frosted with the words "Goodbye and Good Luck," and she blew out the candles. Afterwards, everyone applauded. Even Meyer Lansky dropped in to say goodbye.

It was after one by the time she got back upstairs. Her flight was at ten the next morning. Frankie undressed and got into bed, but she was still awake an hour later when her parents came up and went into their room. Frankie gazed at the three suitcases by the door. They were all neatly packed, along with a trunk filled with her books, records, and collection of painted snails. She would be taking everything home.

Home. The word reverberated. Home wasn't Chicago, not any more. For fifteen years Havana had been her home. And now she had someone to share it with. Someone with whom to wake up each morning, drop off to sleep at night. Cook, eat, spend their days together, reveling in each other's presence. How could she throw that away?

She pushed the covers off and turned on the light. She emptied her Pan-Am travel bag, then repacked it with a toothbrush, three pairs of underwear, a pair of slacks, a long-sleeved shirt, bathing suit, and her hairbrush. She dressed in a skirt, blouse, and sandals and draped her trench coat over her shoulders.

Her father had made sure she had plenty of traveling cash, and she counted over three hundred dollars, a small fortune. She took her purse, her bag, and tiptoed out of her room, across the carpeting, and out of the penthouse. She closed the door quietly.

She couldn't risk the elevator. The casino never closed, and the security staff, though fewer at night, would recognize her. She took off her sandals, padded across to the stairway, and took the steps down eighteen flights to the basement. Then she put her sandals back on and walked across a concrete floor to the back door. She tried to be quiet, but halfway to the door, near the janitor's storeroom, she heard a noise. She froze. Please, God. Not now.

Another noise. Followed by a low murmur and a female groan. Then it grew quiet, except for a persistent thump. A couple was going at it in the storeroom. Relieved, she felt the flicker of a smile. She sneaked past the storeroom to the door.

Outside the rain had fallen off to a light mist. The lights were still bright on the Malecón, but she headed away from them into the darkest part of the night. Objects seemed farther apart here, and mysterious shadows prowled the streets. She wrapped her trench coat more tightly around her, ignoring the occasional whistle and catcall, and searched for a taxi. There should be one; there were drivers who worked all night, ferrying gamblers from place to place, sometimes getting a cut of the action depending where they dropped them.

Within a few minutes, a cab cruised slowly down the street. She held up her hand and waved. The cab slowed; she opened the door and climbed in. The driver wasn't much older than she, and his eyes widened when he saw her. He clearly wasn't used to a young woman traveling alone in the middle of the night. A knowing expression came into his eyes when she gave him the address.

"You are lucky I saw you, Señorita. It is very late, and the streets are dangerous. You are going home?"

"Drive," she said quietly. She was in no mood for platitudes about safety.

Ten minutes later she was there.

She paid, slid out of the cab, and watched it drive away. Then she turned and gazed up at Luis's house. Her plan had only taken her as far as his front door. Now that she was here, she didn't know what to do. She couldn't ring the bell at this hour. Everyone would be asleep. She thought about throwing stones at Luis's window, but there were several windows on the third floor, and she didn't know which was his. Still, she'd come all this way.

She looked up and down the block. It was empty. Dark. Peaceful. She climbed the steps to the front porch, sat down, and propped herself against a column. She would close her eyes for a little while. She was just so tired.

CHAPTER TEN

Luis Perez had never expected to fall in love. Ideology was his mistress, then the *Directorio Revolucionario*. Love was frivolous, for poets, perhaps the Santería goddess Oshun, but not for him. The faction he headed carried out both armed operations and logistics. Logistics involved raising money for the rebels, so when Ramon suggested kidnapping the daughter of a mobster, Luis thought it over.

"She is willful, rebellious, and spoiled," Ramon said at a meeting a month earlier. Cells of underground rebel sympathizers had proliferated over the past few months, and hotel workers were in a unique position to keep tabs on who was coming in and out of Cuba.

"She is due to leave in a few weeks to go back to the States, so we'll have to move quickly," Ramon went on. "But we can use her to make a statement."

"A statement is not as important as weapons and supplies," Luis countered. "Can't we get into the casino?" Ramon had been stealing food and supplies from La Perla when he could, but his take was paltry, usually not worth transporting to the mountains. They needed money, and plenty of it.

Ramon agreed there was a lot of cash at La Perla, but since he'd been working so many extra shifts, he'd learned that getting to it was impossible. "There are armed guards in the casino every hour of the day and night," he said. "Every few hours, the cash goes into a safe. Then every morning Pacelli takes it in an armored Cadillac to the bank."

That's when he'd suggested the alternative. The daughter would be worth at least ten or twenty thousand dollars, he reasoned. Enough to buy new stocks of machine guns, ammunition, bazookas.

They spent hours planning the operation. They would grab her during one of her shopping excursions. One of the bellboys, a sympathizer, had told them she regularly came back to the hotel weighed down with shopping bags from El Encanto. They would nab her as she exited the store at Galiano and San Rafael. Shove her into a waiting car, blindfold her, and drive her to a safe house. Once they had the ransom, they would let her go.

"That's a mistake," said a tall young man who worked in the parking garage. "What if she screams or makes a commotion when we grab her? There are too many informers and secret police on the streets. It would be our luck for one to stop us."

Ramon nodded. "He's right. Plus her father won't let her go out without a bodyguard." He glanced at Luis. "But I have an idea."

"What?"

"What if we could get her to come with us willingly?"

Luis considered it. As their leader, he had the authority to make the final decision, although he put everything to a vote. "How do you propose to do that?"

"She is a vain, silly creature," Ramon said. "You can pretend to fall for her. Make her think you care. She will be intrigued. Curious. You flatter her for a few days. Tell her you love her. Then arrange to meet her somewhere…" He snapped his fingers. "And *presto.*"

"No," Luis said. "I will not do that."

"Why not?"

"Kidnapping is one thing. But deceiving her like that? It is—degrading."

"Aren't you the one who says the revolution requires deception, sometimes towards our loved ones?" Ramon said.

Luis tightened his lips. He *had* said that. More than once.

"I tell you, she's ripe," Ramon gestured. "She has this American boyfriend, but *que mariquita!*" He scoffed. "She needs a real man. Someone *macho*, like you."

The others laughed.

Luis didn't like the idea, but the others were eager to go ahead, and he was outvoted.

It started out according to plan. He intercepted her at the café in Havana Vieja. He pretended to be infatuated. She was young, naïve, and passionate enough to believe him. The next day he took her to the Hotel Nacional for a drink. She was curious, asking so many questions and soaking up his answers that she reminded him of one of Cuba's tiny hummingbirds that consumed half its weight in nectar each day. To his surprise, he found her company invigorating. He looked forward to their next meeting.

Two days later they walked along the Malecón, gulls cawing, the salty spray erupting over the seawall. She was telling him about the Santería dancer she'd seen a few nights earlier. The way she described the woman, with graceful gestures, a sensual smile, and wide eyes, amused him. Her perfume, a sultry, cinnamon aroma, enveloped him. Luis wanted to touch her. That was when he realized he might fail in his mission.

He tried to regain the advantage when he took her to La Cabaña the next day. He was deliberately cool, aloof. Then she asked him about the revolution. He reminded himself of the stakes, what his fellow guerrillas were expecting. He answered truthfully, but she didn't seem shocked. In fact, she seemed to take it in and consider his point of view. Until she spoke up.

"If you succeed you will destroy my family."

She was subdued when she said it. Just a statement of fact. But it sliced through to his core. He was purposely, intentionally planning to ruin her life. And tricking her in order to make it happen.

Luis couldn't face himself. He'd lied to her earlier when he pretended to blame Ramon for not telling him about their three o'clock meeting yesterday. Ramon *had* told him. In fact, Ramon and the others said the timing was perfect. He should walk her out of the coffee shop, and they would be waiting to kidnap her. But he couldn't do it. So he'd stood her up and told his men he couldn't find a car.

But they found one for him, and rescheduled the operation for the next morning. He would meet her at the coffee shop in the morning. All he had to do was drive her to the safe house. Instead he took her to the beach at Varadero, and made love to her in the sand. And now she was leaving.

He told the others she never showed that morning, and that he'd gone for a drive by himself. He knew they didn't believe him, but he didn't care. Operations failed. He'd take the blame. There wasn't time to reflect, anyway—another Havana rebel group was planning to ambush a police precinct that night, set it on fire, and steal their weapons. Luis's faction would drive the get-away car.

The operation went smoothly, and they spent the rest of the night brainstorming their next move. Unlike the rebels in the mountains, urban guerrillas had different tactics. Fidel and his men could make strategic retreats to regroup, care for the wounded, and plan their next attack. But underground guerrillas had to be constant and relentless. The point was to keep Batista's men on the defensive, demoralize them psychologically. But they had to be careful. Unlimited jail time, torture, or outright execution were the consequences if they failed.

It was practically dawn when Luis got back to the house. As he bent down to retrieve the morning paper, something caught his eye, and when he straightened up, he saw Francesca curled up on the porch. She was asleep.

"Ay Dios mio!"

She stirred and slowly opened her eyes. *"Buenos dias,"* she said sleepily.

Luis's jaw dropped. "How long have you been here?"

"Since last night." She stretched her arms and gave him a smile.

"What are you doing?"

Her smile faded. She tucked a lock of hair behind her ear. "I—I couldn't leave you."

"Who—does anyone know?"

"Not yet." Anxiety clouded her face. "It is all right, isn't it?"

He swallowed hard. In one instant everything had changed. It was counter to everything he'd planned, everything he'd worked for. He wrestled with his thoughts, then gazed at her. Whatever he did next would seal their fate.

He climbed the porch steps and took her in his arms. Relief erased her worried expression, and she touched his face. She started to chatter about her escape and the taxi—she liked to talk when she was nervous, he'd discovered—but he shushed her with his lips. She kissed him back, and soon he heard a soft whimper. He unlocked the door and sneaked her up to his room.

CHAPTER ELEVEN

When Tony Pacelli found out his daughter had run away, he didn't yell, and he didn't lose his temper. His wife chain smoked, crying one minute, cursing the next. But Tony stayed in control, if only to prove to himself that no one, including his daughter, could get the drop on him.

First he questioned his wife, not an easy task.

"What happened?" he asked for the fourth or fifth time.

"I—I already told you," she sobbed. "I woke up, went in—into her room to make sure she was up, and she wasn't there."

"What time was that?" he asked.

"*¡Jesù Cristo*! You were there. It was about seven."

He continued to grill her. Bit by bit he discovered she'd been concealing information from him. She tearfully admitted Francesca had been seeing a local. Marlena had forbidden it, and Frankie had promised her mother it was over.

"She swore she would never see him again. Then..." Marlena spread her hands. "...this."

Tony's only external reaction was to raise his eyebrows. But inside his gut roiled. How could his wife have been so gullible? No one in Havana kept their promises these days. Including, apparently, his daughter. As he struggled to maintain his composure, he decided to deal with his wife later. The imperative was to find Francesca.

"And you have no idea who this local was—is?"

Marlena hiccupped and pulled at her hair with one hand. The other, holding the cigarette, was trembling. Tony figured she was remembering the time he'd been betrayed by a capo back in Chicago and what Tony had done to the man. And if this wasn't a betrayal, what was it?

"Is he a friend? A friend of a friend? Someone we know?"

She didn't answer.

"Marlena, we have to consider that she might have been kidnapped."

His wife shook her head. "She went willingly."

"How do you know?"

She gazed at him. "A woman knows."

And does nothing to stop them, Tony thought. Not only were women the most foolish creatures on earth, they were the most useless.

Marlena's eyes narrowed.

Tony caught it. "What is it?"

"The waiter...Ramon..."

"The one you made me fire the other day?"

She nodded.

"Is he is the one?" He felt the cords in his neck bulge. Adrenaline surged through him. A common waiter had his hands all over Tony Pacelli's daughter?

"It is not him," Marlena said. "But I think he knows who it is."

Tony strode to the sliding glass door of the balcony and stared down at the Malecón. He fisted and opened his hands several times to relieve the tension. Those hands had wrung necks in his time, and he'd happily wring more. In fact, he would smash the little spic's face in if—no, *when*—he found him. He turned away from the view and went to the phone.

"What are you going to do?"

He held up his index finger and called down to the hotel manager. "What was the name of the waiter we fired the other day?"

"Which one?" The manager was chatty. "The one who was stealing supplies or the one who couldn't be bothered to come in on time?"

"Ramon."

"Suarez. The one who was stealing."

Tony depressed the switch button and called down to the garage. "Enrico, come up here."

When Enrico arrived, Tony gave his instructions. "I want you to find him and bring him to me."

"*Si*, Señor Pacelli."

"*Pronto. Ahora mismo.*"

***

Frankie was so exhausted she lay down on Luis's bed and promptly fell back to sleep. Luis wanted to lie next to her, but he was afraid to. He wasn't a saint, but he'd never brought a girl to his room before, and he feared she might cry out or talk too loudly if he woke her.

So he sat in a chair and gazed at her. Her cheeks were flushed, and her breath was soft, with a hint of snoring. If he wasn't careful, he might start making mistakes. He knew about the power of women. A woman could weave a spell over a man, rob him of his manhood.

He shifted in his chair. He shouldn't let her stay. She would become a target—everyone would be searching for her. Letting her stay was crazy. But he didn't want to let her go. Or was it that he couldn't? Maybe she was a witch. Maybe she'd already woven her spell over him.

Whatever she was, they couldn't stay here. He'd been planning to leave in any case. The fight against Batista was intensifying, and his group was carrying out more frequent operations. It was only a matter of time before the doctor figured out what Luis was up to. At which point he would kick him out. Or turn him in. Or both. Luis rose and quietly pulled out his suitcase.

CHAPTER TWELVE

Lawton was a crowded working-class neighborhood about a mile south of Havana Bay where cramped tenement buildings crowded each other on the streets. Laundry pinned to clotheslines stretched between windows. Both white and black Cubans lived in Lawton, and there were way too many of both, Frankie thought. But the building exteriors were painted in bright pinks, greens, and yellows, and every so often a tree managed to thrive between them, relieving what might have been a relentlessly dour setting.

A ceiba tree grew on the front lawn of a small house Luis and Frankie were now approaching. "Is this our home?"

Luis nodded.

Frankie had woken with the sun to find Luis packing a suitcase. When he finished they crept downstairs and stole out of the house. On the street, Frankie automatically headed north, the way she'd come a few hours earlier.

Luis called after her. "Where are you going?"

"To La Rampa. To hail a cab."

"No," he barked.

"Why not?"

"We cannot allow ourselves to be seen in public."

"We walked together all over Havana last week."

"That was different. You're a runaway now. Although they will tell everyone you were kidnapped."

"My father wouldn't—" She stopped herself. Of course he would.

Luis emitted something between a scoff and a laugh. "In the end it does not matter who says what. The only thing that matters is that everyone will be looking for you."

"But no one knows who I am."

"Francesca, you must get used to a new way of thinking. You must always be thinking three steps ahead. Sift all the alternatives. Choose the most effective. Or least dangerous."

"It's just a taxi," she said irritably.

Luis gazed at her. "Ramon was right."

"About what?"

"He said you were strong-willed." He explained that her father would be combing the city for her. He would have called the taxi companies, who would have put out calls to their drivers to be on the lookout for someone fitting her description.

Comprehension dawned, and Frankie's irritation vanished. "Of course, *mi amor*. I'm sorry." She paused. "So what do we do?"

"We wait until the buses are filled with people going to work."

The morning air glowed with a warm orange light. They strolled down side streets, and stopped for coffee at a cafeteria. When rush hour was at its peak, they boarded a bus to Plaza Roja. They got off and walked several blocks up a hill. Then Luis turned abruptly in the opposite direction, walked three more blocks, and turned right. He repeated the pattern until they'd circled the neighborhood and ended up near the bus stop again.

Now, Frankie gazed at the lacy canopy of leaves on the ceiba tree. "You know, it's a sin to cut down a ceiba," she said. "You're supposed to ask permission from the Orishas."

Luis looked surprised. "How do you know that?"

"The ceiba is the symbol of Cuban masculinity." She beamed. "My nanny taught me that. And it is the place where *habaneros* come to throw coins when they celebrate the anniversary of Havana."

"Then perhaps you also know that in 1898, the Spanish Army in Cuba surrendered to the United States under a ceiba, which they labeled the Tree of Peace."

She grinned at his one-upmanship. They were a match. She was about to tell him so, but a cautious look came over him, and his smile faded. He crept up to the house and cupped his ear against the thin wooden door.

An icicle of fear chilled Frankie. "Is everything all right?"

He raised a finger to his lips. After a moment, he carefully turned the doorknob. It twisted easily. He poked his head inside, then gestured for her to come in.

"Who owns this?" she said, entering the apartment.

"It belongs to the brother of one of my men. He went to the Sierra Maestra, and his wife went back to her parents, so we use the house for meetings."

"It's safe?"

"For now. But you never know when you may need to abandon a place at a moment's notice. If a neighbor's dog barks too much, if someone doesn't like the look of you. If there's an informant. So don't get too comfortable."

Frankie set her bag down and explored the house. The front room was small and sparsely furnished. No couch, one easy chair, and a few folding chairs. Yellowed window shades. No carpeting. A hall led back to a small kitchen with a table and chairs. Most of the kitchen utensils were missing. Two doors led off the hall. One opened into a tiny bathroom, the other to a bedroom so small it would fit into her closet back at La Perla.

Luis must have sensed her disappointment. "You can still change your mind, Francesca. I will take you back."

"I will never go back."

"But your father will come after you. You know that."

"I will tell him I won't leave."

"He will not believe you."

"How can he not? All he has to do is see us together. He will know."

For a moment his expression made her think they would make love again, the way she'd wanted to last night before she fell asleep. Instead he swept his arm through the air. "It is not much, but the neighborhood is solid." He paused. "Camilo Cienfuegos grew up here."

She stared at him blankly.

"Next to Fidel and Che, he is perhaps the most important rebel. A Comandante now. The three of them met when they were in Mexico City. He's one of the only leaders who comes from the working class, you know."

But Frankie wasn't interested in revolutionary history. "Luis, there's something I need to say."

He cocked his head.

"I love you. More than anything or anyone in the world. I changed the course of my life for you. And I'm glad I did. But there is one thing I require."

"What is that?"

"You need to be completely honest with me. I can understand anything. Forgive anything. As long as I know the truth."

He didn't reply.

"Did you hear me?" she asked.

He took her arm and led her to one of the folding chairs in the front room.

"What are you doing?"

"Sit," he said.

She did.

He gazed at her, his expression inscrutable. What was he going to say? Fear skittered around in her. Was this feeling going to be a way of life from now on? She wondered if she was prepared. Then she thought of the risks she'd taken by running away. The worst was over. It had to be.

"You say you can forgive anything? Well, let's find out." He told her about the kidnapping scheme. His role, Ramon's, and the others.

She listened quietly until he was finished. Then, "I thought so."

A muscle in his jaw pulsed. "How?"

"Before we met in the café the first time, in Havana Vieja, I had the feeling I was being followed. And then after the mix-up with Ramon, I—"

"The plan was to kidnap you that afternoon," he cut in. "And then again the next morning. Yesterday. But I called it off."

"Why?"

"Because—I am in love with you."

She was quiet for a moment. Then, "But you see, Ramon was right. His plan succeeded. You now have me exactly where you want. What's to keep you from carrying out your original plan?"

"Me. I will not let anyone harm you."

She allowed herself a wan smile. "What if you're not here?"

"The only way I will not be with you is if I am dead." He paused. "Which brings us to the thing I require from *you*."

She tilted her head.

"I cannot betray the revolution. If we are to be together, I must continue the fight against Batista."

She pressed her lips together as she weighed the risks. Given who her family was, he must know she couldn't be that shocked. After a long moment, she nodded.

She saw his tense muscles relax.

She rose, went to him, and slipped her arms around his neck. "Now. How long before your men come?" she whispered.

"A day or two."

"So until then, it is just the two of us?"

He nodded.

"There's a tradition in America when two people get married. The husband carries the wife over the threshold."

"We aren't married."

"Didn't we share vows a moment ago?" She broke into a smile, a real smile this time, and went to the door. "I'm waiting."

CHAPTER THIRTEEN

"They are hunting for me all over Havana," Ramon said two nights later. He'd shown up at the safe house after midnight.

"Why?" Luis asked.

"Where have you been, *amigo*?" Ramon looked annoyed. "The Pacelli girl ran away the night before she was supposed to leave Cuba. You didn't know?"

Luis wouldn't meet his eyes.

Ramon's eyebrows arched. "She's not here, is she?"

Luis hesitated then yanked a thumb towards the back of the house. "In the bedroom."

For an instant Ramon's eyes widened. Then he flashed Luis a dazzling smile and threw open his arms. "My brother! You did it! We did it! We are—"

Before Ramon could embrace him, Luis waved his hand. "No. No ransom."

"Of course there is. It's part of the plan."

"No, Ramon." Luis's voice was firm.

Confusion swam across Ramon's face. "What are you talking about?"

"She and I—we—"

"We are together." Frankie's voice cut in from the back of the room.

Ramon spun around. Frankie stood there, in Luis's shirt and not much else. Her hair was mussed, as if she'd just woken up. He sputtered in disbelief. "This—this is impossible. Luis, tell her what is really going on."

Luis met his gaze. "I did."

Ramon's mouth fell open. "Then, it is true? You and she—"

Luis nodded.

Ramon was speechless. Then, "You are mad. You have betrayed us. And the revolution. Everything you stand—stood for—is ruined!"

57

"No, Ramon," Luis said. "I am in love."

"The result is the same," Ramon said. "We are finished."

"Ramon," Frankie said, "Luis has given me his word no danger will come to me. I trust him." She seemed to straighten. "In return, I won't interfere with his—your activities."

Ramon eyed her suspiciously, then looked at Luis. "This is true?"

Luis nodded.

Ramon was quiet for a long minute. "Well, you'd better not let the rest of the men find out. They will not understand."

Luis and Frankie exchanged glances.

Ramon went on. "But there is another, more pressing problem. Pacelli put a dragnet out for me."

"Why?"

Ramon gestured at Frankie. "She used me to contact you. At La Perla they are saying I am the one she ran away with."

"I'm sorry, Ramon," Frankie said. "It's my parents. Not me."

He ignored her. "I haven't been home in days. My mother is going crazy. I was hoping to stay here, but now…" He let his voice trail off.

"Of course you will stay here," Luis said.

"I don't think so."

"Ramon, we must stay together. Events are beginning to accelerate."

"But this is not what we planned." Ramon gestured toward Frankie.

"We will get our money. But not through kidnapping. That's what I want to discuss tonight."

Ramon lifted his chin toward Frankie. "You are going to tell them about her?"

Luis shifted. "In time. But tonight I must ask you not to tell anyone she is here. When the time is right, I will tell them."

"I don't like this, Luis."

"If I thought her abduction would help our cause, I wouldn't have called it off. But they will never fork over the ransom. They will set a trap instead. So I have a new strategy to discuss. Believe me, Ramon, nothing has changed. We are brothers in the revolution. And we stay that way."

Ramon wasn't convinced.

**

The meeting didn't break up until dawn. Luis thought Frankie was asleep when he came to bed, and he tried not to disturb her when he crawled in. But she stirred and with a warm, sleepy sigh twined her legs around his. He breathed in the scent of her, felt her heat. The bed was small, but they didn't need much room. Afterwards, they lay sweaty and hot, the sheet tangled between their legs.

"Francesca, I have a question."

Frankie drew abstract designs on his chest with her finger. She loved the feel of his chest hair, she claimed. "Of course."

"I—I know you are not a virgin, but—"

"I've only been with one other man, Luis, and he was—"

"I don't care that you have been with another man. But," he paused. "Tell me. Were you in love with him?"

Frankie bit her lip. She didn't want to think about Nicky. In fact, she'd been forcing herself not to. She loved Nicky, but not the same way as Luis. Still, Nicky had been a big part of her life, and she hadn't told him about Luis. She stopped fingering his chest. "I have never loved anyone the way I love you. You are my oxygen. My sun. I can not live one day without you."

Luis gazed at her. Then he nodded.

"What about you, *querido?*"

He caught a lock of her hair between his fingers, felt its soft, velvety curl. "There has never been anyone except you."

She smiled contentedly, and snuggled in closer. "How did the meeting go?"

"Ramon did not say anything. I give him credit for that. With everyone searching for him, the pressure must be enormous."

She brushed her hand across his forehead. "Do you trust him?"

"We have known each other since we were children."

"That is not an answer, *mi amor,*" she said. "You are no longer children."

***

A few hours later Tony Pacelli's private business phone rang.

"I have the information you've been looking for," a male voice said in Spanish.

"Who is this and how did you get this number?"

"Do you want to know where your daughter is?"

"Is she all right?" Tony asked.

"She is safe."

"Where is she?"

"In a house. Not far from here."

"You kidnapped her."

The caller was silent. The fact that he didn't contradict Tony spoke volumes.

"How much do you want?"

"Twenty thousand dollars. Half now. Half on delivery."

It was Tony's turn to be silent. Finally, he said, "I need to meet with you."

"No. I will give you a drop for the first payment. Then you will receive further instructions."

Tony clenched his teeth. People saw too many gangster movies in Cuba. Too many movies, period. Batista probably figured the films, which seduced Cubans with their tales of heroism, fantasy, and romance, kept the people docile. Tony might have a piece of a movie theater, he thought. He couldn't remember.

"How do I know you're telling me the truth? Other people know she's gone. You could be a two-bit con man trying to shake me down. I need proof you have her."

"I will leave a piece of her clothing at the drop."

Tony was quick with a reply. "Not good enough. Her mother and I do not know what she was wearing when she left. You could buy a trinket at El Encanto, try to convince us it was hers."

More silence on the other end. Tony wasn't sure if he was winning or losing. The caller clearly had the power. Then again, Tony was a good negotiator. He should be able to regain the advantage. He was trying to think two steps ahead when he realized this wasn't a negotiation to be won or lost. This was his daughter. He had to accept reality. At least for now.

"Where will you leave this 'proof?'"

"Go to the janitor's storeroom at *La Perla* at three PM this afternoon. You will have your proof. But only if the money has been paid in advance." Ramon gave him the address of a Western Union near La Perla and told him to make sure the money was there by two. Addressed to Señor Diego Juarez.

But Tony Pacelli surprised himself. "No. No money until I am convinced you have my daughter and she is unharmed."

The response was a click, then a dial tone. Tony made a call.

***

Ramon debated long and hard before he called Tony Pacelli. On the one hand, Luis was his oldest friend. They'd been inseparable. Ramon's father worked with Luis's father on a sugar plantation in Oriente until he dropped dead. When the boys were eighteen they moved to Havana to attend university together. They scrounged jobs, working as busboys, messengers, and movie ushers to make ends meet. When things were really bad, Ramon dove for pesos off the rocks at Regla. Then La Perla opened and advertised for workers, claiming they'd pay higher wages than any other resort. Ramon, who had never been a good student, dropped out of university and went to work.

Through everything they had been loyal to each other, sharing their adventures and confidences. When Ramon first slept with a girl, he described it to Luis, who, still a virgin, went wide-eyed at his friend's machismo. When Luis started to get involved with the rebel movement, Ramon found himself drawn in.

When they formed the group, Luis was in charge. Ramon didn't mind. He had a lot to learn, and Luis was clever. In fact, Luis reminded Ramon of Che, a doctor and an intellectual. But people change, and claiming to be in love in the middle of the revolution was unacceptable. Everyone knew women were good for three things only: cooking, sex, and babies. Everything else was witchcraft.

What had come over Luis was a sickness, a fever. He was under this woman's spell. If the other cell members knew, they would strip him of his command. And so Ramon convinced himself he was actually doing Luis a favor. Saving him from himself. When this was over, Luis would be grateful.

He took the bus back to the safe house. He could fabricate a pretext for returning: a nonexistent conversation he wanted to share with Luis, perhaps about a potential recruit. He hummed as he got off. By the end of the afternoon, they would have ten thousand dollars, and he would be a hero. He walked the three blocks from the bus stop, taking care to make detours in case of a tail. He couldn't afford to have Pacelli's men or the police following him.

He climbed a fence, trotted down an alley. Satisfied no one was following him, he approached the house. The ceiba tree cast dappled shadows on the walk. Most of the other apartments had their doors open. In this heat, you needed air, even if it was hot and tropical. But the door to the safe house was closed. He knocked. There was no response. He knocked again. Nothing. He turned the knob. It twisted. He went in.

He called out. "Luis? Señorita Pacelli?"

No answer.

Maybe they had gone to eat or buy groceries. Or do laundry. Isn't that what women did? He called out again, to be sure. When no one answered, a rush of energy came over him. He couldn't believe his luck. He could go into the bedroom and take an article of her clothing without having to sneak it out.

As he approached the bedroom, though, Ramon hesitated. He was crossing a boundary. Luis would see it as a betrayal. But it really wasn't. It was necessary. If he'd been in his right mind, Luis would have agreed. The revolution came first. Ramon was doing the right thing. He opened the door, anticipating what he would take. Nothing too personal. A shoe, perhaps. Or a piece of jewelry.

The room was empty. Nothing but the bed, a mattress, and a folding chair.

CHAPTER FOURTEEN

The train ride was only supposed to be four hours, but with the roadblocks and inevitable breakdowns, it took nearly seven hours before they reached Santa Clara. Frankie could tell Luis was nervous. What if her father had men watching the bus and train stations and airports? Frankie tied her hair in a ponytail, bought a cheap dress, and wore dark glasses. The disguise seemed to work; neither she nor Luis sensed anyone looking or following as they boarded the train. Once they were settled in Santa Clara, though, Luis said she'd have to change her appearance more dramatically.

While Luis kept fidgeting and wouldn't meet anyone's eyes, Frankie stared out the window. A team of oxen pulled a plow across a field, farmers in straw hats picked tomatoes, boys dove into rivers. She hadn't been out of Havana much, especially in the past year. And anywhere she went—in or out of Havana—she had always been Tony Pacelli's daughter. Treated with deference and respect. Now, though, she felt like she'd put on a cloak of freedom. The anonymity of being simply another person, no one special, was euphoric.

Still, she felt a twinge of guilt. She knew she was the reason Luis was troubled. Love had destroyed the familiar and ushered in the unknown. The upheaval had to be particularly cruel, given his revolutionary zeal. Her heart ached for him, but she couldn't interfere in the political part of his life. Instead she resolved to manage every other part. She would do whatever it took to build a happy and safe life for them both. A perfect life. He would never regret the decision to be together.

The sun winked off the tops of nearby rail cars as the train slowed. "Why did we come to Santa Clara?" Frankie asked Luis in Spanish. The city, which sprawled along the Central Highway in the province of Las Villas, was supposed to be beautiful, but with only 250,000 people it was a sleepy, more rural version of Havana.

Luis looked around before answering. There was no one in the seat in front of them, and the woman behind was busy trying to manage two children.

"Three reasons," he replied quietly, also in Spanish. He ticked them off his fingers. "One, it was time to get out of Havana—"

"Because of me."

"Not entirely. The streets are dangerous. The cells are conducting more operations, and Batista's men are out in large numbers. If I was caught, they would certainly torture or kill me."

She winced. "And the second?"

"Santa Clara is a university town. We will blend in."

"I thought the university was closed. Like Havana's."

"Yes, but many students are still here living, working, waiting."

"And the third reason?"

"I can be useful." Luis explained that Fidel and the rebels were moving out of the Sierra Maestra mountains. At the end of August, Camilo Cienfuegos set out with a column of men, their mission to march across the island and to Pinar del Rio on the western edge. Along the way Cienfuegos was to organize more rebel units.

"But we're going in the opposite direction."

"That's because the other column of rebels, led by Che Guevara, is heading toward Santa Clara."

Frankie gulped air. "Why?"

"Fidel's plan is to cut the island in half at Santa Clara. So it will be impossible for Batista to prevail."

"Will it succeed?"

Luis nodded. "Eastern Cuba is already under the rebels' control. And Batista is a terrible military leader. The soldiers realize they're fighting a general's war, not their own. The struggle reflects that."

"What do you mean?"

"Batista has played his generals against each other for so long they are interested more in enriching themselves than fighting. Soldiers are deserting in droves. And the rebels treat them well. That's why our ranks are growing. It is merely a matter of time."

The train lurched to a stop. Frankie stood and reached for her bag, but Luis got to it before she could. "After two years," he went on, "and so many false starts and stops, I want to be involved in the final act."

"How?"

"Che's column will need scouts, once they arrive. Food and equipment, too. Maybe explosives and weapons. I will help."

Frankie sat down again.

"You're not surprised, are you?"

"I guess not."

"You know how many people have withdrawn their support for the government?"

"Yes, but I don't know whether it's because they love Fidel or hate Batista."

"Does it matter? Attitudes are changing. Money and manpower are coming into the movement. Everything is on our side."

Frankie thought it over. After the revolution, who knew? Maybe, because of Luis's dedication and heroism, he would be given an important position. For now, though, she had to adjust to a new way of thinking. A thought occurred to her. "What about us? How do we make sure we stay safe? Until it's over?"

Luis didn't reply as they walked down the aisle toward the exit. Only after they had descended to the station platform did he say, "We must adopt new names. New identities, too."

She tilted her head.

"People cannot know who we are, where we are from, or what I am doing. It helps that you look Spanish and you speak like a native. If we're careful, we should not have a problem."

Frankie thought about it, then grinned.

"What is funny?"

"Does that mean we can tell people we're married?"

Luis's face lightened too, and he smiled for the first time that day. "If you want."

"So… what should our name be?"

"What do you think?"

She thought of Señor Wences and his act on the Ed Sullivan show and giggled. "How about Señor and Señora Wences?"

"Too obvious." He paused. "How about Lopez?"

"All right. Luis Lopez."

"No. I will be—Julio. Julio Lopez. You must call me that."

"But I love your name, Luis."

"Then you will be Luisa. Luisa Lopez."

"Perfect."

"We are not from Havana," he went on.

"Oriente?"

"I think to be safe, we should be from Camaguey. Santa Lucia, perhaps."

"It has a beautiful beach."

"Good." They reached the exit, and Luis jumped down to the station platform. He set down the bags and held his hand out. She descended the steep steps carefully. "Francesca… I mean Luisa… one thing you must remember. This is not a game we are playing. It is deadly serious. Our lives depend on it."

Frankie nodded. She knew they were in the middle of a revolution; but they were also in the first blush of love. And love was supposed to be joyful. She couldn't dwell on the possibility that Luis might be captured and tortured, or that she would be found; focusing on the danger would turn her into an anxious, nervous creature, much like—well—her mother. She would not allow that to happen.

"*Comprendo, amorcito.*" She ran her hand across his cheek. "But today... today we are newlyweds."

He cocked his head as if he was wondering "are all women this crazy?" Then he gathered his suitcase and her Pan Am bag. "And we must think of a job for you, Señora Lopez."

She nodded. The three hundred dollars she'd brought with them wouldn't last forever. "I will find work in a store. Or a hotel. A place where I can use my English."

Luis grinned as if he was proud of her. "We will decide later. Now we eat."

***

After a hearty lunch in a café near the station, they stopped in Vidal Park, where the profusion of greenery and flowers contrasted sharply with the gazebo's white columns and surrounding buildings. As they walked, Frankie studied the statue of Marta Abreu, one of the most famous women in Cuban history. Originally from Santa Clara, Marta was a civic hero who donated her entire fortune to the poor and was honored like a patron saint. Frankie learned that the University of Santa Clara was named in her honor. Maybe one day she—no, Luis—would be remembered with that kind of reverence.

They hiked over four miles to the northeast side of city where the university was located. The air had a slightly dusty taste, not the briny tang she was used to in Havana. It was now the middle of the afternoon, but without the bay breezes she was used to, the heat blasted with such force that Frankie felt light-headed. More than once she wondered if she had arrived at the gates of Hell.

When they finally found shade, Luis struck up a conversation with two young people. Frankie fanned herself and listened. Eventually, the subject turned to housing, and the two young people recommended a rooming house a few blocks away. As Frankie and Luis followed the directions they were given, Frankie marveled that finding a place to live could be so simple. As a Pacelli it was never simple. Houses had to be staked out, inspected, cleaned, and renovations made for security.

But once they'd chatted with the woman who owned the rooming house, making sure to tell her they were newlyweds who'd just arrived from

Santa Lucia, the woman told them her sister had a suite of rooms in her home she was looking to rent. Luisa and Julio replied that it sounded like a place they'd be interested in, and politely asked the rent. The woman said it couldn't be much. Did they have jobs?

"I will be looking for work," Frankie said.

"What kind of work?" the woman asked.

"I studied English. I speak it well."

"Ahh...." She turned to Luis. "And you?"

"I was studying to be a lawyer. But the university is closed. So..."

"I want him to continue his studies when the university reopens," Frankie broke in. She took his arm. "So I will be the breadwinner for now."

"I see." The woman winked at her. "But not for long, I suspect."

"Why do you say that?" Frankie asked.

The woman laughed. "The way you two cling to each other, I think you will have a family soon."

Frankie beamed. Luis turned crimson.

CHAPTER FIFTEEN

"*¡Mierda!*" Ramon cursed when he realized they were gone. Now what? He slumped on the folding chair in the safe house, head in hands. He had been so close, and now everything was in jeopardy. He'd worked too hard, accomplished too much, to let this slip through his fingers. He ran his hands through his hair, trying to figure out how to salvage the situation. Clearly, he couldn't produce Frankie. But Pacelli wouldn't have to know that. Ramon would drop off a piece of her clothing, take the money, and disappear. Ten thousand dollars was a significant sum. The rebels could put it to good use.

Yes. That was a good idea. He rose, feeling more in control. He would go to El Encanto, buy something and pretend it belonged to the girl. It would be expensive, but he would reimburse himself after he got the money. He didn't need anyone's permission for that. Indeed, with Luis gone, Ramon might become the new head of the faction.

If Luis was really gone.

Ramon felt his eyes narrow. Of course he was. The question was why he'd chosen this moment to flee. Was it possible Luis had kidnapped the girl himself and was planning to demand a ransom? If so, Luis's declaration of love had been a lie, and he was much more cunning than Ramon had thought. Maybe he was planning to keep the ransom for himself. No. Money wasn't important to Luis. Principles were. But maybe the girl was in league with Luis. Maybe they were playing her father, so they'd have enough money to live together. If that was the case, his friend had obviously changed. Women did that to a man.

On the other hand, obsessing about Luis and the girl wouldn't solve his immediate problem. He needed *something* to give to Pacelli. Perhaps he wouldn't go to the department store. His mother might have something at home. A scarf, a glove, a comb for her hair. No. His house—and his mother—were under surveillance. He couldn't go home.

So he stopped at a small store in Lawton and bought a brightly colored scarf. Pink and orange and flowery, it looked like something the girl would wear. He tore off the tag and hopped on the downtown bus. Instead of the stop nearest La Perla, he got off two stops before the hotel and found a phone booth. He called one of the bellhops at La Perla, who was also a group member. The bellhop agreed to meet him at the taxi stand around the corner from the hotel and take the package to the janitor's room. Ramon would hurry to the Western Union office and wait for the money.

The mid-afternoon sun cast a wan, milky light, and clouds were massing at the horizon, but Ramon was covered in sweat as he reached the taxi stand. He tried to look inconspicuous as he waited. He watched two women, and then a tourist couple—Americans, of course—hail cabs.

Ten minutes passed. Where was the bellhop? He'd promised to come right away. Had he been pulled away? *Mierda*. Ramon couldn't go back to La Perla; he shouldn't even be this close. He turned around, irritated. He'd have to telephone the bellhop again. He hoped it wouldn't delay the hand-off. He had important things to do. He was heading back to the phone booth when they grabbed him.

***

Water poured over his head. Ramon came to. His first instinct was one of relief. That he could think and feel at all meant he was alive. Then the hurt began. Wave after wave of excruciating pain washed over him. He tried to figure out where it was coming from, but it seemed to originate from every part of his body. A sharp ache stabbed his gut. His head felt like a mushy watermelon. He tried to open his eyes, but they were so swollen his eyelids wouldn't crack. Something was dripping from his nose. Perhaps snot; perhaps blood. He wanted to touch his face, to make sure it was still intact, but his hands and feet were tied to a chair. He tried to shift his weight but whimpered at the effort.

A voice emerged from the fog of pain. "I trust our—exercise—has made you more cooperative."

Ramon ran his tongue around his mouth. His lips felt like balloons, and a couple of teeth were loose. He tried to clear his throat, but there was so much spittle—or was it blood—that he started to cough, which made the pain worse.

"You didn't really think your loco plan would work, did you? It was full of holes."

Ramon didn't answer.

"Well…" the voice said calmly. "Are you ready?"

Still hacking, Ramon nodded.

"Where is she?"

With a huge effort Ramon tried to speak. It came out as a wheeze. "Don' know…"

"Oh, but I think you do." The voice paused. "Maybe we should 'refresh your memory.'"

They were going to hit him again. Ramon felt his stomach pitch. He vomited.

"Christ!" a second voice yelled. "He puked all over my shoes!"

The first voice cut in. "You can clean up later." A pause. "Well, Ramon? Where is she?"

Ramon forced his eyes open. Everything swam. He blinked, squeezed them shut, then opened them again. Slowly the spinning stopped. He could see he was in a small, dark room. A desk lamp threw elongated shadows against the wall. Probably the basement of La Perla, in a room that had been designated for this kind of "exercise." Three forms wavered in front of him. He squinted, and the forms turned into men. He couldn't see clearly, but he didn't have to. He knew who was orchestrating the scene.

"Ahh… Good of you to join us, so to speak." Tony Pacelli's body language was relaxed and his voice was casual, as if he and Ramon were about to share a coffee, rather than an interrogation. "I trust you are ready to talk?"

"It—it's the truth," Ramon croaked. "I don't know where she is. They ran away. Luis and your daughter. I—I can prove it."

"How?"

Ramon told him about the safe house. Pacelli promptly sent two men to Lawton. He told Ramon he would be back and turned off the light. Ramon dozed upright, still bound to the chair. When they returned, a man shook him by the shoulder. "This is your lucky day, Suarez."

Ramon blinked himself awake. He could smell his own body odor and piss. He breathed through his mouth.

"You're going to live. For a while. But during that time you're going to help me find my daughter."

"But I don't know where they are. If they're still in Havana."

Pacelli's smile was ice cold. "You will find out. In fact, from now on, that will be your job. Your only job. To find my daughter and tell me where she is. *Comprende?*"

Ramon hung his head. In one way, he wished he'd been caught by Batista's men instead of Pacelli's. The police would have killed him right away. Tortured him, yes, but killed him afterwards. This was worse. Now his life depended on the whim of a gangster. If Ramon didn't produce, he would die, but he would never know when or where. He would wake up every morning wondering whether this would be his last, whether this would be the day Pacelli would extract payback. Why had he thought he could blackmail one of the most ruthless men in Havana? He was a fool.

"Now listen to me," Pacelli said quietly. "Here is what we are going to do."

CHAPTER SIXTEEN

Frankie couldn't believe her good fortune. The Orisha gods were working their magic. It was as if she and Luis were destined to come to Santa Clara. The rooms they rented were perfect, complete with a tiny kitchen. She promptly went shopping for new towels, sheets, and kitchen tools, and discovered she didn't have to spend a fortune. She was able to snag good bargains at the flea market.

Two days after they moved in, she went to a hair salon recommended by her landlady. The "Pixie" hairdo was all the rage in the States, and she asked the hairdresser to cut her hair short. The hairdresser balked at cutting Frankie's long, thick curls, but Frankie insisted. Afterwards the ladies in the shop said she looked like Audrey Hepburn. Frankie smiled; it must be a good disguise. Then she went shopping and bought a few inexpensive dresses, skirts, and blouses. The styles and materials were very different from her wardrobe in Havana, and as she pirouetted before the mirror in the dressing room, she was sure no one could recognize her. Luis had changed his appearance too; she'd helped him cut and dye his hair, and he now wore a pair of fake glasses.

The next day, wearing her new hairstyle and clothes, Frankie interviewed at a bank that needed an English-speaking clerk. She made up a story about her parents sending her to live with relatives in Chicago while they tried to better themselves in Cuba. After seven years, they had scrounged enough money to fly her back for a visit. Which is why her Spanish wasn't quite fluent, but her English was. The man interviewing her asked why she hadn't gone back to the States. She was planning to, she told him, but then she met Julio. Blushing prettily, she added, "And you know how that goes, Señor." The man nodded. He understood the arrow of love. She got the job.

Her new life settled into a routine. In the morning Luisa Lopez went to

71

the bank, while Julio saw to his activities. She was home by evening to cook dinner. Growing up, she'd spent hours glued to her nanny's apron strings, and the nanny was their cook. She always begged to help add ingredients or stir the pot, and her nanny obliged, explaining what she was doing and why. Frankie had clearly absorbed more than she thought, because she developed a flair for cooking. Luis especially liked her *pulpeta*, a Cuban version of meat loaf, and her *ajiaco*, a hearty vegetable soup.

His approval delighted her. For eighteen years she'd led the life of a princess, but it had left her unfulfilled. Now she was simply an ordinary woman, but she had a purpose, and that made all the difference. She would share her life with Luis and fill it with the things they loved, from food to a new home, a family, long, passionate nights in each other's arms. It was odd—ironic, really—that she should feel so blessed while a revolution seethed, but she was practical enough to take her happiness where she found it. Revolution or not, she had no regrets.

It took a few weeks for Luis to forge connections with the rebels, but by the middle of October he was running interference between Che Guevara, whose column had reached the Escambray Mountains south of Santa Clara, and the local rebel leaders in Las Villas province. Unity between the revolutionary factions was not a given, and Enrique Oltusky, the underground leader in Las Villas, had different ideas than Che. The two disagreed about agrarian reform, as well as the future role of the U.S. At one point, Che wanted to carry out a series of bank robberies to augment rebel funds, but Oltusky opposed the idea. He argued that robbing a bank was contrary to the Cuban spirit. Not even Fidel would condone it. As a courier and supplier, Luis was a friend to both camps and became a de facto peace-maker, spending hours trying to ease tensions.

In mid-October Fidel redeployed Camilo Cienfuegos. He was no longer tasked with marching his men to Pinar del Rio. Instead, Fidel ordered him to the northern part of Las Villas to support Che. Luis met Cienfuegos for the first time near the end of the month. Cienfuegos was recruiting workers from the sugar mills, and Luis was asked to help. Luis came home with stories that made Frankie think Cienfuegos, who, like Luis, came from the working class, was the real hero of the revolution. As much, perhaps more than Fidel.

***

By November Luis was either with Che in the mountains or with Cienfuegos somewhere in Las Villas, sometimes for days at a stretch. Frankie wished he would confide in her more; she knew she would understand the tactics the revolutionaries were using. But she also knew that it would be dangerous for her to know too much. Like her father's people, the revolutionaries had their own *omerta*.

So she passed the time when Luis was gone either working—she was beginning to enjoy the job and the respect that went with it—or with her new friends from the bank. On evenings and weekends they headed to the Parque Vidal in the center of town. The custom was to walk around the park several times, the women strolling along an inner circle, the men an outer one. It was an excellent way for young women to check out men and vice versa, and the girls whispered and giggled when they spotted appealing prospects.

Frankie felt like an old married woman compared to the girls, but she joined in; there wasn't much else to do. Her favorite time was Sunday afternoon, when local musicians, in fancy guayabera shirts and polished shoes, played guitars in impromptu concerts.

It was on one of those Sundays that Maria, one of the girls from the bank, gazed at Frankie as they strolled. Maria's expression grew solemn.

Frankie felt her stomach clench. Had Maria figured out she wasn't Luisa Lopez? Was she going to confront her?

"What's wrong, Maria? You look so serious," she said hesitantly.

Maria didn't reply for a moment. Then she cocked her head. "I've been watching you, Luisa." She pointed. "I think perhaps you are becoming a little thick around the middle."

Frankie, who was still at the age where she could eat anything without gaining weight, objected. "Impossible. I can eat anything. It never shows."

Maria shot Frankie a meaningful glance. "I didn't say it was from eating. And your skin—it has a glow I haven't noticed before."

Frankie stopped. When did she last get her period? It had been a while. Before they came to Santa Clara. In fact, now that she was thinking about it, her breasts seemed more sensitive these days. She'd thought it had to do with her new clothes. Tighter fitting. But then there was Luis. When he was home, they were having glorious sex. Often two or three times a night. She turned around and gave Maria a hug.

***

It wasn't until the middle of December that Ramon got a lead on Luis and Frankie. By that time Havana was simmering with rumors, secrets, and conspiracies. Propaganda from both sides churned, the newspapers bragging about the number of rebels captured, while the broadcasts from Radio Rebelde boasted that the rebels were making progress. The truth was somewhere in between. The rebels were advancing, but many thought that timing and luck—as opposed to skill—were the reasons. Batista's army was demoralized. More soldiers deserted, and the rebels made it a point to treat them well, so *their* ranks had swelled. Meanwhile, those who remained in the army refused to mount vigorous attacks. The rebels managed to block highways and blow up telephone and electrical installations, which made travel and communication between Havana and the rest of the island uncertain.

Without Luis at the helm, Ramon's group fell apart—that could happen—which, perversely, made Ramon's job easier. He didn't have to lie to his former compatriots about his assignment. He prowled Havana streets, penetrating as many other cells as he could to ferret out information about Luis. He carefully constructed his approach. He couldn't appear desperate. Just concerned. He and Luis had been best friends since childhood, and he was worried. Had Luis been picked up? Had some misfortune befallen with the girl? He needed to know. Luis's family was going crazy.

But it was dangerous to divulge too much information these days, and if his colleagues had news, they weren't sharing. After weeks of hearing nothing, Ramon's nerves were shot. Tony Pacelli demanded he report in every day and asked detailed questions, including who he was talking to, and where he'd tracked down the contact.

Indeed, Pacelli's insistence on knowing every detail made Ramon wonder if Pacelli was planning to take matters into his own hands, which, of course, would mean the end of Ramon. He lost his appetite, and he couldn't sleep. His house was still being watched, and the few pesos Pacelli doled out to him barely paid for food for himself and his mother. She never complained, but she was looking frail and drawn. If not for her, Ramon himself would have fled. Instead he was trapped like a mouse in a cage. This was how you died, he decided. Not in a fiery ball of violence, but bit by bit. First you lost your power, then your freedom, then your will.

He trudged down the Prado one evening, trying to ignore the glut of Christmas decorations that had sprung up seemingly overnight. Havana was awash in tinsel, lights, Santa Clauses, reindeer, and trees imported from the States. Tinny recordings of American Christmas carols blared out from shops, and store windows were filled with giant packages brightly wrapped with thick red ribbons. Judging by the hoopla, you wouldn't know there was a war going on. Ramon was bitter he wasn't working at La Perla anymore—the holidays were the best time for tips.

He slipped behind a building into an alley. A tall, skinny kid who couldn't be older than eighteen was nervously smoking a cigarette. The kid's hair was slicked back in a D.A. and though it was almost eighty degrees, he wore a black leather jacket. Fake, of course. Still, he looked like one of the characters from *West Side Story*. Marco, the dance director at La Perla, had created a dance number in honor of the Broadway play—what were the gangs' names? The Sharks and the Jets. That was it. Ramon shook it off. How could he be thinking of a New York play when his life was at risk?

He approached the informant and drew out his own cigarette. The kid worked at the Riviera and was part of that hotel's rebel group. Ramon had spent the better part of a day tailing him before he decided to meet, and while he didn't trust anyone, he'd determined the kid was harmless. "Got a light?"

The kid fished in his pocket, brought out matches, flipped them to Ramon. Ramon took his time lighting up. He inhaled, blew out smoke. The kid had half a foot on him, but Ramon wanted him to know who was in control.

The kid waved away smoke.

Finally Ramon spoke. "So?"

The informant dropped his cigarette on the ground and crushed it. "First, the money."

The kid was no dummy. Ramon felt in his pocket, drew out a few bills, handed them over.

"We just got back from the Escambray Mountains." The kid slipped the bills into his pocket. "We made a drop."

That's where Che Guevara was holed up, Ramon knew. Che was his hero. "You were there?"

The kid looked proud. "I was one of the drivers."

Ramon struggled to keep his composure. It wasn't fair. He was the one who should be with Che. Not this skinny little kid. "And?"

"My boss was making the final count, making sure all the guns and ammo were there—"

"Get to the point," Ramon cut in.

"We saw your man."

"Luis Perez?"

The kid nodded. "He looked different. His hair was lighter, and he was wearing glasses, but I remembered him from the job at the police station."

Ramon nodded. Six months earlier, their cell worked with a couple of others to set fire to a police station downtown. It hadn't been successful—the police put the fire out before much damage was done, but it was great for morale and courage. He thought he recalled the kid. Gangly. Scared. A new recruit.

"I'm going to need proof," Ramon said. "And I want to meet your leader."

"That will never happen. He doesn't meet with strangers."

"Then how do I know it's really Perez?"

"Because he said he's only been in Santa Clara a couple of months. Him and his 'wife.'"

Ramon straightened. "His wife? You saw her?"

He shook his head.

Ramon deflated.

"We drove back to Santa Clara together. Me, my boss, and Perez. Perez said how hungry he was and how his wife was such a good cook. But then my boss said he thought he recognized Perez from Havana. Perez said it was impossible. That he was from Santa Lucia. His wife, too. He clammed up after that. Wouldn't say a thing. Had us drop him off on a street corner."

"Do you know where they live?"

"No."

"And you don't know what he's doing."

"All I know is that he spends time with Che. Cienfuegos, too."

"I need to know where they're living."

A shrewd look came over the kid. "I can maybe find out… but it'll cost you."

Ramon fisted his hands. Pacelli had given him money to spread around, and he had skimmed a little to buy food. He didn't have much left. He studied the kid. It was bad enough that Luis was spending time with Che and Cienfuegos while Ramon was stuck in Havana. It was worse that he, Ramon, was in danger of being bumped off if he didn't come through. He was supposed to be by Luis's side. Not the girl. The Santería witch. Meanwhile he had been reduced to doling out bribes. Ramon was so angry he thought his head might explode, with steam blasting out, like in the cartoons. Then he remembered who his boss was. He told the kid he'd be in touch and headed back to Pacelli.

CHAPTER SEVENTEEN

Tony Pacelli put the phone down and rubbed his hands together. The spic had told him about the lead last night. His first instinct was to send his men to Santa Clara right away; stage a late-night raid once he discovered where his daughter lived. Then he'd hustle her out of Cuba with her mother. Perez would be taken out, of course. No great loss. But there was a risk that Francesca might be caught in the crossfire, so he had to consider other options. The phone call he'd ended would be an excellent alternative.

He went to the balcony and looked down on the Malecón. The water was choppy, and the morning sun fired a volley of sparks that danced over the waves. There was no doubt in his mind now that Batista would be overthrown. The only question was when. Castro would take over and there would be chaos for a while, but Tony figured it would be only temporary. The new government would need a steady source of revenue, and the casinos could supply it. It was simply a matter of waiting, figuring out the new point men, greasing the right palms.

Until the dust settled, however, Tony, along with the other casino owners, was flying cash back to the States. On the return trips the planes brought in weapons for the rebels. He'd known about the flights for over a year but only involved himself a few months ago. It was a prudent insurance policy, a way to hedge his bets.

All their bets, in fact, except Lansky's. Meyer Lansky's ties to Batista were too deep. And too public. Once Castro took over, the Little Man's days in Havana would be numbered. Tony felt bad—at least he told himself he did. Lansky had been his mentor. But Tony had his own future to consider, and without Lansky as his filter, he'd be dealing with the top government honchos himself. Not so bad.

Although Tony wasn't prone to outbursts in his professional life, he wasn't a man who smiled easily. He did now. Normally he didn't care how weapons arrived and reached their destination. The important thing was that the rebels knew who their benefactors were. Everything else could be handled by bagmen and underlings, men Tony didn't know and didn't want to. Until now.

***

The day after Christmas Ramon boarded the train for Santa Clara. The kid, whose name was Alejandro, sat beside him, still wearing his fake leather jacket. Alejandro didn't talk for most of the trip. Just slumped in his seat, pale and awkward, a fearful look on his face. He had reason to be afraid, Ramon thought. The kid had to be feeling more pressure than in his entire life. At the same time Pacelli had dangled a lot of money in front of him, so he was motivated.

Pacelli wanted to use Alejandro to bait Luis. At first Ramon thought it was too risky. Luis wouldn't trust the kid, might suspect him, given what the kid said about Luis clamming up after someone thought they recognized him. But Pacelli pointed out that Luis wouldn't deal with Ramon under any circumstances. They had no choice. If the kid failed, well, Pacelli told Ramon to impress on him that this was Pacelli's daughter. Failure was not an option.

Ramon stared out the window. The blur of countryside, small towns, and fields reminded him of the time he and Luis took the train to Havana from Oriente. So much had happened over the past three years. His friendship with Luis had gone cold, just when the revolution was heating up. Which would not have happened if the girl hadn't stumbled into their lives. Ramon was only doing what any good friend would when that friend wasn't thinking with the right body part. And now her father was on his side, too. Luis would thank him one day. He would realize how shrewd Ramon had been to make the deal. Everyone would benefit. The father would get his daughter back, Luis would get his weapons, and Ramon would—eventually—get Luis.

He turned away from the window and started to explain to the kid what he should say to Luis, and more important, what not to say. "Never mention the girl. As far as you know, he is alone. There is no woman."

The kid nodded. Ramon could smell the fear coming off him. Bitter, a little salty.

"Don't mention that you want to come to his house. You don't want to raise any suspicions. Let him suggest a meeting place."

"But how will we find out where he lives?"

"Leave that to me."

"How will—"

Ramon cut him off. "Like I said, leave that to me. Do not talk to him about anything except the weapons."

"How will that work?"

Ramon cleared his throat, straightened up, and laced his fingers together. "I already told you that my people are flying in a cache of weapons from Miami. I've arranged for them to be trucked here to Santa Clara. You are the go-between. You tell Perez they are coming and that he—or someone he designates—should handle the transfer."

The kid bit his lip. "What if he decides to send another man instead?"

Ramon flexed his fingers forward and backward. "He won't. He'll want to supervise it. That's the way he is. By the way, when you first approach him, he'll want to meet in a neutral location. He might bring some of his *compadres* to check you out."

The kid's chest heaved. "I don't know—"

Ramon cut in. "Oh yes, you do. And yes you can. That's why you're getting all the *dinero*."

The train slowed. They were approaching Santa Clara.

"You will give him a deadline to make a decision. Say twenty-four hours. He will talk it over with his superiors. We will stay in a hotel while he does."

"How do you know they will agree?"

Ramon chuckled. "They cannot afford to say no." He jabbed his finger at the kid's chest. "The most important thing is the delivery location. It will be wherever Perez tells you. Before you go there, you and the driver will meet me. There will be several men in the truck. They will come with me. Then you will deliver the cargo. Meanwhile, the others will rescue the girl. If everything goes right, no one will get hurt." He hoped what he was saying would prove true. He was following Pacelli's orders exactly. Pacelli had no reason to turn the tables on him. Or the kid. He hoped.

The kid nodded uncertainly, as if wondering the same thing. "And I will get paid when?"

"When I am." Ramon forced a smile. "I will get your share to you. It will be a very happy new year. For both of us."

The kid looked blank.

"One more thing," Ramon added. "You are never to mention Pacelli's name. Ever. They will ask. Especially Perez. He will want to know who is behind the shipment. You will tell him you do not know. That it was a gift. From friends. It will not be the first 'gift' they've received. He will understand."

The train pulled into the station. It had been a remarkably smooth trip. Even the train was on time.

The kid pulled up the collar of his jacket.

"Why do you wear that?" Ramon asked. "It is way too hot for it here."

The kid shrugged.

Ramon heaved a sigh. *Another* pendejo *who thinks he is what he wears.*

Aloud he said, "You'll have to take it off. You look too obvious. Now, do you have any questions?"

"What do we do now?"

Was the kid really that stupid? Ramon hoped he hadn't made a mistake. So much depended on him. "We contact Perez."

***

Like Havana, downtown Santa Clara was overwhelmed with Christmas decorations. Although it was beach weather, the sidewalks, stores, and buildings were plastered with evergreens, colored lights, Santas, reindeer, fake snow. All American-inspired. Probably brought in from Miami. America seemed to own every square mile of Cuba. What would happen when they disappeared after the revolution? Luis said it meant freedom. Ramon used to believe him. Now he wasn't so sure. He wasn't sure about anything.

He and the kid walked to the university and settled themselves in front of one of the campus buildings. Ramon was the spotter, identifying people—usually young men or women walking alone. When he found a prospect, Ramon told the kid to take the lead while he lurked in the background. The kid did what he was told, but it wasn't easy. They were strangers, and people knew it was dangerous to talk to outsiders these days.

Finally, after a couple of hours, two young women told them about a rooming house where the proprietor knew people who knew "the right people." One girl seemed to recall a couple who came from Santa Lucia.

They followed the directions to the boarding house, but once they got there, Ramon decided their intelligence was wrong. Alejandro asked the woman who owned the place whether she knew a couple who'd arrived in Santa Clara a month or so earlier. The couple were their cousins, the kid claimed. They needed to find them. For the family back in Santa Lucia.

But the woman refused to admit she'd ever heard of them, and she certainly couldn't tell them where they were. Ramon swore softly. What was it about Luis? Why did he always seem to have a cocoon of protection around him? What made him so special?

Frustrated, he and Alejandro checked into a cheap hotel. The next morning he told Alejandro to go back to the boarding house and beg the woman to send word to Luis. They would meet him any place he said. Any time. They just wanted to talk. "Are we still cousins?" Alejandro said.

Ramon thought for a moment. "You can tell her the truth. But say that you are certain Luis will want to talk to you." He told the kid to wait at the woman's rooming house until Luis replied.

"What if she doesn't come through?"

"Then we'll find another way," Ramon said, knowing he sounded more confident than he felt. If this didn't work, he didn't know what he'd do.

CHAPTER EIGHTEEN

High clouds stole across the sky, too shy to drop lower, Luis thought as he headed toward Parque Vidal the next afternoon. The woman whose sister's house they lived in sent him a note last night saying that a young man—a boy, really—wanted desperately to meet with him. "He wouldn't go away," the woman wrote. "He tried to convince me he was your cousin but then admitted he wasn't. But he was certain you'd want to hear what he has to say. He said for you to set the time and place—all he wants to do is talk."

At first Luis wasn't inclined to go. He'd spent too much time and effort creating a disguise. He cut his hair, and Frankie had helped him bleach what was left light brown. He wore glasses too, although they had no prescription, and he dressed in short-sleeved shirts and chinos. Just another bourgeois man on his way up. But the camouflage hadn't been foolproof. A few weeks earlier he'd hitched a ride on a truck back from the mountains with a few rebels who'd delivered weapons to Che. One of them thought he recognized Luis from Havana. Luis denied it, of course, but he made a speedy exit.

Since then he'd been extra careful. If he was spotted, he and Frankie would retreat to the mountains. Frankie wouldn't complain, but he didn't want to subject her to what was essentially an army camp with no plumbing, rough people, and a glut of weapons. Not in her condition.

The baby. A flush of warmth swept through him whenever he thought about it. Since she'd told him she was carrying his child, Luis began to look at the world differently. He was going to be a father. It was nothing short of a miracle. And it changed everything. He and Francesca would marry. He imagined where they would live, what he would teach his son—he was sure it would be a boy. The child would want for nothing. In a way he knew his joy was the natural progression of things, and he wasn't surprised. But at times the force of his emotions caught him unaware, and he had the

82

nagging feeling his priorities were backwards.

Francesca was the one who was working, cooking, cleaning. She couldn't continue after the baby was born. He would need to provide for the family. For the first time since he'd dropped out of university, Luis thought about going back. Becoming the lawyer he'd planned to be.

And yet the note sent to him by the boarding house woman was tempting. It was probably another arms shipment. The timing couldn't be better. Che was about to launch an attack on the city of Santa Clara. If he succeeded, Cuba would be cut in half, with the rebels controlling the eastern half of the island. Batista could not survive. The revolution would be over, the rebels victorious. It was critical that the attack be successful. The rebels could use all the support they could get.

And, if he was honest, there was another reason Luis wanted to meet the contact. He'd been in the area three months now. He'd made connections, but he wasn't much more than an errand boy. If he could broker this deal and pull it off, Che and the others would know he was important. Deserving of respect.

And so he sent word back to the woman at the rooming house that he would meet the boy in the Parque Vidal at four.

***

Tinny renditions of Christmas carols from nearby stores floated over Luis as he crossed the wide bricked pavement edging the park. He'd told the boy to meet him by the gazebo. He'd cased the place an hour earlier, looking for strangers whose expressions were a bit too casual or furtive. He saw nothing unusual.

At four o'clock he sat down on a bench a few yards from the gazebo. A few moments later, a scrawny, gangly young man in a blue t-shirt and khaki pants appeared on the opposite side. He stole a glance at Luis but made no effort to approach him. Instead he strolled across the lawn to the center of the park, to the statue of the "El Niño de la Bota," The Child with the Boot. He studied it, then went to the bronze statue of Marta Abreu. He was trying to blend in as a tourist, Luis thought, but his moves were so obvious it was painful. Luis wondered who had sent such a raw recruit.

He rose and walked over to the statue of Marta Abreu. As he drew near, a relieved expression came over the boy. Up close, Luis saw beads of sweat on his upper lip. He motioned toward the statue. "She was a very important person."

Confusion swam across the boy's face.

"Marta Abreu," Luis said. "She traveled all over the world but never forgot where she was from. She gave all her money to help the poor. You might say she's the first socialist Cuba ever had."

The boy gazed at the statue. Then he cleared his throat. "You are Luis Perez?" He wouldn't meet Luis's eyes.

Luis glanced at his watch. "I only have a few minutes. What is it you want?"

"There is a cache of weapons being flown in from Miami tomorrow. Someone thought you might be interested in them."

"Who?"

"I don't know," the boy said. "I know only what I have been told."

"And who told you?"

"My—my rebel leader at the Riviera Hotel in Havana. I cannot tell you his name. But we are DR. Like you."

The *Directorio Revolucionario* was one of the two major guerrilla groups fighting Batista. They were fighting to restore Cuba's democratic constitution of 1940. The other was Fidel's M-26-7, which stood for the Twenty-sixth of July movement, the date Fidel unsuccessfully attacked an army facility in Santiago de Cuba in 1953. The M-26-7 wanted to create a socialist state.

Luis eyed him suspiciously. "How did you find me?"

"You were recognized during a trip back from the Escambray Mountains."

Luis swore softly. All the effort he'd put into his disguise was for naught.

The boy seemed to understand. "Do not be worried. Our group wants to help. They know how committed you are."

Luis tightened his lips, unsure whether to believe him. "Who is supplying the weapons?"

"I hear rumors."

Luis arched his eyebrows.

"Businessmen in Havana who see the writing on the wall. They want to foster good will."

Luis squinted. "What businessmen?"

"I don't know."

"Americans?"

The boy hunched his shoulders.

"Casino owners?"

The boy hesitated. "As I said, I do not know. But I will be your contact. The only one you will deal with."

Luis thought for a moment. "No. How do I know you are not a traitor? An informer? I cannot consider it without more information. Our conversation is over." He turned and started walking away.

The boy called out. "Two hundred M-1 Rifles. Fifteen Springfields, ten carbines, and seven thousand rounds of ammunition."

Luis spun around and hissed. "You should never say things like that out loud."

The boy hung his head. "I'm sorry. I—I only wanted—"

"To impress me. Get my attention."

The boy nodded. "My brother was with Camilo Cienfuegos. He was killed by the army. I asked for this job. To make sure his death would not be in vain."

Luis shifted his feet, studying the boy, considering. Finally he said, "You have a lot to learn."

The boy made scuff marks in the dirt with his sneaker. It was white, Luis noted.

"When will the shipment arrive?" he asked quietly.

"As I said, they are being flown in tomorrow night. We will truck them here from Havana. You will need your own truck to take possession. Whatever meeting point you wish."

"And what do they expect in return?"

"Only your good will once we are victorious."

Luis scratched his cheek. "I will consider it. You should stay in Santa Clara tonight. Meet me here again tomorrow morning. So that you have time to get back to Havana before dark if we move ahead."

The boy nodded.

"What is your name?"

"Alejandro."

They discussed a few more details, then Luis briskly exited the park. Batista's soldiers were gearing up for the battle with over three thousand troops, he'd heard. The rebels were only four hundred. The army would be supported by aircraft, snipers, and tanks. In fact, the army was waiting for reinforcements which were supposed to arrive by train tomorrow. But Che was planning to attack the city before then. Cienfuegos would have been here too, but he was battling an army garrison on the northern coast in Yaguajay. The rebels were outnumbered and outgunned. They needed support.

Was this offer real? He'd heard reports that Havana businessmen, casino owners, other Americans, the CIA included, were ferrying in arms for both the army and the rebels. Betting on both sides. Luis needed to be careful he wasn't putting himself in a position to be exploited by both sides. And yet he was already thinking where the weapons should be deployed. He would deliver them to Che and his men, who, if everything went according to plan, would reach the university tomorrow.

***

Alejandro watched Luis walk away from the park. Everything went exactly as Ramon said it would. The lie about his brother dying while fighting with Cienfuegos clinched it. Ramon would be pleased.

Meanwhile Luis shuffled down the street, so preoccupied that he failed to notice a figure detach itself from the column of a building near the park and follow him. It would be the most important mistake of his life.

CHAPTER NINETEEN

On the morning of December twenty-ninth a lonely bird chirped as if it might be its last day on earth. Given the circumstances, Luis thought as he made his way home, it might be. Che's column had reached the university late yesterday. Since then steady bursts of gunfire had rung out, threatening to silence the bird's song. The flinty scent of gunpowder hung in the air.

The rebels were clearly outnumbered, but they were positioned for maximum effect. Men from the DR and M-26-7 had crept into the city to attack the army barracks. Bombs and snipers were planted strategically so that army troops couldn't roam the streets. Most of the residents of Santa Clara helped by creating barricades. They had a cache of homemade Molotov cocktails, too.

Che's men had advanced on Capiro Hill, the last obstacle to their entry into the city proper. The men expected to be on a suicide mission, but as they approached the top of the hill, they were stunned to meet no resistance. Batista's troops had fled, taking cover in their barracks and on the train from Havana with reinforcements. The rebels figured the army was buying time for a counterattack. At dusk Che brought in tractors from the university's agriculture department to destroy the tracks, so that the train would be stuck.

As dawn broke, Luis, who had been with Che all night, took advantage of a lull in the fighting. He walked home, his rifle slung across his shoulder. His fatigues were stained with dirt and sweat. Francesca was still asleep. She could sleep through anything, he thought as he slipped the rifle off and sat on the bed. His weight on the mattress woke her, and she greeted him with that wanton smile he'd come to expect. How could this woman make him want to take her whenever he saw her? Maybe Ramon had been right. Maybe she was a witch, and he was under her spell. If so, he hoped it lasted forever. She held out her arms. He took off his clothes and lay on the bed.

When they embraced, she let out that breathy sigh of contentment he'd also come to expect. She kissed his neck, his ears, his face.

"You taste salty," she whispered.

"It was a hot night."

"And earthy. Were you rolling around in the dirt?" She laughed and positioned herself on top of him. Her hands softly brushed his chest. He felt himself harden.

Someone outside yelled, and an explosion shattered the mood. It wasn't a direct hit, but it was close. A Molotov cocktail. They heard the clomp of shoes and boots running down the street. Gunfire erupted. The smell of kerosene and smoke drifted inside. Francesca froze.

Luis tightened his hold on her. They stayed still, not moving for almost a minute. Then he gently pushed her away. In the dim light of dawn he saw fear in her eyes. Fear, and something else. Something sad and haunting, as if she knew what was coming.

"You need to leave Santa Clara for a while," he said.

She was quiet for a moment. Then she rolled off him. "No. I won't leave you, Luis."

Luis snapped, and he stood, a wave of anger flooding through him. He needed to protect her, but she was not allowing him to. "How can you be so stubborn? And selfish? You hear what's going on out there. You have to think of the baby. What if something happens to you? Or him? I cannot permit you to stay. Our landlady is going south to her family this afternoon. She's offered to take you with her. It's settled." He flicked a hand toward the closet. "You should get dressed and pack."

He expected her to react with fury, but she surprised him. She stood, her face hard with determination. "We have never been apart," she said quietly. "Ever since I left Havana. I told you then I would stay with you forever. In good times or bad. War or peace. This is one of those times."

"Francesca, I will be gone all day and most of the night. I wouldn't be able to concentrate if I thought you were here by yourself."

"Luis, stop this foolishness. You know I can blacken the windows. Turn off the lights. Run to the back of the house and hide. We will be fine." She patted her stomach.

Luis tried to choke back his anger. "Francesca, listen. If we win this battle, it will be over. The rebels will be victorious. But the fight for Santa Clara is critical. The most important battle of the revolution. I cannot leave you unprotected." He stopped. "And if you won't go willingly," he added, "I'll arrange for someone to take you."

She planted her hands on her hips. "You still don't understand, do you? If something happens to you, it happens to me. We go through this together. "

His frustration roiled. He'd never told her what he did for the rebels.

Partly because she didn't share his views, partly because it was dangerous to reveal information, but mostly because since they'd left Havana, he had nothing noteworthy to report. Until now. He weighed telling her about the weapons. If it would persuade her to leave and guarantee her safety, it was worth it. He told her.

"Who is supplying them?"

"I'm not sure. That's what concerns me." He told her about the meeting in the park. "There is always the possibility of a trap. If that is the case, I don't want you anywhere near."

"If you are that suspicious, why go through with it?"

He didn't answer for a moment. "Because I want to make a contribution."

Francesca was quiet. Then she went to their bureau, opened the drawer, and pulled on her slip. It was getting tight across the middle. She came back. "Yes, it very well could be a trap. Then again, it might not. And in the end, it might not matter. Whoever is providing the weapons is working toward the same goal as you. At least for the moment. You cannot refuse the deal."

"Which is why you must leave for a few days."

She whipped around. "Luis, I am not leaving my home. Not again. Not without you." She finished dressing in a red skirt and white blouse.

Luis tried to contain his frustration. He had never met such an obstinate woman. He was about to tell her that when another Molotov cocktail exploded outside. Francesca winced, but then went into the kitchen to start breakfast. Eggs, tortillas, and plantains. She had turned into a wonderful cook. He had expected the daughter of a Mafia boss to be a spoiled princess, but she took to the life of a worker like she was born to it. It was impossible to remain angry at her.

She was at the sink washing up afterwards when he caught her around the middle, pulled her to him, and kissed her belly. It was starting to have that rounded look. "This will be the most adored baby ever, you know."

She put down the saucepan and slipped her arms around him. The wanton look came into her eyes again. "When did you say you have to leave?"

"I have a meeting at the Parque Vidal."

"How soon?" Her hands caressed his shoulders and moved down his arms.

He felt himself respond. "Not that soon."

***

News of the battle of Santa Clara reached Havana that night. After the rebels bulldozed the railroad tracks late that afternoon, the army's train derailed, and most of the troops surrendered. That meant the enormous cache of ammunition on the train was now in rebel hands. Tony Pacelli crossed his arms as he waited at a private airstrip outside Havana. His load from Miami, which was due to land in a few minutes, might be superfluous. The rebels wouldn't need them.

Fortunately, that wasn't the goal of his mission. But it might change things on the other end. Luis Perez might cancel the meet; he might laugh at the paltry amount of arms he was getting compared to the cache on the train, which, rumor said, were packed in boxes labeled "Property of U.S. Army." To make things worse, there was the possibility Perez wouldn't show at all, and Tony would miss his opportunity to take him out.

A thick cloud cover spat out a light drizzle, obscuring the view. Tony shifted, feeling droplets of moisture on his cheeks, his neck, his hair. The damn pilot better know where to land. This was an airstrip known only to a few Havana "businessmen." In fact, he should have alerted Lansky he was planning to use it, but he'd somehow forgotten to call.

A hushed but distinct buzz whined in the distance. One of the men with Tony lit a few flares and placed them on both sides of the landing strip. Within a minute, the buzz became a drone and finally a shriek. A bulky shape emerged and descended from the gloom. It was a Piper Comanche. Landing gear materialized, the plane landed and coasted to a stop at the end of the strip. Then it turned and taxied over to Tony's Cadillac and a pickup truck parked mid-strip. The smell of fuel wafted over the men at the vehicles.

Tony's men surrounded the plane. The door to the plane opened. A stepladder appeared. A small wiry man exited the plane and clattered down the steps. Tony walked forward to greet him.

"So?" Tony flipped up his hands.

"Smooth as silk," the man replied. "Everything is under control."

"Good." Tony slipped his hands in his pants pockets. "Is the cargo everything you said it would be?"

The man smiled. "That… and more. Our friends were especially generous this time. Two days ago, apparently, there was a heist at an armory in Kentucky."

Tony nodded. He hadn't asked the identity of these "friends" when he made the arrangements, but he had an idea who they were. Santo Trafficante, Lansky, and Carlos Marcello from New Orleans had all been known to cultivate contacts in the CIA when their interests aligned. The Cuban revolution was one of those times. Both organizations had a vested interest in making sure Fidel, when he did come to power, would be a friend. But relations between the organizations were—to put it mildly— precarious. Tony wanted Santo to guarantee that the CIA wasn't mounting a sting operation designed to net him and other casino owners. But Santo told him the CIA wanted assurances from Tony that he wasn't trying to swindle *them*. It was hard to tell friends from foes. Everyone was playing the Cuba card.

Tony gestured for his men to unload the weapons. He turned around. "Suarez, where are you?"

Ramon, hunched over the wheel of the pickup, jumped down and trotted over.

Tony looked him up and down. "Are you ready?"

Ramon nodded. "*Si*, Señor. Everything is in place."

"You're sure you know where she is?"

"I followed Perez to their home. I can find it in the dark."

"And your boy?" Tony motioned to Alejandro who was helping the men load the weapons into the bed of the truck.

"He is ready. He will meet Perez and transfer the weapons."

"Good," Tony said. "I will meet you at the prearranged place."

"*Si*, Señor Pacelli."

Tony went to his Cadillac and got into the back seat for the drive to Santa Clara. With luck they would make it in about two hours.

***

Frankie yawned as she washed the dinner dishes. Being pregnant was more tiring than she'd expected. She was able to come home early—the bank closed at noon because of the fighting—and washed their clothes. Now she went into the back yard to take the dry clothes off the clothesline. She tried to blot out the noise, but the occasional shatter of glass, distant bursts of gunfire, shouts, and car horns made it impossible. She went inside quickly to fold the clothes, murmuring a prayer that Luis was safe.

It was a crazy, unpredictable time. A friend at the bank said her mother, a teacher, had been visited by a couple of rebels. Dirty and smelly, they'd shown up without warning at the house. They were wearing fatigues, and their rifles were slung across their shoulders, while rosaries hung from their necks. Her friend's mother was terrified until one of them confessed he'd been her student years earlier. The teacher relaxed and offered them coffee. They stayed for an hour, drinking coffee and eating cookies, chatting about everything and nothing. Then they thanked her for the coffee and left.

Frankie went into the bedroom and put their clothes away. When she was home, safe and secure, she could shut out the fighting. She, too, could drink coffee and eat cookies, ignore the chaos. Inside, her world was smaller. More ordered. And once the baby was born, it would shrink more. There would be only the three of them. Their family against the world. She ran her hand tenderly around her belly.

She had to make sure there was nothing but love and safety around them. If God allowed her to.

She realized she'd said another prayer. She hoped God was listening. It had been a while since she'd gone to church. Like her, Luis was Catholic, but not observant. She didn't miss mass, communion, or sermons. They'd made her impatient. But if He was going to protect them, Frankie figured she owed Him something.

Feeling strangely peaceful, she ran hot water for a bath. Afterwards she'd curl up in bed. With luck, Luis would be home before morning. Hopefully he would tell her what happened. She was delighted he was finally beginning to confide in her. They would be true partners. In life as well as love. Sharing their dreams, their plans, their children. She hung her robe on a hook, took off her clothes, and was about to get into the tub when she heard her front door burst open. An eruption of machine gun fire strafed the walls followed by shouts and exclamations in Spanish.

Frankie grabbed a towel and froze. No one broke into *her* house. She wrapped the towel around her and hurried into the front room. Three men, their faces masked by bandanas, quickly surrounded her, all of them pointing machine guns at her. In the face of such imminent danger, her courage evaporated, and her skin prickled with dread.

"Don't shoot!" She screamed. "I am unarmed."

One of the men grabbed her. She could barely keep the towel where it belonged.

"Stop!" she begged. "Don't hurt me. I am pregnant. *Estoy embarazada!*"

The man who grabbed her loosened his hold, but only for a second. Then he ordered one of the other men to take off his shirt. A camouflage shirt. The man stripped it off and held it out. Frankie snatched it, and, with the first man still holding her arm, awkwardly turned away. She dropped the towel and took her time getting the shirt on, trying to think of something—anything—she could do to break free, but she knew it was futile.

"If you do what we say, you will not be hurt, Señorita Pacelli," the man said. Above the bandana, his eyes were chips of ebony.

Frankie's mouth fell open, and in that second, she understood. She didn't know these men, had never seen them before, but she knew who'd sent them. And why. She suddenly felt her new life slipping through her fingers like sand. Her body went slack, and she broke into long wrenching sobs. If the goon hadn't been clutching her, she would have collapsed on the floor.

The man holding her nodded to the others, and the man who'd given her his shirt fished a blindfold out of his pants and slipped it over her eyes.

"You will only wear this for a short time," he said. "We will not hurt you."

The third man went around behind her, squeezed her arms together and tied her hands. Frankie cried hysterically. She tried to go weak again, to sink to the floor so they couldn't move her, but they pushed and pulled and prodded and shoved until they forced her upright and she had no choice. Reluctantly she planted one foot in front of the other.

They steered her outside. Amid her sobs, the spit of gunfire, and the smell of cordite, she was lifted into the bed of a truck and propped against the side. A sharp pain throbbed against her temples. Light trickled through a tiny gap in the blindfold, and she could tell that one of the men was staying with her in the back. The others must have gone in front, because the doors opened, then slammed. The engine revved. A moment later the truck bumped down the road and turned the corner.

***

It had been a long day for Luis, and night would be longer. The rebels had derailed the train earlier, and the army troops had, for the most part, surrendered. So did the troops in their barracks. There was little bloodshed, and Che was already enjoying the fruits of what would be heralded as the defining battle of the revolution. In Oriente province, Fidel and his men had attacked Santiago de Cuba and were winning. The rebels now had control of the entire Central Highway across the island. Everything was coming together.

Luis met Alejandro and the truck from Havana on a dirt road near a farm outside Santa Clara. They transferred the weapons to the pickup Luis had borrowed. He turned toward the truck, ready to jump into the cab, when a series of shots rang out from behind. Luis dropped to the ground and threw his arms over his head. Alejandro didn't.

Luis peeked at the boy and saw a look of complete surprise come over him. A blossom of red appeared on his chest and expanded until it covered the front of his shirt. Luis watched in horror as the boy reached an arm toward him, staggered forward, then sank to the ground.

Behind him, Luis heard a car door slam. An engine accelerated and he heard a squeal as if the car was making a sharp turn. He waited for more shots to tear him to pieces. Nothing happened.

When he was sure the car was gone, he leaped up and threw himself into the truck. It had been a trap. He should have known. The bullet that killed Alejandro was undoubtedly meant for him, and when they realized they'd shot the wrong man, they would come back to finish the job. He and Francesca would have to flee Santa Clara. Tonight.

But first he had to deliver the arms to Che. He raced the truck back to the university where Che was headquartered and hurriedly unloaded the cargo. Although the weapons from the train now gave them more than enough without Luis's contribution, Che clapped Luis on the shoulder and called him a "brother." Luis was too worried to feel a scrap of pride.

He left the truck with Che and hurried home. Wisps of smoke, the remnants of Molotov cocktails, rose in the night air, but that didn't keep the people of Santa Clara from gathering on the street to celebrate. Technically, the battle was not yet over, but the university was in the hands of the rebels, and the streets were full of revelry. Luis pushed his way through the crowd, cursing them for getting in his way.

The farther he got from the university, the quieter it grew, although that wouldn't last. As people in his neighborhood heard the news about Che's victory, they, too, would rush outdoors to celebrate. Paradoxically, the silence made him more frantic and he started to run.

Their apartment occupied the rear of a house. Which meant their front door was in the back yard. As he crossed the lawn and went around to the back, he froze. The lights in the apartment were on, and the door was wide open. It was almost four in the morning. Something was wrong. He raced to the door and called out.

"Francesca?" No answer. His skin was damp beneath his clothes. He burst inside. "Francesca, where are you?"

Still no answer. He sprinted from the front room to the bedroom. She wasn't there, and the bed was still made. He spun around, frantic, and called her name. Nothing. When he got to the bathroom, he saw the tub filled with now cold water. Her robe hung on a hook behind the door. He hurried back to the front room and took in the scene. The reading lamp was knocked over, and the two chairs they owned were on their sides. Then he saw the spray of bullets embedded in the wall.

A knot twisted his stomach, and a wave of horror washed over him. He started to shake uncontrollably. He felt disoriented and weightless, as if his body was held together by only the flimsiest of strings.

He trudged back to the bathroom, grabbed Francesca's robe, and inhaled. Her smell was woven into the fabric, and he wanted to lose himself in it. Then he dropped the robe and sank to his knees. He covered his eyes and began to weep. His anguished cries were swallowed up by cheers from his neighbors outside.

"*Viva la Revolución!*"

PART TWO
1989 – 1992

CHAPTER TWENTY

1989: Angola

Nightfall came hard and fast in Angola. This close to the equator twilight was an illusion. Minutes after sunset, night slammed into earth like a giant boulder, obliterating the day with an explosion of dark. A thick, menacing dark, unrelieved by street light. It was a dark Luis had come to know.

He made his way across the road to a ramshackle bar on the outskirts of Lucapa. Lucapa was the main city—if you could call it that—in Lunda Norte, the province of Angola that bordered Zaire. The city was like a frontier town in the Wild West, full of miners, prostitutes, guns-for-hire, and traders.

And Cubans.

For nearly fifteen years, since 1975, Fidel had been sending troops to help the Angolans preserve their Marxist government. A protracted civil war pitted groups backed by Fidel and the Soviets against insurgents supported by South Africa and the U.S.

Last year a peace accord had finally been signed in New York, and while insurgents were still attacking each other, the Cubans were out of the fight. Luis, a *Coronel* in the Cuban Army, had been promoted to *General de Brigada* after the peace accord and was now the commander of the Lucapa base, charged with the orderly withdrawal of Cubans. He'd been there nearly two years, and he often wondered why they'd been there at all. People called it Cuba's Vietnam; he couldn't disagree. Over fifty thousand Cuban troops and humanitarian forces, mostly doctors, had come halfway around the world, but for what? A primitive country with nothing to offer except diamonds and gold, caught in a proxy war between the superpowers.

He rolled his shoulders and stamped his feet. Almost fifty now, and a bit stooped, flecks of gray were threaded through his hair, and he needed glasses to read. The humid climate was hard on him, and November marked the start of Angola's hot, rainy season. He felt stiff, and his clothes were damp and clammy. The breeze had stiffened, and the air carried a prickly metallic scent, which meant a storm was on the way. Mercifully, Lucapa sat on a high plateau, with an elevation that normally made the heat more tolerable. In Africa a few degrees made the difference between hell and purgatory.

He pulled the door open and walked into Nkiambi's, Niki's for short. It was not much more than a ramshackle hut with a corrugated metal roof. A desultory fan circulated air, but electricity in this part of the world was unreliable, and Luis fully expected it would cut out at some point that evening. A makeshift bar that had once been a tree occupied one side of the room; white plastic garden chairs and tables the other. Two light bulbs overhead threw long, dark shadows that made it easy for people to disappear in the corners.

It was still early, and the bar was half filled. A few soldiers, mostly Cuban; an Angolan here and there. Miners, probably. No women yet, but they usually didn't come until they'd put their children to bed.

Luis went to the bar and ordered a beer from an Angolan with shiny black skin and a permanent air of resentment. Luis couldn't blame him. For fifteen years Niki had contended with Cubans invading his country, drinking his booze, often not paying, and, now that they were withdrawing, stealing whatever they could. Of course, corruption and plunder were never discussed in Fidel's army—officially they didn't exist—but ask any Angolan, and they'd tell you the truth. The Angolans probably held Cubans in the same esteem that Cubans held Americans thirty years earlier.

"You call this shit rum?" a voice called out.

Luis spun around.

"¡Mierda!" Ramon drained his glass, then slammed it on the table.

"Ramon!" Luis called.

Ramon looked up. He had not aged well. Then again, who had? He had lost most of his hair, gained twenty pounds, and his face was both wrinkled and flushed, the mark of a man who drank too much and slept too little. Luis raised his bottle of beer in greeting and joined him at a table. "Relax, *amigo.* Two more months and we're out of this hell hole."

Ramon glowered. "Easy for you to say. I don't have my orders."

Luis sat. "They are coming. I made sure of it. We leave together."

Ramon sniffed.

"Until then, all you have to do is stay out of the way of the elephants."

Ramon had risen to the rank of *Teniente Coronel,* Lieutenant Colonel, mostly because he'd been at Luis's side for years, the Sancho Panza to his Don Quixote. The only time they'd been separated was the few months Luis was in Santa Clara during the revolution, and they no longer talked about that. After Francesca disappeared, Ramon confessed that he had been tortured by Francesca's father to betray the couple. The alternative would have been certain death. Luis admitted he'd probably have done the same thing, but it took years of abject apologies on Ramon's part—he was young; he didn't have any choice—before Luis trusted him again. But that was in the past. In the years they'd been in the army together, Ramon had been steadfast, loyal, and obedient.

"The lions, too, *General*. Once they pick up your scent, you're dinner." Ramon paused. "And the way we stink..." He laughed.

Luis took a pull on his beer. It was miraculously cool. He had no idea how the Angolans kept beer cold in the middle of the bush. "So, did you hear the news?"

"There's a private 747 waiting for us in Luanda?"

Luis grinned. "You haven't been on the shortwave today?"

"I've been on maneuvers with our FAPLA friends."

FAPLA, the People's Armed Forces for the Liberation of Angola, was the Angolan army, and despite the peace accord, they were still fighting the enemy insurgents of UNITA, the National Union for Total Independence of Angola.

Luis nodded. "Well, forget all that. Today will go down in history as a watershed event."

Ramon sat up. "Did the Israelis set off an atom bomb?"

"The East German government announced that East Germans can cross into West Germany any time they want. People in Berlin are celebrating in the streets. They tore down the Wall."

Ramon's mouth fell open. "The Berlin Wall?"

Luis nodded. "It's over. Communism is finished."

Ramon didn't move. His mouth remained open, as if he was still processing the information. Finally, he spoke. "What about Cuba?"

"How long do you think Fidel can hang on without Soviet support?" Luis took another swig of his beer. "Why do you think he was so anxious for peace negotiations?"

Ramon looked confused.

"Fidel is many things," Luis went on. "But he is not stupid. He knows we're in for tough times, and we need to stop bleeding money and manpower here. He wants us home."

"Wait. Are you saying the Soviet Union is no longer giving us support?"

"Not like before. They've cut back on their exports. Especially petroleum."

Ramon scowled.

"East Germany was first, but I expect there will be a chain reaction. Poland, Romania, Hungary. Then Armenia, Georgia, the Ukraine. It's entirely possible that in a few years the USSR will no longer exist."

Ramon splayed his hands in the air. "Where does that leave us?"

"Good question." Luis finished his beer and ordered another.

"¡Jesu Christo!" Ramon said after a pause. He stood up, his chair scraping the floor, and strolled to the bar. "Another round." He tipped his glass to Niki. He brought the drinks back to the table, sat down, and leaned toward Luis. "I've been thinking," he said in a low voice. "And what you said makes it more important. Why should we be the only ones going back to Cuba without—souvenirs?"

"Souvenirs?"

"I have a friend. He's mining for diamonds, and he's willing to stake us to a partnership. All we have to do is get them out of here."

"An Angolan?"

"What does it matter where he's from? If we can smuggle them out and get them to a polisher, we would be rich."

Luis took a long pull on his beer. Through a window a fork of lightning singed the sky. A crack of thunder followed. The storm. "And how do we get them to a polisher?"

Ramon smiled. "He says there are three centers for refining diamonds. Antwerp and Israel are two."

"We can't go to either place. We don't have the money. Or visas."

Ramon held up a finger. "Ah, but the third center is in the USSR. Yerevan, capital of Armenia. You could get yourself a trip there. To inspect the troop situation or something. You're a *General* now. You can go anywhere."

Luis thought about it. Then he leaned toward Ramon. "Just because everyone else is plundering the people and resources of this godforsaken place doesn't mean we should."

Ramon leaned back, slapping the surface of the table. "You are a fool."

Luis didn't answer.

"Look, *amigo*. This is a sure thing. But I can't do it alone. I need help." His eyes swept the room. "But if you're not interested, I'll find another officer." He paused. "You won't say anything?"

Luis hesitated. "Of course not."

Another crack of lightning split the air, followed by a clap of thunder. Then the rain started. Without warning a torrent of what sounded like machine gun bullets pummeled the metal roof of the bar.

Suddenly a shout erupted from the corner behind them. "Goddammit!" someone yelled in English. "On top of everything else, this shithole of a bar leaks!"

Luis and Ramon whipped around. A man in the corner had stood up. He held a glass of what looked like whiskey in one hand, but the other was rubbing the back of his neck as if he'd been punched.

"You get what you pay for, amigo," Luis replied in Spanish.

"*Claro*," the man said, switching to Spanish.

"Join us." Luis tilted his bottle in the man's direction. "During the rainy season it's smarter to sit in the middle of the room."

The man nodded and came over. He was a tall, lean man with pale skin, frizzy red hair and a bushy beard threaded with gray. He didn't appear to be military, and he was dressed in the type of khakis people wore on safari. A scuffed leather backpack was slung over his shoulder. The man's face was flushed, as if he'd been out in the sun too long. That, or he was drunk. Maybe both.

Still mumbling in English, he sat down. "Sorry." He switched to Spanish again. "Everything is soggy here. *Empapado.* The air, the clothes, the food, even the booze."

"Where are you from?" Luis asked. "Your Spanish is good."

"I was born in Sweden but I've lived in the U.S. most of my life."

Ramon and Luis exchanged a look.

The man caught it. "Don't worry. I'm not CIA or army or any military, as it happens. I'm a geologist."

"Geologist?" Ramon cocked his head.

"A scientist who studies rocks and other materials deep in the Earth," Luis explained.

Ramon's eyes narrowed. "Ah, a miner."

"You could say that."

"Diamonds or gold?" Ramon waved a hand. "Or do you plan to make your fortune in both?"

The man smiled and extended his hand. "I'm Ned Swenson. And with whom do I have the pleasure of drinking?"

Ramon and Luis introduced themselves.

"How long have you been in Africa?" Ramon asked.

"About a month," Swenson said.

"You have to be careful," Ramon said importantly. "You must make sure your guide is trustworthy. Despite the peace treaty, there is still fighting. And UNITA is the largest diamond miner in the area. If they think you're invading their territory, they'll kill you." He snapped his finger. "Like that."

"If the land mines don't," Luis added.

"So I understand." For having heard such a dire prediction, Swenson looked remarkably serene.

"You're not the first to find your way here, you know," Luis said. "Now that the war is winding down, everyone is trying to exploit the area. Except the poor Angolans."

"Spoken like a true Marxist." Swenson clapped Luis on the back. "Of which there will be fewer after today."

"You heard about Berlin?"

"Of course." Swenson got up. "In fact, let me buy the next round. To celebrate."

The rain still pounded the roof, and wet air drifted inside, curling Luis's hair and ringing his neck with sweat. When Swenson came back with their drinks, Luis saw bubbles of condensation on his bottle. Niki's electricity was stretched to its limit. This should be his last beer.

"So," Ramon tossed back his rum. "Which is it? Diamonds or gold?"

Swenson gazed at Ramon and Luis with bloodshot eyes. He'd probably been drinking for hours, Luis thought. "Actually, neither," he said.

"Then, why are you here?" Ramon said. "Surely, not for the climate." He guffawed and poked Luis with his elbow.

Swenson took his time answering. "The world is changing." He glanced at Luis. "In fact, today might be the first day..." He glanced up. "...or night of the new order."

Ramon nodded. "That's what Luis was saying."

"Not just a political order," Swenson went on. "An economic one, as well. Twenty years from now, the world will do business very differently."

"How?" Luis asked. For being half-drunk, the man was articulate.

Swenson took a long swig of his drink. "*Electronica.*"

Ramon scoffed. "Computers? They're nothing but a fast adding machine."

It was Swenson's turn to laugh. "Gentlemen, the world is on the brink of a new industrial age. Everything we use will be different in a few years. Imagine a telephone as small as a pack of cigarettes."

"You mean one of those cell phones?" Luis said. "I've heard of them. But they're expensive. A rich man's toy."

"Now, yes. But in ten years? Or twenty? You've probably seen the price of computers come down, perhaps in Cuba as well. Well, imagine a day when you will have access to a phone you can take anywhere in the world. Or an electronic device you can read books on. Or watch films. Or play games more complicated than any arcade. It's all coming."

He was starting to slur his words, Luis noted.

Ramon rubbed the back of his hand across his mouth. "So what? What does that have to do with mining in Angola?"

"All these devices will require a new type of battery."

Ramon pointed two fingers in the air and hopped his hand across the table. "They have them now."

"Not the bunny type." Swenson laughed. "Actually, they're called capacitors. Sort of a cousin to a battery. They help stabilize and store an electrical charge more efficiently than a battery. Because of that, they need to be made from materials that will conduct and preserve that charge."

Luis connected the dots. "And you discovered that material here."

A flush crept up Swenson's neck, and he flashed a Buddha-like smile.

"You don't expect me to confirm that, do you?"

He was definitely slurring his words. "You just did," Luis said.

Swenson flipped his palm up and down. "Maybe, maybe not. But I doubt I'm the first man who's not looking for gold or diamonds here."

Ramon curled his lip. "I don't understand."

Swenson shot Ramon a patronizing look. "Of course you don't."

Another torrent of lightning and thunder exploded.

Swenson leaned forward and whispered in a theatrical voice. "All right. I'll tell you. It's called coltan."

"Coltan?"

"Coltan. There is only a limited supply of this mineral in the world, and eighty percent of it is in Zaire. I predict that within ten years, people will be mining—and fighting over—coltan more fiercely than diamonds or oil or gold put together."

Ramon rolled his empty glass on the table. "If this mineral is so wonderful, why haven't we heard about it? And why haven't you found it?"

"Who says I haven't?" Swenson emptied his glass.

The door to the bar opened and an Angolan came in, spotted Swenson, and came over. "A break in the rain is coming, sir," he said politely. "We should be on our way."

"Ah, Tobias." Swenson nodded and stood unsteadily. "You've been excellent company, my friends, but now I must bid you good-bye. My driver is never wrong."

Luis watched him settle his tab with Niki, then lurch out the door. Suddenly Ramon got up too and went over to Niki. Luis couldn't hear their conversation, but he saw Ramon point toward the door.

Niki called out to his eighteen-year old son, Kambale, who worked the bar with his father. When Kambale came over, Niki whispered in his ear. Kambale nodded and exited the bar.

CHAPTER TWENTY-ONE

The next morning Ramon and Luis drove out of Lucapa on its only paved road. It smelled like damp asphalt, but that wouldn't last. Shimmering waves of heat were already rising from the ground. Luis was in the passenger seat, and Kambale, Niki's son, sat in the back of the Jeep they had borrowed.

"It is sure he went this way," Kambale said in broken Spanish. He pointed north.

Zaire lay to the north and east, but a corner of Angola's Lunda Norte province, where they were stationed, stretched farther north than the rest. This made the border between Angola and Zaire in that area hazy and imprecise, a fact that both miners and rebels had taken advantage of over the years.

After driving nearly sixty miles, they reached Dundo, a mining town a few miles from the border. The surrounding area was drained by several rivers with African names. At one time Luis had known their names, but now all he remembered was that the best mineral mines in the world could be found in the river basins.

If Lucapa was a Wild West town, Dundo was its outpost. Except for one anomaly. Diamonds had been discovered in its riverbeds in 1912, and part of the town had been developed as a planned community. For over sixty years, until 1977, an international consortium held the monopoly on mining, supplying ten percent of the world's gem-quality diamonds from the region. But the consortium was gone now, and the mining area was in the hands of the government, which effectively meant it was up for grabs.

Luis had been sent here when he was first posted to Angola. His assignment was to inspect the border crossing and recommend whatever fortifications he thought necessary. He knew it was a test—officially the border was supposed to be protected by Cuban forces. But the reality was that Cuban soldiers spent most of their time drinking, whoring, and acquiring contraband. Luis reported back that everything was in order. His Cuban higher-ups were pleased. No one wanted any trouble at this stage of the conflict.

Ramon drove past a ramshackle building that in Dundo was called a hotel. It was a place in which it was safer not to sleep, since you never knew how many of your belongings would still be there when—or if—you woke up.

Poverty, disease, and ignorance were rife in this corner of the world. And yet Angolans were among the most beautiful souls Luis had known. Simple folk, friendly, spiritual, and full of magic. They loved their dancing, and they loved their masks. They reminded him of the Santerías in Cuba.

They passed a development where roads bisected each other to form precise square lots with homes perched on top. The planned community. East and west lay a sprawl of huts that, by their lack of design, indicated a studied indifference, perhaps even a mutiny against the rigidity of the planned community. The locals lived there.

Leaving Dundo, they stayed on the main road, which roughly paralleled the rivers. The terrain rose and became rocky, with pockets of valleys in between. It wasn't mountainous, at least not like the mountains at home, but the unevenness of the plateau created rapids and waterfalls on the rivers, a few of which were used to generate power. When the wind blew in their direction Luis was sure he could hear the distant churn of the water.

Eventually Kambale gestured for them to turn west. As they jerked and bumped down a dirt road, the forest encroached on both sides, turning from brown to different hues of green. It smelled of rotting leaves, and Luis spotted a few trees that looked like the ceibas of home. Monkeys jabbered, insects buzzed, and a macaw, no doubt alarmed at their arrival, shrieked. Another bird responded, and the macaw screamed again. Luis felt a chill.

"How much farther?" Ramon asked Kambale.

Ramon must be uneasy, too.

"Small." Kambale pointed forward.

The road narrowed to a trail hardly wider than the Jeep. The forest seemed anxious to reclaim the road and swallow it whole. Luis noted they hadn't seen another human for miles.

"Where the fuck are we?" Ramon asked.

"Near the border," Luis said. "We might have crossed over." There would be no border guards here. "You need to be careful. There could be land mines."

"Or snakes." Ramon grimaced. Without warning a partial clearing materialized, as sudden as the advance of the forest moments earlier. Fifty yards ahead a mountain stream burbled over pebbles. Unlike the river water, which was muddy and brown, this stream was remarkably clear. A boulder surrounded by smaller rocks in a rough circle sat a few yards away from the stream.

"We are here," Kambale said.

Luis and Ramon hopped down from the Jeep and walked gingerly toward the stream. Kambale stayed in the Jeep. He was the smart one, Luis thought.

But nothing exploded and he saw no snakes. After a time Ramon stopped and kicked the dirt. "I don't get it," he said. "Why here?"

Luis studied the clearing. "If he's going to sink a mine, he's going to have to deforest the area and bring in machinery, like the diamond miners. Clearly he hasn't started yet."

Ramon called back to Kambale. "You sure this is the place?"

Niki's son nodded. "White man stop here. He have big light. He walk around. Take measures with feet. Sit on big rock." He pointed to the boulder and the circle of stones around it.

Ramon shaded his eyes with his hands. "Do you remember how we got here?"

Luis nodded.

"Can you make a map? You're good at those things."

"Why?"

"In case we need to find this place again."

"Ramon, it doesn't belong to us. I—"

"I'm not saying it does," Ramon said. He ran his tongue around his lips. "Consider it a personal favor, okay? It won't take long."

Luis slapped at the mosquitoes, considering. Sometimes Ramon did have good ideas. He was certainly more opportunistic than Luis, but he didn't always see the long-term implications of his actions. Which was why he got in trouble and relied on Luis to bail him out. But sketching wasn't a difficult or dangerous task. Luis enjoyed drawing, especially in Africa. So many exotic scenes.

He went to the Jeep and retrieved his backpack. He walked back toward the clearing, pulled out paper, and started sketching. He didn't know the coordinates, but he sketched the long road they'd driven up on, the Congolese border, as best he could, and the nearby rivers. He drew the boulder and circle of rocks in an inset on the lower left of the page, although it was not to scale.

"Would you say we went west or northwest after we turned off the main road?"

"I'd say—" Ramon's words were cut off by the whine of an engine. For an instant, all the other sounds in the forest ceased, as if the animals, birds, the insects too, were listening. Then, like a film that was paused and then advanced, everything spun into motion. A bird cawed. An animal yowled. The stream splashed against its banks. The drone of the vehicle grew louder.

"*¡Mierda!*" Ramon ran to the Jeep, jumped in, and started the engine. He shifted into reverse. With a jerk he backed up.

"Ramon, where are you going?" Luis called out. "Wait!"

"I need to hide the Jeep!" He motioned with the back of his hand. "Go hide in the bush. I'll be back."

Before Luis could answer, the Jeep screeched backwards out of the clearing and disappeared. Luis looked for a place to hide. He spotted a thicket not far from the stream, jogged over, and squeezed inside. He dropped to a crouch. The brush cast dark shadows over the thicket, but he had a view of the clearing.

A horn blasted, but Luis couldn't tell where it was coming from. Brakes squealed. A door slammed. Luis heard shouts about a hundred yards away. He could only hear snippets of the conversation, but it was obvious a heated argument had developed. He heard Ramon's voice, and a voice that sounded like Ned Swenson, the geologist from the bar. They were yelling at each other in Spanish.

"What are you doing here? Get out! *Ahora mismo. Immediatemente!* You have no right!"

Ramon shouted back. Luis frowned. It wasn't smart to scream at the top of one's lungs in the bush. Unwelcome ears could be listening. He drew his service revolver. Ramon was a hothead. Luis usually had to talk their way out of trouble.

Luis emerged from the thicket and was heading toward the quarrelling men when a shot rang out. Then another. He froze. New voices he hadn't heard started to yell. Luis ducked back into the thicket. Two minutes later Ramon, Swenson, Swenson's driver, and Kambale backed into the clearing, hands clasped behind their heads. Swenson's expression was pure panic. Ramon scowled and glanced around as if searching for Luis. Luis retreated farther into the bush. Something was very wrong.

A group of six soldiers appeared in the clearing. The soldiers were in khaki uniforms, and two of them wore bush hats, but all of them were pointing automatic weapons at Ramon and Swenson. UNITA rebels. And Ramon was driving a FAPLA Jeep. FAPLA was UNITA's sworn enemy. As the rebels forced the men back toward the stream, Luis gulped air. He felt like he'd been punched in the gut.

The rebels screamed, argued, and jabbed the men with their rifles. Luis brought up his automatic. Now they were only twenty yards away from him. He could probably take down three, maybe four, but the others would mow him down before he could sprint to safety. Luis hesitated.

Ramon called out to Swenson. "Tell them you're an American!"

Swenson looked at him as if Ramon was crazy.

"Quick. They think you want their diamonds!"

Swenson started babbling in English, making sweeping gestures with his arms. But his voice was between a sob and a wail, and Luis realized no one could understand him. Kambale tried to explain in one of the Bantu dialects, Luis guessed, but the rebels' frequent interruptions indicated he wasn't having success. Swenson's driver and Ramon kept their mouths shut.

Luis thought about creating a diversion so that Ramon could run to the Jeep and grab his rifle, but logistics were against them. There was no way Ramon would make it out of the clearing alive. At the same time he couldn't allow his best friend to be shot. He didn't know what to do.

The rebels kept barking at the men, jabbing and harassing them with their guns. Tears were now streaming down Swenson's cheeks. Kambale had stopped talking, but a look of terror stretched across his face. Ramon's back was to Luis, but he thought he saw Ramon shake his head. A signal. But for what? Was Ramon telling him to stay where he was or to take a stand? Luis shifted. As he did, he heard the snap of a breaking branch.

Suddenly there was a rush of movement. Swenson's driver made a break and tried to flee. Two of the rebels spun around and fired. The driver went down. Kambale dropped to the dirt and started crawling toward the thicket. Luis felt a whoosh of air as one of the rebels pumped several rounds into the boy. Kambale flopped on the ground like a fish that doesn't yet know it's dead. Blood pooled under his body.

Swenson raised his hands in supplication, but the Africans must have misunderstood. Maybe they thought he was preparing to attack because one of the rebels shot him through the head. Swenson sank to his knees, still crying, his palms clasped together. Then he slowly drooped sideways and fell.

Ramon hunched his shoulders, bent his head, contracted into a hard ball, and plowed straight into the men. He'd been a wrestler as a teenager, and he knew how to use his body as a weapon. But his odds against six armed rebels were nil. One of the rebels fired. Ramon clutched his side and sank into the dirt. The other rebels grabbed his arms and pinned him to the ground.

Luis saw him writhing in pain. He wanted to rescue his friend, but he was outnumbered and outgunned. He watched as two of the men dragged Ramon out of the clearing. A trail of blood followed their path. The others marched behind Ramon, disappearing from view.

Luis heard more jabbering among the rebels, this time from a distance. Then two engines roared to life. Apparently the rebels were stealing *their* Jeep, along with the vehicle they'd come in. Luis was ashamed at the relief that washed over him. He'd taken his backpack out so he could sketch the map. Nothing of his tied him to the Jeep. No one knew he was there. Except Ramon.

He waited until the drone of the Jeeps faded and the chirr of insects took its place. A macaw screeched. The stream splashed. The light bleached the forest's colors to a dull waxy green. Luis emerged from the thicket. He wasn't sure if minutes or hours had passed. It was still hot and humid, just another day in Africa, but Luis felt unaccountably cold.

CHAPTER TWENTY-TWO

1991 — Chicago and Miami

A shrill sound pulled Michael out of his dream. It was a sweet, bucolic dream. He was fishing in a stream that was supposed to be in Wisconsin but was really in Europe. His former Dutch girlfriend was helping him bait the hook. He was about to cast his rod when the high-pitched jangle intruded. A bell? A siren? Why would a siren wail in the European countryside?

As he swam up to consciousness, he realized his phone was ringing. He threw a pillow over his head, but he heard the muffled click of the answering machine.

"Michael...." There was a pause. "Michael DeLuca. Get out of bed right now. It's the middle of the afternoon."

How did his mother know? He heard her sigh—partly irritated, partly resigned. A sigh that could only come from a mother. "Call me when you're up. We're expecting you for dinner. Of course, it will probably be your breakfast, but don't assume it will be pancakes and bacon."

He tossed the pillow aside, rolled over, and opened one eye. The clock said almost two. He threw the covers aside and sat up. A wave of nausea climbed up his throat, and his head started to pound. He swung his legs over the side of the bed, and propped his elbows on his knees. Holding his head in his hands, he let the queasiness wash over him. Eventually it passed.

He tried to remember what he'd been doing last night. Another Saturday night. He'd gone bar hopping on Rush Street with Arnie. It was coming back. They were getting wasted as usual, but this time they'd met a couple of women. What was her name? Tracy? Stacy? She was blond. He remembered that. He liked blondes. He thought he remembered a teddy bear on the bed. He must have gone back to her place. He felt his cheeks get hot, then shook it off. He was single and almost thirty-two; she was over twenty-one. So, what the hell was she doing with a stuffed animal on her bed?

He stood up slowly, found his balance, and went to the window. A bleak November gray had descended on his Lakeview neighborhood. Unlike the fiery passion of October, November was a dreary old maid. He turned on the tube, went to the kitchen, and brewed a pot of coffee. He sipped it while watching the mindless TV chatter that passed for intelligent discourse these days. What do you get when you combine predictable questions and talking point answers? Ersatz communication. He knew all about that.

In the bathroom he idled under a hot shower. Afterwards, he felt tolerably well enough to shave. His mother hated the scruffy look that was popular on men these days and let him know it. Frequently. He shared the same dark hair as she, and lots of it. He'd shaved it off when he was in the military, but now it was back, long, thick and curly. Women described his brown eyes as soulful, whatever that meant. A patrician nose and a scar under his chin from a fall when he was young were enough to make his face not quite handsome, but interesting. Hard to look away from, he'd been told. He was big enough to be tall, fit enough to be buff. He'd never had problems attracting women. Men, either, although he didn't swing that way.

He finished shaving and threw on some clothes. He'd come back from the Persian Gulf in May and was still at loose ends five months later. Not that he hadn't been offered opportunities. He'd been an MP with the 285th Military Police Battalion from Illinois, headquartered in Kuwait, but he'd made several missions into Iraq. Now the Agency was extending their hand, thanks to his grandfather, but Michael wasn't interested. Like other bureaucracies, climbing the ladder at the CIA was increasingly a matter of who you knew and whose ass you kissed, and Michael had never been a team player.

He finished dressing, rinsed the mug in the sink, and put on a jacket. He'd have to drive forty minutes to Barrington where his parents lived. He wasn't anxious to go. Not that he didn't enjoy seeing his mother. But his father, well, that was another story.

***

The men at Miami's Maximo Gomez Domino Park in Little Havana were at least twenty years older than Ramon. So much for a place where he wouldn't be conspicuous. He wove around crowded tables that were shaded by a permanent portico, listening to the clack of tiles and the occasional grunt. The scent of Cuban cigars wafted through the air. He'd been to the cigar store a few blocks away; the owner always seemed to have a supply on hand, but they cost three times as much as they did back home.

He sat on a bench painted green at the edge of the portico and pretended to read a newspaper. He was waiting for a meeting with a man he'd hoped he would never see again. He'd been living in the States almost two years now, but he still didn't know whether it was a blessing or a curse. A blessing because he'd assumed his life was over when the UNITA rebels shot him in Angola. A curse, because he could never go back to Cuba.

He recalled how the Angolan rebels had slapped a blindfold on him, tied his arms and legs, threw him in the back of the Jeep. How, after being jostled and bumped for what seemed like hours, he arrived at an unknown location, a dark, dank, stifling hut. Someone dressed his wound, but over the next week the beatings, the sleep deprivation, and the waterboarding took him to the edge of death. All because the Africans didn't speak Spanish, and he didn't speak Portugese or Bantu.

Then, just when he thought he wouldn't survive another day, two white men appeared. From their accents, he guessed one was South African, the other American. A second interrogation followed, this time in Spanish, with no pain. Ramon spilled everything: what the Cubans were doing in Angola, how much longer they would stay, their relationship with the MPLA, Swenson's discovery of coltan, and what he and Luis were doing at the site of the future mine.

A week later, the American returned. Suddenly Ramon was treated better. There was no more torture; he was fed. When his wound healed, he was given asylum and flown to Miami. A new year, a new decade, a new life. A new name, too. Like a snake shedding his skin, he was no longer Ramon Suarez. He was Hector Gonzales. He received a monthly stipend, too. Just enough to live on. When he asked why, the American, who told Ramon to call him Walters, said it was a down payment. "You never know when we might need you again."

Which was why "Hector" was in Domino Park today. Walters had called him last night. By now Ramon had figured out he was CIA. The Americans had been quietly working around the edges of Angola for years, allying themselves with UNITA and the South Africans, hoping to take advantage of the anarchy.

Now, as he waited in the hot Florida sun, rings of sweat dampened his shirt. The hottest part of the day in Miami was still cooler than Havana, but the absence of the trade winds turned Miami into a boiling cauldron. What a difference ninety miles made.

A few minutes later a man sat down. Ramon glanced up from his newspaper. The man wore wrap-around sunglasses, a fancy sports shirt, pants, and well-shined loafers. Although he was heavier and his hair was longer, Ramon recognized Walters. He went back to his newspaper, but smells carried in this heat, and he picked up the scent of Walters' aftershave. Brut, he thought. Figured.

Walters stretched his arms across the back of the bench and looked away from Ramon. Still, his words were clear. "How you been, Hector?"

"Not bad. All things considered."

"You getting by on that pension?"

"*Sí. Es muy bien.*"

"*Bueno.* You suffered a lot."

Ramon nodded. "I wish I could say it was worth it. But I don't know. I thought I would be going back to Cuba."

"I understand." Walters cleared his throat. "Well, I have news that will make you feel better. At least, dull some of that pain."

Ramon turned to him, skeptical.

Walters subtly shook his head. It was only a tiny movement, but Ramon lowered his eyes.

"You remember telling me about that coltan mine you and your buddy found?"

Ramon nodded, wondering where this was going.

"Well, I have a—client—who is interested in it."

"Client?"

"A guy in Boston. I'm not with the Agency anymore. But I'm in the same business. You know what I mean?"

Ramon didn't know, but he played along. "I see."

"We want you to go back over there with us. Show us where it is. There's a big cut in it for you. In fact, you'll probably make a fortune. You'll be set up for life. Your kids too."

"I don't have kids."

"Well then, this could be a reason to start."

Ramon pretended to think about it, but knew what his answer would be. After a moment, he said, "I'm sorry, but I'm never going back to that place. Not for all the fucking money in the world. You know that movie— *Apocalypse Now* or something? When they go up that river to that hell on earth? That's how I feel about Africa. If you hadn't come along, I would be dead. So I'm grateful to you for that. But I can't—I won't—ever go back."

Walters persisted. "It's different now. You won't be in danger. My friends and I will be with you."

Ramon thought about the scars on his back from the beatings. The limp he still had from the time they broke his leg. The ache in his side that started whenever he was tired. The sheer terror of not knowing whether he would make it through another hour, much less a day. "I know I owe you, but this would be like death. I want to forget it ever happened. Even if you take my stipend away."

"You do owe me," Walters said. "You know that."

Ramon massaged his temples, wracking his brain. Then it came to him. He looked over. "What if you could get a map instead? A map that would lead you right to the mine?"

Walters' eyebrows arched. "It's a possibility. But how will I know it's accurate? And how would I know you're not leading us down a blind alley?"

"It's the real thing. I'll swear to it. On my life."

Walters was noncommittal. "It's tenuous, but it might work. At least it's a first step."

"Good." Ramon smiled. "That's good."

"So?" Walters asked. "Where is it? When can you get it to me?"

"Ahh…" Ramon said. "Sadly, I don't have it."

"Then why the fuck are we talking about it?"

"Because I know who does."

Walters snickered. "And I suppose he's going to hand it over, no questions asked? We're not playing games here, Hector. My client is prepared to pay for the information, and I'd like to cut you in, but not if I can't come up with the goods."

"I understand. I do. And I know someone this man *would* hand the map over to."

Walters faced Ramon. "And who would that be?"

"You ever hear of Tony Pacelli? He's an old friend of the Agency's."

"The name sounds familiar. But, like I told you, I'm not there anymore."

Ramon waved a dismissive hand. "Doesn't matter. Pacelli used to run a casino in Havana in the old days. Meyer Lansky was one of his friends. Anyway, Pacelli has a grandson. He's your guy. He can get the map."

"How do you know?"

"I can't tell you. But my information is good."

Walters flashed him a doubtful look. "So let's say I get to this guy, Pacelli, and I use your name. What's he gonna say?"

"You can't use my name. I worked at his hotel, but—we didn't part under the best circumstances."

"Then why the hell would he let me use his kid?"

"Because I know something about Pacelli he doesn't want out. And I guarantee he'll cooperate if you bring it up."

"Is that so?" Walters leaned back, extending his arm on the back of the bench. "What?"

Ramon held up a finger. "First, we negotiate."

The two men haggled for a few minutes. Then Ramon said, "Yes. That will do."

"So, what is this information?"

"I can provide information that proves Pacelli supplied arms to the rebels during the revolution."

"Fidel? Not Batista?"

Ramon nodded.

"So? He wasn't the only one."

"Yes, but I have dates and times. Details on shipments, too."

Walters rubbed his hand across his chin. "Well, now, given our current relationship with Castro plus all the Kennedy assassination, Mafia and CIA crap, I can see that might be information Pacelli doesn't want to get out."

This time Ramon didn't try to hide his smile.

"But what about the kid? His grandson? Why can't I send one of my own men?"

"First off, he's not a kid," Ramon said huffily. "He's in his thirties, was an MP during the Gulf War. But now I hear he doesn't know what to do with himself. More important, though, he's about the only person in the world who can get you that map."

Walters narrowed his eyes. "What's so special about him?"

Ramon hesitated. "He'll get the job done. That's all you need to know."

The ex-CIA officer looked like he was weighing whether or not to believe him. "And if he doesn't?"

"Then both of us will lose a fortune."

Walters stood up and left. Ramon leaned back, wondering if he'd sold out Luis along with Pacelli. Back in Havana during the revolution, Pacelli's men had tortured him. No one could withstand that agony without spilling everything. Not even Luis. Pacelli deserved whatever was coming. But Luis? He had abandoned Ramon in Angola, leaving him to die with the rebels in the most godforsaken place on earth. If Ramon did sell out Luis, it was no more than he deserved.

CHAPTER TWENTY-THREE

The security guard waved him through the gate, and Michael parked in the circular driveway at the Barrington house. Instead of going in through the front door, he walked around to the side and slipped in through the kitchen. The scents of sauteed onions, garlic, and cumin came at him before he closed the door. His mother loved to cook, especially on Sundays when the chef was off. She was a great cook too, and Michael had memories of delicious Caribbean meals like *langosta rellena*, *frijoles negros*, and *platanos en tentación*. She often sang when she cooked. In fact, Michael realized, cooking was the only time his mother seemed content. She was humming now.

He hung his jacket in the mud room and headed into the kitchen. The white walls, splashed with swaths of bright red, blue, and green, took him back to his childhood when he'd spent hours in here with his mother. His father never joined them; in fact, he'd usually complain she was spending too much time in the kitchen—that's why they paid a small fortune for a chef. Which only made Michael and his mother whisper and laugh like members of the Hole in the Wall gang.

"Hi, Mom."

Her face lit when she saw him. It always did. He went to her, and she hugged him fiercely, as if it might be the last time. She did that a lot. Which puzzled him. She was over fifty, but she looked years younger. She'd kept her figure, colored her hair, and did whatever other wealthy women did to preserve their youth. On her, though, it all looked natural. He was proud to squire her around when they went out for the occasional brunch or drink. Her behavior was somehow younger, too, when they were together. She was more talkative, girlish, and often funny. Pretty much the opposite of how she was around the house.

"I got you out of bed, didn't I?" she said.

"Guilty."

"Who was it? No. Actually, I don't want to know. We're supposed to respect each other's boundaries. Isn't that what they say these days?"

"I don't know what *they* say, but *I* say my mother is a busybody."

She slapped him playfully.

He changed the subject. "It smells great."

"I'm making a Havanaise. With lobster."

"Fancy."

"Burhops had a sale. And your grandfather is coming when he's finished working." She turned back to the stove. "He wants to talk to you."

"About what?"

"He didn't tell me. But you know how he—"

"Fran? What are you doin'?" A voice with a Brooklyn accent broke in from another room. Michael tensed. A moment later the kitchen door swung open and a tall man with styled but thinning gray hair entered. He wore a leisure suit, but he was impeccably groomed.

"I thought we were going to grill steaks." He stopped when he saw Michael. "Oh, hello, Mike." He nodded, his voice noticeably cooler. "I didn't know you were here."

Michael nodded back, equally cool. His father knew he hated to be called Mike.

His father turned to his mother with a frown. "This doesn't look like beef." He gestured to the food on the stove.

"I found lobster on sale at Burhops yesterday, so I thought I'd make a Havanaise."

"Fran, you know I don't like seafood."

"Carmine, Papa is coming tonight and he does."

"What's wrong with pasta? He likes that, too."

His mother didn't answer. His father watched his wife break the shell of a lobster. With his sharp features and flat expression, he looked like someone who could break a man's neck as easily as his mother did the lobster. Which, as a former capo for the Mob in New York, he'd undoubtedly done, Michael thought. Before he came up in the world and stripped the dirt—and blood—from beneath his fingernails.

His father turned back to him. "You find work yet?"

Carmine DeLuca had the unique ability to engage and insult at the same time, especially his son. If you didn't know him well, you might gloss over the words, not realizing his insinuations and how deeply they cut. But Michael knew him well and had developed strategies to deal with their passive-aggressive warfare. He gazed at his father.

His father kept his eyes on his mother. "Oh, I forgot. You're still waiting for the right opportunity." His smile was as insincere as his words.

Michael managed a tight smile in return.

His father wheeled around and left the kitchen.

Michael fought back the bile in his throat. This was why he hated to come home. Every time he stepped across the threshold, he was not the skilled military officer who took little at face value and trusted no one. Instead he was the little boy he'd once been, desperately—unsuccessfully—seeking his father's approval.

He stole a glance at his mother. Her lips were pursed. She turned back to the Havanaise. She wasn't humming any more.

***

An hour later Michael helped his mother clear the table. The Havanaise was delicious, but it had been an awkward meal. His mother tried to make small talk with his father and grandfather, but his father left the table when they finished the main course.

"You don't want dessert, Carmine?" Michael's mother asked. "I made rum cake."

"Please bring it to me in my office." He motioned toward his den, a room off the living room where he spent most of his day, and, increasingly, his evenings.

"Of course."

Michael's father had always "worked" from home, but he wasn't one of those stay-at-home dads people talked about. In fact, Michael never understood why his mother married him to begin with. He guessed she'd become pregnant—Carmine had once been handsome, Michael had to admit—and in those days, it was a sin to be unmarried and pregnant. But times were changing, and Michael wondered why she stayed married when it was clear there was no love between them. Was it because she was Catholic? He didn't think so. Was it simply habit, honed over thirty years of living together? He wanted to ask but knew the topic was *prohibido*.

As soon as his father left the table, the mood lightened, and his mother and grandfather started to chat. Tony Pacelli wasn't a tall man, and at eighty, he was stooped and gnarled. But he still had the same round face, olive complexion, and lots of thick silver hair. His mother once told Michael they'd called him Silver-Tongued Tony, but Michael thought it should change to "Silver-Haired Tony." His mother got a good belly laugh out of it.

Michael cleared the table while his mother brewed coffee. "Get the red plates for the cake, the ones from Grandma Marlena, would you darling?"

Michael took four dessert plates out of a cabinet. Made of red beveled glass in an Art Deco style, they were so old they were new, his mother said. He brought them out to the dining room. His mother served cake and coffee.

His grandfather took a bite of cake and chewed slowly. A beatific smile spread across his face. "*Delizioso*, Francesca."

"*Grazi*, Papa."

He sipped his coffee. "This too."

The joy of simple things. That must be what comes with age and a life well-lived, Michael thought. He wondered if he'd ever feel that way. He smiled at his grandfather.

"What's so funny?"

"I enjoy watching you."

His grandfather raised his fork in Michael's general direction. "Good cake, coffee, and family. What more could a man want?"

His mother rolled her eyes, but she was smiling. "This, from the busiest eighty-year old man I know."

"What else am I gonna do, Francesca? Your mother's gone, you've got your own life, and our young man here is in his own world."

"You could retire. At least slow down."

"And do what? Play cards all day?" He pointed his finger at Michael's mother. "All those years at La Perla, and I never gambled. Not once. I should start now?"

"Well in that case, we need to talk about the supplies for the restaurants. Prices have skyrocketed, and it's because of the Teamsters. They keep hiking their rates. They're killing us."

Michael started to tune out. Although his mother had her "own life" as his grandfather put it, she was shrewd, and as a formidable cook, she enjoyed working around food. She'd stepped into the Family's restaurant supply business and was now running it. Two of the nonfood operations, as well. When his grandfather allowed her to. He was still coming to terms with the idea of a woman—even one who happened to be his daughter—managing his business.

"Francesca, I've told you before. We can't force them. They are our friends."

"They may be, but there's got to be a limit. How can we charge ten dollars for a damn salad?"

But Tony Pacelli was old school. "Pick your battles, Francesca. You need to know when it's time to mount an offense, and when to go along. There are times when loyalty trumps all."

Michael caught his mother's exasperated expression.

But Michael couldn't care less about Family business. "Grampa, Mom said you wanted to talk to me," he cut in.

His grandfather waved his fork. "Later."

That was code for "I want to talk to you in private."

His mother kept bickering about the Teamsters, and his grandfather parried. Michael decided he might as well go home. Finally, his mother noticed his disinterest, ducked into the kitchen, and came back with a plate of cake. "Here. Take this to your father."

Michael took the plate and headed into the den. With dim lighting, oil paintings of the Italian countryside, and a silver pen and pencil set his mother had given his father years ago, the den was an imitation of a respectable WASP's room. His father was on the phone, talking quietly. Probably catching up with his bookies, going over the spreads of the Sunday football games, sorting out who lost what. The noise from the TV blared, covering the conversation. Curious that his father had never become an integral part of the Pacelli Family business, Michael thought. Had that been his father's decision or his grandfather's?

Michael cleared his throat. "Here's your dessert."

His father looked up but didn't reply. Michael set the plate down and flicked his eyes to the TV. A James Bond movie. Timothy Dalton, the new Bond, was on some Caribbean beach while a beautiful woman worked her wiles on him. Dalton wasn't nearly as appealing as Sean Connery, whom his mother declared was the only Bond worth watching. Michael was heading back to the dining room, when his mother's voice rose above the TV. She sounded angry.

"You can't be serious. I won't permit it."

At first he thought they were still discussing the Teamsters.

His grandfather's voice was soft, and Michael had to concentrate to make it out. But his tone was conciliatory. "Francesca, you're being unreasonable. You said yourself he doesn't have any plans. He needs to do something until he's ready for the family business."

Michael stopped.

"He's never going into the family business. Don't you realize that?"

There was a long pause. "Never is a long time. But we don't need to discuss that now. What we do need to discuss is this—this proposition."

"I won't let him go. Is your memory so short?"

"Is yours that long?"

Michael knew his mother and his grandfather had been estranged when he was a little boy. They didn't speak, and when they were forced to be in the same room, they avoided each other like the plague. When Michael asked his mother why, she'd say it was something that happened a long time ago and she wouldn't discuss it further. It was only after the death of his grandmother, Marlena, that his mother and Grandpa Tony reconciled. Still, it was an uneasy truce, as he could sense.

"Someone has something on you, don't they?" his mother said sharply. "You're in trouble."

"You know better than to ask that."

"Why not? You've always sacrificed family for business." His mother sounded bitter.

His grandfather's voice rose. "Don't talk to me like that. I am still your father. And the head of this Family."

But his mother refused to back down. "I swear to you, if you raise this with him, I will never speak to you again. I can't believe you have the nerve to suggest it after all we've been through."

Michael ran his tongue around his lips. What the hell were they talking about?

"You live in the past, Francesca."

"That's a joke, right?" His mother's voice quieted, but it was thick with tension. "It's not *me* who's living in the past. I'm moving forward—with or without you. That part of our lives is over. If you bring it up, I guarantee you'll regret it."

Michael decided whatever they were arguing about had gone on long enough. He strode purposefully back into the dining room. "What are you talking about?"

Both of them started, as if they'd been caught red-handed. Each flashed recriminating glances at the other.

"What's this about me going somewhere?"

His mother said nothing.

"Mother, whatever is going on, don't you think you ought to talk it over with me, rather than Grampa?"

"You—you…" His mother stared at his grandfather, so angry she couldn't make her lips form words.

"You see?" Michael's grandfather snorted.

"You have no idea what you're doing," his mother finally spat out.

"If one of you doesn't tell me what's going on, I'm out of here." Michael didn't intend to make good on his threat, but it sounded good. Forceful.

His grandfather pushed himself back from the table. "All right. Here it is. I got a call from an—associate. He has a job I think you might be interested in."

"Papa—"

"*Silencio!*" Tony Pacelli yelled. "Go into the kitchen."

His mother flared her nostrils but didn't move. Michael expected her to defy her father. Then, after a long pause, she rose, stomped into the kitchen, and slammed the door. Michael could hear her throwing pots around. Noisily.

There was still a difference between women of his mother's generation and his, he realized. His mother's generation was caught between two worlds: the world of the obedient wife and daughter and that of the independent woman. It was clear his mother didn't like it, but ultimately, she obeyed her father. At least this time. Was it because Tony Pacelli was still the Don? Was it because she knew her father wanted to talk to him in private? Didn't matter. No way a woman in Michael's generation would do that.

Michael cleared his throat and turned to his grandfather. "Now… what's this all about?"

His grandfather drew a cigar out of his pocket and held a match to it. "I hear you turned down the job at the Agency."

"It's not the kind of place I want to work."

An Ivy League graduate, fluent in four languages, Michael had drifted around Europe and Asia after college. Much to his mother's chagrin, he ended up in the military and was sent to the Persian Gulf as an MP. Now his tour was over, and his mother, alarmed at his lack of direction, had asked his grandfather for help. Michael had few illusions. He knew Tony Pacelli's history; the man had practically been best friends with Meyer Lansky in the Fifties.

Still, when Tony set up a meeting at the Agency for him, Michael realized his grandfather's contacts ran deeper than he'd thought. Maybe all the way back to the Second World War when the Mafia helped the OSS plan the invasion of Sicily. History had proven there was a thin line between the hunters and the hunted.

His grandfather puffed on the cigar. Wisps of smoke corkscrewed up, turning the air milky. "Maybe it's better. Your mother hated it when you went to Iraq. It drove her crazy."

"Except the Agency wanted me to be an analyst. Sit in an office and translate articles. I can't think of anything worse."

"Still the buccaneer."

"It's not that. Since Iran-Contra, everyone in the business is looking over their shoulders, covering their asses, wringing their hands."

"Not your—what do they call it—your M.O." His grandfather puffed on his cigar.

Michael nodded. Both his grandfather and mother wanted him to join them in the Family "business." Michael had mulled it over, but he knew he could never be a part of the Outfit. It wasn't simply a youthful rebellion, although he'd been told countless times he was a cliché straight from *The Godfather*. All he knew was that the path they wanted for him was too easy. Too orchestrated. Whatever he ended up doing, wherever he ended up going, he wanted to do it on his own. Not inherit it. Plus, the fact that he'd been on the right side of the law in the army didn't exactly square with the Family business.

"So." His grandfather sucked on his cigar. "I have a—friend. Actually he's a friend of a friend. He has a job that needs doing in Cuba."

"Cuba?"

"It has nothing to do with the time we lived there."

Michael had always been curious about his mother's life in Cuba. She'd told him stories about growing up in Miramar, an affluent suburb, before they moved into La Perla. Her stories made him want to see the island. But every time he suggested a trip, perhaps through Canada or Mexico, she'd shake her head and say, "Not while there's an embargo. Anyway, from what I hear, Cuba has changed. The life I knew is gone."

Now Michael focused on his grandfather. "Your 'friend' is with the Agency?"

"He was. He went private. So did *his* friend, I'm told. Has a client near Boston."

It was happening more and more. Recruits no longer stayed in intelligence organizations for their entire career. Instead, they used the CIA, FBI, and the other alphabet soup security groups as stepping-stones for more lucrative jobs. Some started their own companies, hiring themselves out to lobbyists, corporations, and international conglomerates. Others went freelance, picking up surveillance and undercover work for foreign governments. He'd heard a few former MI officers were involved with a couple of law firms in D.C.

"Where did this friend of a friend come from?"

His grandfather threw up his hands. "I'm an old man. I don't keep up anymore. But I trust *my* friend. He says *his* friend, name of Walters, needs a man to go down there."

"To do what?"

"I don't know."

"It's not another one of those crazy-ass plots to kill Castro, is it?"

Tony chuckled. "Not this time."

"How long will I be there?"

"I don't know that either." He tapped the end of his cigar in the ashtray. "But if you're interested, I'll give you his number."

"Is that why you and mother were arguing?"

His grandfather furrowed his brow and raised his eyebrows in the Italian way that meant maybe, maybe not.

Although Michael hadn't wanted to use his family connections, deeming them tainted, he hadn't been called back for second interviews except at the Agency. And despite his experience, he doubted any police force would willingly hire a mobster's son, except as an informant, which he had no desire to be. He was, in a word, stuck.

"Okay. Give me the number."

Tony was digging into his wallet when his mother stormed back into the dining room. Her cheeks were red, her eyes black as coal. Her body language was rigid, and her breath came so fast and shallow Michael thought she might start to hyperventilate. Michael had never seen her this worked up. Not since he was seventeen and he'd wrapped his car around a telephone pole on Christmas Eve.

"I won't allow it, Michael. You go to Cuba over my dead body."

"Francesca," Tony said, "the revolution ended thirty years ago. And despite Fidel, Cuba is one of the safest places in the world. Now that the Soviet Union has collapsed, there's a good chance relations with the U.S. might warm up. I don't—"

His mother planted her hands on her hips. "Cuba is in the middle of a severe depression. Even Castro calls it a 'Special Period.' No one has enough food. Or oil. Or anything. People are dropping dead in the streets. You won't—"

Michael cut in. "Both of you, stop it. Right now. I'm going. And that's the end of it."

He turned to his grandfather. Pacelli was looking at his daughter with pity, as if he felt sorry for her and wanted her to know it. Michael looked back at his mother. "Mom, I make my own decisions. Besides, I want to see where you lived. So I'm going."

Whatever he said or didn't say, his attitude wrought a marked change in his mother. Like a pin piercing a fat balloon, the fight suddenly went out of her. Her body slumped, as if she was Atlas with the world on her shoulders. She seemed about to speak when his grandfather cut in.

"You see, Francesca? Let him make his own way."

Michael prepared himself for a fresh burst of temper from his mother. Something about undue influence. Or forcing someone to bend to his will. But when he looked over, her anger had dissipated. Now she looked scared. More scared than he'd ever seen her.

CHAPTER TWENTY-FOUR

1991 – Havana

Sunlight crashed down onto the street, bounced off metallic objects, and flared into Michael's eyes. He was wearing wrap-around sunglasses, but he had to squint.

He'd been in Havana less than a day. The city looked much like he'd expected, a seedier, more Spanish version of Miami, trapped forever in 1959. Few cars cruised the streets, and those that did were mostly vintage Chevys, Fords, or Soviet Ladas. Crowds of people queued patiently at bus stops and stores. The only billboards and posters were either profiles of Che Guevara or ads for rum.

But the biggest difference between Cuba and the States was the pace. Here everything was unhurried and languid, as if people knew they had nothing very important to do. Part of it was the heat, of course, but Michael couldn't help noticing the absence of hustle and bustle. Not that there weren't as many people as Chicago or New York. There were. But they seemed content to spend the day waiting for rations that inevitably ran out before they made it to the front of the line, after which the line would dissolve and form again around the corner for something else. Some rode bicycles, but no one pedaled quickly. The beat of an Afro-Cuban tune spilled into the street from somewhere, lending a perversely festive air to the surroundings.

He'd checked into the Hotel Nacional, probably the best known hotel on the island, but he didn't plan to stay more than one night. Half the population in Cuba informed on the other half, and a stranger, especially a single man, was news worth reporting. He would leave as soon as he found smaller, more private accommodations. *Casas particulares*, they called them, Cuba's version of the B&B. They weren't legal, at least not yet, but Cubans were inventive when it came to survival, and the state pretended they didn't exist. There were small restaurants too, *paladares*, which were operated out of private homes and served excellent food. Michael planned to find both so he could melt into the background before anyone figured out who he was.

He'd come to Cuba through Mexico, where he boarded a private boat that took him from Cancun to Bolodron. From there his plan was to make his way to Pinar del Rio on the western edge of Cuba, then Havana. When he flashed his fake American passport, the customs officials, as expected, didn't stamp it. It was a practice they followed for any American visiting Cuba. But they did question him. Michael had to ask them to repeat themselves; Cuban Spanish was faster and differently enunciated than the Spanish he'd been taught. His college professor used to call it "Hillbilly Spanish."

Once he got the hang of the dialect, he told them that he'd sailed to the island from Mexico. One of the officials told him that's how Fidel returned to Cuba in 1956 to start the revolution. Fidel's boat was the *Granma*, the other official said proudly, which was now the name of Havana's main newspaper. Michael thanked them for the history lesson and asked the best way to get to Pinar del Rio and then Havana.

"There used to be a bus," one said. "A train, too. But now…" he said, "…who knows?" He yanked his thumb in the air. "This is the best way. If you find a truck that will stop."

Michael thanked them and made his way to the highway where a large truck eventually picked him up. The back of the vehicle was crowded with other Cubans, all of whom, he learned, used hitchhiking as their primary means of transportation. The truck broke down an hour later, so Michael didn't reach Pinar del Rio until dark. He spent the night in a sugar cane field after watching farmers methodically plow the field with oxen. He didn't make Havana until the next afternoon.

By the time he'd checked into the hotel and showered, he was famished. But he couldn't eat in one of the Nacional's restaurants—too many prying eyes—so he decided to take a walk. Not wanting to call attention to himself by using a map, he ambled down the Malecón, then turned toward Vedado. His grandfather's hotel was supposed to be nearby; he'd have to check it out.

He walked by older buildings with narrow balconies, many of which had crumbled and were supported by cinderblocks or other patchwork fixes. The decay made him think of an apocalyptic French Quarter. Porticos stretched around the corners of many buildings, offering shade, but they too were in need of structural repair. Pastel painted buildings, originally braced by columns, were now buttressed by wooden planks. Part of his brain tried to remember the difference between Doric, Ionic, and

Corinthian—these were Ionic, he thought. The other part of his brain was monitoring his surroundings and the people on the street. And that part said he was being followed.

He slowed, knowing whoever was tailing him would slow too. Who the hell was it? No one knew he was here, except his family. And Walters, his contact. Was he making sure Michael was doing the job? Or was his tail involved with the Cuban authorities? Spying was the only industry not affected by Cuba's Special Period. Intelligence always thrived, no matter what shape an economy was in. In fact, the worse things got, the more clandestine operations flourished.

For a split second he almost wheeled around to confront whoever was stalking him. Then he realized that would be rash—the tail might simply be an overeager *jinetero* trying to take advantage of a tourist. Or it might be no one. A healthy paranoia was the hallmark of a good MP, and Michael was jittery from lack of sleep.

As he turned the corner onto La Rampa, a faded sign on a building announced he had reached "Cafeteria Cubana." He ducked inside. The blast of cold air that usually slaps people when they enter an air-conditioned place in the States didn't happen, and for a moment Michael, who'd already started sweating, was irritated. But no one followed him in, and three large ceiling fans circulated air. He decided to stay.

The room was large and well-lit, but paint was peeling off the walls, and on one side a crack ran from floor to ceiling. A radio droned with a rant about Cuban rectification, Fidel's reaction to the growing divide between Cuba and the Soviet Union.

Only two of the fifteen tables were occupied. He realized why when he went to the counter. Most of the steel serving tubs behind the glass shield were empty. Only three bins at the far end near the cash register were filled, two with rice and beans, the third with some kind of stew. Behind the counter a woman in a stained yellow uniform stood up from a stool as he slid a tray towards her. He nodded. She took a plate, scooped up stew, rice and beans, and set it on top of the counter.

"How about a Coca-Cola?" he asked in Spanish.

"We don't have any."

He looked around. No vending machines but he saw a pot of coffee, and a carafe of water on a small table.

"What do you have?"

"Mango juice."

"Okay. *Gracias.*"

He paid, picked up his tray, and went to a table. He slipped off his backpack and dropped it on the floor beside his chair. The meal was surprisingly good, and he wolfed it down in less than a minute, so he went back for more. Once he'd polished off a second helping, he sipped his juice and looked around. An elderly man with sienna skin sat at one table, alternately smoking an unfiltered cigarette, then taking a forkful of rice. At the other was a young woman reading a book.

Michael took off his sunglasses. Despite the fact that the old man had soft food, it looked like he was having a hard time chewing. He realized why when the man opened his mouth. He was missing nearly all his teeth. Michael looked away. The woman was studiously ignoring her surroundings. She had beautiful skin, a long nose, and from what he could see, nice eyes. She reminded him a little of Barbra Streisand, except she was shorter, and more compact, with short brown-blonde hair in a bob. She was attractive, but her expression, though absorbed in reading, said she'd take no bullshit from anyone.

He decided it was safe enough to take out his map of Havana, so he leaned over, unzipped the backpack, and pulled it out. As he did, the door of the cafeteria opened. He glanced up. A young man, hands in his pockets, came in. Michael couldn't tell if it was the guy who'd been tailing him, but he looked like he had nothing to do, which was suspicious. Michael went on alert. He figured the guy for an informant, maybe the head of the neighborhood CDR, a huge network of spies the State had created to report on the activities of their neighbors. Maybe he'd been called by the woman behind the counter. Michael decided he should probably take off.

He was about to get up when the woman from the other table rose and started toward him. The guy who entered looked like he was heading his way, too. With two people approaching from opposite directions, Michael was cornered. Was this an ambush? He swore softly. His hunting knife and the small 9-millimeter he'd bought in Cancun were in his backpack. He was about to grab it when the woman passed by his table. She tripped on the backpack and flailed her arms.

"*¡Mierda! Que es eso?*" she cried angrily.

Michael jumped up to steady her. "I'm so sorry. Please, sit down." As he was talking he bent over to grab his backpack. "Are you hurt?"

She sank into an empty chair and massaged her ankle. "I don't know," she snapped. Then she lowered her voice. "Keep talking."

Michael didn't miss a beat. "Should I take you to a doctor? Or the hospital? I'll go find a taxi." And then disappear.

"I *am* a doctor," she said in the same low voice. Then she spoke normally. "I twisted it, no thanks to you." She glared. "The least you can do is help me out of here."

"Of course." He made a show of helping her get up. "Put your arm around my shoulders."

She rose and draped her arm around him. The man who'd come in a moment ago stopped when she tripped, but called out. "Señorita, may I be of assistance?"

She replied with a stream of invective so rapid that Michael had trouble understanding it. He did pick up the words *"estupido," "turista,"* and *"venda,"* bandage. She turned to Michael. "Get my bag." She pointed to the floor where she'd dropped it when she lost her balance. He complied.

The man who'd come in kept his distance, apparently deciding it wasn't worth getting involved. Michael led her to the door, the woman hopping on one foot. With his backpack and her purse slung over his shoulders, he awkwardly maneuvered her out to the street.

"Take me around the corner." She lifted her chin slightly to the right. Michael continued, half carrying, half supporting her. Their bodies were so close he could smell her. Sweet and sweaty. They rounded the corner, and halfway down the block, the woman stopped and turned around. So did Michael. No one else in sight. The woman put her foot down and took a few steps, with no limp whatsoever.

"Muchas gracias," Michael said.

"I didn't like the look of that man." She studied him. "But with your American clothes and map, you certainly were *dar la nota.*"

He cocked his head, surprised she was so observant.

"You made a spectacle out of yourself."

"Ahh…" He nodded. "I didn't know the cafeteria would be that empty. I was trying to ditch him."

"Then it's a good thing I was there," she said drily.

"Who do you think he was?"

"Probably nobody. But he'll tell the CDR about you."

Nothing he could do about that. He took out his sunglasses and slipped them on. "Are you really a doctor?"

"*Sí.* But I am not working today."

"Your day off?"

"My schedule is—irregular—these days."

He held out his hand. "I am Miguel."

She took it. "Carla Garcia."

He held her hand a beat longer. "A pretty name. For a pretty woman."

She dropped her hand. "Do you say that to all the women you trip?"

"Only the ones I want to see again."

She tried to scowl, but little crow's feet danced in the corners of her eyes. Up close, those eyes were emerald green, he noticed.

They continued to walk and chat. An hour later Michael decided he didn't want to find a *casa particular.* He knew where he wanted to spend the night.

CHAPTER TWENTY-FIVE

Michael sat on Carla's balcony at dusk that evening, watching a brisk wind whip the fronds of palm trees. Her apartment was off Calle Ocho in Vedado, on the fourth floor of a building that at one time had been a mansion. Vedado, in uptown Havana, was the heart of the city's financial and commercial district, but its residential parts reminded Michael of Chicago's Lincoln Park. Unfortunately, many of the buildings, built years ago in the graceful Spanish tradition, had deteriorated so much a feather could knock them down. And while the Soviets had built their share of buildings since the revolution, they were little more than ugly boxes that lacked architectural sophistication. One apartment building, near the former Riviera resort, was particularly unattractive and clashed with the expansive American-style structure behind it.

Inside, Carla's furniture was old and shabby; her TV was a cheap Soviet model, and her radio looked older than the revolution. But the walls were a cheerful red, and except for the cracks that were becoming all too familiar, looked freshly painted. She also had plenty of plants, which were all flourishing. And the apartment wasn't too far from the Malecón. Michael smelled a faint tang in the air.

Carla brought out two drinks and handed one to him. He took a sip. Rum and some kind of juice. Slightly chilled and sweet. "You live by yourself?"

She sat in a chair, took a sip, and nodded. "The rent is not expensive. It's all subsidized. Of course, there's nothing worth buying, even if I did have money." She said it matter-of-factly, without anger or regret.

"I know you work for the state, but you're a doctor. Shouldn't you be at the top of the pay scale?"

A puzzled expression shot across her face, as if she couldn't make up her mind whether to scold him or explain. "We *are* at the top of the scale.

Seven hundred pesos a month."

Michael made a mental calculation. "That's only about thirty-five dollars. How do you get by?"

"Many don't. People are starving here. There's malnutrition. And disease. And no medicine. Or vitamins. People have asthma, they go blind, they can no longer have babies. That's why I do not work full time. My hours have been cut. And when I do work, all I do is send people home to die."

The wind kicked up again. An open door or shutter banged. Then the lights inside snapped off.

"¡Mierda!" Carla whipped around. "It happens all the time." She went back to her drink, took another sip. The dim light from the street threw long shadows across her face. "So who are you, Miguel? Why are you here? Are you visiting family?"

"In a way."

She stared at him. "Let's get something straight. I don't like *pendejadas.* Bullshit. I can smell it a mile away. Cubans have a sixth sense for it."

Chagrined, Michael leaned forward and swirled his drink. "My mother lived here when she was a child."

Carla perked up. "Really? What province was she from?"

"She's American. Her father ran one of the hotels and casinos before the revolution."

"Which one?"

"La Perla."

"I know it. I have snapshots of my parents there. They used to go on special occasions. It was a luxurious place." She laughed. "You know that today the casino is a convention hall, no? In fact, I was—"

A knock on the door cut her off. Michael tensed.

She waved a hand. "Do not worry. It is probably my upstairs neighbor. She will be needing a candle, and I have a secret supply. From the clinic," she added.

He let himself relax.

She got up and went to the door. "You asked how we get by. Cubans are quite creative at survival. There is an expression for it. 'Resolver.'"

"To resolve?" he asked.

She held up a finger on one hand and opened the door with the other. He heard the murmur of a woman's voice.

"Come in," Carla said. "We're on the balcony."

While Carla rummaged around inside, the woman came out. Michael couldn't see clearly in the dusky light, but he thought she looked emaciated, with limp hair that hung past her shoulders. He had the sense she had been attractive at one time, but that was in the past.

"*Buenas tardes,*" he said.

When she smiled, her mouth opened. She was missing two teeth. *"Buenas tardes."*

Carla returned with two candles. "For you, Juliana."

"Muchas gracias, Carla." She wrapped her arms around Carla and hugged her tight. "You are my angel." Then she waved to Michael and disappeared through the door.

"She doesn't look good," he said.

Carla brought another candle out to the balcony, lit it, and sat. "She is sick."

"With what?"

"The disease you call AIDS."

He took in a breath. "It's spread here? How did—"

Carla cut him off. "How do you think? Tourists come, and Cuban women do what they must. It's all part of *'resolver.'"* Then as if realizing what she'd said, she added, "I choose not to go that route, of course."

Michael decided to believe her. Or maybe he wanted to. "Does she know how sick she is? She must stop what she's doing."

"I have told her she should go home to Camaguey. But her parents say she has disgraced them and is no longer their daughter." Her voice rose, sounding close to despair. "I can do nothing. We do not even have simple antibiotics."

"I'm sorry," he whispered.

Carla blinked several times, as if blinking would blot it out. Or perhaps she was fighting back tears. Then she cleared her throat. "You were saying, you are here... why?"

Michael picked up her cue. "To see where my mother lived. They had a house in Miramar before they moved into the hotel."

"Your father, he is Italian?"

"Yes."

"So he lived here too?"

"No. We—well—it's not important."

"I see." This time she picked up *his* cue. "And where are you staying?"

"My bag is at the Nacional."

She let the silence grow between them. Her gaze was cool. Then, "Why are you really here?"

Michael hung his head, like a student who's been chastised by the teacher. He didn't want to lie. "I'm looking for someone."

In the candlelight he saw deep lines crease her forehead. She looked like she was trying to make a decision. He realized he hoped it would be in his favor.

"OK. I understand you are not ready to tell me the truth. *Entiendo.* Do not tell me. But be forewarned. What I cannot bear are lies. You must never lie to me, okay? Not—how do you say it in English—a little white lie."

He nodded. Her eyes didn't move from his face. Had she extended an invitation?

As if she read his thoughts, she added, "Now, why don't you get your bag from the hotel?"

***

A morning sun brushed the clouds with rose and gold as Michael and Carla sipped coffee the next morning. In daylight the view from the balcony was mostly other buildings, but the hint of the bay behind them was a tease.

"That's the last of the coffee until next month." Carla's cup clanked as she put it down on the saucer.

"My mother loves Cuban coffee," Michael said. "Maybe I can find some."

She laughed. "You will need to be a magician. The only coffee around is black market, and it costs more than gold." She stood. She was wearing a ratty Yankees t-shirt. Michael imagined the curves underneath the shirt, curves he had come to know well last night.

But Carla was all business. "I must dress. I work at the polyclinic until seven."

"Where is it?"

She gestured off the balcony to the left. "A few blocks away. Off La Rampa. In an older building that's covered with murals. What are you going to do?"

"I guess I'll start looking for the man I need to contact." He got up too. "He's in the military, and he spent time in Angola. Would you happen to know any bars or *paladars* that cater to soldiers?"

She frowned. He liked how her brow furrowed, then smoothed out when an idea came. "One of the doctors I work with was in Angola. Come with me, and we'll ask him."

CHAPTER TWENTY-SIX

Michael hopped down from the taxi at the gates of Havana's Chinatown. A cross between a rickshaw and a golf cart except that a man pedaled a bicycle in front, vehicles like these were common in the oil-starved capital. This must be what Carla meant by "*resolver*," he thought.

He paid the driver the equivalent of a dollar in pesos, including tip, and went to the entrance arch. He hadn't known there was a Barrio Chino in Havana. In fact, the very idea seemed bizarre. How did the Chinese get to Cuba? When? And most important, why? He peered at the gate. If he blinked, he could have been back in Chicago. The entrance arch was gray, not red, and the pagoda roofs gold, not green, but otherwise he might have been standing at Cermak and Wentworth, not Calle Dragone.

He walked through the gate and down the street. He'd met Carla's doctor friend, Mario, earlier that morning at the clinic. Mario had spent almost two years in Angola. He knew of a *paladar* in Miramar for officers, but you had to be a *Coronel* or higher to get in. There was also the Hotel Habana Libre in Vedado. It had housed Fidel's soldiers for several days after they took Havana; Michael might find an enlisted man or two hanging around. And, Mario said, he'd run into a couple of officers in Chinatown— one of them lived above a restaurant, he thought.

The Miramar *paladar* and the Hotel Libre weren't far from Carla's apartment, so Michael decided to try Chinatown first. Now, as he wandered down Calle Dragone, he noticed the same Chinese shops as in Chicago. Stacked almost on top of each other, he smelled the same greasy aromas and spices, although here they were mixed with the cloying scent of overripe fruit. The same red lanterns dangled above the doors, and the same junk was for sale in the shops. Curiously, there were more black Cubans than Chinese in Chinatown, but the Chinese who were there spoke Spanish and seemed to have lost the sharpness of their Asian features.

Their faces, the result of generations of intermarriage, made Michael think of an ink stamp that's been imprinted too many times.

Mario couldn't remember the name of the restaurant where he'd seen the soldiers but thought it was halfway down the first street to the right. It served Italian food, he added. Amused at the thought of an Italian restaurant in the middle of Chinatown in Cuba, Michael turned the corner. The side street was so narrow he doubted a small car could navigate through, much less a restaurant supply truck.

Nevertheless, halfway down the street, a banner hanging from a second story window flapped in the breeze. The words *"La Traviata"* in capital letters were printed on a background of red, white, and green. Michael opened the street door and climbed up a flight of stairs. The door to the restaurant was slightly ajar. He pushed through.

A woman with curly black hair, brown skin, and features that looked part Asian, part Hispanic was setting tables. She scowled at him.

"We do not open for another hour."

He eyed the tablecloth she was smoothing out. Yellowed and stained, it wasn't much more than a remnant of fabric. "I'm not here to eat. I'm looking for someone."

The woman tensed. Michael wondered what secrets she was hiding. Then, as if she'd decided it was wiser to attack than submit to a stranger's request, her eyes narrowed and her voice tightened. "Americano, no? What do you want?"

Michael stood his ground. "There is an officer here who was posted to Angola. I need to talk to him."

"Why?"

"It's personal."

A wily glance spread across her face. *"No esta aqui."*

Michael decided to up the ante. "But we had a meeting."

Confusion swam across her face. Michael repressed a smile. Now she wasn't sure what to believe. Exactly what he wanted.

She looked around as if taking inventory, should he try to steal the room's belongings. "Stay here." She ducked through the door and climbed a second flight of stairs.

Michael sat at one of the tables, facing the door in case there was a problem. So far, so good. He drummed his fingers on the table.

A moment later, he heard raised voices upstairs. A man was cursing. "I don't know any *malditos* American! It's a trap!" The woman's voice was pleading. "He says he knows you." Michael heard a snort. Followed by a snarl, and a curse directed at the woman. There was no reply, but a moment later footsteps clattered down the steps. The woman, probably, judging from the tread. Then a heavier step.

The woman burst into the room. She refused to look at Michael and disappeared into the kitchen. She was followed by a man who looked like he'd just woken up. Middle-aged and swarthy, he needed a shave. His hair, and there was a lot of it, was turning gray, and chest hair stuck out over a yellowed undershirt. He'd thrown on a pair of pants; still, he looked like an older Marlon Brando in *A Streetcar Named Desire*.

He peered at Michael through bloodshot eyes. *"¿Quién eres tú?"* Who are you? *"¿Qué carajo quieres conmigo?"* And what the fuck are you doing?

"I am Miguel DeLuca. We've never met. I apologize. But I didn't know any other way to get you to talk to me. I'm looking for a man. I was told you might be able to help."

The man cursed under his breath—Michael couldn't quite catch it—then rubbed his hand over his chin stubble. Then he walked to the bar on the other side of the room, took a glass, and poured himself a generous shot of rum. He appraised Michael. "What's in it for me?"

Michael smiled inwardly. "Twenty-five dollars. American."

The man tossed back his shot and poured another. "Make it fifty."

Michael appeared to consider it. Then, "If the information pans out... okay."

The man made another snorting sound, as if he realized he probably could have wangled another fifty out of him. Then he wiggled his fingers, motioning for the money.

Michael went over, slipped out a fifty from his billfold, and handed it over.

The man looked satisfied. "So?"

"I'm looking for an officer who was posted to Angola in '88 and '89."

The man scowled. "Angola is a big country. Over 50,000 Cubans were stationed there at any one time. What was his name?"

"Luis Perez."

"Where was he posted?"

"Lucapa."

Recognition lit his face. "Lunda Norte."

Michael nodded, daring to hope.

"Too bad. I wasn't anywhere near there."

Michael suppressed his disappointment. "Where were you?"

"In the south. Cuito Cuanavale. I was there during the run-up for the last battle."

It had been a long shot, Michael thought.

The man called to the woman in the kitchen. She came out with a Montecristo cigar. *"Uno mas,"* he ordered. She retraced her steps, returning with another. He motioned for her to hand it to Michael. "It's the real thing, Americano. None of your Yankee imitations."

Michael nodded his thanks and took the match the man offered.

They smoked in silence for a minute. Then, "Why are you looking for this man?"

"He has something that belongs to me."

The man smirked. "Cubans have nothing of value these days."

"Let's just say it has—sentimental—value."

The man tipped his head to the side. "Are you CIA?"

Michael choked back a laugh. "No." That much was true.

"Mafia?"

"Nothing like that."

The man's expression said he didn't believe Michael, but he kept puffing on his cigar. The overt hostility was gone, Michael thought. That was good. In fact, with the cigar smoke curling up, Michael was reminded of his grandfather.

The man's gaze turned calculating. "It's possible I might know men who were stationed up north."

"Is that so?"

The man nodded.

"How do I know you'll steer me in the right direction? As you said, there were a lot of soldiers in Angola."

"Up to you. You don't want? You take the cigar and go."

Michael appraised the man. Then he put his cigar in an ashtray, withdrew another ten, and put it in the man's palm. It was probably another long shot. The man fingered the cash and arched his eyebrows. Michael pulled out another twenty.

The man nodded and closed his hand around the money. "There is a man. We flew back from Luanda together. He was stationed in the north."

Michael's pulse sped up. "What is his name?"

"That I do not know. But he runs a small shop in La Havana Vieja. A print shop. In a warehouse. Near the Cathedral. Of course, he might have closed. The economy, you know."

Michael stubbed out the cigar. He wondered if the man was telling him the truth or whether, after he left, the man's nose would lengthen like Pinocchio's. Then again, he didn't have a choice. This was his only lead. He nodded at the man and headed for the door.

CHAPTER TWENTY-SEVEN

A hot tropical sun glinted off the handlebars of the bicycle taxi as Michael rode to La Havana Vieja that afternoon. After his encounter in Chinatown's Italian restaurant, a paradox he would find forever ironic, he hailed another bicycle taxi, which took him to another Havana—not the Havana of the Malecón, or that of Carla's apartment. Parts of Old Havana, especially near the port, were almost a shanty town. Streets had crumbled from neglect, laundry was strung up across yards, and telephone pole wires were strung so haphazardly it was no wonder the Cuban phone system was unreliable.

Michael asked how much he owed and was astounded when the guy told him the fare was less than two dollars American. He gave the guy a huge tip. The cyclist's eyes widened as he stuffed the cash into his pocket. Michael hoped the guy's family would eat well that night.

As he stepped down from the taxi, Michael pulled out his map. The officer in Chinatown said the shop was near the Cathedral of San Cristóbal. Michael set off. Burrowing deep into Old Havana, he wound around narrow cobblestone streets and buildings that reflected Cuba's Spanish heritage. Eventually he reached a wide plaza.

Before him was the cathedral. He stood in front, studying its elegant baroque stone façade and the asymmetry of its two towers. Someone had a sense of humor, he thought. He remembered his mother telling him she used to light candles inside, so he went in. No one was there, but the marble floor, granite columns and gentle arches cast a cool hush. He walked around the nave, admiring the ornate carvings and artwork. Sure enough, in the rear of the church, near the door he'd entered was a table filled with flickering votive candles.

He exited the church and turned right. The thought that his mother had walked these same streets filled him with a curious sensation. What was she doing here? Who did she spend time with? A small café sat about a hundred feet down from the plaza, and he had a feeling he should stop in for a coffee. He started towards it, but then remembered he had a job to do. Coffee would have to wait.

He retraced his steps to the plaza and made a circuit around its wide perimeter. The buildings on and off the plaza weren't as architecturally sophisticated or well-maintained as the church; in fact most looked downright seedy. Michael peered down one area off the plaza. It wasn't long enough to call a street. It was more like a recessed alley or alcove and ended abruptly at a three-story building with two wide doors that might be the entrance to a warehouse.

Was this the place?

Michael crept closer. The doors had once been painted white, but like everything else in Havana, the paint was chipped and peeling. He looked up. The eaves of the roof sagged, and there were no windows. He let his gaze wander and spied a narrow walkway to the left of the doors. He went over. Dark shadows dimmed his view, but twenty yards down, the walkway spilled into a tiny courtyard surrounded by dilapidated buildings. On the second floor balcony of one, a black-skinned woman in a white gown and turban stared down at him. As soon as they made eye contact, she disappeared inside so quickly Michael wasn't sure she'd been there at all. What was that about?

He backtracked to the doors of the warehouse and leaned his ear against them. A radio blared jazz from inside, but it was competing with a high-pitched whine, which periodically started then stopped. Michael took note of his surroundings, in case he had to make a hasty retreat. Then he took his nine millimeter out of his backpack, pulled out his shirt, and stashed the gun under his waistband.

He approached the doors, knocked, and waited.

Nothing happened.

He wasn't surprised; if someone was inside, the noise of the radio and whatever machine was working probably drowned out his knock. He grasped a door handle. It turned easily, and the door opened. Cautiously, he peered inside.

A light bulb swung from the ceiling, providing dim illumination, but it was helped by bars of light slanting through the open door. The floor was cement with spider-web cracks running through it. The fact that it was cement suggested that at one time, the place must have been a working factory. The walls, down to studs in places, were corroded and bare, and an assortment of wires ran randomly across them. One cord led to a self-standing fan, which, by its screech and rattle, was responsible for much of the noise.

At the back of the shop two men hunched over what looked like an old-fashioned printing press. Two huge wheels turned a drum that was attached to an elaborate metal frame. Their backs were toward Michael, but the men looked to be in their fifties, maybe older. One was practically bald with droopy jowls. The other had a mop of greasy gray hair. Both wore sweat-stained undershirts and baggy pants. The bald man went to the wall, plugged in a cord, and the high-pitched whine Michael heard outside resumed. The wheels turned for about three rotations, then stopped.

"*¡Mierda!*" one of the men snapped.

Absorbed in whatever the press was—or wasn't—doing, the men didn't notice Michael, so he rapped on the door again, this time from inside.

"*Buenos dias, Señores.*"

The men turned and looked at him. Frown lines appeared on the bald man's face. The man with all the hair stuck out his lower lip in disapproval. Neither replied.

Michael continued in Spanish. "I was told by a former army officer in Chinatown that the owner of this shop served in Northern Angola."

The bald man's frown deepened, and he exchanged a glance with the other. They both stared at Michael as if he was a space alien.

Michael persevered. "I'm looking for a man. A colonel who was stationed in Lucapa two years ago."

Another look passed between the men. The bald man rubbed his chin, which had at least three days' worth of stubble. "*Quién carajo es usted?*" he asked. Who the fuck are you?

Michael had prepared his cover story on the way. "I was also in Angola. Not a soldier. A doctor."

The bald, jowly man arched his eyebrows. "Where?"

"Dundo."

"A hell hole, that place. The whole country, in fact."

Michael nodded his agreement. "So you're the owner of this—factory?"

The bald man laughed, but it was a hollow, raucous sound. "You call this a factory?" He waved a hand. "No lights. No power. No money." He shook his head. "And I don't own it."

Of course he didn't, Michael thought. The state owned everything. He tried to smile away the mistake, but the second man, who'd been watching him carefully, broke in. "So who is this colonel you're looking for?"

Michael turned to him. "His name is Luis Perez."

"And who are you?" His gaze turned calculating.

"I am Michael DeLuca."

"DeLuca? *Italiano?*"

"My father. My mother is Cuban," Michael lied. "She almost left in fifty-nine. Then changed her mind. My father was a sailor," he said. "I didn't know him."

The second man's eyes narrowed. "Why are you looking for this colonel?"

"He has information I need."

The man's face darkened. A gust of wind—or was it the fan—swept the scent of burning rubber across the room.

Michael could tell the men weren't buying his cover. They probably suspected him of being CDR. Maybe secret police. He wondered if they might try to take him down, although he wasn't too worried. He was thirty-two, well-trained, and armed. They were in late middle-age, paunchy, and looked like they could throw a punch about as far as a goat. Still, they might have friends around the corner who were in better shape. He should play it cool. After all, they didn't have to believe his cover; they only had to believe he was no threat.

"What kind of information does this—colonel—have for you?"

Michael looked around the shop, as if searching for bugs or other surveillance equipment. "You know how walls have ears. But it is nothing illegal, and nothing political. It is simply something this man saw in Angola. Something that's important to me." He hesitated. Then, "I am prepared to compensate you for the information."

The second man snorted. "I thought so. Your accent is not Cuban. Or Mexican. You are Americano?"

Michael didn't answer. They probably figured he was CIA. Even so, he sensed they were considering his offer.

Finally the bald man said, "How much?"

Michael tilted his head. "Depends if you find him."

"You pay in dollars?"

"If you want."

The men exchanged another glance. The second man dropped his arms. It was a signal.

Jowly Man rubbed his chin again. "I will ask," he finally said. "But people—you know how it is here—they don't talk."

Michael nodded. "How much to loosen their lips?"

They bartered and came to an agreement. It was more than Michael expected. Then again, Cuba was in a bad way. Still, as he forked over the cash, he didn't doubt for a minute that he was being conned.

"Come back in day after tomorrow. *Viernes.* Maybe I will have information for you."

"And if you don't?"

The man licked his lips, then broke into a grin. "Then you will have contributed to the betterment of the *revolución.*"

***

At Carla's apartment that evening, Michael said, "Let's go to dinner. I'll take you to a *paladar* in Old Havana."

Carla, who was changing out of her work clothes, stopped, her blouse half-unbuttoned. "No."

"Why not?"

"It's not a good idea."

"What's the problem?"

She took off her blouse and put on a t-shirt and shorts. Then she turned to Michael and planted her hands on her hips. "You Americans! You think all you have to do is come to our country, flaunt your dollars, and we will bend over backwards to serve and obey."

Startled, Michael stepped back. "It's just dinner, Carla. To—thank you for letting me stay here."

A flush crept up her neck, and she ran her hand through her short brown-blond hair. Michael wasn't sure what to say. The anger bubbling under the surface gave her a perversely attractive quality, and in her shorts and t-shirt, with her hair swept back, she looked sexy. But she must have sensed his thoughts, because she wheeled around and stomped into the living room.

"Think about it, Miguel," she called over her shoulder. "The *paladars* are for foreign tourists or high government officials. When they figure out I'm a nobody, and they will as soon as I open my mouth—with my Havana accent—they will report me."

"For what? Having dinner with a friend?"

"For consorting with a foreigner who flashes around money. Technically, the *paladars* are still illegal, you know. At least for Cubans. Someone will tell the CDR official in that district they saw me. That official will report it to my CDR, and they will start watching me. Who knows? Maybe they already are. They know everybody's business. So." She turned back to him. "That is why it is not a good idea."

Michael opened his hands in a gesture of frustration. Living in Cuba was clearly difficult for many reasons, only one of which was the failing economy. How could people survive in such an oppressive environment? He moved in on Carla, hoping to wrap his arms around her.

But she stepped back. "Why do you play at these deceptions?"

"What deceptions?"

"Who are you, Miguel DeLuca?" Her eyes blazed.

"A man who cares about you."

She let out a snort. "*Que pendejada.* Bullshit. We just met. We had good sex. That is all. I am not stupid."

Surprised, Michael stepped back. He lowered his voice. "I never thought you were. But it's better that you don't know what I'm doing."

"Are you CIA? FBI? Or maybe Mafia? If you are any of those, they will find out. The CDR… the police…" Her tone softened, but worry lines dug into her forehead. "I'm sure they are already watching. I was a fool, *una tonta.* I should never have let you stay."

He cleared his throat. "Carla, I'm not CIA. Or FBI. I have a job to do. When the time is right, I will tell you." He paused. "Look. I understand your concern. If we can't go to a *paladar,* why don't you take us to a more 'appropriate' place? I want to buy you dinner."

***

They ate at a small Cuban café with rickety tables and linoleum surfaces that were chipped and marred. The menu, written on a sheet of cardboard tacked to a wall, consisted of rice and beans with a morsel or two of pork, or rice and beans with a morsel of chicken. Michael chose the pork, Carla the chicken.

"They used to have *ropa veija,*" Carla said wistfully.

"What's that?" Michael asked.

"It's a stew. Lamb or beef, slow-cooked with peppers, tomatoes, onions, and garlic. *Muy ricos.*" She smiled dreamily for a moment. Then she said matter-of-factly, "I suppose we are lucky it is still open."

"I'll bet he does." Michael motioned toward the owner, who was bussing trays at another table. Despite the meager menu, the place was almost full.

He understood when their meals arrived. The food was excellent: generous portions, perfectly cooked, aromatic, and spicy.

Michael watched Carla wolf down her food. He knew food was a scarce commodity in Cuba. The average Cuban had lost twenty pounds during the Special Period, particularly in Havana, where farms and arable land were rare. People had begun to grow their own fruits and vegetables on rooftop gardens and whatever plots of earth they could scrounge, but it would take time before those efforts became self-sustaining. Michael was glad that, at least for today, Carla's stomach would be full.

It was after eleven when they finished dinner, and they wound through the narrow cobblestone streets of Old Havana. Despite the late hour, it was crowded. Shops that were still in business remained open, although they didn't have much on the shelves. *Jineteros* and prostitutes, both white and black, advertised their wares. Stray dogs—and there were a lot—begged for food. A gentle breeze carried the scents of cheap perfume, musky sweat, and body odor, and everywhere was music: guitarists, singers, and percussionists.

Beneath the festive atmosphere, though, it was clear everyone was either looking for a handout or to trying to *"resolver"* their way to survival. It reminded Michael of what he'd read about Germany during the last days of the Weimar Republic, when the partying grew increasingly desperate, forced, and hollow. Then again, Cuba wasn't always like that. His mother had walked the streets of Old Havana thirty years ago when Cuba was thriving. He wondered what she'd think of the place now.

Carla, whose good humor seemed to be restored now that she'd been well fed, turned to him with an impish expression. "I have an idea."

"What?"

"You'll see." She led him around a corner and down a narrow passage. She threaded her way around other streets until Michael was hopelessly lost. Finally she stopped halfway down a narrow alley. The odor of incense floated out from an open door.

Carla stuck her head in and spoke to someone. A moment later she beckoned Michael.

The breeze stopped at the door, and Michael walked into a room cluttered with so much furniture, junk, and kitsch he felt claustrophobic. In the middle at a small covered table sat an enormous black woman dressed in white. She wore a white turban. Her wrists and ears jangled with jewelry, and her lips were so red they made her teeth look as white as her robes. Michael blinked. It wasn't the woman he'd seen in the courtyard near the Cathedral, but it could have been her sister.

"Come Miguel, Yelina will tell you if your job will be a success."

He hesitated. Many Cubans flocked to Santería priests and priestesses to find out about their health, relationships, and finances. A blend of voodoo, Catholicism, and African-based faiths, Santerías were famous for their prophecies and fortune telling. They were the Cuban version of gypsies, although they were slowly being replaced by machines that spat out fortunes, like the one at Coney Island. In other words, scams.

Yelina, the priestess, must have sensed his uncertainty because she flashed him a wide smile. She was missing two teeth. "Come, my son," she said in Spanish. "Sit."

Michael sat. He told himself he was only doing it to please Carla, especially since they had quarreled earlier.

"You do not want to be here, do you? You are only doing this for your woman."

He was taken aback. Was it that obvious?

Yelina smiled at his discomfort, then got up and went to another small table covered with a cloth and strewn with beads. Two candles sat on top, as if the table was a tiny altar. Yelina lit the candles, chanted, and made circles with her hands. Michael had once dated a Jewish girlfriend, and had watched her mother do the same thing on Friday night when she blessed the candles.

She picked up a small bag on the altar, came back to Michael, and sat. She opened the bag and spilled over a dozen shiny egg-shaped seashells across the table. Again she chanted. Then she moved a few of the shells around, studied them, moved a few more. She looked up at Michael, then murmured in an unfamiliar language.

"What are you doing?" he asked.

"I am inviting the saints and disciples of Orisha to join us." She paused. "You know who the saints are. I can tell."

She knew he was Catholic. So what? Most people here were. Or had been.

She moved a few more shells, then looked up at Michael again. "You will be lucky at love." She stole a glance at Carla and smiled. "In fact, you have met the love of your life."

That was par for the course.

She glanced down at the shells. "You have come to Cuba to search for something. And someone."

Also pretty easy. His clothes weren't threadbare or shabby. She probably guessed he was a foreigner.

She went back to her shells. "You have no money problems. Indeed, someone close to you… will be giving you more wealth. Quite soon."

That could be his mother. Or father. Or grandfather. They were all well off.

She was rearranging a shell when Michael heard a gasp. The woman sat back in her chair, then looked up at him. Her smile was gone.

"What?" Michael asked.

She glanced at Carla. Michael twisted around. Carla's face registered fear. He turned back to Yelina. "What is it, dammit?"

She spoke rapidly to Carla in Spanish.

"I do *not* want to ignore it," he said, making sure she knew he understood. "I want to know."

Yelina's eyebrows arched, and Carla's cheeks reddened.

"I apologize, Miguel," Carla said. She motioned for the woman to proceed.

The woman ran her tongue around her lips. A speck of lipstick ended up on a tooth. "You will meet the person you came to Cuba to find. Very soon. This person has the answers you have been seeking."

Michael canted his head. "What answers would those be?" he asked skeptically.

"That I do not know."

"Well, that sounds about right," he said, figuring he'd wasted a few dollars.

Yelina and Carla studied the shells, then exchanged a glance.

"Why are you looking at each other?" Michael asked.

Yelina hesitated. "Because you may decide afterwards that you did not want to know those answers."

"Why not?"

She laced her fingers together on the table. "Because the shells say the answers may spell your doom."

CHAPTER TWENTY-EIGHT

Friday afternoon Michael went back to the warehouse in Old Havana. It was hotter than his first visit, and despite the fan, he felt like he was entering hell. Sweat dripped down his neck and clung to his shirt. Instead of music, the radio was blasting out a baseball game with lots of static. Cubans loved their baseball, he recalled his mother telling him. Fidel himself had been a professional ball player once. In fact, many Cubans swore the game had been invented here.

The two men were frozen in the same positions as his first visit. The same bald jowly man and his grizzled partner, both hunched over the press. If he didn't know better, the scene could have been a still life. This time, though, the men nodded as he knocked, as if they'd been expecting him.

"Welcome back, Señor DeLuca," the bald man said. "I trust Habana has been good to you?"

"I can't complain." The guy was trying to be social. Odd, given his coolness before. Michael went on alert.

"So my friend, where in America are you from?"

Something was up. Michael squinted. "Why do you need to know?"

The bald man let out a nervous laugh. "Just curious. I have cousins in Miami. But I know others in New York, and Chicago."

Michael smiled. "Refugees from Cuba are always treated well in my country."

"That is what we hear."

Michael looked around. The warehouse was as dim as before, and nothing seemed different. Still. "So?"

The bald man spread his hands. "Ahh... *Lo siento. Mucho.* I tried but I could not find anyone who was in Lucapa or Dundo during the war. I talked to many people." He nodded vigorously as if it would attest to his efforts. "But no one was posted that far north."

"Perhaps you didn't try hard enough." Michael rolled his thumb and fingers together, indicating the international symbol for money.

The man drew himself up with an air of feigned indignation. "Señor, we Cubans are not that desperate. I tried. I failed. I am sorry."

Michael would have to start over. Maybe go to the hotel Carla's friend had suggested a few days ago. Or take an entirely different tack.

The second man flicked his eyes to the back of the warehouse, then back at Michael. Michael caught it.

"How long will you be staying in Havana?"

"I don't know."

The bald man cut in. "Well, if one of my contacts does come through, how can we reach you?"

Michael thought about it. He'd told them the other day he was a doctor. "I am helping at the neighborhood clinic in Vedado. If I'm not there, leave a message. They will give it to me."

"*Bueno*. Again, I am sorry we could not locate your—associate. But do not give up hope. In Cuba one never knows."

***

After Michael was gone Luis Perez stepped out of the shadows. He knew who Michael was the moment he saw him. A younger version of both him and Francesca, right down to the dark eyes, prominent nose, and high cheekbones. Even his posture, straight with his head canted a bit to one side, was like her. Seeing his son, however, didn't prepare him for the wave of sorrow that washed over him; a feeling so raw it was as if Francesca had been taken from him only yesterday, not thirty years ago. He tried to erase the image Michael's presence had conjured up. He couldn't.

The two men's faces filled with curiosity. "So?" the grizzled man said. "Do you know this man?"

Luis tried to focus. Why was his son here in Cuba? Did Francesca send him? Was she delivering a message? And if she hadn't sent him, who did? His mind was suddenly reeling with possibilities. But prudence dictated he keep his thoughts to himself. The bald, jowly man had been under his command, but Luis trusted no one.

"*Gracias, Sargento*. I appreciate that you contacted me. It has been a long time since Lucapa, no?"

The bald man nodded. "When he mentioned Dundo, I knew I should look you up."

Luis nodded back. "You were right to do that. It is an interesting situation. Unfortunately, I do not know this man. I have never seen him, not in Angola, not here, not anywhere."

The bald man cocked his head. "But he is so certain he knows you."

Luis turned up his palms. "That does not change the facts. I fear he has made a long journey for nothing."

CHAPTER TWENTY-NINE

Michael stood in line for hours to get Carla's food rations for the month. He was fortunate to snare a scrawny chicken and a few fresh vegetables that had been trucked in from Camaguey. He plucked the chicken, peeled the vegetables, and put everything in a pot to simmer, as Carla instructed. The meal turned out to be quite good. After dinner, they went for a walk.

As usual, the Malecón was crowded with people: boys in shabby clothes and sneakers with no laces, prostitutes in tight shorts and tank tops, musicians playing for food. The light from their candles threw a muted glow up from the rocks. Many were living on the other side of the seawall, Carla said. As night fell, masking the despair, they saw dark smudges bobbing on the surface of the bay.

"What are those?" Michael pointed.

"*Neumáticos,*" Carla answered. "People lash together the inner tubes from tractor wheels, throw a board on top, and use them as fishing boats."

"Tractor wheels?"

"They are no longer being used to farm. At least they are being put to use."

Another case of "*resolver,*" Michael thought grimly. He watched the fishermen paddle the *neumáticos* farther out into the bay. "The doom... it's right here."

"*¿Que dices?*" Carla asked.

"Remember what the Santería priestess with the shells said?"

"Of course. But what is this doom?"

"The *jineteros,* the hookers, the *neumáticos*... all of them were probably teachers, engineers, technicians before. But now..." His voice trailed off. "Where is your family?" he asked.

"My father is sick, so my parents went back to Santiago de Cuba. That's where they came from. There is family there to help them." She was quiet. "He has cancer," she added.

"But you stayed here?"

"I have my job. And the apartment. At least for now."

"What do you mean 'for now?'"

"The house originally belonged to a man who got out of Cuba thirty years ago. His son was a friend of my mother's. My parents moved in to be the 'caretakers.' Of course, it belongs to the state now. They can reclaim it anytime they want."

"But they haven't?"

"Most likely because I am a doctor." She snorted. "At least it is good for something."

"What happens if they do take it one day? What will you do? Where will you go?"

"I will '*resolver.*'" She paused. "But let's not dwell on unhappy subjects." Carla smiled. "Come. We will go to La Perla, so you can see where your mother lived."

***

The tour of La Perla was bittersweet. A convention center now, the place was locked and they couldn't get in. Instead they peered through glass doors. Michael saw an expansive lobby with floor to ceiling mirrors and plenty of chandeliers. Carla said it was one of the first resorts to be fully air-conditioned.

Michael imagined what it must have been like thirty years earlier when it was one of the jewels—the pearl, in fact—of Havana's resorts. Again, he wondered about his mother's life. Cuba had been her home for nearly fifteen years. She'd grown up here. How did she feel about leaving? Did she have regrets? Is that where *his* restlessness came from? She'd never spoken much about her life here. Then again, he hadn't asked.

They turned back towards Carla's apartment. As if she knew he needed a distraction, she started to chatter. "I like the dry season better than the wet. It's not so hot. And the breeze is so lovely."

"What is it now… December?" Michael went along with her. "I'll bet it's snowing back home."

"Where is home?" Carla asked.

Shit. It had slipped out. He didn't want her to know. The less she knew about him, the better. Although with every passing day, that was becoming more difficult. He tried to cover his gaffe. "If you were in the States now, you'd see a frenzy of materialism. Lots of men dressed like Santa Claus, Christmas trees, lots of money being spent. They call it 'the holiday spirit.'"

For his mother Christmas was the most important holiday of the year.

151

She always made sure there was a ridiculously huge pile of presents under the tree. And there was the party. His mother threw an annual Christmas Eve party with lavish decorations, a catered dinner, and a band that played swing music in the early hours, switching to rock and roll later. His grandfather and father would each wear a tux. Now, though, as he strolled down the Malecón, comprehension dawned. The frivolity, the food, the music—it must have reminded his mother of Havana; of the time when there was a party at La Perla every night. Michael slowed his pace, so caught up in his thoughts he didn't hear Carla.

"Well?" she said. "Miguel?"

He forced himself back. "*¡Perdone!* What did you say?"

"I was saying that Christmas in Cuba is a religious holiday. But, before the revolution—I was quite young, maybe three or four—I remember the stores and hotels were decorated. They imported fir trees and dressed them with those big balls of color. And lights. After 1959, of course, the holiday was banned as a symbol of imperialism. But every now and then you see a red sock on a door. Before the CDR makes them take it down."

Michael took her hand. She let him. It had to be the first time, he thought.

"The New Year is our big celebration. It coincides with the success of the revolution. The country goes wild. Fireworks, parties, drinking, fiestas." She nodded. "It is better that way."

"Why?"

"Because of what you said. You Americans are consumed by material things. You should hear the letters my patients get from their relatives. Full of how much money they have, what they have bought, what they are going to buy. They try to make you feel the streets are paved with dollars."

Michael was about to say "what did you expect" when it occurred to him that like Carla, there had to be many Cubans who didn't want to be in thrall to America, politically or materially. Who might actually resent the people who left or escaped when Fidel came to power. People like his mother. He wondered what Carla would think of his mother if they met. Probably not much, he thought. But aloud he said, "You don't like Americans much, do you?"

Carla corrected him. "I don't like greedy people. Or those who try to control others because of where they live or how much they have."

"Like I said, you don't like Americans much."

She dropped his hand. "Miguel, I grew up with Fidel. We were taught Americans cannot be trusted. There was the exploitation before the revolution, then the invasion afterwards—what you call the Bay of Pigs—then the Missile Crisis. And embargo. Why should we trust you?"

"What about all those letters your patients get from their relatives?"

She made a brushing aside gesture. "Much of what is written is a lie. It's intended to make us resent Fidel and long for America. But it doesn't work. Your country has problems. War-mongering, racism, discrimination. In America, Cubans are treated as badly as your blacks."

"That's not true." Michael felt his cheeks get hot. "Cubans are always given asylum."

"Yes, but after that, a man who was once a doctor in Havana washes dishes in Miami. Or drives a taxi in New York."

"So, you'd rather stay here and barely survive? Use all your energy to 'resolver?'"

"Cuba is home." Her expression went flat, and she picked up her pace.

Michael followed. This was their first fight.

They continued down the Malecón in silence, Carla a few feet ahead of him, as if determined not to bow before the almighty fortress of capitalism that Michael represented. For his part, Michael, who was jaded by nature, had to admire her tenacity. And, because she was a few steps in front, he couldn't help but admire her ass too. Small and beautifully shaped.

As if she'd read his mind, she stopped and wheeled around. "Oh. I almost forgot." Something in her tone told him she hadn't forgotten at all but was waiting for the right time to bring it up. "Someone came looking for you today at the clinic."

Michael was jolted out of his fantasy. "Who?"

"He wrote down his name and address." She fished in her bag and pulled out a scrap of paper.

"Was it Luis Perez?"

Carla's eyebrows arched as she gazed at the paper. "How did you know?"

"He's the man I've been trying to find."

She handed it over.

He held it up to a lamppost and read the address. "Where is this?"

"Lawton." At his questioning look, she added, "It's a neighborhood a bit south of here. A working-class neighborhood." She hesitated. Then, "I suppose that now that you know where he is, you will conduct your business."

Michael nodded.

"And then you will go back to America?" Her expression was unreadable.

Michael didn't answer. The night air that had seemed so refreshing a moment ago suddenly grew close and stifling. His plans were to get the map, deal with Perez, and leave Cuba before Christmas. But he couldn't tell that to Carla. The thought of lying to her filled him with guilt.

CHAPTER THIRTY

Michael and his contact, Walters, had prepared a cover story back in the States that wasn't far from the truth. The gist of it was that Ramon Suarez was still alive, living in Miami, and wanted to reestablish ties with Luis. When he finally did meet Perez, Michael would case Perez's home and decide how best to get the map.

It was a shoot-to-kill mission. If Perez resisted before Michael had the map, he would be eliminated. If not, he would be dispatched afterwards; they'd agreed it was better not to leave loose ends. Michael had killed while he was in the Gulf; he could do it again. Especially because, despite his grandfather's denials, he suspected he was helping get Tony Pacelli out of a tight spot.

Michael spent a sleepless night planning his strategy. He decided to carry out the mission the next morning. Lawton was working class; people would be on the streets; he wouldn't stand out. Once he arrived at Perez's house, he would try to win the man's trust. Maybe swap war stories. Perez had been in Angola; Michael in the Middle East. He mentally brainstormed the questions Perez would ask. Questions like what happened to Ramon after the rebels kidnapped him... why he never came back to Cuba... why he never got in touch. Michael rehearsed his answers. He didn't know what happened to Ramon, but he knew it had been gruesome. Ramon settled in Miami because the South Africans turned him over to the Americans who granted him asylum. He didn't write because the mail—telegrams and telephones as well—couldn't be trusted. And Ramon didn't want to make trouble for Perez if the wrong people discovered they were communicating.

Dawn seemed to take a long time coming, and when it did, streaks of clouds strafed the sky with pink and purple. Two gulls that resembled vultures circled above Carla's balcony. Michael watched them as he drank what Carla called coffee, a weak and watery brew that tasted like chicory.

Carla told him the P-2 bus would take him to Lawton but warned it might take a few hours because of the erratic schedule. Michael made sure his pistol was in his backpack along with a change of clothes. He kissed Carla goodbye but didn't tell her this might be the last time they'd see each other. Still, something made her turn away from him.

***

Carla was right about the bus, and it was too early for bicycle taxis, so Michael waited over an hour. When the bus finally lumbered up, belching black smoke from the exhaust, it was standing room only, and he hung onto the overhead bar during the entire trip. He got off at a major intersection in the 10th of October neighborhood where buildings with crumbling columns flanked the streets. He imagined how grand and imposing the buildings had once been; now laundry was suspended on a line between them.

He turned the corner and started walking. He was in what looked like a barrio, although in Havana, what wasn't? Eventually he reached the intersection of Camilo Cienfuegos Avenue and San Francisco, and headed up a hill. He found himself in a residential area. It wasn't prettier: a canopy of telephone wires marred the view, and the pavement was cracked with weeds poking through. But a copse of healthy-looking trees stood in the center of the block, and ramshackle buildings were grouped around them. He recalled Carla telling him every house was technically the property of the state. He couldn't imagine anyone wanting these.

He'd been right about the people on the streets. Most of them, caught up in the activities of their day, paid him no heed. The faces he passed were black or tan and looked like they needed a good meal. He passed only a few white faces. Which made him wonder why Perez lived here. His military status could probably get him a nicer home, along the lines of Carla's place. Then he remembered the officer from Chinatown and the enlisted men at the warehouse. Maybe not.

He followed the street numbers and came to a drab, one-story house with slatted European-style shutters on the windows. One or two were missing, but the rest were partially open to let the light through. The door was open, and the smell of coffee—real coffee—wafted out. Maybe there *was* something to being an army officer. Maybe they got the first pick of rations.

He strolled past the house and circled the block, passing three women and one man. No one took any notice of him. Looping back around, he returned to Perez's house. The street was empty. He wanted to race to the door and break in, but he forced himself to walk up and knock.

The man who came to the door had no shirt on, just pants. He was about the same height as Michael, but thinner. His face looked especially gaunt, but he looked—familiar. Thick dark unruly hair. A Roman nose that was too big for his face Full lips but an unimpressive chin. Olive skin. His eyes were dark and smoky, but Michael couldn't read his expression. It was part knowing, part kind. Why? Michael felt uneasy.

"*Buenos dias, Señor.*"

The man nodded.

"You are Luis Perez?"

He didn't miss a beat. "You must be Michael DeLuca."

Michael nodded. "I've been looking for you."

"So I hear." A smile tugged at his mouth. "I wasn't expecting you this soon." He stepped back from the door and motioned Michael inside. "Make yourself at home. Let me get my shirt."

He led Michael into a small room. The living room. Perez disappeared into the back. Michael couldn't believe his luck. He had the opportunity to case the place. He started to explore. The furniture was worn, but the room was immaculate; everything seemed to have its place.

Bands of light poured through the slatted shutters, but the only colors came from a collection of books, which lined two walls of the room. Plain wooden planks supported by cinderblocks; the kind of thing you'd see in a college dorm back home. He scanned the titles. They were all in Spanish, but he could see works of literature, poetry, as well as non-fiction. Michael ran his tongue around his lips. Perez was exceptionally well-read. Practically an intellectual.

He surveyed the rest of the room. A tiny sofa, a chair. A lamp. An open sketchpad on the sofa. A set of pencils sat on a small table, and a framed photo lay on top. He went to take a closer look. The photograph was of a woman and a man. They were both quite young. The man had his arm around the woman. The man was tall, slender, fit, and looked very much like Michael in his twenties. The woman looked to be barely out of her teens. Dark hair. Slender but curvy. High cheekbones. Dark, luminous eyes that sparkled through the frame across time. As Michael stared at it, he felt his eyes widen, and his jaw dropped. He felt as if he'd been struck by lightning.

Perez came back into the room. Michael spun around. Perez was buttoning his shirt. He peered at Michael, the photograph, then back at Michael.

Michael blurted it out. "What the hell are you doing with a picture of my mother?"

CHAPTER THIRTY-ONE

Michael. Miguel. It was a sturdy name; strong, Luis thought. His son—how strange to say that word after so many years—would need that strength now that he knew the truth. But his son's reaction was not what Luis had expected. He'd prepared himself for disbelief, denial, anger. None of that happened. After his initial outburst, Miguel's face went white, and he stiffened in the same way people told Luis *he* did when he was upset. He blinked rapidly, but his expression was blank.

Luis guessed it was a learned response. Someone—the army, perhaps—had trained him well. Never reveal yourself, especially in enemy territory. Never let them know what you're thinking until you strike. Luis waited.

After a moment, a puzzled look came over Michael, as if he was trying to piece something together. That was followed by a suspicious glance around the room. And then, as if everything was suddenly too overwhelming, he sagged and sank down on the sofa.

"I wouldn't mind coffee," he said.

Luis hesitated. This was an unexpected request. Was it an act? If he was going to strike, this would be the moment. Should Luis go into the kitchen? What would be waiting for him when he got back? He had no idea why his son was here in Cuba. Then again, Michael *was* his son, and he'd gone to a lot of trouble to find him.

He weighed his options. Whether the news was good or bad was, of course, important, but his son likely wouldn't have come all this way and not deliver it. So he took a leap of faith and went into his kitchen. He returned a moment later with two steaming cups of coffee.

Miguel was still on the sofa, but he had the photo in his hands and was studying it. Relief flooded through Luis. Relief, and a glimmer of hope. He set the coffee down on the tiny table. Miguel looked up.

"Where did you get this?"

"Excuse me?"

"The coffee."

"It is the only luxury I allow myself. I buy it on the black market."

Michael nodded as if he, too, would break the rules for a cup of good coffee. But it was a strange comment to make at such a moment, Luis thought. Miguel put the picture down and picked up his coffee. He took a sip. Then, "When was that taken?"

"In 1958."

"Where?"

"In Santa Clara. That's where we were living. Before the *revolución*."

"You and my mother?"

Luis nodded and sipped his coffee. They were both silent, but Luis felt an odd intimacy between them, as if they had been drinking their morning coffee together for years. He pushed the thought out of his mind. He must be imagining it.

Michael set his cup down and gazed at Luis. "Tell me. Why should I believe you?"

"Believe what?"

"That you—and my mother—lived together? Were—are—you..." he stumbled over the words, "...my parents?"

This was the reaction Luis had been waiting for. "You should believe it because it's the truth," he said.

"How do I know you didn't fake this photo? And the story? To lure me in."

"Lure you? Where? For what purpose?" Luis spread his hands. "You found me." At the same time, Michael's question intimated he had not come to Cuba simply to connect with his father. Something else was driving him. Something that involved risk—perhaps danger. Luis briefly thought about retrieving his service revolver, then decided against it. This was his son.

Michael gazed at him, searching his face. What did he see, Luis wondered. Was it the same thing Luis had seen when he eavesdropped on Michael's conversation with the men in the warehouse? How much they physically resembled each other?

Then, "So what was the relationship between my mother and you? Were you married?"

Luis didn't bother to keep the surprise out of his voice. "She never told you?"

Michael shook his head.

"I see." He paused. "She—your mother, Francesca—was the only woman I have ever loved. And she loved me."

"But you weren't married."

"We would have—but the revolution..."

"I don't understand. I was born in the States."

"Your mother ran away from La Perla to be with me in Santa Clara. We were there a few months. But then her father—your grandfather—discovered where we were, came in with a squad of men, and kidnapped her. He forced her to go back to America. It was during the peak of the revolution. Everything was in chaos. Everyone was frightened. She was pregnant when she left."

"Were you?" Michael's tone was almost accusatory.

"Was I what?"

"Were you frightened?"

Luis hesitated again. He had to tell his son the truth. "No. I was with the rebels. I was overjoyed. Cuba was finally going to be free."

"Except it didn't turn out that way."

"Nothing turned out the way it was supposed to." Luis stared at him. "Except you."

A faraway look came across Michael's face. He was quiet.

After a long moment, Luis asked, "What are you thinking?"

Michael looked startled. Luis wondered if Michael thought he was presumptuous to have asked the question.

His son flicked his eyes to the photograph of his mother. His expression hardened. "My mother..." he said, eyes narrowing, "... had a secret life. A life she never shared. How could she be so selfish? Why didn't she tell me that man she married—that man..." he spat out the word, "...wasn't my real father?"

"It was a difficult, complicated time. She was probably forbidden to say anything."

"Yeah, sure," Michael said caustically in English. Then he switched back to Spanish. "Since when would that stop her, once she'd made up her mind?"

Despite the seriousness of the conversation, Luis smiled. "That's the Francesca I remember. Willful. Spoiled. But so beautiful. And such spirit..." His voice trailed off.

"You did love her," Miguel seemed surprised.

"And I can only imagine how much she loved—loves—you," Luis said. "She was consumed by the times. Do not be angry with her. She had no control."

"If you loved her so much, why didn't you go after her? Bring her back? Or move there?"

"Forces were beyond my control as well. I fought for the revolution. I became part of the new regime. I never heard a word from her in those early years, and, after a while, I realized I never would. Until now." He shifted. "Tell me, Miguel, when did your mother change her mind? Why are you here?" Despite the toll of so many years and so much disappointment,

Luis couldn't suppress the hope in his voice. "Does she have a message for me?"

His son looked away.

Something was off. Luis leaned forward, hands on his thighs. "You are here because of her, no?"

Michael put his coffee down, stood, and started to pace the small room.

"She didn't send me," he finally said.

"Her father, then? What does Tony Pacelli want from me after so long?"

Miguel didn't reply.

"Not your grandfather, either?"

When Miguel still didn't answer, Luis straightened. "There is only one other person in the world that knows who you are. But he died in Angola...." As comprehension dawned, Luis broke off. "Perhaps he didn't."

Miguel wiped his brow with the back of his hand. He started toward the door. "I must go."

Luis stood. "Why?"

Miguel didn't reply.

"When will you come back? We have much to discuss."

But his son bolted through the door and sprinted away from the house. He didn't look back.

CHAPTER THIRTY-TWO

The morning sun burnished the city with a shiny, bright glitter the next morning, but Michael kept his head down. The streets were full of potholes filled with dirt, not concrete. That would never be tolerated in the States, he thought absently. At the same time he knew his analysis of Havana's road conditions was just a way to avoid the storm of confusion washing over him.

His instinct told him to get in touch with Walters back in the States, but he was shrewd enough not to trust it. He needed actionable intel before he proceeded. And the truth was he had nothing. He didn't really know Walters; his grandfather had made the connection. All he knew was that the man had been CIA and was now private. Working for a concern that wanted the map for commercial reasons. Walters wouldn't be concerned with Michael's personal issues. He might not know about them.

But the man who'd put Walters and his grandfather together might. Was that the man Perez believed died in Angola? The only other person in the world who, according to Perez, knew he was Michael's father? Who was that man? How had he managed to connect them? Was it a benign or sinister motivation? The man had to know he and Perez would figure out their connection. Was he counting on that? Was he hoping to double-cross Walters and Tony Pacelli? Whoever this man was, he had to know Michael wouldn't kill his own father, especially when he'd just discovered him. Wouldn't he?

Michael ran a hand through his hair. Too many questions, too few answers. The bottom line was that Michael didn't know who to trust. He sensed Perez wasn't lying. There was no reason for him to. But if his father—he had a hard time thinking of Perez that way—was telling the truth, it meant his mother and the man he'd called father for thirty years had lied to him. His grandfather, too. They had all kept secrets from him.

For decades. And that, Michael wasn't sure he could ever forgive.

***

A watery breeze, carrying away the day's heat, brushed their faces as he and Carla took a walk that evening. But Michael was still weighted down by his thoughts, and he ignored the gathering crowd of musicians, prostitutes, and people with their hands out.

"You are quiet," Carla said.

Michael looked over. How could he tell her his world had imploded? "How was your day?" he asked instead.

"Like all the others."

They continued to walk. Dusk threw a soft mantle of purple over the bay. Waves smacked against the rocks. Two or three lights, fishing boats probably, blinked through the darkening water. Suddenly Carla stopped. Before Michael could react, she grabbed his hand and pulled him down over the seawall. She crouched down on the rocks, forcing him to do the same.

"What is it?" Michael asked. His pulse was pounding.

Carla put a finger on her lips and pointed. Above them a group of men in blue shirts, dark pants, and what looked like berets with tassels approached from the opposite direction. Police. As they marched past, Michael could see they were not in formation, and their voices were boisterous. They were laughing, clowning around, leering at the whores. Feeling no pain.

Michael waited until the thud of their footsteps was gone. "What was that all about?"

Carla planted her palm on her chest, as if to slow her racing heart. "One never knows with La Policía. I panicked. I am sorry."

"What's going on?"

She went to a spot where they could climb back over the seawall to the Malecón. "There's something I haven't told you."

Despite the heat, an icicle of fear prickled his skin.

She hesitated then blurted it out. "Juliana—you remember. My upstairs neighbor..."

He cut her off. "The one—who's—who is sick?"

She nodded impatiently. "She told me the CDR knows you're American."

"Who is the CDR official?"

"An old woman. She lives next door. It's her job to know everybody's business."

"How did she find out?"

"How does anyone know anything in Cuba?"

Michael nodded as if he'd expected it. "It was bound to happen. You and I—we haven't been making a secret of my presence. Juliana is a prostitute, desperate for money. She probably told the old woman. She—"

Carla cut him off. "Maybe yes, maybe no. But that does not matter. If they find you... I do not want to think what will happen. To us both."

Michael glanced at the seawall, then back at Carla. "How long before they send the security police?"

"Maybe one or two days. They will arrest me for harboring an enemy of the state." She paused. "What they will do to you, I have no idea. They will assume you are—what do you call your intelligence service?"

"CIA." Michael extended his hand and pulled her up over the wall. Together they climbed up the rocks back to the pavement. "I will go. I should never—"

Again she pre-empted him. "I invited you, remember?"

He looked at her. "But... what are you going to do?"

"I have been thinking. I will go to Santiago de Cuba. To my family."

"Are you sure that's wise? Won't they come after you there?"

"Perhaps. Perhaps not. But I cannot stay home. And I cannot go back to the clinic."

Michael gazed at this fiery woman whose spirit hadn't been crushed by the hardship, the poverty, and the sickness she confronted every day. He remembered how, when they met, she'd faked a sprained ankle to get him out of trouble. To *"resolver"* was second-nature for her. He admired her resilience, her ingenuity, her fatalism in the midst of danger. A danger that he had caused. It occurred to him that this was the first time he had ever felt this way about a woman. He took her hand, and they resumed their stroll.

"So..." he said, "it would seem we both have reasons to leave Havana."

"Have you completed your mission—whatever it is?" she added acidly.

"The reason I haven't told you about it is precisely because of this. I did not want to put you in a compromising position."

"It's a bit late for that, don't you think?"

"I agree. It's time I told you my story." As they walked he told her everything: why he'd come to Cuba, what his mission was. It was dark now, but someone had lit candles on the rocks, and Carla's expression was wide-eyed and at the same time knowing. When he told her his target had turned out to be his father, her hand flew to her mouth. A salsa beat thumped close by. It ended as Michael finished his story.

"So, when my contact discovers I walked out on my mission—"

"You have made that decision?"

"How can I kill my father?" He hesitated. "It's strange, you know? The man I *thought* was my father, Carmine DeLuca... he hated me. I never understood why. What I had done to provoke it." He tightened his lips.

"Now I understand."

She inclined her head. "But Miguel, if you do not complete your mission, what *are* you going to do?"

"I want to get to know my father. But I need to tread carefully. Part of me thinks this is a fairy tale. The other part of me suspects it could be a set-up."

"I do not believe in fairy tales," Carla said.

He looked over. "Nor do I."

She was quiet for a moment. Then, "Miguel, it is clear you're involved in things I know nothing about. And I do not want to. But family—that I do understand. And family must always come first."

He felt his jaw clench. "You think so? My mother kept the truth about *my* family a secret over thirty years. She has been living a lie. And forced me to do the same. I don't call that putting family first."

"She was trying to protect you."

"She was selfish," he snapped. "Trying to paper over the past, pretend it never happened."

Carla stopped, turned, faced Michael. "You have much to learn about women. If I had a child, I would do anything to keep it safe. Anything."

"Yes, well, she failed." He spread his hands. "I am about to be hunted by the security forces of two countries."

Carla picked up her pace. "*Terco como una mula*," she muttered.

Michael caught up to her. "Stubborn? Who is the stubborn one? You only have a day or two left of the life you've always known, and yet here you are, sauntering down the Malecón like you don't have a care in the world."

She didn't answer for a moment. Then, "We are where we are supposed to be. We do what we are supposed to."

Was this more of her Santería nonsense? Or wisdom? The breeze picked up, and Carla turned into it, letting it ruffle her hair. Despite their bickering, he was surprised at how natural it felt to stroll down the Malecón holding her hand. Like he belonged.

And with that came another insight that seemed to explain everything. Michael had spent his life as an outsider, eavesdropping on other peoples' lives, literally and figuratively. Picking up crumbs of happiness when he could. He'd never been content. Now, though, despite the circumstances, or maybe because of them, he felt as if he was home. As if the pieces of an enormous puzzle were finally clicking into place. Was this destitute island the place *he* was supposed to be?

CHAPTER THIRTY-THREE

Michael didn't go back to the States for Christmas. Or New Year's. He sent a telegram to Walters saying the mission had been delayed and hoped no prying eyes saw it. Then he and Carla discussed their options. They couldn't stay at her apartment, and she couldn't go back to the clinic. They needed a safe house. And time.

"What about your father?" Carla asked.

"You read my mind," Michael said. "They'll have no reason to look for us there. At least for a while."

An hour later their bags were packed, and they fled the Vedado apartment. At dawn they showed up at Luis's home in Lawton. He seemed surprised but pleased and welcomed them in. Fortunately, he had an extra room. It was scarcely bigger than a closet, but they moved in a mattress that afternoon, and the room became theirs.

The more time Michael spent with his father, the more surprised he was at his feelings. Luis Perez was intelligent and thoughtful; soft-spoken but articulate. Michael began to admire him, something that had never been the case with Carmine DeLuca. In fact, it was a feeling so new and tender that Michael wasn't sure whether to trust it. Was this the way families who actually liked each other behaved?

At the same time, Michael sensed an underlying sadness in his father, a sorrow Michael suspected had been caused by his mother's departure. He recalled a similar regret in his mother at times. And while he understood how and why his grandfather tore them apart, he also realized his grandfather's actions thirty years ago were the reason he came to Cuba in the first place.

New Year's Eve was a bawdy celebration marked by an excess of rum and firecrackers and music. At one point Luis, Michael, and Carla trudged to the top of Lawton's highest hill, where the neighborhood gathered to watch the fireworks.

But the tentacles of the state's CDR stretched into Lawton, and the neighbors' curious glances practically guaranteed that the CDR would follow-up on Luis's "guests." So the next morning Luis announced it was a good time for a trip: Michael should see his native land—despite where he was born, Luis considered his son a Cuban—as well as the places where Luis and his mother had been together.

They would start at the beach in Varadero and end in Santiago de Cuba so Carla could visit her parents. Luis would show Michael where he grew up in Oriente. By the time they returned, Luis said, perhaps the CDR would have moved on.

The next day, on a sparkling, seductive morning, they set out in a borrowed '58 Buick. The car sputtered and whined and coughed, and Michael was sure it would conk out before they drove twenty miles, but that failed to dampen their spirits. Michael felt like a kid who'd discovered a new world full of wonder, and Carla's grin said she shared his enthusiasm. Even Luis looked energized.

Luis drove. Once they were out of Havana, the scenery changed. Gone were the revolutionary murals and buildings with images of Che and Fidel; the tangle of telephone wires; the maze of trolley tracks. They were in the countryside, but if Michael expected to see acres of sugar cane and tobacco, he was disappointed. The landscape was mostly abandoned fields and grasslands.

"The remains of the sugar cane crop are south and east of here," Luis explained.

"But I thought—"

Luis cut him off. "Fidel told us we were going to harvest our way out of the Special Period. Unfortunately he neglected to tell us that we need fertilizer, herbicides, and fuel. All of which, of course, we do not have. The sugar crop is down ninety per cent."

Gradually the grasslands turned into woods, then marshland, and an hour later they crossed a tall bridge high above a twisty river the color of emeralds. Though Luis pronounced the bridge stable, Michael swore it swayed as they drove across. Relief washed over him when they reached the other side. He'd never told anyone he had a fear of heights.

Soon a huge sign welcomed them to Varadero, and twenty minutes later they were gazing at a perfect beach: turquoise water, white sand, and a golden sun. Children supervised by watchful parents frolicked in the water; lovers snuggled on blankets and towels; older adults relaxed under thatched umbrellas. The beauty was so absolute, so flawless, that Michael's throat went tight.

Luis was watching him. "I brought your mother here," he said softly.

Michael spun around. "Where?"

Luis pointed. "There is a secluded area down by the nature preserve."

Michael shaded his eyes with his hand. "I want to see it." He started off toward the nature preserve, but Carla stayed him with her arm. She smiled and shook her head. Did she sense it was a private memory? Not to be shared?

Michael dropped his hand. "Never mind."

Luis seemed relieved. "When I was young, I used to spend the night on the beach in Oriente. The stars were so close I was sure I could reach up, grab a few, and put them in my pocket. Along with my marbles and lizards." He paused. "A boy and his dreams." He smiled and touched Michael's shoulder. "Tell me about your dreams, son. I want to know."

No one, man or woman, had ever asked Michael about his dreams. This must be how a real father behaved. A father who loved his son.

***

The car did break down on the way to Santa Clara, and Luis abandoned it outside Matanzas. They hitchhiked back to the train station and bought tickets instead. The train was three hours late, which was considered on time these days, and when it pulled into the station, it was teeming with people. They had to stand in the aisles for most of the journey, peering out at the road that paralleled the tracks. Occasionally a truck packed with hitchhikers passed them, but more often they saw wagons and carts pulled by oxen or horses. The signs on the road were painted on slabs of wood or rock, all of which was a grim reminder that progress in Cuba was moving in the wrong direction.

When they arrived in Santa Clara, Luis took the same route he and Michael's mother had walked when they first came to the city. He showed them the university, and the house where he and Francesca had lived. Carla had brought a camera, and they took pictures in front of the house: Luis with Michael, Michael with Carla, the three of them together.

In Santiago de Cuba they met Carla's parents. And her aunt and uncle. And their children. Carla's mother, an energetic fiftyish woman, was beside herself with joy, but whether that was because she was seeing her daughter, or the fact that Carla had brought along a boyfriend, and her boyfriend's father, wasn't clear. Carla's father, sick and frail, was less fervent, but shared his stash of Cohibas with Luis. A teenage nephew bounced a basketball the whole time they were there. When he learned Michael was from Chicago, he wanted to know if he knew Michael Jordan. He was crestfallen when Michael admitted he did not.

Carla stayed with her parents a few extra days. No one said anything, but they all knew this was the last time Carla would see her father. Meanwhile, Luis took Michael to Alto Cedro, the village in Holguin province where he'd been raised. He also took Michael to Biran, a neighboring village, where Fidel had grown up. They had known each other as youngsters, Luis told him. They played baseball together. Fidel's father was a self-made man, a farmer who became wealthy, so Fidel's upbringing had been relatively affluent. Michael seemed surprised.

It was on the train back to Havana a few days later, the train having been four hours late, that Luis looked over at Carla. She was dozing.

"I want to tell you why I came to Cuba," Michael said softly.

When Michael told him his mission had been to kill him, Luis flinched. "After I gave you the map?"

Michael nodded.

"And how were you to convince me to give it to you?"

"I was to tell you Suarez was alive in Miami, and wanted to re-establish ties."

"How did he know I'd kept it all these years?"

"Good question," Michael said. "Maybe he knows you better than you think."

Luis thought about it. "You have a point."

"Maybe he knows that you remain loyal to the people you love."

Luis shrugged it off.

"Anyway, they prepped me how to respond to the questions they expected you to ask." He paused. "If that didn't work, I was to use whatever means necessary."

"Did you see Ramon? Meet him?"

"There was no time."

"I see." Luis, who had been reading a book, closed it. 'From the first day to this, sheer greed was the driving spirit of civilization.' He peered at Michael over his reading glasses. "Friedrich Engels. The father of communism."

"He wasn't—isn't—altogether wrong," Michael said.

Luis smiled.

"Luis... Father..." This was the first time Michael had called him "Father," Luis noted. "My contact and the people he works for believe there's a fortune at stake. They have put a plan in motion. A plan that won't end even if I don't complete the job. They are relentless, and—"

Luis raised his palm. "Before you go on, I want to tell *you* a story." Luis told him about the geologist who thought coltan was black gold, and how he and Ramon had tailed him to the mine. How Ramon had told Luis to sketch a map of the location. How they were attacked by rebels, Ramon was shot, and taken away. How Luis thought he was dead. And how he'd kept the map all these years as a tribute to their friendship.

"When did you learn it could be valuable?" Michael asked. "I mean, why did you decide to hide it?"

Luis smiled. "We may be backward compared to America, but we are not stupid. I read. And since I spent time in that part of the world, I try to keep up. I realized a few years ago that the map might be of interest to some. Ramon certainly thought it would be. So I thought I should protect it." He flipped up one hand. "One never knows."

Michael cleared his throat. "Look. I've been thinking. I want you to come to America with me. You and Carla. We will deal with this—together. As a family."

Luis blinked back a sudden wetness in his eyes. It occurred to him that he'd been waiting for a declaration like this for years: a public recognition that the woman he loved had borne his son, that they were joined through that son forever. But this wasn't the time for sentiment. He needed to focus. "*Resolver*," as they said. He took a moment to compose himself, then placed his hand on Michael's shoulder.

"What you have said means more to me than anything I can remember. But I cannot go to America."

"You do not understand. As soon as my contact figures out I've aborted the mission, he will come for the map himself. He will kill you."

"He has no idea where I am."

"I found you."

Luis pressed his lips together. "I am old. Closer to the end than the beginning."

"*¡Mierda!*" Michael shot back. "You are not old. But you *are* in danger." He rubbed the back of his neck with his hand. "You cannot refuse. It would be suicide."

"But I must," Luis said patiently.

"Why?" Irritation laced his son's voice. Then he stopped. "You're worried about seeing my mother, aren't you?"

Luis didn't reply.

"We will deal with her. And my grandfather. Together. After Suarez."

Luis looked up. "What about Ramon? Are you going to kill him?"

It was Michael's turn not to answer.

"You see? I cannot ask the son I just discovered to avenge his father."

Michael started to argue, but his father persisted. "You have a life now…" he gestured toward Carla. "You will have your own family. You should not carry my burdens on your shoulders."

"But they are going to *kill* you."

"Perhaps not." Luis explained how Ramon and he had been childhood friends in Oriente. How they came to Havana together to study. How they both drifted into the revolution. How Ramon, not much of a student, dropped out of university and landed a job at the hotel. "That was how I met your mother, you know."

Michael listened, albeit with a skeptical expression.

Luis told him how Tony Pacelli tortured Ramon thirty years ago to find out where his daughter had fled. And, more recently, how the Angolan rebels tortured him as well, for the sole reason that he was on the wrong side of the war.

"Ramon has had a hard life, an impossible life. I am glad he is alive, and I am sure he considers the map and the riches it will bring him his due. And this may surprise you, but I do not disagree. He deserves his reward. I have no interest in the mine. I never did." He leaned forward. "What's more, I do not harbor any ill will toward him, except as it concerns you. I do not like that they used you to deceive me. So perhaps, if I explain this, Ramon will change his mind."

"Father, you cannot be that naïve."

Luis smiled. "Why do you think Ramon chose you for this mission?"

"Because he knew you wouldn't give the map to anyone else."

"Exactly. But what if he engineered this so you and I could find each other?"

Michael nodded. "I wondered about that, but—" He was quiet for a moment. "At this point it does not matter. If you are right, Suarez's generosity ended with him. My contact, Walters, has different motives. He's a danger to us."

Luis was about to reply when Carla opened her eyes and stretched.

***

After they arrived back in Havana, Carla went straight to bed. Luis motioned for Michael to follow him into his room. "I want to show you where the map is."

"I don't want to know."

"But you must." He led Michael into a small room with a bed not much larger than a cot. A brightly colored woven rug, about as big as a bath mat, lay on the floor next to the bed. Luis picked it up. Underneath was a loose floorboard. He raised it and rooted around. He pulled out a large white envelope.

"*Aqui.*" Luis made sure Michael saw it, then put it back under the floorboard. He pressed down until the board snapped back in place. He spread the rug back on top.

Michael spoke up. "It's hard for me to believe you care nothing for the map. It could make you wealthy. Change your life."

"It already has. It brought you to me."

Michael put his hand on Luis's arm. "Thank you. But this is only the beginning. I know you are retired from the army, but your pension is not nearly enough. Please, Father. Put your affairs in order. You and Carla and I—and the map—are going to the States. In the next few days, in fact."

"How do you propose to do that? It's not easy for Cubans to leave the country. We will need a *tarjeta blanca*, Carla and I. They take time. Months, perhaps years."

"Leave that to me."

Luis gazed at Michael. Clearly there were things he had yet to discover about his son. "Why so soon?"

Michael hesitated before answering. "I sent a telegram to my contact saying I needed more time. But I'm not sure he will give it to me. If he doesn't, he will—as I've said—come here himself to complete the mission."

"When?"

"The original plan was a month after I arrived." Michael hesitated. "The month was up three days ago."

CHAPTER THIRTY-FOUR

Why the fuck would anyone want to live here, Walters thought as he stared out at Havana Bay. Whitecaps sparkled in the Caribbean waters, but the beauty of the bay was lost on him. He'd only been here twenty-four hours—he'd sneaked in from Mexico—but he was already disgusted by the poverty, the come-ons from both sexes, the incessant din of the music. This place was no better than the African jungle. Well, maybe one step up. At best a third world society, where desperation leaked from walls like water from broken pipes. Even the hotel he was staying in—one of the best in the city, he'd been told—wouldn't rate two stars back in the States.

He turned away from the view and rummaged in his suitcase. Although he was furious, he wasn't entirely surprised the operation had gone south. He should have realized when you dealt with spics, it was never smooth. He should never have listened to that punk Gonzalez or Suarez or whatever he was calling himself now. Fucking Cuban lizard turncoat. Like all of them. They told you what they thought you wanted to hear. Just enough to snatch the money you dangled in front of them or a free ride to Miami. His pals back at the Agency had warned him. At least the rebels in Angola were honest. Stupid but honest.

On top of that DeLuca had disappeared. Taken off. The kid sent him a telegram when he'd arrived in Havana. And another a few days ago asking for more time. But when Walters replied, he never got a confirmation reply. The little wop had vanished into the fog that shrouded the harbor at night. Either he'd decided to rip off the map for himself, or he had fucked up the assignment and was dead. Too bad. Either way, *his* client would be enraged. He might have *him* taken out.

A wave of anger rippled through him. He should never have brought Suarez to the States. But his superiors back in Langley were hot for the chance to turn a Cuban Army officer. They'd debriefed Suarez "aggressively," as the Agency put it, when he arrived, but the guy had no intel worth passing on. He could have told them that would happen. Angola was a hemorrhoid on the continent of Africa. Nobody cared about FAPLA or UNITA or the South African Army. They were unimportant. A footnote in history. The day he'd been relieved of duty in Angola was the best day of his life.

Not like today. He scowled. To make things worse, the Outfit was breathing down his throat. The guy who'd hooked him up with Pacelli kept telling him Pacellli wanted updates on his goddamned grandson. Sure, he'd replied. He had shit to report. But if he didn't give him something, Pacelli might send *his* thugs after him. Not good, the guy who'd made the connection kept saying. Not good at all. Like a fucking parrot. Like Walters didn't already know?

He sat on the bed, head in his hands. What had he gotten himself into? All he wanted was a decent living. Too old for the Agency, too smart for a desk job. This was supposed to be his swan song. His "I'll-never-have-to-work-another-day-in-my-life" reward. God knows he'd earned it. Listening. Currying favor. Making things happen. But now he didn't know a goddamned thing about his own operation. If there weren't so much money involved, he'd shitcan the whole thing. Leave this godforsaken place and get back to America.

But he couldn't. He had to find the asshole with the map. He hoped it wouldn't take long. When he did, he'd find out if DeLuca made off with it, and, if so, where. Then he'd take care of them both. He opened his suitcase, removed two pistols, a revolver, and a hunting knife. Checked to see they were all in working order. As he did, he realized he'd never be done with clean-up operations. At the Agency he was the guy who made everything neat and tidy. And untraceable. He snapped his suitcase shut. Some things never changed.

***

The chirp of birds woke Carla at dawn the next morning. Most likely a family of trogons, the blue, red, and white national bird of Cuba. She didn't mind. She'd slept well, which was unusual for her. It must have something to do with sorrow. Knowing she would never see her father again, she'd bid farewell to him in Santiago de Cuba. They'd both shed tears. Hugged each other close. Afterwards all she wanted to do was sleep.

But now she felt rested and energized. Perhaps there was a limit to the amount of sorrow a soul could absorb. Whatever the reason, she decided to get up and make breakfast for Michael and Luis. In the kitchen she found eggs, bread, and enough coffee for three cups.

She went to the stove to heat water and toast the bread, but when she turned the knob for gas, nothing happened. Like the electricity, the gas often shut off without warning. There was no way to tell how long it would last. She would slice fruit instead. Still, her mood didn't dampen, and she hummed as she searched for a knife.

She'd known Miguel barely a month, but her life had changed dramatically. And now irrevocably. She went back into the tiny space they used as a bedroom. Miguel was still asleep, his legs tangled in the sheet. She watched the rise and fall of his chest and breathed in his scent; she loved knowing their smells had blended together. Was it love? Perhaps. Perhaps not. She'd never been in love before.

A moment later, as if he'd felt her presence, he rolled over and slowly came awake. His thick hair was tangled, and a cowlick stuck out on top. His eyes were still hooded and smoky with sleep, but they tracked her up and down. She sat on the edge of the bed, leaned over and kissed him. His lips were sweet and full of desire. She felt herself become aroused. She forgot about breakfast and crawled back into bed.

Afterwards, she brushed the thatch of hair off his forehead.

"*Buenos días*," he said, still on top of her.

She grinned.

He rolled off, leaned back, and laced his hands behind his head. "We have an expression in English: 'You look like the cat that swallowed the canary.'"

"What does it mean?"

"It means to be very pleased with oneself."

She nodded. "Ahh. In Spanish we say "*Estar más ancho que largo. No cabe en sí de satisfacción.*"

Michael tickled her chin. "I think I see your whiskers," he teased. "Why so happy?"

"Because I am two weeks late with my period. And I am never late."

She watched as it sank in. His brow furrowed. He looked pensive. Then comprehension dawned. "You are pregnant?"

She nodded tentatively.

His face lit. "This is wonderful!" He gathered her in his arms.

Carla hadn't realized how tense she'd been. Now she sagged against him. She couldn't have hoped for a better reaction. Maybe it was love. Her eyes filled.

He tipped up her chin with his fist. "No," he whispered. "This is a time for joy, not tears. Let's tell my father. We'll wake him up."

She giggled and stroked his brow, aware she was laughing and crying at the same time. "Oh, let the poor man sleep. There is plenty of time."

Michael clasped her to him, planting kisses on her neck, her chest, her breasts. When at last he stopped, she whispered, "Now who is the *gato*?"

He slipped his arm around her neck and nestled her into the crook of his elbow. "Maybe there is something to your philosophy."

"Which one?"

That everything happens the way it is supposed to." He made tiny circles on her stomach.

She stretched to give him more of it to rub.

"There is only one thing," he said. "We cannot have the baby here."

"Not in Havana, you're right. We should probably go to—"

He cut her off. "Not in Cuba. You are coming with me to America. My father, too."

"America?" She extricated herself from his arms.

He nodded, still patting her belly.

She tensed. His stroking ceased. "Are you crazy? How will we get there? I do not have a *tarjeta blanca*, and they are impossible to get if you are not connected."

"You won't need one."

She removed his hand from her stomach. "What are you suggesting?"

"There are—other ways."

"What other ways? I am a doctor. They will never let me leave."

His confident expression faded.

"I know it is dangerous, but perhaps we could find a place to hide here. Cuba is not perfect…" her voice trailed off, "… but it is the only home I know."

"Carla, you have no life here; at least no life worth living anymore. If the CDR finds you…"

It was her turn to interrupt. "But—your mother… she will never accept me. And your grandfather. They do not want to be reminded of Cuba. I will be—"

"Carla. You are going to be the mother of my baby. Our baby." His expression was solemn. "I want our child to grow up in America. I was planning to take you with me anyway, before I knew about—this. But now…" he got out of bed. "…it is more important."

"Miguel, this does not feel right. It is not the time. Perhaps in a while…"

His voice sharpened. "Are you still putting stock in what that Santería priestess said?"

When she didn't reply, his voice spiked. "Don't you realize she was a total charlatan? A fake? All she wanted was our money. She was making it up. All of it. "

Carla kept quiet. Her mouth felt as dry as dust.

CHAPTER THIRTY-FIVE

Michael thought it through before he fell asleep. He didn't expect Luis or Carla to help him find a way back to the States. As an MP in the army he'd never started an assignment without knowing how he would finish it, and an exit scenario had been part of the plan. Walters was going to send a tiny plane out of Miami when Michael was ready; it would land near Pinar del Rio in the middle of the night to pick him up.

But now he had to scramble for another plan, and he couldn't burden his father or Carla. Whatever they might suggest would put them at more risk; they needed to keep a low profile. He'd come into Cuba through Mexico, but they couldn't leave that way; neither Carla nor his father had passports.

Which left either a private plane or boat. If he'd had more time, he could have arranged a plane without Walters. In the army he knew people who knew people in the Keys who were flying in and out, picking up and delivering "cargo." The addition of human "freight" wouldn't be a big deal. But he had no time to track them down or coordinate logistics.

So a boat was the best option, but he'd have to use his resources here to find one. He went back over everyone he'd met since he'd come to Cuba. There was Carla's doctor friend at the clinic—the one who'd been to Angola and told him where soldiers hung out in Havana. Mario, his name was. But Carla wouldn't be returning to the clinic, and her colleagues would be under orders to report any contact with her. She had become a traitor. A *guzano*, a worm. He doubted Mario could withstand the pressure.

There were the two old men in the warehouse, the ones who'd cheerfully taken his money, and then lied about knowing Luis. Going back to them was worse than stupid, even if they hadn't known Luis, which of course, they did. Then there was the Santería priestess. Michael wouldn't go back to her if his life depended on it. She was the kind who would take his money, make wild promises, then give him a bullshit story when it all fell through.

That left the former army officer in Chinatown, the one who'd first led him to the print shop. He had willingly taken Michael's money, too, and would undoubtedly demand more, but his information had panned out. What's more, his threadbare living conditions made it unlikely he was politically connected. He was probably one of the forgotten ones, Cubans who had done their duty, thought they would be taken care of afterwards, and had come back to a country that was broke and helpless. The guy was scrounging now, trying to "*resolver*." He was probably as close to a mercenary as Cuba had.

So, after breakfast Michael borrowed Luis's bike and rode it down to Chinatown. Luckily, the officer was there, in the same dingy yellow undershirt, with the same chest hair sticking out. His ornery mood hadn't changed either, until Michael flashed a wad of cash at him.

His face brightened. "What can I do for you, Americano?"

Michael explained what he needed. The man scratched his hairy chest, then wiggled his fingers for the money. Michael peeled off a few bills. He was down to his last few thousand. The man counted the money, then stuffed it into his pants pocket. He went into another room and came back with a scrap of paper and pencil. He scribbled something and handed the paper to Michael.

"I do not know if this man is still in Sierra Chaquita," he said. "Maybe yes. Maybe no."

If he heard that one more time, Michael thought he might slug someone. The Cubans' blasé attitude toward life would never work in the States. Then again, this was life in Cuba. Maybe yes, maybe no. Never good.

"What—or where—is Sierra Chaquita?"

The man laughed. "It is our name for Regla. You will see."

Michael heaved a sigh.

The officer seemed to understand Michael's frustration. "Take Marti to the first side street beyond the power plant. You will be behind a warehouse. Walk around to the front. You will see an office. Go inside. If the man is still there, tell him I sent you."

"I don't know your name."

He smiled. "Tell him Chinatown sends regards."

Like the movie, Michael thought.

"Yes. Chinatown." The officer nodded as if he'd read Michael's mind. "That's all you need to say."

***

The view from the ferry that chugged across the bay framed Regla as an industrial area with dingy warehouses, smokestacks of varying heights, and a shabby wharf. Regla was home to those who couldn't afford Havana prices. In return for the lower cost of living, its residents shared space with shipyards, a power plant, and an oil refinery, which belched a stomach-churning stench into the air. Once a center for Cuban rebels, over the years Regla's energy had dissipated, like a balloon that had lost its air.

Michael walked the bike off the ferry and started down Avenue Marti, Regla's main street. At a square past the Church Nuestra Señora de la Virgen, famous for its statue of a black Madonna, he dropped the bike. Not only was it slowing him down, but it was calling attention to him. He might as well have a target painted on his back. He didn't expect the bike to be there when he returned—he'd buy Luis a new one when they got to the States.

He asked a gnarled black woman in the square for directions to the power plant. She vaguely waved toward the right. He started down the street. At intersections, he caught glimpses of crumbling houses and streets, old American cars on blocks, and people, mostly black, not doing much of anything.

Ten minutes later he passed the power plant. Solid wood walls cordoned off the side streets adjoining the plant, and guards stood at attention. Michael tried to appear inconspicuous and kept walking. Remembering Chinatown's directions, he eventually got to a side street that wasn't walled off and turned down it. A little black girl pushing a doll in a baby carriage eyed him curiously as he passed.

At the end of the street to his left was a field where a group of boys were playing baseball. The thwack of the bat as it connected with the ball, the ensuing shouts and cheers sounded familiar and comforting, and for a moment, Michael imagined he was back in Chicago. Then he looked the other way. To his right was a rocky, uneven patch of tall weeds and grass, and beyond that, the wharf. He started across the grass. As he got closer, the briny smell of salt water and dead fish assailed him.

A moment later he was in front of the shipyard. It was a dreary-looking place, with rundown piers, docks, and warehouses. A few freighters were docked near the piers, but it was eerily silent. It was nothing like Chicago's Lake Calumet harbor, which his grandfather had taken him to when he was a kid. The opening of the St. Laurence Seaway a few years earlier had triggered an expansion of the entire harbor, and shipping in South Chicago was booming.

Here, though, the despair was almost palpable. Which made it a place to keep your wits about you. With one eye on the dark water, he shook off his backpack, retrieved his pistol, and stashed it in his waistband. The movie *Chinatown* had stayed with him, especially the scene where Roman Polanski slashed Jack Nicholson's nose. That had to do with water, too, he recalled.

He made his way to a small office in one of the warehouses. So far Chinatown's information had been spot on. The door to the office was open, and Michael could hear a fan inside blowing air. He knocked. No response. He knocked again. This time a voice, sounding disgruntled, almost hostile, replied.

"*Estamos cerrados.* We are closed."

Michael stuck his head in the door anyway. "Your door is open."

Behind a shabby-looking desk was a middle-aged man, bald, with a mustache. He didn't look up from what he was doing, but there were only a few papers on the desk, and no pencil, pen, or computer. Not even an adding machine. He'd probably been napping. Finally he looked up.

Michael didn't attempt to explain but read the name on the scrap of paper from Chinatown. "I'm looking for Esteban Diaz."

The guy raised his eyebrows.

"Chinatown sent me."

The man straightened. Michael didn't know if that was a good sign or not.

"I feel like some air," the man said after a pause. "Walk with me."

Diaz strolled to the edge of the pier. Michael followed. A gull lifted off, flapping its wings, as though surprised to have been disturbed in such a lonely, desolate spot.

"What is it you're looking for?" Diaz appraised him.

"I need to arrange a boat out of Cuba. To Miami. For three people. As soon as possible. Can you help?"

Diaz rubbed his chin, covered with about a week's worth of stubble. He tipped his head to the side, appraising Michael. Then, "Chinatown, eh?"

Michael nodded. He wondered how the two men knew each other. Angola? He didn't ask. It was irrelevant. He waited for Diaz to continue. It seemed like a long time. Then, "You may be in luck. I have a shipment coming in from the Keys."

Michael didn't ask what Diaz was bringing into Cuba. Certainly contraband. Weapons or drugs? Or more prosaic things, like gourmet food or stereos? Which they could store unobtrusively at the warehouse. The less he knew, the better. Regla was known to be a smuggler's paradise.

"When?"

"I expect them any time. Maybe tonight."

Michael's pulse sped up. It couldn't be that easy, could it? But apparently it was. Chinatown and Diaz's bond must run deep.

"How much?" Michael asked.

The guy held up two fingers. "Thousand. In dollars. One now. One later. Come back tonight. After midnight. With your passengers."

If he paid Diaz, he would be broke. Still, he would soon be back in the U.S. The hard part would be persuading Carla and Luis to pack up their entire lives in a few hours and flee. He promised himself he would replace their belongings with bigger and better things. Then again, Carla didn't care about material possessions. Nor did his father.

But that wasn't his chief concern. Why did Diaz want them to come back here? The wharf was practically next door to the heavily guarded power plant. And the lighthouse at El Morro, which wasn't far away, had a powerful searchlight that raked the bay every night. A vessel leaving Regla after dark might be spotted, stopped, boarded.

Almost any other wharf would be a better choice. Maybe he should case the Mariel Harbor west of Havana, although it was heavily guarded too, since the boatlift a decade ago. Or one of the beaches outside Havana. Maybe this was a set-up. Maybe he should walk away. He tried to keep his suspicion in check.

"Will we be leaving from here? Is it safe?"

Diaz nodded. "Security police patrol the entire coastline. Which, oddly enough, makes Regla one of the safer places."

"How is that?"

The man gave him a cagey smile. "The guards you should worry about are at the power plant. But they like their rum. Especially when my friend, who is one of them, brings it to them for free. By two in the morning, they will be falling down drunk."

"What about the searchlight from El Morro?"

"The boat captain will hug the shoreline until you are well out of the bay. The light will not reach you."

Michael wasn't convinced. "I don't know."

"I do not know when there will be another boat," Diaz said. "As you know, it is not easy. But, of course, it is your choice."

Michael weighed the risks. The timing. The location. The people involved. But he didn't really have a choice. They had to get out of Cuba. He handed Diaz the money.

***

Luis scratched his cheek in amusement. Miguel was so much like his mother, at least the Francesca he remembered: full of grandiose plans and determined to carry them out, no matter what the consequences. He recalled the time he found her at dawn curled up on the porch of the house in Havana where he'd lived. She'd simply run away so she could be with him. He realized then that she would do anything and everything to get what she wanted. Now her son—their son—was the same way.

He went into his bedroom and rummaged through his wardrobe. If, by some miracle, Miguel were able to put together an exit plan, what would Luis take? Aside from his books, which he knew he couldn't bring, there wasn't much. A few shirts, pants, shoes. He considered the Makarov he'd been issued in the army. It had been stashed in the back of the wardrobe since he'd come back from Angola. The pistol needed a thorough overhaul; he wasn't even sure it would fire. He even gazed at the rug over the loose floorboard where the map was hidden and wondered whether to take it. It didn't have any meaning for him; it had been Ramon's scheme, not his.

He was still debating when he heard a muffled noise from the front of the house. Someone was opening the door and trying to be quiet about it. He called out. "Carla? Miguel? Is that you?"

There was no answer. Luis started out of his bedroom, but before he had taken two steps, a blur of khaki flew at him. He had the impression of a beefy Caucasian man, stocky but surprisingly nimble. The man rammed into him, knocking him to the floor. The man promptly threw himself on top of Luis and started pummeling him. The first blow, to his gut, made Luis groan in pain. The attacker followed it up with another into his kidneys. Luis gasped and tried to curl into a defensive position to block the assault, but the man's weight prevented it. Luis cried out at a particularly sharp blow to his head, turned his head to the side, and squeezed his eyes shut. When he opened them a moment later, he saw that the man had a gun and was using it as a cudgel.

Luis tried to roll back and forth on the floor in an effort to gain momentum and extricate himself from underneath the man. If that didn't work, at least he might be able to wrestle the gun away. But the man outweighed him by at least fifteen pounds, and the most Luis could do was to free his left arm. Although he was right-handed, he threw up his left hand trying to grab the gun. A tug of war ensued, both of them rolling on the floor, each with a hand on the gun, looking for purchase. Then, with a huge effort, the attacker grunted, snatched the gun from Luis, and fired point blank into his head.

CHAPTER THIRTY-SIX

Michael was surprised to find Luis's bicycle in the same spot he'd left it. As he pedaled from the square back to the ferry, the weight that had been pressing down on him started to lift. The bike hadn't been stolen, and by tonight they would be safe, well out of Havana on a boat bound for Florida. If Carla were here, she would say it was a sign. That his meeting with Diaz had been the right move. That they were supposed to leave Cuba.

As he rode back to Lawton the sky lowered. Brooding clouds squeezed the air into a humid sludge as heavy and thick as a wet blanket. Sweat poured off Michael as he pedaled up the hill to Luis's home. When he arrived, he laid the bicycle down in front—there was no kickstand—and went to the front door.

Then he stopped.

Luis's door was open wide. He knew his father often kept the door partially open during the day to catch the breeze. But not this wide. Was a visitor there, a visitor Luis was trying to make more comfortable? Or was his father trying to signal something by leaving the door open? And if so, what?

Michael crept to the door and leaned his ear against it. It was quiet. No movement, rustles, thumps, or other sounds inside. Where was the idle chatter between Luis and Carla? The sounds of cleaning up, washing dishes, cooking? He spun around. The street was clear of people. No one strolling past. No children playing. No birds singing, either. Fear ballooned in his gut.

He backed up and circled the yard. Nothing seemed out of the ordinary. He came back to the front of the house. He took another look down the street. Still no one. He took out his gun, released the safety, and slipped inside.

When he saw what had happened, his stomach pitched.

Everything in the front room had been tossed. The tiny sofa lay on its back, its cushions ripped to shreds. One of the two chairs was upside down. His father's books had been hurled everywhere. The lamp was on the floor, its light bulb shattered. Shards from the bulb stuck out between books.

Michael called out for his father. Then Carla. No one answered. He racked the slide of his gun and started to case the house. The kitchen was empty, the breakfast dishes stacked in a drain-board by the sink. But the cabinet doors were open, and the few cans Luis had stored had been flung on the floor.

He stopped outside the tiny bedroom he and Carla shared. Aiming the gun, he pivoted fast into the room. No one was there. But someone had been. Their mattress had been slashed and the few clothes they'd brought were scattered on the floor. He checked the bathroom. Nothing, but the bathroom cabinet was empty. A half-used tube of toothpaste lay on the floor.

He aimed the pistol again and swung into his father's room. The doors to Luis's wardrobe were open, his clothes strewn on the floor. The bed was torn apart too, the mattress humped in one corner of the room. The chair beside the bed, the only upholstered chair in the house, was ripped. Michael sank down on the bed frame and covered his eyes. He thought for a moment maybe the police had paid them a visit, but he didn't think they would have trashed the house.

Someone was clearly looking for something. Walters. Still, he wanted to believe that Carla and his father had escaped. He dropped his hands and scanned the room more carefully. When his gaze rested on the mattress, he went cold. Red blotches stained the mattress. He got to his feet. He'd assumed his contact, in his rage, had hurled the mattress into the corner, but now he could see it was partially covering something. As if to conceal it. His jaw clenched, his hands shaking, Michael went over and raised the mattress.

His father's body was crumpled underneath. A gunshot had blown off most of his head. Streaks of red and brown spattered the walls. A second shot to the chest had produced a pool of blood on the floor that, in the tropical heat, was already congealing. Flies were beginning to settle on his father's face—which meant Luis had not been dead for long. Michael dropped the mattress and ran to the bathroom.

***

By the time Michael pulled himself together, the only remnant of his grief was a profound exhaustion and a trembling in his hands that wouldn't stop. He tried to compensate with precise movements designed not to waste any energy. He forced himself to compartmentalize. Detach.

Strategize.

When the police found Luis's body—which would happen sooner than later—his father's neighbors would pretend to know nothing. That was Cuba. Eventually, though, with enough pressure, they would crack. They would tell them about the visitors who'd been staying at the house: a young man and a woman. He and Carla would become the prime suspects and targets of an investigation. Unless Carla was dead, too. He squeezed his eyes shut. God couldn't be that cruel. Still, he had to put as much distance between himself and Lawton as he could. He shouldered his backpack and slid his gun in his waistband.

Steeling himself, he walked back into Luis's bedroom. He kept his head down so he wouldn't have to look at the body. He went to the side of the bed. The woven rug was still in its place. It was probably the only thing in the room that hadn't been touched. Michael squatted down and picked it up. He pressed the heel of his hand on the floorboard; it snapped up. He peered inside. The envelope containing the map was still there. He lifted it out and slipped it into his backpack. Then he snapped the floorboard back in place, and put the rug back.

He headed to the door. He was almost out of the house when he stopped, turned around, and went back to the front room. He didn't see what he was looking for, and he didn't have time to hunt for it. He was ready to give up when he caught a metallic glint peeking out from under a pile of books on the floor. He went over and pulled out the picture of Luis and his mother in Santa Clara, the one that Luis kept on the tiny table by his sofa. Michael turned over the frame, removed the photo, and put it in his backpack, too.

Outside, he kept close to the side of the house and edged around to the back. He should make his way back to Regla. But he still didn't know what had happened to Carla. Did his contact kidnap her? Take her hostage? Or was she lying somewhere bleeding her life away? He tried to remember what she said she'd be doing today. He thought she would be standing in yet another endless line for rations. But maybe he was making it up. Either way, how could he leave until he knew?

He couldn't. She was going to be the mother of his child. He would find cover and wait. He crept away from Luis's home. Lawton was one step up from a shanty town, and the houses were as crowded together as people on a Havana bus at rush hour. But the street was strangely silent. The neighbors were probably glued to their windows, hidden behind their shutters.

He looked for a place to hole up. He remembered where he, his father, and Carla had watched the fireworks. It was farther up the hill. A couple of palm trees blocked the view, but if you pushed aside the fronds, you could see the front of Luis's house.

Michael jogged up to a tiny plaza now broken into chunks of concrete with weeds growing through the cracks. In the center was a small stone monument, its markings covered with so much graffiti that Michael couldn't tell why or for whom it had been erected. He crossed the plaza and crouched down beside one of the palm trees. He was almost hidden from view, and a telephone pole in front of him provided more cover. No one could spot him unless they were looking.

He stared at his hands. They were still shaking. He refused to consider the possibility that he was making the biggest mistake of his life. All his training and common sense said to flee. Instead Michael settled in to wait. And grieve the death of what might have been.

***

Angry storm clouds painted the late afternoon sky with shades of gray and white and purple. Carla had not shown up. Michael was close to despair. It would be dark in an hour. He debated whether to check her apartment on his way to Regla. No, that wasn't a good idea. The local CDR was looking for her. Carla knew that. She wouldn't have gone home. He pushed aside the fronds of the palm tree. People were starting to come home for supper. They would find his father.

Walters was reputed to be an excellent cleaner, but he had left Luis's body, knowing Michael would find it. It was a message: "Look what I can do." Still, it pained Michael not to bury his father. He hoped his father's soul would forgive him.

At the same time, though, Walters hadn't taken the map. Why not? He should have discovered it: a loose floorboard was a flimsy hiding place. Had Walters been interrupted? Had Carla suddenly come home and surprised him? And if so, did Walters kill her too? Or take her hostage? Or did he flee, thinking it might have been the police?

No matter what the situation, Michael knew he couldn't stay in Lawton any longer. He gathered his backpack and stood up. The irony was he'd sworn to Carla he'd never do to their child what his mother did to him. Their child deserved to know his father. And that it had been conceived in love. But now, like Luis, he would never know his child. With a heavy heart he started to trudge down the hill.

Which was when he saw Carla hiking up. She was carrying a string bag with packages wrapped in brown paper. Relief flooded through him and for the first time that day he smiled. He hurried down to meet her, so grateful she was alive that he almost failed to check whether he was being tailed. Then he remembered and whipped around. He saw the woman pushing a baby stroller, and the black man with a bicycle tire around his neck.

But he didn't see Walters, who eased out of the shadows after Michael had turned back to Carla.

CHAPTER THIRTY-SEVEN

By nightfall the weather cleared and only a few clouds remained. They scudded across the dark sky, their undersides lit by the moon, throwing hazy shadows over everything. The breeze picked up, and it was chilly enough that Carla was glad she'd picked up a sweater.

On the ferry to Regla, Michael told her what happened to Luis. She cried out and covered her mouth with her hand. She had only known Luis for a few days, but she'd taken a liking to his gentle nature. She wasn't prepared for this.

"But why?"

He stared out over the water. Despite his grief, she knew he was trying to decide how much to tell her. A cold fear gripped her.

"No," she said. "I do not want to know." She hesitated. "We are in danger, aren't we?"

He tightened his lips. It was answer enough.

Another chill spread over her. What had she fallen into? This man, this strange but familiar man, had brought her passion and intimacy, but he had also put her life in jeopardy. Because of him she was about to abandon the only place she'd ever known. She had been taught America was the source of Cuba's problems. Now she was about to enter the maw of the enemy. The irony threatened to overwhelm her.

Once they got off the ferry, Carla made Michael stop at the church with the black Madonna, where she lit two candles: one for her own father and one for Luis. Outside a Santería priestess perched on a concrete wall beckoning them over, but Michael steered them in the opposite direction. They kept to the warren of back streets, so as not to attract attention. They didn't talk much; Michael's anguish radiated out; Carla nursed her own sorrow.

When they reached the field behind the wharf, a fishy smell wormed itself into her nostrils. They crossed the field and walked around to a ramshackle building across from the pier. An overhead light on one of the walls was broken, but illumination from the moon and clouds cast a dim pool of light. Michael rapped on the door. A moment later a man came out. Thick around the middle, bald, a mustache. He nodded at Michael, then glanced at Carla. In the dim light she saw his brows knit together.

"You said there would be three."

Carla heard a hitch in Michael's voice. "There—there has been a change of plans."

"Ahh…" the man nodded solemnly. "With me as well."

Michael jerked his head up. "What do you mean?"

"It is a minor change. In fact, it will be better for you. The boat is here. But it cannot enter the bay. I will take you to meet it. It is waiting as we speak."

"What happened? You couldn't deliver the rum?"

Diaz laughed. "That has been taken care of." His smile faded. "But Havana security guards are patrolling the bay tonight. I did not expect that. So I want to be cautious. This is the best solution. As I said, I will take you myself."

Michael shifted. Worry and fear warred on his face. Carla's pulse sped up. She was hungry, cold, and tired. And, despite Diaz's assurances, this was obviously a problem. The beginnings of a full-bore panic edged up her spine.

"How will you get us to the boat?" Michael asked.

Diaz motioned toward the pier. Floating on the water below was a contraption that included three inner tubes lashed together with rope, covered by a wooden plank. A *neumático*. "It is what the fishermen who have no boats use," Diaz explained. "I borrowed it from a friend. He built it himself." He tried to paste on a reassuring smile.

Carla grabbed Michael's arm. "No!" she cried sharply. "I will not go on that. It is not safe. We will drown."

"Señorita, keep your voice down," Diaz said. He cleared his throat. "I told you I will take you myself. I would not go if it was not safe. It is only a short trip. A few minutes. And the bay is calm. The boat will pick you up past Regla." He pointed out across the bay. "You see? Hardly any distance."

Carla gazed at Diaz, then at Michael. She knew there was no choice. Still, her stomach clenched. She started to mutter prayers.

Michael slipped his arm around her. "Carla, do not be afraid." His voice was soothing. "I can handle a raft, and if I need to, I will jump in the water and push us to the boat. I am a strong swimmer."

But Carla kept shaking her head as if by doing so, she might wipe out the entire situation. This wasn't how she expected her life to unfold. Perhaps sensing her unease, Michael stroked her hand, which was still clutching his arm.

Diaz headed over to the pier, pulled out a short wooden ladder, and hung it over the edge. He grabbed a couple of oars and lowered himself onto the raft.

"*Venimos, ahora,*" he called in a dramatic whisper.

Michael gently edged Carla forward, but she refused to budge. "Carla, there is no other way."

"I know."

"Please."

"I—I do not know how to swim," she said.

Michael stroked her neck. "You will not have to."

"How do you know?"

He studied her for a moment, then slid his backpack off his shoulders. "I almost forgot. I need you to do something for me."

She eyed him suspiciously. "What?"

"I am so sure you will be fine that I want you to keep some important—documents—for me."

"What documents?"

He fished in his backpack. "One is a photo of my mother and father in Santa Clara. I want my mother to have it. The other is the map."

She felt herself scowl. "The map? After everything that's happened, you're taking the map?"

"You do not want to know, remember? Don't worry. You can give it back to me when we are ashore. In America." He handed over the papers.

"You are trying to distract me."

"Maybe." He leaned over and kissed her cheek.

What was he not telling her? "Why must I take them? Where will you be?"

"Right beside you. But they may not search you when we get to the States. I know they'll search me."

"A search?" Her voice rose. "Miguel, what is this? Why do we have to go to America tonight? I do not—"

"Shhh!" Diaz cut her off and raised a finger to his lips. "It is time."

Reluctantly Carla took the papers and stuffed them in her bag. She took a step forward. Michael went to the ladder. She followed. Michael stepped back so she could go down the ladder first. He stood above her, Diaz below on the raft. She descended the ladder gingerly, took Diaz's hand, and stepped onto the plank. It listed to one side. Carla let out a shriek.

"Señora!" Diaz's whisper was tense. "Please! You must be quiet. This is perfectly natural. The tires—they do that. Do not be alarmed."

The panic she'd been trying to hold at bay rolled over her. Diaz helped her find a spot in the center. She wrapped her arms across her chest. Diaz looked up at Michael.

"Señor. Now you."

***

Michael dropped his backpack into the *neumático*, flashed Carla a smile, and started down the ladder. He was on the first rung when a voice yelled out of the darkness.

"Halt! Do not move!"

Carla gasped. Michael drew his gun and called out. *"Quien es usted?"*

The sound of a weapon being racked echoed across the pier. *"La guardia de Frontera!"* The Cuban Border Guard. "Drop your weapon! *Ahora! Immediatamente!"*

"Shit!" Michael spat out. Diaz was right. The police were patrolling the bay.

Why, he wondered. Who had informed on them?

Diaz lifted the rope that tied the *neumático* to the pier and whispered to Michael. "Hurry... get in! I will catch you."

"No. Take her. I will swim to you."

Carla started to scramble out of the raft. "No, Miguel! I will not go without you!"

But Diaz had already grabbed an oar and was using it to push away from the dock. "After we pass the freighters, there will be a boat. He has a light. He will flash it three times," he hissed. "We will wait."

"Miguel!" Carla reached out to Michael. "Señor, please. Go back!"

"Take care of her," Michael called.

Diaz's gaze slipped from Carla to Michael. "Do not worry."

Michael clung to the ladder with one hand until the raft was out of range. Then he raised his pistol.

"Put your weapon down," the same disembodied voice barked. "Or I will shoot."

He must have a night scope, Michael thought. He aimed into the dark and fired. A second later, a rifle blast exploded out of the dark. Michael dropped his gun and fell off the ladder. He never heard his body splash into the water.

***

Walters watched as Michael's corpse slowly turned onto its back like a jellyfish. The guard was already at the edge of the pier. Walters patted the revolver in his holster and emerged from the shadows. He stalked over and barked in perfect Spanish. "What is this? What happened?"

"Señor, two people were trying to escape on a raft. This one tried too, but he had a gun. I told him to put down his weapon. He wouldn't listen."

"The raft," Walters said. "Who was on it?"

"A man. And a woman," the guard said.

Walter pointed to Michael's body. "I know this man. He is a conspirator against the State. You did the right thing. But we must go after the woman."

The guard cocked his head, as if he'd just realized the contact was not a security officer. "And who are you, Señor?"

Walters pretended he didn't hear. "But first we need to search his body."

The guard gazed at him, clearly puzzled.

"Help me get him back up on the dock." When the guard didn't move, Walters peeled off a wad of cash and held it out.

The guard hesitated, then slipped it into his pocket.

Walters took off his jacket and the holster and climbed down the ladder into the water. He grabbed Michael by his shirt and pulled him over to the ladder. Together they managed to lift him back onto the pier. Walters promptly searched Michael's body. No map. He picked up his jacket and holster, making sure the revolver was in easy reach, and stood up.

"Who are you?" the guard repeated.

Walters pulled out his gun. "You never saw me. *¿Comprende?*"

The guard raised his rifle, aiming it at Walters. "Put your weapon down, Señor, and identify yourself."

Walters fired, but his shot went wild. The guard returned fire, point blank. Walters' last thought was one of surprise. He never thought it would end like this.

***

Perhaps sobs could be heard, but whether it was the cries of a woman or simply a night animal was unclear. The waves lapping against the pier made the other sounds extraneous, and whatever the noise was, it faded away. Silence reclaimed the bay.

A man in a uniform jogged toward the pier. "I heard shots. What happened?"

The young guard explained. He couldn't stop shaking. This was the first time he'd fired his rifle. And he'd fired twice. The CDR official who'd got him the job a year earlier said it would be easy. You walked around and wore a uniform. But he'd be first in line at the rations store. He'd have other perks, too. That's what he'd signed up for. Not this.

"What do I do now, Capitan? It was self-defense. I know there needs to be an investigation. Reports. Inquests." He hesitated. "I am—I am—"

The captain raised his palm to stop the guard's babbling. He gazed at the two bodies, then back at the guard. The guard was a young man, well under thirty. A baby. And this was the first shoot-out they'd encountered in

Regla. Usually escapees were meek, not gutsy. They surrendered quickly. This would put a blemish on the guard's career. His, too. Especially since the raft got away.

He squinted out over the dark waves, as if trying to see where the raft had gone. Then he turned back to the guard.

"This didn't happen. Understand? This was just another routine patrol."

The young guard motioned to the two corpses. "But—but, what do I do with them?" He looked panicked.

The captain didn't answer for a moment. Then he said, "Throw them into the bay. And make sure they never come to the surface."

CHAPTER THIRTY-EIGHT

Chicago — May
Four months later

Frankie would always remember the day she realized Michael was dead. It was the beginning of March, and the jonquils were already forcing their way through the snow. There had been no word from him in two months, which was a month longer than they'd ever been out of touch, even when he was in the Middle East. She begged her father to make inquiries, but when he came to the house one night, his face ashen, and told her he couldn't locate Michael or the contact who'd arranged the mission in the first place, she knew.

At first she raged against her father. "You taught me never to trust the government. How could you?" she yelled.

"My contact wasn't with the government," her father said.

"But his contact was, and you always said 'the apple don't fall far from the tree.'"

For one of the only times in his life, Tony Pacelli's silver tongue was silent. There was nothing he could say. Frankie shouted, cried, threw things, then sank into a despair so wide and deep she wanted to drown in it. Her father wasn't much better. The loss of his grandson, the successor he'd always hoped and expected Michael would become, crushed him. He took the blame, apologized profusely, and told Frankie he had nothing more to live for.

He didn't. A month later Tony Pacelli died of a massive coronary. Although Frankie was grateful he hadn't suffered, she was furious. Why was God punishing her? She'd loved only three men in her life, and two of them were dead. As for the third, Luis—well, who knew what had happened to him? Pain gnawed at her like a rat feeding on a carcass, so fierce and raw it threatened to eat her alive. At times she wanted it to.

But Frankie had to put aside her grief temporarily. With her father gone, she was the *de facto* head of the Family, and if she wanted to keep her position, she would have to fight for it. She wanted it. Why had she suffered so much, if not to assume the mantle of power? Perhaps God was rewarding her by making her the captain of her own ship. It was time. She'd learned from her father, and she knew she could steer it well. But there had never been a female head of any *Cosa Nostra* Family, and there would be threats to her succession.

After the funeral she closeted herself in her office with Roberto Donati, her father's *consigliere*.

"Roberto, I want you to analyze all the high-ranking *soldati* in the Family. Who am I going to have problems with?"

Donati leaned back in his chair and templed his fingers. A tiny smile unfolded across his face. "Your father asked me the same question a few weeks ago."

Frankie arched her eyebrows. "He did?"

Donati's smile broadened. "I will tell you what I told him. I see two threats."

"Only two?" She tried to smile, but the corners of her lips wouldn't move.

"One will be from Benito Albertini. You may be too young to remember, but his father tried to unseat yours years ago. He failed." Donati flicked his hand. "Albertini thinks with other parts of his body, rather than his head."

Frankie nodded. She didn't know Albertini well, but he was a weaselly runt of a man, and she didn't like him.

"And the other?"

"Gino Capece. Your *sotto capo*. He is a capable and ruthless man. But he is shrewd. An altogether different situation than Albertini."

"What do you advise?"

Donati was quiet for a moment. Then, "Offer them their own squads, reporting only to you. Better to turn an enemy into an ally than the other way around."

This time Frankie did smile. He sounded so much like her father. "Set up meetings with both."

Albertini came in an hour later and declined her offer. "The Family rightfully belongs to me." He flashed her a contemptuous smile. "A woman cannot do the job. Even your father agreed with me. As do most of my *capos*."

Frankie knew he was lying but said she'd consider his advice carefully. When he left the room, she nodded at Roberto. Albertini wouldn't make it home that night.

Gino was another matter. "Your father and his were friends. They respected each other," Roberto said. "He will bide his time, but you will have to earn his respect. If not, he will stage a coup."

"When?"

Donati shrugged. "That I do not know."

Frankie told him to bring Gino in. He was a tall muscular man who'd seen so much action over the years that his natural expression was one of suspicion.

"Please sit, Gino," she said. She explained that she wanted to offer him his own unit. "In fact, I want you to consider yourself my second in command."

Gino cocked his head and narrowed his eyes—he was known as a man of few words—then nodded. Frankie could tell he knew what she was doing and that while he didn't mind being bought, he would be watching her every move.

By the next day, for the first time in history, a woman was named the head of a major crime Family. Despite her grief Frankie couldn't suppress her elation. This was the way it was supposed to be. She would take the Family's businesses to new heights.

After everyone had left the Barrington house, she wondered if *this* was why the men she loved had been taken from her. Why she had suffered so much. Since she couldn't have love, she would take power instead. And God forbid any man—or woman—tried to take it away from her. They would pay a price. She was finally free to make her own decisions. Do as she saw fit. Without interference.

There was only one issue in her way. Carmine DeLuca had been a distant husband and a worse father. Her father, calling in a few favors, had arranged the marriage to shield her from the stigma of bearing an illegitimate child. She couldn't go back to Nick; she'd broken his heart once, and she knew he wouldn't let her do it again. She had no choice. So she married Carmine and tried to be a dutiful wife, if only for Michael's benefit. But now Michael was dead, and so was her father. There was no reason to keep Carmine around. He might even prove to be trouble. So around midnight she picked up the phone and made a call to a man known only to her father, and now, Frankie.

"Hello, my friend. I have a job for you."

***

Miami — September

The sun broke through a swollen overcast, and weak light spilled across

Carla's one-room apartment. Efficiencies, they called them. Studio apartments. Why didn't they call them what they were, she thought. A box inside a box for people with no money. Still, she spent as little time outside as possible. Even in September the oppressive Miami humidity left her gasping for air. Florida was only ninety miles from Cuba, but it was another world. No trade winds, no Malecón, no bay. Instead there was the intercoastal, which was usually clogged with nausea-inducing exhaust from power boats. Although mired in poverty, Havana was more delicate and graceful. Everything in America was big, brash, and dirty.

Including her. Carla felt like a cow: all nipples, stomach, and cud. She never realized that being pregnant would be so uncomfortable. Like lugging around a twenty-pound sack of rice. She felt a pang of guilt for all the pregnant women she'd treated so cavalierly back in Cuba.

She squeezed her eyes shut. She couldn't think about home now. She had to get to work. She slowly lumbered down the stairs and out of the small building on NW Avenue Twelve. Sweat promptly beaded on her neck. She picked her way across a wide street that was more highway than road, dodging the cars that barreled past. She hoped they were on their way out of Little Havana forever. She waited for a bus that took her to her job at a Spanish-speaking drugstore. The irony was, she was earning minimum wage in the U.S., but she still took home more in a day than she had in a month in Havana.

Forty-five minutes later, she stepped off the bus and walked the two blocks to the pharmacy. The owner, a Cuban doctor originally from Pinar del Rio, was somewhere in his sixties, with thick salt and pepper hair. She'd met him at the Catholic Church six months earlier. He'd asked her a few questions, which she'd obviously answered to his liking, because he offered her a job. She would not be a doctor, he said. He could not practice medicine in America without returning to medical school, and neither could she. But she could work in his pharmacy. She was grateful. She had no papers, money, or ID.

Now, he looked up from the vial of pills he was filling in the back of the store. "*Buenas tardes*, Carla. A man came here looking for you."

Carla, who'd already started towards the cash register in front, jerked her head around. Her father had passed after she arrived. She hardly ventured out of the barrio except for an English class at the community college. She'd learned that, like Havana, it wasn't wise to speak out in the U.S., but for the opposite reasons. No one in America wanted to hear how Cuba was more beautiful, egalitarian, and less materialistic than the States. Especially from someone who'd grown up under Fidel. She'd learned to be circumspect and to keep a low profile. In fact, she only knew two or three people in Miami, and, with the exception of her boss, none of them were men.

"Who was it?" she asked nervously.

"He was—perhaps—a bit younger than I. But fat. Not much hair. Olive skin. Red-faced." The pharmacist shrugged. "The heat, you know."

"What did he want?"

"He claimed he knew your husband." Her boss motioned to her belly.

A sudden fear skittered around in her. She'd told no one about Michael. No one. In fact, she'd given people the impression that her pregnancy was "one of those things." She hadn't been careful. She didn't think it was that time of month. She certainly never claimed to be married. She ran a hand through her ponytail. She'd let her hair grow long, but she mostly kept it pulled back in a band.

"What did you tell him?"

"That you had the afternoon shift and to come back."

Her expression must have betrayed her apprehension because her boss extended his palms. "I am sorry. Did I make a mistake?"

She unlocked the register, thinking it through. She'd figured out by now that the documents Miguel had given her were related to his mission. She'd also figured out the mission had fallen apart and that both Luis and Miguel were killed because of it. But she still had no idea what the mission was, or why the map was important. Now, though, it didn't matter. If someone had tracked her here, it wasn't good.

As if to emphasize the point, the baby kicked.

The baby. Her landlord's wife claimed to know a midwife. Carla herself knew enough to deliver a baby, and had bought all the supplies through the pharmacy. It would be born soon. Any day, thank god. But now a new danger was flashing as brightly as one of those huge American neon signs. Her survival, and that of her baby, might be at stake.

When would it end? The past nine months had been a nightmare: from the night Miguel had been shot and she'd begged Diaz to go back and he'd refused; to the crossing when a sudden squall had nearly capsized the boat; to the horror of being left on the shoals of American soil with no papers or money; to eking out a living while trying to stay healthy for the baby. She might have survived worse in Cuba, but that was her home. In the land of plenty, her life was harsh and difficult. Almost desperate.

She almost shed a tear but forced it back—it was merely the result of hormones. Still, part of her wanted to surrender. She was exhausted with the daily struggle to survive. She was, as they said in English, at the end of her rope. She needed help. Especially once the baby came. But now, she had to flee. Find a new safe haven. She didn't know if she could. How much could one person stand?

She closed the register and told the pharmacy owner she needed to take a break.

"But you just came in."

"I'll be back in an hour," she lied.

She took the bus back to her apartment. There wasn't much to pack. It had come furnished, and she'd been frugal with her paychecks. She picked up a duffel bag and started back down the stairs. At the bottom of the steps a pain as sharp as a knife tore through her abdomen. She had run out of time.

***

Over the next twelve hours she swam through an ocean of pain. She had dim recollections of biting down on towels. The midwife making her walk around. The smell of blood—her own—worming its way up her nose. There was temporary relief, but only for a few seconds. Then the agonizing pain came back. She lay back down and slipped into a dream-like trance where everyone shouted for her to push. She did, but she couldn't remember why. All she wanted was the pain to go away.

And then, finally, it did.

"You have a daughter, Carla," a voice said through the dream. "A beautiful baby girl. With such rosy, chubby cheeks!"

PART 3
THE PRESENT
CHICAGO

CHAPTER THIRTY-NINE

"Such rosy, chubby cheeks!" Francesca DeLuca sat on the edge of the bed and pinched her granddaughter's face.

Although she was twenty-two, Luisa Michaela DeLuca scrunched up her nose like a little girl and raised her hand as if to ward off the devil. "Gran, you promised to stop that when I graduated."

Francesca laughed. "So I did. I apologize, *preciosa*. I'm sorry."

"No you're not."

"You're right." Her grandmother smiled in that hapless way people did when they admitted to guile. It didn't matter whether they were Italian, French, Jewish, or Latino, Luisa thought. Every culture shared the same *"je ne sais quoi."*

She stretched and threw the covers off the bed. She'd been staying with her grandmother in Barrington while her mother attended a medical conference in Cleveland. Technically Luisa was an adult, but her mother still insisted she stay with her grandmother when she was out of town. Overprotective was not the word for Carla Garcia. Strangulation was more like it.

Still, Luisa didn't mind. Gran treated her like a princess. For five years when she was little and her mother was in medical school, they'd lived here, and her grandmother had turned one of the guest rooms into a pink and white castle for Luisa. It was a wonder Luisa wasn't spoiled rotten, her mother would sniff.

"So, what are your plans today, Luisa Michaela?"

Gran was the only one who called her by both her names. Luisa smiled. Her grandmother was somewhere in her seventies—she'd never confess her exact age—but she barely looked fifty. Trim and athletic, thanks to the personal trainer who came every morning, Gran was impeccably dressed, thanks to the personal assistant who came every afternoon. Her hair was also perfectly coiffed—with nary a strand of gray—thanks to the hairdresser who came three times a week. In that respect, Gran was the opposite of her mother, who couldn't be bothered with make-up or expensive clothes and belittled the thought of someone coming to the house to help move her body through space.

Now Luisa threw her arm over her head. "I'm meeting with friends to go over a flyer for the demonstration next month."

"You're still—involved—in those activities?" Gran pursed her lips.

Luisa propped herself up in bed. "Of course I am. You should be too. We're all on the same side."

"What side is that?"

"The side that wants to stop poisoning the planet and purge the toxins we've spread in, around, and on top of it. We've got to stop reckless corporations from destroying what's left of our air and water and land. They know they're doing it, too. And then they try to whitewash it with the golden fleece of jobs and American self-sufficiency," Luisa said. "Everybody knows all they're after are profits."

"Ahh, the idealism of youth," Gran said.

"You were young once."

"Thankfully, I grew out of it."

Luisa expected Gran to smile when she said it, but she didn't. Luisa let it go. "And then I have a meeting with my advisor to go over my summer plans." She was studying for a Master's Degree at Northwestern's School of Civil and Environmental Engineering.

"I told you I could help."

Luisa pretended she hadn't heard. "And Mom's coming home later, so I'll go home afterwards."

Gran cleared her throat. "That means you have nothing planned for this morning, correct?"

Luisa cocked her head. "Why?"

"Oh, nothing." Gran's tone was offhand, and she hunched her shoulders in another shrug.

Luisa tried to gauge her grandmother's mood. Bland. Casual. But there was a catch in her eyes. Gran always had an agenda. "Gran…"

"All right," Gran said. "You know I can't lie. At least to you." She paused. "Do you remember our discussion last night?"

Luisa's pulse sped up. "About my father?"

Gran nodded. "I have work to do this morning, but then I want to show you something." She hesitated. "The only problem is… it's a secret. Between you and me. Okay?"

Luisa thought about it. Her mother and grandmother didn't get along well. Her mother said it was because grandparents and grandchildren were natural allies against the parent. But Carla, Luisa's mother, was blunt, honest, and prickly; she would admit to it occasionally. And her grandmother, despite her claims otherwise, was just this side of cunning. Luisa tried to keep her balance between the two, but it wasn't easy. The one thing both women had in common was their stinginess with information about her father. But now, apparently, Gran was ready to open up. Luisa's curiosity won out. Like Gran knew it would, Luisa thought.

"So what's the secret? Does it have to do with my father?"

Gran nodded. "Something that belonged to him."

Her father, Michael, had died before she was born, but she'd been told the stories. How Gran met her grandfather Luis in Havana, but had been snatched away from him by *her* father. How she'd been forced to marry Carmine because she was pregnant. How, thirty years later, their child, her father, was sent to Cuba. How he met her mother. How he'd been shot when they tried to escape.

"What is it?"

Gran's expression turned conspiratorial. "It's in my safe deposit box. Down at the bank."

Luisa wondered what it could be. Jewelry? Stock certificates? A souvenir from his time in Iraq?

Her grandmother leaned over, stretched out her hand, and smoothed out the lines on Luisa's forehead. "You go ahead and get dressed, Princess. There's coffee in the kitchen. Armando will drive, but we'll take three cars to the bank. Then you can go to your appointments."

Luisa showered in her bathroom, which, like the bedroom, was pink and white. Over the years she'd come to agree with her mother. It was too much: the opulence, the luxury, the pink—it was suffocating. After toweling off, she threw on jeans, a thick sweater and work boots. It was early April in Chicago, but the temperature was only a few degrees warmer than winter. Spring in Chicago was brutal. And then it was summer.

She attempted to wrestle her hair into place. A rich brown, it was thick, long and curly, and rarely did what she wanted. Her bad hair genes came from both sides of the family: her mother's hair was wavy in all the wrong places, and her grandmother's tended to kink into tight curls. Although people told her she was attractive, Luisa considered herself average. Petite. Sturdy. Widely spaced hazel eyes. A patrician nose. OK features, except for the chubby cheeks her grandmother never let her forget.

***

An hour later, accompanied by their bodyguards, Gran and Luisa were greeted by Gran's bank manager in Barrington, who insisted on personally ushering them down to the safe deposit vault. Gran went through the rituals of signing the cards and producing a key, which the manager matched with another. He opened a small metal door cut into a wall of similar doors, lifted out a box, and took it to an area curtained off from the rest of the room. Gran nodded at the bodyguards and the bank manager, and told them all to wait outside.

Once they were out of sight, Gran slid the box open. Inside were three small white boxes, several business envelopes, and several large manila envelopes. Gran lifted one of the manila envelopes out of the box, opened the clasp, and withdrew a sheet of paper. She handed it to Luisa.

The paper was eight by eleven inches. Thick. Off-white originally, it was yellowed now. On it was a sketch of three squiggly vertical lines about an inch apart. In the middle was a straight line that angled right. A jagged horizontal line bisected all the lines near the top of the page. Near two of the squiggly lines were three dots. One was below the horizontal line. A second was below and to the left of the first. The third dot was about three inches farther down the page. At the bottom of the page the letter "C" was written twice. The "C's" were followed by the letter "L" which was circled. On the lower left was another sketch: a circle of dots with something in the center.

Luisa couldn't make any sense of it. "What is this?"

Gran didn't answer for a moment. Then she looked up, her eyes bright. If Luisa didn't know Gran was one of the toughest women alive, she could have sworn those eyes were wet. Then Gran blinked, and her expression reverted to normal.

"Your grandfather could have been an artist," she said softly. "But he had—other interests."

"Granpa Luis drew this?"

"He gave it to your father when they were in Cuba." Frankie didn't add that Luisa's mother was sure it was the reason her father died. Frankie kept that to herself.

"It's a map," Gran continued.

Luisa held it up. The squiggly lines, the dots, the letters were unreadable. "Of what? Where?"

"We don't know."

Luisa gazed at Gran. "Really? Ma doesn't know?"

Gran shook her head.

"You don't, either?"

Gran arched her eyebrows. "By the way, if your mother finds out I showed this to you, she'll be furious."

Although Gran had a propensity for the dramatic, Luisa's stomach knotted. Her entire life she'd been aware of secrets held, stories untold. Gran and her mother told her only what they wanted her to know. Memories that had been approved and sanitized. Why couldn't they be like other families, sharing their histories, warts and all?

"So why did you? Show this to me, that is?"

Gran shot her a sidelong glance. There was something she wasn't telling Luisa. "Because I think you have an adventurous spirit. Like me."

Luisa was about to say she knew Gran wasn't telling her everything when Gran smiled.

"You're always asking about your father. This sketch was important to him. Your grandfather, too. Over the years I have kept wondering why. I'd like to know, wouldn't you?"

Her smile was too broad, Luisa thought. "You want me to find out what this is all about and report back, don't you? That's why you showed it to me."

"Aren't you curious? It could be a quest." Gran paused. "Of course, if you don't want to…" She let her voice trail off.

Luisa knew her grandmother. "Of course, I'm curious, but why now?"

"I was thinking with your engineering background, you probably have access to better resources than me."

"Are you sure you want me to look into this? What if we find out something we don't want to know?"

"*Querida*, whatever this represents is over twenty years old. Who would care after all this time?" She paused. "Still, you probably shouldn't say anything to your mother." She paused again. "So, what do you say?"

Luisa studied the map again. Then she looked up at Gran. "Why don't you ask the bank to make a couple of copies?"

"Good idea." Her grandmother beamed. "I knew you were the right person for this."

CHAPTER FORTY

"So everything was okay while I was gone?" Carla asked her daughter that night as they were finishing dinner. Carla had returned from a medical conference on developmental disorders in children and spent the afternoon preparing *arroz con pollo*. Unlike Cuba, in Chicago the ingredients for any recipe she dreamed up were permanently stocked at an enormous grocery store only five minutes away.

Carla still couldn't get over how large and shiny and prosperous everything in the U.S. seemed. She knew it was mostly a mirage, that poor people were crammed into substandard housing; that gangs roamed the streets of the South and West Side; and that the American murder rate was one of the highest in the civilized world. But living, as they did, in an affluent part of Evanston, it was easy to ignore the flaws. In fact, with both she and Luisa coming and going all the time, a peaceful evening at home, without security guards invading their space, was a rarity.

"Everything's fine, Mama." Luisa smiled through a bite of the chicken.

"And your grandmother?" After twenty years, Carla could almost say the word without any particular emphasis.

"Oh, you know Gran."

Carla nodded. She had a love-hate relationship with Francesca DeLuca. She never doubted her mother-in-law loved her granddaughter more than life itself. But the woman's values were so different from hers. It wasn't the conflict between socialism versus capitalism. Over time Carla had grudgingly come to believe that a capitalistic system was healthier and—shockingly—more reasonable than what Fidel had in place. She couldn't complain about her treatment, either. The day she arrived in Chicago with Luisa in her arms, scared, destitute, and desperate, she'd showed Francesca the photo of her and Luis taken forty years earlier in Santa Clara. Francesca broke down and from that moment on treated Carla and Luisa like royalty.

She helped Carla become proficient in English, sent her to medical school, but made sure she still had time for the baby. She found Carla a job at a hospital as a pediatric resident, and when it was time for Carla to start a private practice, was there to help her launch it. There wasn't a dollar she didn't spend, a connection she didn't use, a string she didn't pull.

Which was the problem. Francesca wasn't happy unless she controlled the lives of everyone around her. And Carla did not like being controlled.

"Gran wants to help me find an internship this summer," Luisa said.

Carla picked up the dishes and took them into the kitchen. She had to be careful in her responses to her daughter about Francesca. She didn't want Luisa to feel torn between them, although she suspected her attitude seeped through anyway.

"I told her that my advisor already set me up with some interviews."

Carla called out from the kitchen. "Really? How nice of him." She returned with a little cake, a *gateau* the store called them, and set it on the table.

"He likes me," Luisa said.

Carla couldn't suppress a smile. Luisa was so like her father that way. What some might call boasting was simply a matter of fact for them. For about the millionth time, Carla wished Michael was alive to see what they had created. She retrieved a knife and sliced the cake.

***

Carla was relaxing in the recliner later that night, poring over a conference abstract on radical hemispherectomies in children, when Luisa came out of her room. She'd been inside with the door closed for over an hour, which was unusual for her. Carla looked up and smiled. Evenings like this when she was doing one thing, her daughter another, but they still managed to connect, were small miracles. Carla knew Luisa would move out soon, and she was trying to mentally prepare herself for that day, but for now she cherished their shared moments.

"What are you doing?" she asked as Luisa plopped down on the sofa.

"Putting the finishing touches on a flyer. And surfing the net."

"A flyer?" Carla frowned. She still had trouble with idiomatic English.

"You know. For the protest next month."

Carla smiled faintly. Although her daughter had not grown up under a Marxist government as she had, Luisa shared her belief that society should not focus on the accumulation of wealth at the expense of public welfare. She hoped Luisa's desire to become an engineer would contribute to that welfare one day. It was an ambition that Carla supported. She wasn't sure Michael would have. He had been independent, a lone ranger, more interested in personal than societal goals. But in his heart? Who knew?

His father, Luis, had been different. In fact, Carla found it curious the way values often skipped a generation. Or two. She never said much about Luisa's activism, but secretly she was proud of her. Although she suspected that part of her daughter's commitment was due to her boyfriend, a long-haired computer student named Jed.

Now Luisa cleared her throat and sat up straight. A serious expression came over her.

"What is it, *Luisita*?" Carla asked.

She seemed to choose her words carefully. "Mama, tell me about Granpa Luis."

Carla closed the abstract she'd been reading.

"Your grandfather was a wonderful man. Intelligent. Curious. Firm. But gentle. He was a man everyone looked up to. The kind of man everyone should have as a father. Or grandfather," she added.

"But he was killed, right? Shot in his bedroom."

Carla hesitated. "That's right." Neither she nor Francesca had hidden that part from Luisa. Her daughter knew about the Pacelli Family. She knew about their history in Cuba. She knew how Francesca's father, Tony, had torn Francesca away from Luis during the Revolution. And how Michael, after being raised by Carmine DeLuca, discovered who his father really was. How their reunion had been cut short by tragedy.

Now that Carla knew the whole story, in fact, she often thought the family was cursed, like the Kennedys. The evils of the fathers—or in both cases, the grandfathers—had been foisted upon the children. But Carla was determined that the curse ended with Michael. Luisa would not be exposed. And from her behavior, she assumed Francesca felt the same way. Still, an unsettled feeling bordering on fear made her straighten and cross her legs.

"Why do you ask?" Carla hoped her voice sounded casual.

Luisa tucked her feet under her. "Why was he killed?"

Carla remembered asking Michael the same question on the way to Regla twenty years ago. A few minutes later, he'd handed her the photo and the map. And then *he'd* been shot by the border guards.

"I don't know, Luisa," she lied.

Luisa looked as if she couldn't accept such an inadequate response.

"What was his life like? Before you met him?"

Carla remembered the mornings at Luis's home when Michael was out, mornings she and Luis had talked while drinking contraband coffee, the only luxury Luis allowed himself.

"Well, I know he was in the army for a while."

"The Cuban Army."

"Of course. He knew Fidel from Oriente—I mean Santiago de Cuba. They fought together. Well, maybe not together, but like Fidel, Luis fought against the Batista government."

"I know all that," Luisa said impatiently.

"What?"

"That Papa Tony couldn't bear the thought of his daughter being with a revolutionary. It's why he broke them up."

Carla nodded.

"And that Gran was already pregnant with my father."

Carla inclined her head. "Why so curious all of a sudden?"

"We have a—a colorful family. Full of drama. I want to know the characters better."

Carla shifted, reflecting on her daughter's question. "Well, as I said, I always felt Luis was more of an intellectual than a soldier. I was surprised when he said he spent time in Angola. It didn't seem—"

"Angola? Granpa Luis was in Angola?"

Carla nodded.

"You never told me that."

"I suppose it was not important. Half a million Cubans went to Angola. Soldiers, doctors, social workers… Fidel would never admit it, but Angola was Cuba's Vietnam."

"Where was Granpa stationed in Angola?"

Carla furrowed her brow. "I am not sure. It was so long ago. Let's see. He was a *General de Brigada*, I know that. And he was there for two years. Then a peace accord was signed, and he came home. Although he said the rebels were still fighting each other in the jungle."

"But you don't know where?"

"No. Why?"

"No reason." Luisa went into the kitchen. A drawer squeaked open, and Carla heard utensils clanging.

"What are you doing?"

"I'm getting another piece of cake. Do you want some?"

After four days of starchy hotel food and sugary drinks, Carla felt like a cow that had been led to the trough. "Thank you, no."

***

Luisa slid a generous piece of cake onto a plate and carried it back to her room. She set it down by her computer and pulled out a copy of the map her grandmother gave her. She jiggled the mouse to wake up her computer, closed Word and the flyer she'd been editing, and opened up Google Earth. When prompted to enter where she wanted to "fly," she typed in "Angola". She watched as the globe on the screen slowly rotated across the Atlantic Ocean, dipped south, and closed in on a mass of land in Southeastern Africa.

She tapped the mouse for a closer view, but the colors on the map—

green, muddy brown, and gray—made it difficult to determine the topography. Plus Angola was huge. She zoomed in close enough to see riverbeds, forests, and mountains, but nothing resembled the map her grandfather had sketched. In fact, she had no idea what the scale of his map was supposed to be. She pored over every inch of Angola, looking for the three skeletal fingers that snaked down from the top of her grandfather's map. She assumed they were creeks or rivers or streams but nothing revealed itself. And the letters, two "C's" and an "L," written on the bottom of the page, were equally baffling.

She sat up, stretched her arms, then dug into the cake. She'd examined maps of Cuba that afternoon at the library, but hadn't found anything that approximated the sketch. She supposed she could hunt for more detailed maps of Angola tomorrow, but she wasn't hopeful. Whatever her grandfather had drawn might be lost to history.

CHAPTER FORTY-ONE

The next morning dawned April balmy, warm enough for Luisa to ride her bike to campus. That was spring in Chicago: prepare for the worst, then praise the weather gods when given a reprieve. A female security guard followed Luisa in a car. By now the guards were as familiar to her as her shadow—someone had been with her since she was a baby—and she'd learned to ignore them. She locked the bike in the iron bike rack and strolled across a wide plaza.

McCormick Technological Institute was one of the more modern buildings on Northwestern's campus, at least architecturally. In fact, the building's only link to the past was some stone carvings above the door. Luisa wasn't quite sure what they were and was too embarrassed to ask, but one looked like an ancient Greek using a primitive lever to move a boulder. Another could have been chemist John Dalton or Sir Isaac Newton sitting beside an unknown machine.

She went inside and walked down halls marked by linoleum floors and fluorescent lighting. When she turned right, the interior changed dramatically, and she crossed a sunlit glassed-in bridge that took her to the Mudd library. Like the bridge, the library was relentlessly bright and modern. It wasn't crowded, and she was able to get on a computer right away.

She entered "Angola" and "maps" and clicked on search. A moment later she was crestfallen. Most of the maps and information about Angola were in the main library, not Mudd. She searched again, adding the terms "engineering" and "technical" but nothing materialized. She took the steps up to the stacks on the third floor where a small collection of maps was housed. She found nothing.

She came back outside. She'd have to go to the main library. She was unlocking her bike, her back to the sidewalk, when a male voice called out.

"Hey Lulu!"

She turned around. A gangly young man in threadbare jeans and a bulky jacket was heading toward her. His brown hair was thick, curly, and flyaway, giving him an Albert Einstein look, which was magnified by rimless glasses. Behind the glasses was a pair of bright blue eyes.

"Hey you." She slipped her arms around his neck and gave him a long, slow kiss. His body relaxed into hers, and when they broke apart, those big blue eyes were squeezed shut, and she saw his languid smile. Jedidiah Collins, from Montana, was as different from Luisa as a horse from a rattlesnake, he joked. He grew up riding the range and helping his father herd cattle. He was a direct, easy-going cowboy, and she'd never seen him in a bad mood. It was as if coming from Big Sky country had imbued him with a permanently sunny disposition. With her intensity, complicated family history, and activism, Luisa was the exact opposite, an exotic hothouse flower. Which made them a perfect match.

She finished unlocking her bike. They were a match in other ways, too. They were almost exactly the same height, which meant their pace matched when they walked arm in arm or jogged. In bed, too, they were a match, and she felt herself warm as she remembered the nights in his apartment when she was supposed to be at the library.

"What're you up to, Lulu?"

She loved his nickname for her. "I was looking for a map of Angola."

"Angola? What for?"

Although Jed knew her family history, and liked to hear the stories—he was the first to admit that everything he knew about the Mafia was from the movies—Luisa made a brushing aside gesture. "Just a little family business."

She was surprised he didn't follow up. She realized why when he spoke.

"Um, do you have any classes this afternoon?" There was a catch in his voice.

Luisa knew what that meant. It had been a few days since they'd been together. She looked up. "None that I can't miss."

They walked the bike back to his apartment. The security guard knew better than to tell her mother.

***

After making love, Jed dozed off. Luisa wondered if she should be irritated but decided it gave her an opportunity. She slipped out of bed, threw on one of his t-shirts, and went to the blinking laptop on his desk.

If only she knew where her grandfather had been stationed in Angola. Her mother didn't know, and she doubted Gran did, either. She Googled "Cuban soldiers in Angola" and was surprised at the number of hits that came back. She started reading. Apparently, Cubans had been posted all over Angola in virtually every province. She remembered her mother telling her half a million Cubans had been there over the years. Which didn't help. Why couldn't the Cubans have been squeezed into a smaller, more enclosed area? South Vietnam, for example? Or a place so desolate there were only a few options, like Afghanistan?

She went back to Google and searched maps of Angola, drilling down on the images. She scanned dozens of maps, some topographical, like the ones she'd found the night before, some political. But she didn't find any places that looked like her grandfather's map.

Twenty minutes later, Jed stirred. "What are you doing?" He stifled a yawn.

"I told you."

"Yeah. I know. A map of Angola. But why?"

She turned in the chair. "My grandmother gave me a map that her—my grandfather—drew in Angola. He was stationed there when he was in the Cuban Army. But we don't know where. I've been trying to find out. Without much success."

"Nothing in the library?"

"Not in Mudd. I thought there might be engineering maps but I didn't find any. There could be more at the main library, which is where I was headed before I got—waylaid."

"You know, I might be able to create a computer program that would let you scan in the drawing and compare it to existing maps."

Jed was a graduate student in computer science. For a moment Luisa's hope flared. "That would be way cool. How long would it take?"

"I don't know. A week or two."

She screwed up her mouth. "I was hoping it'd be more like an hour. I'd like to figure this out."

He leaned over his bedside table, grabbed his glasses, and put them on. He brushed his hair back, a habit he'd adopted when he was pondering something. Then he rolled back and stretched out his arms. "You know, Lu, for a smart girl, you're not using your head."

"What do you mean?" she said in an irritated tone.

"Think about it. What's in Angola? And the Congo? And all over that part of the world?"

"I—I don't know."

"Yes, you do." He paused. "And I'll bet your grandmother does, too." He held up his fingers and wiggled them.

She stared at Jed for a moment. Then her mouth opened. "Diamonds!"

"Bloody and otherwise."

She smacked herself on her forehead. "Of course! I am so stupid. Mining maps!"

"Now you're thinking."

Luisa swiveled back to Jed's laptop and entered "mining," "maps," and "Angola." Several websites popped up. They weren't in color and they weren't much more than pen and ink drawings. Which was exactly what she needed. A few moments later Luisa whistled.

"Jed. Look at this!"

CHAPTER FORTY-TWO

"You found it?" Gran stopped chewing mid-bite.

"I think so." Luisa and her mother were having dinner at Gran's in the dining room. Her grandmother had redecorated the entire first floor of the Barrington home after her husband, Carmine, died in a sudden car accident not long after Gran's father passed. Luisa was a baby during the renovation—they had just arrived from Miami—but her mother told her about the heavy dark furniture, thick rugs, and air that reeked of cigarette smoke. Now the house was light and airy, with shiny hardwood floors, rich oriental rugs, and lots of crystal that made the light sparkle. Gran was a wonderful cook, and although she had help—so many secretaries, bodyguards, and assistants that they usually tripped over each other—she still enjoyed cooking. Tonight was lasagna with a salsa twist.

Her mother looked up from her plate. "Found what?"

Luisa and Gran exchanged glances.

"Luisa has been on a treasure hunt," Gran finally said.

Carla looked puzzled. "For school?"

Luisa looked at Gran, who gave her a brief nod. "Um, not exactly, Ma."

Carla stiffened almost imperceptibly, but Luisa caught it. Her mother only did that when she was disturbed. And no one disturbed her more than Gran. Especially when Gran managed to make her mother feel excluded. Luisa didn't know if it was intentional on Gran's part, but her mother clearly thought so.

Gran cut in, apparently oblivious to Carla's discomfort. "What did you find?"

Luisa rose from the table, went to her backpack, and pulled out what she'd printed. Her mother followed her with her eyes. Luisa came back and handed it to Gran.

Gran studied the paper. Then she looked up. "I'm sorry. What am I looking at?"

"It's a map of a small area in Angola."

"Angola?" Both Gran and her mother said the word at the same time. Gran's eyes widened. Her mother's narrowed.

"The northeast part of the country, near the Congo border," Luisa said.

Gran's eyebrows arched.

Luisa pointed over her grandmother's shoulder. "These three squiggly lines are rivers. Two of them begin with the letter 'C.'" She pointed to the two 'C's at the bottom of the page. "Look at their names. 'Chiumbe' and 'Chicapa.' And the one in the middle is 'Luachimo.' That's the 'L.'"

Gran's mouth opened. "Unbelievable!"

"Jed helped me figure it out. And these…" She gestured to two dots on the page. "Those are cities. One is Lucapa, which is one of the bigger cities in that part of Angola. The other is Dundo, which is in the northeast corner, practically in the Congo." Luisa went back to her seat at the table. "I researched it, and it turns out Cuban forces were posted in both places. Most were in Lucapa, but there was an outpost in Dundo."

"So Luis could have been there?" Gran murmured.

"It's possible. The only thing I don't know is what the third dot at the top of the page represents." She hesitated. "But the area is known for diamonds and other minerals. It could be a mine. Maybe Granpa Luis found a diamond mine. And I'm not sure what the circle of dots around the larger circle is on the bottom of the page. It might be an inset—you know, a close-up of a portion of the area."

Gran opened her mouth, about to say something, when a sharp voice cut in. "What the hell are you doing?"

Both Luisa and Gran looked up. Her mother's features had gone rigid, and her face was crimson.

Oh no, Luisa thought. *Ma's pissed.* Aloud, she said, "Gran asked me to take a look."

"And this map. Where did you get it?"

Gran spoke up. "I gave it to her. Well, a copy." Luisa heard a trace of defiance in her voice.

"Why?"

"Because it's time we knew the truth."

Now Luisa was confused. "Truth? What truth?"

"I don't believe it, Francesca. How could you?" her mother cried.

"It's long overdue, Carla."

Her mother's face darkened.

"What's overdue?" Luisa asked. "What's going on?"

"I'll tell you," Carla sniffed. "Your father—and your grandfather—were killed because of this map. Both of them murdered. On the same day. All because of…" She waved her hand, unable, apparently, to finish her thought.

Luisa whipped around to face Gran. "Is that true, Gran?"

Gran didn't answer, but she didn't have to.

"It's the truth," her mother said. "But your grandmother can't leave it alone. I should have burned the damn thing when I got to the States." She looked at Gran. "I almost did, you know. But I thought you'd want something tangible. A memento that belonged to the man you loved." She sniffed again. "The more fool I."

Gran extended her palm. "Carla. I am grateful for what you did. As I am for the photo." She gestured to a small glass-covered table on the end of a black leather sofa where a photo of herself and Luis in a sterling silver frame sat in the place of honor. "But we have to discover the truth."

"Francesca, this happened over twenty years ago. It was another lifetime. A dangerous one at that."

Gran straightened. "No one gets away with killing the people I loved." Her tone was harsh, imperious. "No matter when it happened."

Carla pushed away from the table and stood. The cords on her neck stuck out. Her eyes turned steely, and her voice was cold fury. "You have no right to expose my daughter to danger because of your need for revenge."

Luisa gazed at her mother, then her grandmother. Two alpha women, both protecting their turf. She hardly dared to breathe.

Then Gran relaxed, smiled sweetly, and softened her voice. "Carla. Be reasonable. Do you think I would put Luisa in any jeopardy? She did a little research. That's all. Nothing dangerous."

But her mother wasn't buying. "I know you want to control the universe, but sometimes things happen that you cannot anticipate. You have no idea what could be unleashed. What if it opens—how do you call it in English?" She looked at Luisa.

"A Pandora's box," Luisa said softly.

"*Sí.* A Pandora's box," her mother repeated.

"That's simplistic, Carla," Gran said. "I would expect it from someone whose beliefs are mired in superstition and rigid ideas about destiny." It was a jab at her mother's penchant for Santería beliefs, Luisa knew. "But you're far too intelligent for that. We make our own destiny. And we have. Both of us."

"You weren't there, Francesca. I saw it happen."

Luisa pulled on a strand of hair. "Is that true, Gran?"

"The map was why your father went to Cuba in the first place," her mother jumped in. "Someone wanted it. His mission was to bring it back. At any cost."

Luisa frowned, half in shock, half in anger. "You never told me that."

"You were too young, and there was no need. Your father did not know

Luis was *his* father. But whoever sent him did. And knew that Michael would be the only person Luis would give the map to. When your father discovered the truth, he aborted the mission."

"But they killed him anyway," Gran said, as if that explained everything. "It's time to hold them accountable."

"Who?" Luisa asked.

"Your grandmother doesn't know," her mother said. "But if you find them, she will put us all in danger."

Luisa looked from one woman to the other. "Gran, Ma has a point. Maybe we should leave it alone."

But Gran didn't answer. An absorbed expression came over her, as if she was making connections, putting things together.

"Francesca, did you hear me?" her mother said.

Gran didn't answer.

Her mother folded her arms. "You're trying to figure out who sent Michael, aren't you?"

Her grandmother focused, then, and cleared her throat. "Carla, my life has been filled with men taking advantage of me. Using me. Controlling me. They tore me away from Luis. They killed my son." Her expression grew steely. "No more. I'm done with that."

"What men?" Carla snorted. "Strangers like the people Michael was working for? Or your father? You could have gone back to Luis."

"My father would have killed him if I tried. Plus, I was pregnant."

"You could have escaped. Like you did when you went to Santa Clara. Babies are known to have been born in Cuba."

"Like yours?" Gran's voice was heavy with sarcasm.

Her mother's eyes flashed. "We are not talking about me. It was your father who ruined your life, Francesca. Not the people behind Michael's mission. If you want revenge, start with him."

But Gran's father, Grampa Tony, was gone, Luisa thought. He'd died before she was born.

"You're playing with fire, Francesca," her mother went on. "You'll endanger all of us. And for what? Because you can?"

Francesca's voice was quiet but held such a firm resolve that Luisa grew unsettled. "Carla, I will not tolerate being talked to this way. We're done here."

Gran left the room and headed to her office. The office used to belong to Carmine, but Gran took it over after he died. When Luisa was a little girl, she would sneak past the bodyguards—or so she thought—into the office. Sometimes her grandmother would be arguing with someone, but they'd stop as soon as she crept into the room, and Gran, all smiles and sweet words, would offer her a lolly-pop. She learned later that the guards had been instructed to allow Luisa free rein in the house.

Neither her mother nor Gran had been sweet tonight.

"Let's go," her mother said tersely, cutting off her memories. Luisa went to the closet to get their coats.

***

In her office, Francesca picked up the phone.

CHAPTER FORTY-THREE

It had been over fifty years since Nick Antonetti flew to Havana to propose to Frankie Pacelli. Although she didn't say yes at the time, he was confident they would end up together. His parents hadn't been in favor of the union. They knew whose daughter she was, and the Antonettis were already two generations on the right side of the law. But Nick was crazy about Frankie, and they must have realized that putting up a fight would only have fueled their son's desire.

Nick had been packing for the University of Pennsylvania when he heard she'd run off with a Cuban revolutionary. It was a knock-out blow to his gut and his dreams. At the time he doubted he'd ever recover. But his parents made him go to Philadelphia anyway. They expected great things from him; he was the first in his family to go to an Ivy League school. They thought he'd be a lawyer, but he surprised them by majoring in finance at the Wharton School and going into investment banking.

In his senior year he met Bonnie Hamilton from Westchester County. They married and moved to Chicago, where Nick worked for Mesirow for two years. Then he started his own firm. It flourished, and they bought a house in Lake Forest where they had their two and a half children—Bonnie always said their beagle, Shiloh, was their half-child.

But Bonnie had passed away a year earlier after a long battle with cancer. Nick hated the word battle. People didn't battle cancer, they held it at bay until the poisons in the chemo and radiation made them so fragile that almost any infection or virus could fell them.

After Bonnie passed, Nick came out of semi-retirement and redoubled his efforts at Nicholas Financial. Part of it was the economy, but part of it was that he had nothing else to do. He wasn't the type to spend the day on the golf course, and he didn't gamble, drink, or carouse. Making money was the only thing he knew how to do. And he did it well. Despite the economic climate, Nicholas Financial was surviving nicely, probably because it was small, selective, and fiercely independent.

Although his life was layered with loss, Nick was not bitter. Over the years he and Francesca had talked occasionally, and in his mind, they'd mended the damage to their relationship. When her son Michael died, he and Bonnie attended the memorial service, and when Bonnie passed, Francesca came to the wake. So when the phone rang at home that evening, as he was finishing his coffee and weighing whether to read a book or watch TV, he wasn't shocked to hear her voice.

"Good evening, Frankie," Nick said. "This is a nice surprise."

"I realized we hadn't talked since—since Bonnie's wake. It's been too long."

Nick gazed around his giant kitchen with the island in the middle. He'd been thinking he ought to downsize. Move into the City, maybe Lake Shore Drive. Lake Forest, with its acres of landscaped property dividing up what amounted to estates, was possibly the most affluent suburb on the North Shore. He'd been proud to afford to live there. But now, without Bonnie to share it with him, it was too grand, too showy, too exclusive.

"How are you coping, Nicky?"

"You know how it goes. I work. I come home. And then I work more."

"I want you to come for dinner."

Nick picked up a spoon and twirled it between his fingers. Barrington, where Frankie lived, was the equivalent of Lake Forest in affluence, but situated farther west. "That's very sweet of you. But you don't have to."

"Nonsense. You and Bonnie were so kind to me after Michael... and then Carmine..."

"You've had your share of sadness too, Frankie." He didn't add that given her family business, death and misfortune were inevitable consequences. He'd managed to steer clear of the Outfit, politely refusing the offers they made, and they'd left him alone. Probably because of his ties to Frankie. Which was another reason he was grateful rather than bitter.

"We all have," she said.

To be honest, Nick was happy on his side of the fence. It hadn't been a bad thing, he'd come to realize, when they broke up. Not marrying Frankie had simplified his life. Kept him from a host of ethically compromising positions.

Frankie cleared her throat.

Nick remembered that sound. It usually preceded a request or a suggestion. "So, Mrs. DeLuca. I'm happy to come to dinner, but I have a feeling that's not the only thing you have on your mind. What can I do for you?"

Frankie giggled, maybe a little too brightly for ten at night. "I'm not sure I like that you know me so well." There was a pause. "But I do have a question. And you're about the only person I trust enough to ask. I need total discretion."

He rubbed his fingers across his chin, knowing she was flattering him. "Of course."

Frankie told him about the map and that Luisa had traced it to the northeastern part of Angola. "I think this is an important document, Nicky. But I need to know more about the area."

"How did you get it?"

She paused again, as if carefully choosing her words. "My daughter-in-law brought it with her from Cuba. They found it when—after—Michael was killed. We think the map might point to a mining operation or something similar. But we're not sure. You have experts who handle these things, don't you?"

***

After extracting a promise that she and Nick would talk the next morning, Frankie got ready for bed. She'd never told Nicky how Luis died. Everyone knew Michael was shot by border guards while trying to escape, but she and Carla had kept the details about Luis's death quiet. Not even Luisa had known the entire truth until tonight.

She understood Carla's concerns. But the map had once been important to Luis. And if it was important to him, it was important to her. Luis was the love of her life, the only man she had given herself to without reservation. If the revolution hadn't intervened, she would still be in Cuba, a contented wife and mother, cooking for Luis, scolding the children, keeping each other warm at night. This map was the only link to her past, a past where the possibility of happiness was still alive.

She went into the bathroom to remove her make-up. She washed her face, thinking how Luis had died because of the map, and her son, the product of their passion, had too. It was time to settle accounts. Anyone with her resources would. Her father had taught her that. She was in a position to make it happen. After decades of his guidance, she was no longer a naïf. Anything she might salvage from the mine, moreover, would be an unexpected, but not unwelcome, windfall. She would have completed Luis's and Michael's mission. Reclaimed a little piece of both of them. She was sure they would approve.

She came out of the bathroom, threw back the down quilt on her bed, and burrowed underneath. She was doing this for all the right reasons. By the time she turned out the light, she'd convinced herself.

***

Nick called promptly at ten the next morning. "Good morning, Frankie.

I've put us on speaker-phone. There are two associates I want to introduce to you. They're two of my best people."

"Are you sure this is a secure line?"

"Absolutely. We made sure of it. And the door to my office is tightly closed."

"Thank you, Nicky. I'm forever in your debt." Francesca never went out if she could conduct business by phone. That, or have people come to her. It was safer that way. Her people swept the phones and electronic equipment daily.

"The first person I want you to know is Hamilton Snower. He's my grandson, my daughter's son. He's twenty-three and came to work as a research analyst here at NF. His specialty is natural resources, as it happens."

"Good morning, Hamilton."

"Call me Ham. Everyone else does. Just don't add Swiss on rye."

Frankie made an appropriate chuckle.

"And Ham's boss, George Trevor, is here too. He was a director over at Bear Stearns, but it was our good fortune to snag him when they fell apart."

"Good morning, Mrs. DeLuca," Trevor said.

"We've done a bit of preliminary research," Nick said, "and your granddaughter may be right. The area of Angola that the map corresponds to is heavily mined. But exactly what is being mined has changed over the years. Do you have any idea when the map was drawn?"

"It was during the Cuban intervention in Angola."

She heard a few soft clicks. Someone had a laptop. Ham's voice piped up. "Cubans were in Angola from 1975 through 1989."

"If you say so," Frankie said.

"Frankie, do you have any more specific dates?" Nick asked.

"No," she said. "But we think it was toward the end of the conflict."

"Well," the third voice, George Trevor, spoke up. "Those years were the thick of the blood diamond era. Or, as they are also called, conflict diamonds." His voice was nasal and reedy. She imagined him with glasses and a pocket protector.

"Refresh my memory," she said.

"Of course. Everyone was mining for diamonds then. Mostly to fund the rebel insurgency forces in Angola and neighboring countries. Unfortunately, legal or ethical means were not a priority. You've heard of 'blood' diamonds?"

"Wasn't there a movie about that?" Frankie said.

"Yes. About ten years ago. It was fiction, of course, but it did explore the horrific human rights abuses that took place. The rebels in the Congo exploited children and women as a matter of course, forced them into the mines, and tortured—and slaughtered them—if they didn't come out with stones. Cutting off a young boy's hands or one of his legs was a daily event. And if they couldn't get diamonds that way, they'd simply steal them from legitimate mining companies. They attacked and raped villagers and accused them of stealing diamonds, to deflect attention from what they were doing. If your son was—"

"No," Francesca cut in. "Michael would never have been involved in that."

"Excuse me?" George Trevor's tone was that of a man not used to being interrupted. Maybe he didn't have a pocket protector.

"My son would never have taken a job that involved brutal tactics. He had principles. He wasn't materialistic. He knew the difference between—"

Someone coughed, cutting her off. Frankie didn't know who it was. But in the uneasy silence that followed, she realized she was wasting her breath trying to defend her dead son. No one, including a friendly consultant, would believe anyone connected to the Outfit had a shred of social conscience.

In Michael's case, though, it was true. Frankie had always wondered why Michael didn't care about accumulating power and wealth. In her more narcissistic moments, she thought perhaps her own rebellion, albeit short-lived, had something to do with it. But when she was honest with herself, she knew it was his nature, a nature he'd inherited from Luis. And while being in the army, as Michael was, could—and often did—lead to a yen for power, Frankie didn't want to spoil her fantasy that Michael wasn't pursuing it. She hadn't been either. Back then.

Nick's voice, gentle but firm, cut in. "Didn't you tell me last night that Michael wasn't in charge of the mission? That he was simply carrying out instructions? Perhaps he didn't know what the map represented."

Francesca had to admit Nicky could be right. But it had been Luis who'd drawn the map. And if Michael was disinterested in power and wealth, Luis had actively resisted both. The acquisition of assets went against everything Luis Perez stood for. Or did in his youth. Frankie remembered their discussions about Marxism and the social equality Fidel would bring to Cuba. Luis believed it wholeheartedly. For a moment, her heart cracked and she thought she might tear up.

As if he knew what was going through her head, Nick said softly, "If Luis sketched the map, he did that thirty years after you knew him, Frankie. People change."

Francesca was quiet for a moment. "So you think the mine could be diamonds?"

"It fits," Trevor said.

"Is there a way to confirm that?"

"Short of going there and taking a look? I doubt it," Trevor said.

"But you must have international contacts. People who scout those kinds of things."

"It's outside our line of business, Frankie," Nick said. "I don't doubt we could come up with the right contacts, but you need to ask yourself whether it's worth it. It will be quite expensive. And what do you expect to find?"

Frankie couldn't tell Nicky the truth. Let him think she was greedy rather than vengeful. It was easier. "A fortune, of course."

There was silence on the other end of the speaker-phone. Then someone cleared his throat again.

"I guess we could put out some feelers. But it's entirely possible it's already been developed."

"Well, that would be my misfortune, wouldn't it?"

"Francesca, may I make a suggestion?" Nick asked.

She ignored him. "I want to know what's there. I want to know if anyone else has developed it, who they are, and..." she hesitated. "...whether it would make a difference knowing we had this map."

Nick went on. "I can't recommend this, Frankie. You could come into contact with all sorts of people and groups you might not want to know. People who—" He stopped.

Frankie knew why. He was describing the people she dealt with every day.

More silence.

Finally, Nick said, "Okay. George, why don't we get the map, take a look, and have Ham make inquiries? Discreetly, of course."

"There is a possibility it's not diamonds, you know," Trevor said. "Angola has other resources and minerals. Gold, metals, that sort of thing."

"Are they as profitable as diamonds?" Francesca asked.

"Possibly."

"All right, Frankie," Nicky said tiredly. "Let us look into it for you. You'll fax over the map?"

"Um... I'd rather messenger it. The fewer eyes the better. Actually, I'll make a copy and have it personally delivered. My granddaughter can bring it down."

"That's fine. Have her ask for Ham. He'll be your contact person. Okay?"

"Bless you, Nicky."

He was slow to answer. "I certainly hope so."

CHAPTER FORTY-FOUR

Late afternoon sunlight filtered through the vertical blinds in Ham Snower's office. His window faced west, and now that daylight savings time was back, he usually closed the blinds to keep out the glare. Despite that, stray bands of light seeped through, splashing strips of butterscotch across his desk.

He was finishing an article on mining operations in the Congo when his phone buzzed. Joanie, the receptionist.

"You have a visitor," she announced in a voice that managed to be both sultry and articulate, and was the reason she'd been hired. When he asked who it was, her voice held a note of amusement. "She says her name is Luisa DeLuca."

Ham tried to place the name. He'd been clubbing down on Rush Street with a buddy two nights ago, and they'd had more than a few. He recalled meeting two women, both of whom slipped cards into his pocket.

That happened a lot. Ham was a hottie, or so he'd been told. Women admired his athletic build, sandy hair, and frank blue eyes. He also had a dimple in the cleft of his chin that convinced more than one girl he was related to the swoon-worthy Viggo Mortensen. When he told his mother about that before she died, she'd joked and said the only cleft chin that mattered was Kirk Douglas's.

Joanie brought him back. "What should I tell her?"

He still couldn't place the name but it didn't matter. It was the end of the day; he would meet her, see what she wanted, and if necessary, tell her he was on his way to an appointment. "Tell her I'll be right out."

"I certainly will." Joanie said in a tone that made him think he shouldn't waste any time.

He realized she was right when he pushed through to the lobby of Nicholas Financial, and a young woman rose from the couch. She couldn't have been much taller than five three, but in tight jeans, a heavy sweater, and knee high black leather boots, every inch was perfectly accounted for. Lots of dark hair was gathered up on her head, but a few curls had slipped out and framed her face. She was slender but curvy in all the right places, and her face was part cherub, part siren: round cheeks and small nose, but a pointed chin and dark eyes he could dive into if he wasn't careful. Those eyes were appraising him now.

She extended her hand. It was cool and soft. "Thank you for seeing me. I'm sorry to be so late."

For a fleeting, uncharacteristically awkward moment, Ham was at a loss for words. The receptionist cleared her throat.

Ham took the hint. "Um, Ms. DeLuca, isn't it?"

She nodded, seeming pleased he remembered her name. "My grandmother said you'd be expecting me."

Ham was about to ask what the hell she was talking about when it came to him. His grandfather's friend. The morning meeting. The Mafia Queen. He blinked in surprise. "Of course," he said, trying to recover. "I didn't expect you this soon. You're fast."

She smiled. Her lips were soft and full, her teeth blazing white. Ham realized he had lost control of the conversation. It was a new experience.

"When Gran makes a decision, she doesn't waste any time. She wanted me to come down earlier, but I had classes."

Classes? Where? In what? Suddenly he wanted to know all about this woman. "Well, in that case, come on back to my office." He held the door open and ushered her to the hallway where the staff offices were located. Joanie tried hard not to smile, failing miserably. Was it that obvious?

***

The exchange of the map took about five seconds, but Luisa was in no hurry to leave. Ham—what a peculiar name for a man, she thought—didn't seem to be either, so they chatted. Shafts of light marched across the room, eventually hitting her in the face. When she shaded her eyes, Ham jumped up to shutter the blinds.

"No, don't," she said. "You have a western exposure. Let's watch."

"You sure?"

She nodded and watched him pull back the blinds, moving her chair so the sun wasn't in her eyes. It had turned fiery orange, spitting out beams of light that bounced off skyscrapers, glinted on windows, and suffused the Chicago air with a rosy glow.

"Sunset is the best time of the day, don't you think?"

Ham cocked his head in a way that made her think he'd never thought about it. She went on. "I mean, mornings are nice too, especially here in

Chicago when the sun rises over the lake. But there's something special about sunset. It's almost as if the sun is burning off all the dust and dirt accumulated during the day. You know, preparing the city for a soft, gentle night."

She regretted the words as soon as she'd spoken them. He probably thought she was pretentious. An aspiring literary snob.

But Ham's smile widened, and his Adam's apple bobbed, making her wonder if he was as nervous as she. She ran a hand down the sleeve of her sweater. He was just another guy. Doing work for the family. She had Jed anyway, and she was happy with her cowboy. Wasn't she?

They continued to talk. He'd gone to Penn, he told her, like his mother and grandfather before him. And like his grandfather, he'd majored in finance. He played football, joined a fraternity, became part of the Ivy League old boys' network. He asked about her.

Most times she didn't divulge much about herself. People either knew who she was, or kept their distance when they learned. It had taken Jed months to crack through her shell. But Ham was the grandson of Gran's friend. And he was so damn easy to talk to. Dusk had descended by the time she stopped.

She leaned back, surprised that she'd talked so much. He was probably bored out of his mind. Couldn't wait to get out.

Instead he leaned forward. "Would you like to have dinner?"

***

The next morning Ham arrived at the office early. As he passed Joanie, he smiled.

She eyed him. "Now that's a shit-eating grin if I ever saw one."

Ham didn't reply.

"You're not talking? Uh-oh. Did our young analyst get hit by the thunderbolt?"

He left her with what he thought was an enigmatic smile and went toward his office. Strange what twenty-four hours could do. Yesterday he would have told Joanie she was a romance junkie. Things like that only happened in movies. Today, he wasn't so sure.

When they'd realized they both lived in Evanston, north of Chicago, dinner turned into dessert, then after-dinner drinks, and then coffee, each at a different place. Empty-nester Boomers had "discovered" Evanston, and a new restaurant seemed to open every week, each one more European and pretentious than the next. Neither Ham nor Luisa was interested in ambiance, though, and it was after midnight when she dropped him at his condo.

He wanted to invite her up, hell, he wanted to take her to bed and never let her leave, but it was way too soon. Plus, her bodyguard had been following them in a second car. The guard was a woman, ex-military Ham thought by her behavior. She kept a low profile, but her presence was enough to intimidate him.

So they sat in Luisa's Prius and talked. At one point he tentatively slipped his arm around her. She inched closer to him and tilted her head up. She hitched the strap of her expensive-looking handbag on her shoulder, leaned across, and kissed him on the lips.

"Time for me to get home."

He nodded and scooted toward the passenger door. "Tomorrow?"

She nodded.

"Would you..." his voice cracked. "... consider coming to my place? I'll cook ."

"And what can you cook?"

"Um, er, I can broil a mean steak."

***

Now Ham sat down, leaned over, and opened the drawer in which he'd locked the map. He was anxious to get started. Other projects would wait. If he was lucky, maybe he'd have something to tell her tonight.

As a research analyst, Ham was in an entry-level position, but he didn't mind. He understood that his grandfather would leave the firm to him and wanted him to know it from the ground up. In fact, Ham enjoyed research. The acquisition of knowledge for its own sake was a noble pursuit. And his area, natural resources, was relevant and made for great stories.

He'd about exhausted the links to articles on the web about mining in Angola when his boss, George Trevor, minced into his office. Trevor was unmarried, and on more than one occasion, Ham wondered if he was gay. Not that it mattered. Trevor was tall and slim, with thinning brown hair and glasses that gave him the look of a dead fish. But he was impeccably dressed, and while he'd taken off his jacket, his tie was knotted tight, and the creases in his shirt were crisply ironed. Those creases would stay crisp all day. Ham figured he must sit at his desk without moving like—well, a dead fish.

"What's up, George?" Ham asked.

"Just wanted to touch base on the project Nick assigned you." Trevor sat down. "You need any help?"

Ham held up the map. "I got the map from Grandfather's—er—friend." Ham tiptoed around the word. He didn't know the history between his grandfather and Francesca DeLuca, but he wondered if they had once been more than friends. He realized he'd never know.

Trevor snorted. "You know who she is, right?"

"Mrs. DeLuca?" When Trevor nodded, Ham said, "Grampa said she was Mafia, right?"

"The Pacelli Family," Trevor went on. "Francesca DeLuca is one of the few Chicago families who can trace their lineage from Rothstein straight to Capone."

"Really." Ham rocked back.

Trevor's lips thinned to a smirk. "Her father was Tony Pacelli. Silver-tongued Tony, they called him. In the Fifties he could have gone to Vegas with Bugsy or Cuba with Lansky. He chose Lansky and ended up running a big resort in Havana. He and his family barely got out in '59. Over the years Pacelli rebuilt the family business in gambling, narcotics, hooking. Legitimate businesses, too. The daughter is head of the Family now."

Ham's eyebrows rose sky-high. "You're telling me a woman heads up an Outfit family?"

"Why not? They're in every other industry."

"But—but..." Ham sputtered. "The Mob?"

"Her husband was a jerk. They say she offed him when her father made her the don. Or donna, I guess we should say. "

"No shit."

"No shit," Trevor said. "No Mafioso, man or woman, can afford to look weak. So in case you were wondering, that's who you're working for. I'd advise you not to forget it."

"You're working for her too."

"Nick asked you to be the liaison."

Ham expected Trevor to add "thankfully," but he didn't. Trevor was white bread, a WASP from Connecticut. Ham came from Italian stock on his mother's side, and while his family wasn't connected, he saw things differently. Part of it was the Mob's history. Dirt-poor Sicilian peasants, oppressed by the rich, came to the New World and within a generation, prospered. How could you not respect them, at least a little? Despite their tactics, which ranged from brutal to foolhardy, theirs was an ethnic Horatio Alger story.

Part of it, too, he knew, was his youth. Gen X and Y'ers were both casual and cynical. They took it for granted that corruption was rife, and they didn't have the same idealism their parents did. Practical and flexible, they didn't want to cleanse the system. They wanted to profit from it.

Ham leaned forward. "Well, I guess she couldn't be any worse than a governor or two, could she? And, unlike the politicians who hired us in the past, she'll probably pay her bills."

"We can hope. In the meantime, I know a guy who can tell you more about African mining operations."

CHAPTER FORTY-FIVE

Ham called Trevor's contact at the Canada National Bank in Toronto. Over the years Canadian financiers had carved out a special expertise in mining and energy resources. Unlike the U.S., Canada hadn't soured on shale oil and tar sands, and they were interested in moving oil through their pipelines. They were also on the lookout for the next best mineral that would capture the investment world's attention. And one of the only places in the world that still brimmed with opportunity was Africa. Trevor had met Tom Corcoran at a conference in Florida a few months earlier, and they'd exchanged business cards over martinis, he told Ham.

"Tom Corcoran's office."

Ham introduced himself and explained he was calling at the suggestion of his boss, George Trevor. "I'm an analyst in natural resources and I'd like to pick his brain."

The receptionist said that Mr. Corcoran was out until late afternoon but she'd give him the message. Toronto was an hour ahead of Chicago, so Ham said he'd be in his office for a while.

He was about to pack up and head out to buy steaks for his dinner with Luisa when his outside line burred.

"Hamilton Snower?"

"Yes?"

"Tom Corcoran. You called?" He spoke with a clipped British accent.

"Thanks for calling back. My boss George Trevor said he met you in Marco Island a few months ago and recommended I get in touch."

"Trevor, Trevor…"

"He's a VP with Nicholas Financial in Chicago," Ham said.

"Yes, of course." Corcoran's tone sounded cool and artificial. "Well then, what can I do for you?"

"A client of ours is interested in potentially investing in a mine in

Angola. George says you're an expert in mining and I'd like to ask a few questions, if you don't mind."

"Not at all. Happy to help. Where in Angola is this mine?"

"It's in the northeastern part of the country."

"Near the Congo border."

"Yes. In fact it's supposedly near a town that's very close to the border."

"What town is that?" Corcoran asked.

"Dundo."

There was a momentary pause. "I know Dundo," he said.

Ham's pulse sped up. "What can you tell me about it?"

Corcoran chuckled. "It's trying to become civilized. For about three blocks. They have a hotel. But that's a cover. You can't really call it a city. The place is wild."

"In what way?"

"You need to remember in that part of the world, borders are—shall we say—porous. There is usually a tug of war. More than one, actually. Especially when minerals are concerned. It makes for a dangerous situation. There's still quite a lot of fighting."

"What are they fighting over?"

"What do you know about that part of the world?"

"I know there is supposed to be gold there. And diamonds, of course. Copper. A little quartz. That's about it. That's why I'm calling."

"You're working with old data, my friend. Diamonds are considerably less desirable since the conflict diamonds mess blew up. Gold is too expensive and unpredictable, and the other minerals you mentioned aren't worth the investment. There's only one substance everyone wants."

"What's that?" Ham asked.

"Coltan. It's short for columbite–tantalite. Ever heard of it?"

"Sure. It's mined in the Congo."

"So they say. You know what it's used for, right?"

"Something to do with computers."

"Lad, you need to bone up on your intel. Coltan does not simply have *something* to do with computers. It has *everything* to do with them. Laptops, cell phones. DVD players. Game systems. Computers. Pagers. Pretty much any electronic product on the market."

Ham leaned back. "I didn't know."

"Most people don't," Corcoran said. "Coltan is an essential ingredient in electronic capacitors. It holds a strong electrical charge for a long time. Which makes it ideal to control the current inside all those miniature circuit boards. It can be recycled, but, as you can probably imagine, demand for it has exploded. Companies like Sony and Nokia will do anything for a stable supply of the stuff."

"Wow." Ham knew he sounded like a rube, but this was news to him.

"Yes, wow. And the problem is, there isn't very much of it. In fact, it's extremely rare, except in the Congo. Which means whoever has the coltan has the power. It's why rebel militias in the Congo, who are backed by Rwanda and Uganda by the way, as well as multi-national corporations, are tripping all over each other to get it. The rebels, incidentally, are the same bloody bastards who exploited the diamond market fifteen years ago. They're back now, and there's smuggling. Child labor. Pillage and rape. Not to mention what's happened to the environment."

"But that's the Congo," Ham said. "Right?"

"Ah. But what country borders the Congo?"

"Are you saying there are deposits of coltan in Angola?"

"Now that's the big question, isn't it?" Corcoran chuckled again. "I know people who would like nothing more than to find a supply of coltan a good distance from the exploitation and the fighting."

"So if someone had a map of an area near Dundo, they might be looking for coltan?"

Ham heard the man clear his throat.

Shit. He was sure he wasn't supposed to mention the map. Mrs. DeLuca had demanded strict confidentiality. He smacked himself on his forehead. Had he blown it?

But Corcoran went on as if it hadn't registered.

"Well, they don't call it black gold for nothing." Corcoran paused. "Now, time for you to tell why you've been interrogating me."

"I told you. We have a client who may have an interest in exploring the area but they want more information."

"I see." Ham knew Corcoran wouldn't ask who the client was, and he didn't. "Well, tell them it's dicey. Not only because of the rebels but also because of the rival companies trying to edge each other out. Even the Chinese are dipping their toes into the market. There's no question it is enormously lucrative, but I'd advise waiting until things are more settled. If they don't know what they're doing, your client could lose his entire investment."

"I get it. And thank you, Mr. Corcoran. I appreciate your time."

"Glad to help. Tell Trevor I send my best."

***

Tom Corcoran only vaguely remembered George Trevor, and he didn't have a clue who Ham Snower was, but the mention of Dundo and a map triggered an alarm. He looked at his watch. It was after seven in Boston, but he had his client's cell. His biggest client, the guy was CEO of a company whose volume of investment business with the bank had helped Tom get promoted to VP. Of course, the company wasn't doing so well these days;

then again, who was?

But that's not what was on Tom Corcoran's mind. The CEO had said if he ever heard anything about a map in Northern Angola near a tiny little fucked-up place called Dundo, he should call right away.

Corcoran picked up the phone.

CHAPTER FORTY-SIX

David Schaffer hung up the phone after talking to Tom Corcoran. He tried to curb his emotion. He'd had plenty of leads before that turned out to be zilch, so until he could check it out, he couldn't afford to let himself get excited. Still, he couldn't resist a little daydreaming. He'd been trying to track down the map for years. And each year he didn't find it made it more valuable. Not because he wanted it and couldn't get it. Coltan was one of the most valuable substances in the world today.

He went downstairs for dinner. As his wife, Carol, poured him a glass of Cabernet, he smiled. It was a rare event.

"Good news?" Carol asked.

"Maybe."

"Well, that's nice." She went back into the kitchen to get their meal. As he heard her opening and closing the refrigerator, he realized they'd reached the state of détente of couples who should never have married. There was no overt aggression, no hostility towards each other. They shared mostly—indifference. Which wasn't unusual. At least for David.

He hadn't been born with a silver spoon in his mouth, but it was better than stainless steel. He was the only child of upwardly mobile parents: his mother a doctor, his father an insurance executive. By the time he was six, he'd become king of the household, and used his position to manipulate his parents. "Boundaries" were not words in the Schaffer family vocabulary, and David was given everything he wanted, mostly to ease his mother's guilt for not being home during the day.

Still, he was a shy child, and slow to develop social skills. At one point his mother thought he might have Asperger's, but the kid shrink she took him to said he was lonely and needed to socialize.

As he grew up, though, David preferred to be home and by himself for one important reason. When his babysitter was on the phone or watching soaps, which was almost all the time, he had the opportunity to go through his parents' possessions. He was twelve when he found out his father had a mistress on the side; fourteen when he figured out the combination of the wall safe in their bedroom. And on the day his mother accidentally left her cell phone at home he learned she had a significant prescription drug addiction.

David never used the secrets he'd uncovered, but they made him realize that information was power, and he vowed to always have the right information. In high school, he wasn't a bully, but he always seemed to have dirt on the other kids. Most didn't like him much, but figured it was safer to keep him close than to make him an enemy.

After four unremarkable years in college, David decided to build a career in electronics. He was no Steve Jobs or Mark Zuckerberg. David didn't have their vision or ambition. The best place for him, he figured, would be to copy what others built.

By the mid-eighties he'd convinced his parents to take a second mortgage on the house so they could underwrite his business: a company that would manufacture components for all the electronic devices that were turning from drawing board dreams into reality. It turned out he had a good head for business, and within five years, Schaffer Electronics turned a profit.

His most important task was to acquire a steady supply of raw materials, and David scoured the world for vendors. When he started the company, he needed plastics that were both light and heat resistant to house electronic components. By the nineties, however, the market had changed. Smaller, more portable devices like cell phones, game systems, and laptops dominated, and David expanded into electronic capacitors, essential components for the new power supplies. And for those he needed a supplier who could sell him coltan at a reasonable price.

David found that company in Macedonian Metals, a huge conglomerate headquartered in Delaware. As usual, David did his due diligence before he approached them. He had plenty of resources at his disposal, mostly former intelligence operatives who were now infiltrating the corporate world to ferret out information about a company's competitors, suppliers, and strategic partners.

Through them David discovered that Macedonian was using child labor in Africa to work the coltan mines. Through them David also found out Macedonian was supplying African rebels who were mining the stuff with arms so they could overthrow whatever government happened to be in power. Armed with his intel, he approached Macedonian executives and managed to snag a contract for coltan at a very attractive price.

It was an astute move, but David knew it wouldn't last. He was at the mercy of a huge company that could jack up their prices at any time. He needed a stable supply, preferably his own, if he was to become a major player.

His break came from a retired CIA official who was doing corporate espionage. David had hired him to find out where more coltan could be found. The man told him about one of his former CIA buddies named Walters who knew about a map of a mine in Angola that supposedly held the key to the future. David had his guy get in touch with Walters to find out what the substance in the mine was.

When he learned it was coltan, David rejoiced. This could be his salvation. If David could control the mine, there would be no limit to his fortune. He would get contracts from Motorola, Apple, and Sony. At the very least, he would no longer be dependent on Macedonian. He decided to underwrite an operation to get the map.

Then all hell broke loose. The map, which pointed to a shithole outpost called Dundo, apparently belonged to a Cuban who had become an asset to the agency. But Walters, who had run the asset, was unexpectedly gunned down in Havana, and the map—as well as the asset—disappeared. To make matters worse, as he'd feared, the price of coltan spiked, increasing almost six hundred percent in less than a year. Everyone was going after the stuff, including the Chinese. Schaffer's profits tanked, and the future of the company was suddenly in jeopardy.

Because it was the one thing he couldn't have, it became the only thing worth having. Over the next twenty years, David downsized his company, laid off employees, and made do with a meager—but overpriced—supply of coltan from Macedonian. But he continued to obsess over the map. It became his holy grail, a beacon obscured, luring him with salvation.

Over the years he commissioned satellite photos of Angola, put out feelers to the intelligence and financial communities, and sifted through reports from geologists and analysts. He never entertained the notion of failure. He had no doubt that he would eventually locate the map, mine the territory, and reap the rewards.

So when his banker Tom Corcoran called, David knew this was his chance.

CHAPTER FORTY-SEVEN

Luisa's kiss was still on Ham's lips twenty-four hours later. All day his thoughts had been full of her. What her skin would feel like. How her nipples would feel between his fingers. How he would feel when he entered her.

So, after his conversation with Tom Corcoran, he raced up to Evanston on the El to buy steaks, potatoes, salad fixings, and two bottles of Merlot. Luisa arrived promptly at seven, and he turned out a damn good dinner, if he said so himself. They made their way through one of the bottles of Merlot and halfway through the second before she waved off the bottle.

"I can't eat or drink another thing," she said. "This was incredible."

Ham smiled and led her into the living room. He put on Dave Brubeck—he was a jazz lover—and they lounged feet to feet on his suede-cloth sofa. After an hour he inched across to her side and kissed her, more deeply than their kiss last night. She responded, and within a few minutes, they were in his bedroom, and he no longer had to imagine what she felt like.

Afterwards, curled up together, they talked. She told him about Jed.

"What are you going to do?"

"Break up with him tomorrow. Unless... you don't want me to."

"Are you kidding?" He gathered her close. Her hair smelled like cinnamon and honey. Sultry, not flowery.

"Consider it done." She gave him a solemn look.

He kissed her softly, and fluffed up two pillows. He slid one behind her head, the other behind his. "I've been doing work on the map. I talked to a guy today who seems to think the mine might be coltan."

"What's that?"

He explained.

Luisa brightened. "A pot of gold!"

"Well, don't get too excited. There are—issues."

"What do you mean?"

"Well, first off it's not certain that it is coltan."

"That's a risk we have to take."

He held up his palm. "Hold on. If it is coltan, you need to know that everyone and their brothers are scrambling for the stuff. It's incredibly valuable, and all sorts of bad things are happening because of it." He paused. "Do you remember the blood diamond conflict?"

"I saw the movie. With DiCaprio, right?"

"Right." He nodded. "What's going on now is similar. There's a huge tug of war between the armed rebels in the Congo and the government. The rebels have control of the coltan mines and are reaping huge profits which, of course, they use to further their fight."

Luisa shifted.

"It gets worse," Ham went on. "The rebels are also working with huge corporations who need the stuff badly. Companies like—well—a lot of them are Fortune 500 companies. And they're in cahoots with the rebels. The rebels sell to them, they refine it, then resell it for an exorbitant profit."

"Oh, come on. It can't be that bad."

"Farmers in the area have been kicked off their land and forced to work in the mines. Children, too. And the miners slaughter any elephant or gorilla that gets in their way. Actually, from what I read, gorillas are nearly extinct in that part of the world. The whole ecosystem is screwed up. And, of course, the rebels are torturing, raping, and killing civilians."

She propped herself up on an elbow. "All because of this coltan?"

Ham nodded.

"But that's—that's totally unacceptable."

Ham almost laughed at her tone. As if everything would automatically halt because Luisa DeLuca denounced it.

Luisa said, "I told you last night how I was involved in the Occupy movement, right?"

He nodded again.

"Well, one of the reasons I decided to go for a masters in engineering is to fix what these giant corporations have fucked up. And I do mean fucked up."

"But you're part of the one percent."

"Who cares what percent I am? I have a conscience, don't I? I can't stand by while corporations poison our water, land, and now, if what you're saying is true, kill innocent people. Before you know it, the planet will be a giant strip-mined desert. It's already happening. The fracking they do for gas? It's incredibly destructive. People right here in Illinois are getting cancer right and left. If we don't stop it, eventually society will break down, like it has in the Congo, apparently. We'll all be fighting for the few resources that remain. And the few healthy people left will be leading the charge. It's reprehensible."

Luisa was worked up now, her cheeks red, her eyes glittering with determination. "I'll talk to Gran tomorrow. I'm sure once I explain it to her, she'll reconsider."

Ham raised his eyebrows. It must be nice to have such faith.

***

It was after midnight when Luisa called her mother to tell her she wouldn't be coming home that night.

Carla was not pleased. "And why not?"

"Mother, I'm an adult. Let's keep our boundaries intact, okay?"

Carla made a blowing-out sound. "Boundaries. What *pendejada*! So I'm not supposed to ask where you are and with whom?"

"That's right."

"What about the bodyguard?"

"Marta's outside. I'm going to tell her to go home. I'm well protected." She smiled at Ham.

"No. You cannot do that."

"But Mom—"

"But nothing," Carla cut in. "She stays. Outside. But on duty."

Luisa made a face, knowing her mother couldn't see. "All right," she said sulkily. "By the way, Mama, I need to talk to you. I've found out some really bad things about the map and the part of the world it's in. I don't like it. I want Gran to back off."

Carla laughed. "And you think she'll listen?"

"Maybe. If we put up a united front."

A snort from Carla. "She'll subcontract the job. That's what they do these days. Form subsidiaries, create branches, contract with other organizations. That way they keep their hands clean."

Luisa knew her mother didn't approve of Gran's activities, but this was the first time she'd been so openly hostile. At least to Luisa.

"Well, then, I guess we'll have to persuade her she's wrong. I'll see you tomorrow."

Luisa hung up and rolled over towards Ham. Underneath his lean hard body was a core of softness, and she couldn't get enough. He was what she'd been looking for, except she hadn't realized she'd been looking. She tossed her cell into her purse and snuggled closer. She stroked his cheeks, his neck, his shoulders, his chest and then moved her hands lower. He moaned softly. She rolled on top of him and a moment later he moaned again.

CHAPTER FORTY-EIGHT

Ramon Suarez, aka Hector Gonzalez, and now Tomas Martinez, was peeling an orange when he heard the thrum of an engine. He put the orange down with a sigh of regret. Florida oranges were better than any others, including oranges from Cuba. He went to his living room window and peered through the shade. A black limo was idling in front of his house.

An uneasy feeling rushed through him. Limos didn't come to his Tampa neighborhood in Ybor City, the Cuban district. Most of the area was commercial and reminded him of Miami's Little Havana, but the residential section was beginning to be re-gentrified, and Ramon had rented a small *casita* near Columbus Drive and 17th Street. A swath of woods cut across his back lawn, conferring a rustic feel. For the first time in his life, he was living in a nice place with decent amenities. Leaving Miami had been a good move.

Until now. Had Miami followed him here? He gazed at the limo. The windows were dark, but he thought he saw three people inside: two in the front, one in the back. He tried to convince himself they weren't a threat. If they were, they wouldn't have come in the middle of the day.

The man in the passenger seat got out. He was a beefy guy with a shaved head and an empty expression. Muscle. He went to the rear door of the limo and opened it. The man who climbed out appeared to be early to mid-fifties. Trim. Not tall. Battleship gray hair, and lots of it, nicely styled. Expensive-looking clothes, but casual. Fancy sunglasses.

Still, you never knew.

Ramon went to his closet and fished out his Russian Marakov, the one he'd been issued by the Cuban Army. He shoved the pistol into his waistband and pulled his shirt out to cover it as the doorbell chimed.

Ramon opened the door but kept the screen closed. The man who'd been in the back seat was flanked by his goons. The driver, now that

Ramon could see him, was big and burly like the other guy, but had wavy blond hair. They didn't look like Mob. But if they weren't wiseguys, who were they?

The man between the bodyguards smiled. "Hector Gonzalez?"

"Sorry. You have the wrong man." He was about to close the door when the man said, "But you *were* Hector Gonzalez, once upon a time."

Ramon felt his eyes narrow. "Who's asking?"

The man patted his shirt pocket and pulled out a business card which he offered to Ramon. When Ramon hesitated, the man said, "It's okay. I won't force my way in."

Ramon hesitated for another moment. Then he opened the screen door enough to take the card. He scanned it. After thirty years in the U.S. he could read English, but barely. Luckily, a name and title was all that was written. David Schaffer, CEO Schaffer Electronics, Boston.

Ramon looked up. The security guys made no move to rush him. He allowed himself to relax a bit. "You've come a long way."

The man called Schaffer spread his hands. "It's a no-brainer, as the kids say. It's snowing in Boston."

If Schaffer was trying to get him to let down his guard, he was doing a good job.

"I'd like to talk to you," Schaffer said.

Ramon shifted his gaze to the goons.

Schaffer caught it. "Wait for me in the car, boys."

It was the bodyguards' turn to hesitate, but they retreated to the curb and leaned against the limo, arms crossed.

Ramon opened the screen door, stepped back, let his guest come in. In his late seventies now, Ramon was stooped with arthritis, and he had a limp. His doctor had told him he would need a hip replacement soon, but Ramon wasn't eager to be cut open.

Schaffer must have seen the limp. "Whoever said you get old gracefully is a liar, aren't they? This aging shit takes guts."

Schaffer was trying to be likeable. Why?

They sat in matching easy chairs. The chairs, a taupe velvet, had been one of the few things Ramon had bought new. Usually he got furniture from Goodwill or the Salvation Army. But surviving the life he'd led was grounds for a reward, wasn't it? A pair of goddammed chairs at least.

Schaffer took his shades off, slipped them into his shirt pocket. Despite his smile, his eyes were gray thunder. "You remember the man who brought you out of Angola over twenty years ago?"

Ramon had to force himself not to reach for his Marakov. Aloud he said, "Of course. He was with the Agency."

Schaffer nodded. "Right. Well, after he got back from Africa, he quit the CIA. A guy who worked for me knew him."

Walters. The map. He'd told Ramon he'd quit the Agency.

"We launched an operation based on his intel, but, unfortunately, it failed."

Ramon remembered Michael DeLuca's death. He'd heard about it through the Cuban exile grapevine. Walters had been killed too, but the woman with DeLuca had escaped. Ramon suspected that if anyone had the map, she did. Or knew where it was. He recalled that she was pregnant and was working at a Miami pharmacy. He'd actually gone to see her but missed her. And when he went back, the pharmacist said she'd left. Just up and disappeared.

Ramon wasn't happy, but what could he do? When, after a few months, nobody contacted him to give him his share of the proceeds, he figured the map had been lost. Or that he'd been cut out. It wasn't fair, but in a way it was a relief. The map had become a curse. He wasn't sorry to let it go. *Lo que a uno cura, a otro mata.* One man's meat was another man's poison. Still, given that he'd endured his fill of poison, he decided to play it safe. He moved north, changed his name yet again, and melted into the Cuban community of Tampa.

That was over twenty years ago. Now he eyed his visitor. The fact Schaffer had tracked him down could only mean one thing. The map was back in play.

"How did you find me?" Ramon asked.

"My staff is skilled in all sorts of security activities." Schaffer motioned toward the window.

Ramon knew about the thriving high-tech security business. Ex-military and intelligence operatives working for corporations. Getting paid ten times as much. With unlimited resources, they could *buscar una aguja en un pajar.* Find a needle in a haystack. Anywhere on the planet.

He got up, went back to the window, and raised the shade. The two goons were still leaning against the limo. Fidel had been right. He'd predicted that corporations would run the world. In his more thoughtful moments, which seemed to come often these days, Ramon wondered if the pursuit of profit was more or less evil than a dictator's policies. He didn't know. Luis would have had an opinion. Funny, Ramon hadn't thought about Luis in years.

But his attention had wandered. He went back to his chair.

"A map of a mine in Angola has surfaced in Chicago," Schaffer was saying. "The satellite photos indicate it looks promising. But I am a cautious man. Especially since I've been disappointed in the past. I want to make sure it's the same map I've been looking for all these years. That's why I'm here. I understand you were the one who told us about it in the first place."

"It was a long time ago. I do not know where it is." Meanwhile, Ramon was furiously thinking. How had the map resurfaced? Who had it? He could only think of one family in Chicago. One family with the money and clout to pursue it. But aloud he said, "Why have you been looking for it? You are already a rich man."

Schaffer smiled. "I want to stay rich. And I have a feeling you'd like to be rich too, yes?" Before Ramon could answer, Schaffer added, "Theoretically, the map belongs to you. And the partner you sold out. Who is now dead." He paused. "You want your share of the proceeds, don't you? It will give you more money than you ever imagined."

Ramon blinked. He knew a con when he heard one.

But Schaffer must have taken Ramon's silence as tacit approval. His lips curved in a smile that failed to reach his eyes. "You and I have business to conduct. I need you to tell me who has the map."

Ramon needed time to think, but Schaffer wasn't giving it to him. If Tony Pacelli's family had the map, as he suspected, Ramon was screwed. The Pacellis would kill him as casually as they'd crush an ant. But what about this guy? With his two goons and high-tech security? Why didn't Schaffer already know where the map was?

There was only one reason. Ramon was the only other person on earth still alive who knew about the map. Which meant he was expendable. In fact, it was preferable that he be eliminated. That would make things nice and tidy.

As if Schaffer had read Ramon's mind, the man said, "I was hoping we could strike a deal. Your information in return for a sizeable—call it a finder's—fee."

Ramon's heart started to bang in his chest. The man wanted him dead. Would it be a clean shot? Or a slow, protracted death? If there was one thing Ramon knew he couldn't stand, it was torture. He had survived it twice. The third time would be his last. He weighed his options.

"So, do you want to take me up on my offer?" Schaffer turned toward the window and dipped his head. Out of the corner of his eye, Ramon saw the two bodyguards move leisurely toward the door. He was nothing more than a speck of black on a white surface. A speck of dirt to be wiped away and disposed of.

"Well?"

Ramon glanced through the window. The men were closing in.

Schaffer flipped up his palms. "It doesn't have to be like this, you know." He stood up and turned toward the door, as if he was going to open it for his bodyguards. Ramon pulled out his Marakov, racked the slide, and pointed it at Schaffer.

"Stop," Ramon said. "You're not going anywhere."

Schaffer spun around. When he saw the gun, his face registered surprise.

"Call off your goons," Ramon said. "And get your hands up."

Schaffer raised his arms.

One of the bodyguards reached for the handle on the screen door.

"Tell them!" Ramon barked.

"Boys…" Schaffer's voice was thin. "Back off. He's got a gun."

A stunned silence wafted in from outside. Even the chirr of insects went quiet.

Ramon flicked his eyes to the door. "Tell them to get the hell out of here."

"You heard him," Schaffer said.

Ramon couldn't see the men, but he heard scuffling at the door. They weren't leaving. In fact, they were probably planning an assault. Two against one. He had no chance.

He backed up, still aiming the gun at Schaffer. What Schaffer and his men didn't know was that there was a concealed garage door behind the *casita*. When developers built the place, they decided to experiment with a door that looked like two windows. When the homeowner pressed a button, the exterior wall with the windows quietly pivoted up to expose the garage. Which Ramon used for storage.

If the guards split up, one covering the front and the other the back, the one in back might miss the door and continue around the side of the house. And if Ramon could open the garage door quickly, he might be able to sprint across the lawn to the cover of the woods behind.

Ramon retreated down the hallway that led to the garage. Schaffer's arms were still in the air, but he didn't look scared. Ramon thought he saw a hint of a sneer.

"You're not going to make it, you know," Schaffer said. "My guys are good."

Ramon didn't answer. He was three steps from the door to the garage when one of the goons crashed through the front, clutching a pistol. Schaffer stepped aside. Ramon threw open the door and ducked out as the guard sprayed the hallway with a volley of bullets. Ramon pushed the button that raised the garage door.

The door seemed to take forever to rise. Ramon couldn't breathe. He heard a shout from inside, then the thump of heavy shoes pounding down the hall. *Jesu Cristo! Open, you mother-fucker!*

At last Ramon saw daylight and started to run. Immediately his back screamed at him. Was he hit? No. His arthritis. He almost slowed, then realized if he did, he would die. He forced himself to keep going. The trees were only about twenty yards away, but they seemed like a mile to the seventy-five year old man.

He was halfway across the yard when he heard a snick. The second bodyguard was racking his slide. A spray of bullets whizzed past him. Ramon wanted to twist around and return fire, but that would take time. Time he didn't have. He had to reach the woods. His legs were on fire—

again, he wondered if he had been hit—but the trees were only a few yards away. Shouts hammered out behind him. The goons were chasing him. He started wheezing and gasping for air, but he only needed a few more seconds. *Por favor, Dios!* He stumbled the last few yards and threw himself into the woods.

CHAPTER FORTY-NINE

Over the next few days, Frankie learned more than she wanted to know about coltan. Nicky arrived at the house one rainy April morning with Trevor and Ham in tow. They also brought with them, after doing a thorough background check, a mining engineer who had started his own company but used to work in the Congo. Somehow, between the four men, they'd snared recent satellite photos, mining reports, and other information that made the prospect of working the mine near Dundo, Angola, across the Congo border, look promising.

With Frankie at the meeting was her *consigliere*, a mild-mannered lawyer with snow white hair. He had advised her father for years, and Frankie kept him on. Her personal accountant was there, too, and while neither offered an opinion, they asked all the right questions. How much capital investment was required, what was the window of time, the potential return on her investment, the engineer's expectations and fees. Frankie knew her *consigliere* was figuring out how to launder the necessary funds for a legitimate project, while her accountant was thinking through the tax consequences. But they knew her well enough not to advise her or discuss it in front of strangers.

Nicky, though, was another matter. As an old friend and her former fiancé, he cautioned her to go slowly. She should first commission a study of the specific mine. Nicholas Financial recommended the engineer they'd brought, but if she had access to other sources she trusted, that was, of course, her decision. The engineer would evaluate the environment, the soil, and the water, and develop a plan and timetable. She could then commit or not to a preliminary exploration. If that proved fruitful, they could expand. Frankie nodded her agreement. Nicky concluded by saying that if it panned out, she would be one of the richest and most powerful women in the electronics industry.

She shifted in her chair, temptation washing over her. Frankie's goals had always been to expand the Pacelli Family businesses. Make them legitimate. To a large extent she had. She'd taken them out of restaurant management and supplies into real estate and construction. She had contemplated creating—or buying—a financial services firm and had been secretly eyeing Nicholas Financial. But mining was an opportunity she'd never considered. An opportunity that was simple, do-able, and tantalizing.

Still, if she'd learned anything over the years, it was to proceed with caution. She gazed at the engineer, Trevor, and Ham. "So far you've been telling me all the benefits of excavating. What are the downsides?"

The three men exchanged glances. Trevor cleared his throat. "You would be involving yourself in an industry fraught with politics, eco-terrorism, and armed militias who steal, torture, exploit and kill to get what they want. As soon as they learn there's a new player in the market, they will come after you. You need to prepare yourself. It could—" he hesitated— "prove fatal. These are not people you want to tangle with."

Frankie, seated behind the same oak desk in the same office that had belonged to her late husband, leaned her elbows on the surface. A small smile curved her lips. "Apart from that, however, the operation is legal?"

"Superficially, yes. But the means and methods your people will likely encounter are—"

Suddenly Trevor cut himself off, as if he'd remembered who his client was and the activities she condoned. He cleared his throat and sank back in his chair, all nervous decorum.

But Hamilton, the young man with them, watched her with interest. If she didn't know better, she thought he might have suppressed a smile.

Frankie studied him. Carla had told her Luisa was dating him and had made her displeasure known. Which, of course, made Frankie predisposed to like him. He looked like an earnest young man; blond, blue eyes, and handsome, like his grandfather used to be.

Frankie remembered the times she and Nicky had shared. He'd been terrific in the sack, and he'd been loving and respectful. She remembered when he gave her his fraternity pin, remembered their plans to spend their lives together. But then she had met Luis, and everything changed.

Now, though, because of Luis, their descendants had the chance to pick up where she and Nicky had left off. In a way, it was fitting. The circle would be complete. Perhaps, after she made her decision about the mine, she would plan a celebratory dinner party with Ham and Nicky, Luisa, and Carla.

And with that, Frankie realized she had decided to go ahead with the mine. Luis had discovered it, sketched it, marking it for further exploration. Their son had died trying to protect it. It was her duty to finish what they had started. Fate, or God, or the Santería priestesses she used to consult had given her the opening. It was up to her to make it happen.

This would be her tribute, her legacy to Luis and Michael. And how appropriate that Nicky, Ham, and Luisa would be part of it. After all, the mine would belong to Luisa one day. As Frankie's granddaughter and only heir, Luisa would inherit all the family businesses.

Frankie propped her chin on her hand, reflecting on the oddities of life. An avid socialist, Luis had discovered something that promised untold wealth. Their son, who had been raised with wealth, had risked it all to make certain the good guys won. Now his daughter, a young woman with lofty ideals, like Luis, would reap the benefits.

Frankie thought back to her own suffering: the spic who'd informed and torn her away from Luis; her forced marriage to a cold, distant creature; the tragic death of her son. Perhaps there had been a reason for it all. Frankie had survived. Become strong and powerful. Ensured that the family would persevere and flourish. Now, if the coltan mine produced, she would be richer and more powerful. No one could get in her way.

She flicked her gaze to Ham, then Nicky, then her legal and financial team. She was doing this for the Family. "Let's proceed."

***

Luisa was putting the finishing touches on a flan that night when Ham came into the kitchen and wrapped his arms around her from behind.

She yelped, jumped back, then sagged against him. "Don't do that!" she cried. "You scared me!"

He spun her around. She was breathing hard, her pulse racing, and her eyes held a mix of fear and anger. She pulled away, grabbed one of his hands and pressed it against her heart. "Feel it?"

When he felt how fast her heart was thumping, contrition washed over him. "I'm sorry. I thought—"

"No. You weren't thinking." She paused. "See, that's the problem with someone like me. We—I—don't take surprise well. It's been drilled into me since I was little. Routine. Order. Predictability. Anything that deviates from that is a red flag."

He nodded. She let him draw her close.

"You're probably wondering what kind of mess you got yourself into." She looked over. "It's not all fun and games, is it?"

"I don't regret a second. The last thing I want is to hurt you. Or scare you. Or make you uneasy. It will never happen again."

He kissed her. She closed her eyes, seeming to savor it. Then her eyes flew open, and a grin burst across her lips. "Gotcha!"

It was Ham's turn to be startled.

"I was giving you a load of b.s.," she laughed.

"About what?"

249

"I don't cook very often, so when I do I need to concentrate. I was so into it I wasn't expecting you or—"

"Are you kidding me? The rest of it was—made up?"

Her smile was full of impish glee. "I guess you don't know me as well as you think."

Ham stepped back. "Really? That's the way it's gonna be? You owe me, sister. Big time."

"Wait for the flan. It'll be ready soon."

"Well, then," Ham said. "I intend to make the best of the next couple of hours." He grabbed her arm. "Let's go."

"Where are you taking me?" Her voice rose in mock fright.

"To the woodshed. You need to be punished."

"I can't wait."

***

Afterwards they lay half-drowsy in each other's arms.

"I want to feel like this forever," Luisa whispered.

Ham's arms tightened around her. "You sure I don't have to worry about a jilted lover, crazy with jealousy, coming after me?"

"I told you. Jed goes with the flow. Whatever will be will be. He's kind of Zen that way. He'll have a new girlfriend in a week. Women find cowboys irresistible."

Ham arched his eyebrows.

"But not as irresistible as you." Luisa snuggled into the crook of his arm. She loved the way she felt with Ham. As if she could melt into him. With Jed she'd kept herself separate. As if her subconscious knew he was only a dalliance until she met the real thing. And Ham was the real thing.

"Is the flan ready?"

She giggled. "Thinking about your stomach already? Well, I have news for you. I'm not a great cook. Funny. Both Mom and Gran are. I guess the gene skipped me."

"Speaking of your grandmother, I met her this morning. We had a meeting in Barrington."

"I know."

"News travels fast."

"Always with the DeLucas."

"Well?"

She played with the hair on his chest. There was just enough for her to run her fingers through. Most of it was blond. "My grandmother thinks this is the best thing since sliced bread."

"What is?"

"You and me," Luisa said. "She said it was destiny. Fate. She used to date your grandfather when they were young, you know. They were pinned."

"What's that? A ritual involving blood-letting and leeches? Like Angelina Jolie and what's his name?"

She laughed. "Apparently back in the last century a guy would give a girl his fraternity pin. It meant they were more than going steady. Just this side of engaged."

"My grandfather never mentioned it."

"No reason to," Luisa said. "But now, Gran wants to have a dinner party. You me, your grandfather, her. To celebrate the circle of life. Of course, my mother isn't so happy about it."

"Your mother doesn't like me?"

"She doesn't like anyone I go out with."

"Then my mission in life will be to make her happy."

"No. Your mission in life is to make me happy." She kissed his chest.

"In that case, I guess we'd better get started." He pulled her on top of him.

***

They were nodding off when the doorbell rang. Ham groaned and covered his head with a pillow. Luisa checked the clock. A little after midnight. Not that late.

"Ham, aren't you going to get the door?"

"It's probably my neighbor. He gets high, then goes out and forgets his key. I have an extra." Ham got out of bed and threw on a pair of sweatpants.

"It could be my security guard. She has orders to be in the hallway outside the apartment, not in the car, when I'm—um—sleeping out."

The doorbell chimed again.

"Just a minute, dammit," Ham called and trudged toward the front door. On his way he closed the door to the bedroom.

Luisa pulled up the sheets and spread out on the mattress. His side of the bed was still warm.

A moment later she heard a scuffle followed by sounds of a struggle. Then a soft thud and a muffled cry. Luisa shot out of bed. She grabbed Ham's t-shirt and threw it over her naked body. Adrenaline surged through her. She wanted to run into the living room to see what was going on. But years of training—learned from her mother and Gran—kicked in.

The truth was she hadn't lied to Ham earlier. She'd been taught to be wary of any unexpected sound or movement. It usually meant trouble. If she ever confronted it, she'd been taught, she should make herself as small a target as possible. Hide. Run. Whatever was necessary.

Now heavy footsteps clomped across the marble floor. Not Ham's tread. Luisa grabbed the quilt off the bed. She thought about her training. She should hurry into the bathroom and lock the door behind her. They were coming for her. Which meant her security guard was either gone or dead. No help there.

She thought she remembered a window high on the bathroom wall that she could probably squeeze through. She had no idea if there was a window ledge or exterior support, and Ham's apartment was on the fifth floor. Climbing out might kill her as fast as staying put. But it was her only chance.

Then she changed her mind. Ham was out there by himself. She couldn't leave him alone. She would be the worst kind of coward. It was that simple. If she surrendered to the thugs who were out there, maybe they'd spare Ham.

Someone jiggled the bedroom doorknob. "I'm coming," Luisa said, trying to keep her voice calm. "I'm putting on some clothes."

The jiggling stopped, but she knew it was only for an instant. Whoever was out there would guess she was scrabbling for a weapon. She was right. Seconds later, the door banged open and two men lunged for her.

She gasped but didn't scream. "I know you want me. I'll go with you. But please, don't hurt him."

A grunt from the man closest to her was her only response.

He grabbed her and pinned her arms behind her back. The other lashed them together, threw something over her head that made it hard to breathe. They dragged her out of the bedroom.

She heard a moan from someplace in the living room.

"Ham. Are you all right? Sweetheart?" Her voice sounded muffled.

Another moan. A queasy feeling shot through her. She wanted to collapse, break down, comfort him. But she couldn't. "Please," she pleaded out loud. "You've got what you came for. Don't hurt him."

Another grunt in response. As they hauled her across the marble floor, a sharp crack arced through the room. Ham's groans suddenly stopped. Luisa screamed. Something stung her arm. For an instant she felt cold and dizzy. Then she went limp, and everything went black.

CHAPTER FIFTY

Carla wasn't especially worried when Luisa didn't answer her cell. There were times her daughter deliberately refused to pick up. It was her little rebellion. Sometimes the urge to be unknown, just another anonymous soul, was overpowering. Carla could relate.

She didn't worry when Luisa failed to come home that night. She knew Luisa was annoyed that Carla hadn't warmed to Ham and was expressing her displeasure. So Carla called Luisa's bodyguard instead. The woman, stationed discreetly down the hall from Ham's condo, affirmed that Luisa was inside and had given no indication she'd be leaving. Carla double-checked what time the guard went off duty. She would be there until 2:00 AM, Marta said, at which time the overnight guard would relieve her.

The guards never called unless there was a problem, or Luisa's schedule changed, and they thought Carla should know. Still, Carla checked in daily, particularly when she hadn't heard from Luisa. This wasn't the way she'd expected to live her life, and, like her daughter, she occasionally resented it. It was another way Francesca DeLuca controlled her. But, over time, it had become routine.

Yet Carla couldn't help but wonder what their lives would have been like if she hadn't come to Chicago so many years ago. If she could have found a way to make it work in Miami. She indulged herself in flashes of—not regret—but fanciful thinking. She wouldn't have become a doctor, but she might have stayed at the pharmacy. Perhaps one day, she might have been able to buy it from the old man. She would have scrimped and saved, but she'd done that her entire life. She and Luisa would have led a modest, respectable life. Not this life, of course. The luxuries and opportunities Francesca lavished on them were way beyond anything Carla could have provided.

Still.

She forced herself to stop thinking about what might have been. *Ni modo, así es la vida.* Life was what it was, and tonight, thankfully, nothing was amiss. She made herself a cup of herbal tea, watched the news, then read for a while. As she turned out the light, she had to admit, albeit reluctantly, that Francesca's vigilance was generally a blessing for a single mother with a willful daughter.

She was dreaming about performing an operation on a child except that she wasn't a surgeon when her phone trilled. She came abruptly awake and checked the time. One AM. Her stomach turned over. She picked up.

It was a man's voice, muffled and abrasive. "We have your daughter. If you want her back alive, listen carefully. There is a map…"

***

Francesca sent a car, and less than an hour later, Carla was on her way to Barrington. Sharply etched clouds illuminated by a pale wash of moonlight scudded across the night sky. They had twenty-four hours to surrender the map, the man said, and they should expect a call tomorrow afternoon to set up the exchange. He didn't have to add the inevitable "Or else."

When the driver turned into Francesca's semi-circular gravel driveway, every light in the Barrington home shone, as if daring the darkness to retreat. But Carla took no comfort in it. For her, time and space, light and dark would have no meaning until Luisa was safe.

Inside, she collapsed in a chair in Francesca's study. She was in a pair of sweats, and her hair, short and spiky, flew out in all directions. Francesca, sitting behind her desk, wasn't much better. Wearing a dark robe, her hair down, her mother-in-law was a ghostly specter, Kabuki-like with her wan, pale face. She was on the phone non-stop, as if gathering information and issuing orders might give her control over the situation. But Carla knew the frenetic activity was a ruse. Neither of them had any control.

Between calls, Francesca supervised the arrivals and departures of her men. She'd dispatched two soldiers to Evanston, where they'd found the body of the security guard. But when they broke down the door and found Ham, they discovered he was still breathing. Francesca called the paramedics and Nicky, who immediately started down to Northwestern Memorial. Meanwhile, her *consigliere* and *sotto capo* were on their way to Barrington. "So are my group captains. We'll figure out our plan of attack."

Plan of attack? Had Francesca lost her sanity? They had no idea who'd kidnapped Luisa or where she was. Swinging between fury and panic, Carla felt both chilled and feverish. She hated the woman sitting across from her. But she feared her, too. On a good day, she could disengage enough to see her mother-in-law's good points. But this was not a good day. This woman had almost killed a young man her daughter cared for, and Carla had the uneasy feeling that the killing was just beginning.

"What did you do?" she spat out.

Francesca looked up from the phone.

Carla motioned her to hang up. When she did, Carla repeated very slowly, "What—did—you—do?"

Something on Carla's face must have registered with Francesca, because she hesitated before answering. Then she drew herself up, as if she could not allow any challenge to her authority, especially from the mother of her son's child. "You think *I* caused this?"

There was no time for prevarication. "My daughter has been kidnapped. Her boyfriend is lying in a pool of blood. I want to know what you did to bring this on."

Francesca's stare tore into Carla. When she finally replied, her voice was ice. "When this is resolved—and it will be—you and I will have a conversation." She paused. "A conversation we should have had twenty years ago."

But Carla had had enough. "No. This time you are wrong. I want my daughter. Call the police."

Francesca sat back in her chair. "No police. We will handle this."

Carla rose angrily. "Then I will call. This is *my* daughter. *Mi vida.* Not some—some territorial dispute between mobsters." She started to storm out, but from the corner of her eye, she saw Francesca nod at a bodyguard outside the study. He blocked the door.

Carla whirled around and faced her. She wanted to tear Francesca apart. Instead she glared, her body rigid with fury.

Francesca flinched. It was a slight movement, and very subtle, but Carla knew for an instant that Francesca had let down her guard. And in that instant Carla knew her mother-in-law was as frightened as she. Ironically, that knowledge triggered no empathy. In fact, it scared Carla more. If the head of one of the most powerful Outfit Families was cowed by fear, what hope was there for her daughter?

Events intervened before their conflict escalated. Francesca's *consigliere* arrived, looking sleepy and disheveled. The cook prepared food, and a maid brought in a tray of freshly baked croissants, sandwiches, and a pot of coffee.

Francesca asked Carla to go into the living room and made sure a security guard stayed with her. Carla curled up helplessly on the black leather sofa. Though the door to Francesca's study was closed, Carla heard the trills of the phone and the low murmur of conversation.

The activity inside the Barrington enclave sped up. Several burly men arrived and went into the study. Carla knew they were waiting for orders from Francesca. Her throat tightened. All she wanted was her daughter, but she was increasingly afraid that wasn't going to happen. Francesca DeLuca would turn it into a battle royal between herself and her enemies. Like her father before her. And his father before him. Luisa would end up as collateral damage. Carla wanted to be wrong, but nothing about the situation inspired confidence. Her earlier composure evaporated, and her stomach roiled. She ran to the bathroom and threw up.

***

Frankie was all nervous energy and motion, as if to slow down or stop was to admit defeat. When Nick called, she flew out of her chair, grabbed the phone, and started to pace.

"Thank you for calling. I am so sorry, Nicky. Had I known this would happen, I would never have involved you. This is a—" She cut herself off. "But we'll make it right. I promise. I already have—"

"His mother, my daughter, is—well, you can imagine…" His voice cracked. "He's in surgery. They don't know if he's going to make it."

Francesca bit her lip. She hadn't asked how Ham was. She tried to cover her blunder. "Nicky. I know the doctors are doing everything they can. And you can rest assured that I will too. I am going to get to the bottom of this. We will prevail. Ham's—injuries—will not go unavenged."

Nick kept his mouth shut.

Francesca leaned against the front of her desk. "I know you're thinking you should never have gotten involved in this. But there was no way to predict this would happen. And as I said, we will—"

Nick cut her off. "If anything happens to Ham, I will never forgive myself."

"Nicky, you can't think like that. You didn't do anything wrong."

He was quiet for a moment. Then, "You really don't get it, do you?"

"I get that these are terrible people who will stop at nothing to get what they want."

Nick didn't answer.

Taking his silence as acquiescence, she blathered on. "Attempted murder? Kidnapping? All for a shitty little mine in the asshole of the world? Not a chance."

"Who, Frankie? Who's behind this?"

"Well, actually, that's where I might need your help. To be honest, at first we thought it might be our own people. Or the other Families. Or the government. Someone tapping the phone, bugging our meeting. But…" She cleared her throat. "After we… uh… investigated…" she hesitated "…we're confident it's not. Our people are actually pretty satisfied since the Family reorganized."

"Investigation?" Nick asked. "You mean a police investigation, right? You called them, didn't you?"

It was Frankie's turn to keep her mouth shut.

"Well, don't worry about it. I will."

"Why, Nicky? I can handle it—"

He cut her off. "Frankie, like you said, this is a kidnapping. And attempted murder. You can't cover it up. "

"I don't intend to. I want whoever did this to burn in hell. But I must insist that you not call the police. I need to figure out who's behind this. I want to deal with them myself," she said. "And I don't have much time." She went back to her chair and sat. "OK. Here's where I'm at, Nick. My people are clean. Which leads me to think your side leaked it."

Nick's voice went hard. He was getting riled up. Good, Frankie thought. Anger could be an excellent motivator.

"You know me better than that," he spat out. "No one at my firm would go behind my back."

"Nick, I believe you," she said. "I'm sure your people are loyal. But it might not be an employee. It might be someone your people talked to. Someone who knew something, put two and two together, and passed it on."

"I don't care who it was, Frankie. Let the police handle it. I can't leave the hospital anyway."

"Nick. Help us find out who your people talked to and what they said. Before the police get involved. Please. Just this once."

Despite the word "please" and the tone of her voice, Frankie could tell he knew this was not a request.

He sighed heavily.

"It's as much in your family's interest as ours," she added, trying to soften the order. "I know you want to find out who attacked Ham. Make sure he—they—pay. The police won't do that. But I will. You know that."

Nick started to say something, but apparently thought better of it. Was he going to attack her? Tell her what he really thought of her? Frankie wondered if he was mentally thanking God he had never married her.

But all he said was, "All right. I'll make a few calls."

CHAPTER FIFTY-ONE

Tom Corcoran slept in that morning. Yesterday had been abnormally warm for spring in Toronto, and the forecast today was for another. Because it had been such a brutal winter, he and three colleagues at the bank decided to play eighteen holes instead of going to the office.

Tom couldn't wait to get back on the greens. He'd planned a golf trip to Bermuda last January, but he'd broken up with the woman he was planning to take, so he hadn't been on the links since October. The first outing of the season was always special, even if the ground was still brown and bleak.

He smiled as he shaved, then put on his golf shirt, dockers, and windbreaker. He gulped down coffee, and grabbed his wallet. His gear was stowed in his locker at the club; he would buy a box of balls and tees at the pro shop.

He was rinsing his coffee mug in the sink when his doorbell chimed. Reflexively, he checked his watch. Barely nine. Probably the Korean dry cleaners delivering his shirts. Or the man on the desk downstairs with a package that wouldn't fit in his mailbox. He threw the door open, about to offer a genial good morning, when two burly men rushed in. One, wearing a peacoat, grabbed him, while the other, in a down jacket, pinned his arms behind him.

"Hey!" he cried. "What the fuck—Stop! You're hurting me!"

Peacoat closed the door to the apartment. The man in the down jacket tightened his grip.

"Who—What is this?"

"Shut the fuck up," Peacoat muttered.

Tom winced and tried to squirm out of DownJacket's grasp, but the goon had at least fifty pounds on him. Then he started to twist Tom's arms in a way no arms should ever be. Agonizing pain shot through Tom. "Okay, okay," he gasped. "Stop! I'll give you my money. I have a wall safe. Just—

stop."

Peacoat moved in close and watched Tom writhe. His expression was detached, even bored.

"Please—make him stop." Tears welled in Tom's eyes. "You're killing me."

Peacoat arched his eyebrows, his face still wearing the same dispassionate expression. Then he nodded at DownJacket. Tom felt the pressure on his arms ease. He sucked in air.

"Does that mean you're ready to talk?"

Tom blinked. "Who are you?" His voice was ragged. "What do you want?"

Peacoat seemed to consider the question. A tiny smile curled his lips. "We're—investigators."

Tom stared at the man, uncomprehending. "What—what the fuck does that mean?"

Peacoat smashed his fist into Tom's face. The pain exploded. He heard his nose crack. Blood filled his mouth and spurted out his nostrils. A tooth came loose. He screamed and sagged against DownJacket. Peacoat's face was only inches from his. Tom smelled sour coffee breath.

He coughed up blood. The tooth came with it. "Oh, Christ…" He was almost crying.

"Tell us all about your conversation with Hamilton Snower."

Tom's brain was fuzzy with pain. He couldn't think.

DownJacket tightened Tom's arms behind him. Tom whimpered. "All right. All right. Lemme think."

"I'll make it easy for you," Peacoat hissed. "Snower's an analyst from Chicago. Nicholas Financial. He called a few days ago to ask you about coltan."

It came to him slowly, like a train rolling leisurely over the tracks, and despite his misery, Tom made the connection. Coltan. Schaffer. Something about a map. He'd called Schaffer after the conversation. What the hell had Schaffer done? Tom tried to think it through, but the pain made all but the most basic thoughts impossible. Still, something told him not to admit what he knew. "I don't know what you're talking about."

"Then let me remind you." Peacoat nodded to his partner who gripped Tom. Peacoat slammed a fist into Tom's midsection.

Tom folded like an accordion. He would have collapsed if DownJacket hadn't been holding him upright. Excruciating pain crowded out any thoughts.

"You ready now?"

Tom grunted.

"Good." Peacoat nodded and looked around the living room. His gaze lit on a sliding patio door. "Since it's such a nice morning, why don't we go out on your balcony?" He didn't wait for an answer. "Take him out," he told DownJacket and slid open the door.

It was a small balcony, just big enough for two loungers and a grill. A couple of flowerboxes hung over the railings, but they were bare, filled with hard, cold dirt. The men pushed and dragged Tom outside. Peacoat sat on a recliner and motioned for DownJacket to drop Tom on the other.

Tom groaned at the movement, twisting back and forth until he found a position that didn't make him want to lie prone on the cement.

"So, let me give you some news about the man you spoke to," Peacoat said. "He's in critical condition. Someone shot him late last night."

Tom stiffened in shock. But along with the shock came something worse. A premonition. "What—what happened?"

"We think you told someone about your conversation and we want to know who."

Tom had enough presence to understand if he admitted calling Schaffer after he talked to the analyst, the shit he was wading in would get a lot deeper. He tried to recall his conversation with Snower. The kid was from Chicago. Tom had told Schaffer that. Again he wondered what Schaffer had done—or arranged—that aroused the wrath of the Outfit. Because that's who these people had to be. He blinked his eyes shut.

How could the Outfit be working with this guy Snower? Thugs were supposed to keep to thuggish business. Not insinuate themselves into legitimate concerns. Although no one would ever argue that mining in Africa was legitimate. Dirt begot dirt. And corruption. No matter where you were. Tom's thoughts were cut short by Peacoat.

"Well?"

Tom tried to shake his head, but it wouldn't move.

DownJacket cleared his throat.

"It will go easier if you tell us now. You know you're going to eventually."

Tom tried to figure out what to say to the mobsters. Before he could, though, they pulled him off the recliner and leaned him against the porch railing. Tom felt as flimsy as a ragdoll. His muscles were loose and rubbery. This was silly. He should be able to stand up. At least lean against the railing. He almost laughed.

Peacoat raised his eyebrows again. "Glad you're finding this funny, Corcoran. Look, I know you want us to leave. And we will. All we want is the name of the person you called after you talked to Ham Snower. How tough is that?"

The men began to close in on him again. This time he was able to shake his head. He tried to speak but all that came out was a squeak. Then he felt the railing sway. People didn't realize that winters in Toronto were warmer than Chicago. Even so, mountains of snow and frigid temperatures had put the words "climate change" on everyone's lips, and a sudden warming, after a solid freeze of three months, wreaked havoc on wood and metal. That's what Tom's porch railing was made from.

He tried to straighten up. The railing swayed again. He ignored it. "Look, guys," his voice sounded almost normal, he thought. "I don't know what you want."

"I'm losing patience, Corcoran," Peacoat said. "How much plainer can I make it?"

"How do you know it's me? Your people in Chicago talked to a lot of other people, too. Snower said so."

Tom realized his mistake as soon as he said it.

"So you did talk to him." Peacoat's chin jutted out. "Okay. We're making progress. Now tell us who you called afterwards."

Schaffer was Tom's only respectable client. He'd been lucky to land him. To be honest, Tom knew he was only average. Maybe a bit of a douchebag. He'd never had much talent. But he couldn't tell these guys. They'd go after Schaffer, and it would only take a second for Schaffer to figure out who'd led them to him. If he lost Schaffer, he was done.

He shook his head.

That must have been the final signal, because the men flanked him on both sides. Then they lifted him up by his hips and tilted him up and over the railing. His head hung below his feet, anchored by nothing. They held him by his torso. Air was all around him. Blood rushed to his head, making him dizzy. For some reason, he smelled fresh earth. But he was eighteen floors above ground. Where the hell was that coming from?

"Wait, wait!" he shouted. He started to panic.

The men's response was to tilt him farther over the railing.

Now he could see the sidewalk below. The cars looked tiny, but morning sunlight glinted off their bumpers and shot up eighteen stories. He had to squeeze his eyes shut. Maybe this was a nightmare. When he opened them again, he was still in mid-air.

"Okay, okay." Tom was hyperventilating now. "I'll tell you."

"That's better," Peacoat said.

He nodded to DownJacket and they tightened their grip on Tom and started to pull him back onto the porch. As they did, though, a loud crack exploded from the balcony railing. It splintered and collapsed. The men's grip on him came loose and Tom began to fall.

"Oh Jesus. Help me!" he yelled.

They tried to grab him, but everything happened too fast. Tom's body, already halfway over the railing, slipped out of their reach. DownJacket lost his balance and staggered backwards. Peacoat tried to grab Tom—at least afterwards he swore that he did—but it was too late. They heard his terrified shriek as he fell.

CHAPTER FIFTY-TWO

"So you never got a name?" Burning with rage, Frankie felt her vocal cords go tight. This had been her one chance to find out who was behind the kidnapping, and her men had screwed up. She slammed down the phone.

It was ten past noon in Chicago, twelve hours since Luisa had been snatched, twelve to go until the deadline. She propped her elbows on her desk and covered her forehead with her hand. Her head felt like it was caught in a steel vise.

She forced herself to take stock. They wouldn't kill Luisa before they got the map—that was a no-brainer. And Frankie might have to surrender it to them. But they had to realize she would make a copy before she handed it over. So what was the point? Unless she was wrong. Maybe it *was* a rival Family flexing their muscles. Or another organization racing to mine the land. Whatever the case, if she was forced to surrender the map, this wouldn't be the last battle. A lot could happen after Luisa was safe.

Still, this was her granddaughter. And now it was personal. What's more, if they'd been searching for the map for decades, as she now suspected, they had to be behind the murders of Luis and Michael. Which made it more personal. Who were they? Did they know who *she* was? She tried to imagine what her father would have done. He would have gone full bore attack, assuming his enemies were Mob. But what if they weren't? Would he be that aggressive? Would he save Luisa at any cost?

Frankie wondered if her enemy thought that because she was a woman, she would capitulate. If they did, they'd made a serious mistake. Frankie had watched her father before her. Male or female, as the head of a powerful Mob family, she knew the consequences of war, and she was on intimate terms with death. She would go after them with everything she had. If they thought she would break, they had the wrong woman.

But first she had to find out who *they* were. The most frightening part of any battle was the unknown. Once you knew your enemy, could put a name or a face to them, you could formulate a strategy. Implement a plan.

Clearly, something or someone had tipped them off to the re-emergence of the map—probably the moron in Toronto. But he was dead, which meant they would have to show themselves. And when they did, she would regain the upper hand. She would regroup, bide her time, retaliate. They would get what was coming to them.

Buoyed by her thoughts, she pulled herself together and emerged from her office. Carla was curled up on the leather couch, this side of catatonic. Frankie's *soldati*, unsure where to go or what to do, milled around. Gino, her *sotto capo*, was on his cell. She sat down on the other end of the sofa. In a quiet voice, she said, "We're going to have to get the map. The original. Not a copy. It's at the bank."

Carla roused herself, and for the first time since the kidnapping, looked alert. She nodded.

"Well then," Frankie said. "Let's go."

***

Frankie and Carla returned to the Barrington estate with the map around three. The kidnappers were due to call at six. En route Frankie asked Carla about Luis and Michael's death: exactly what happened and how they were murdered in Cuba. After hearing the story, Frankie was more convinced that the people who kidnapped Luisa were the same people. She was about to tell her crew, so she could prime them for tonight, when one of the guards called from the front gate.

Gino picked up the phone, then called across the room. "Mrs. DeLuca, there's a man at the gate who says he needs to see you."

Frankie arched her eyebrows. She wasn't expecting contact from the other side for two more hours. She crossed the room and took the phone. "Who is it?"

The guard said, "He says his name is Ramon Suarez."

Frankie scowled. "I don't know anyone by that name."

She heard a murmured conversation in the background.

"He says you knew him in Havana."

Frankie thought. Then she sucked in air. Ramon. The waiter who informed on her. Who tore her away from Luis. She felt her eyes narrow. "What does he want?"

"He says he has important information."

She snorted. "What information could he have?"

Another murmured conversation. Then, "He says he knows about the map. And who is looking for it."

She thought about it. After a pause, she said, "You searched him?"

"Yes, ma'am. He's clean."

***

The man who entered the house had skin as brown and withered as a dead leaf, Carla thought. He was using crutches, and his right thigh was heavily bandaged. He'd had an accident, and it was still causing him pain; she saw it in his eyes. Francesca, on the other hand, appraised him coolly.

"Hallo, Miss Pacelli." He spoke English with a thick accent. It was an accent Carla recognized. He was Cuban.

"What are you doing here?" Francesca said.

"I come to warn you."

"About what?"

He inclined his head. "The map."

"What do you know about it?"

He looked around as if he was afraid to go on with so many people—and guns—in the room.

But Francesca had no patience. "I didn't think so." She spun around. "Gino, I need—"

"Wait!" Carla threw her hand up in the air. "Don't." She started to talk rapidly in Spanish. His face lit when he realized she was talking a language he understood. "What happened to you? Why are you here?"

He answered in equally rapid Spanish.

Carla nodded and asked more questions. He answered, but in the middle of one of his responses, Francesca cut in. "My Spanish is rusty. What is he saying?"

Carla turned to her. "He says he knows you hate him. That you blame him for everything."

More words poured out from him, as if they'd been bottled up for years. Maybe they had, Carla thought. "He says he could not stand up to the torture your father inflicted. That he was—he is—not a strong man."

Francesca stared at Ramon as if he was a creature who'd crawled out of the sewer.

"He says the same man who killed Luis came after him in Florida a few days ago. They shot him in the leg when he tried to escape."

"What man? Why were they after you?" Francesca said in English.

Ramon switched back to English. "Because I was the one who tell Luis to draw map."

Francesca's mouth dropped open. "You were with Luis? In Angola?"

"He forgive me when he hear what your father do during the revolution," he said. "But there was—another problem."

Francesca threw up her hands. "I'm in the middle of a crisis. I have no time for this." She started to turn away. Gino and another *soldati* closed in.

But Ramon stood his ground. He clearly wanted to tell the story. "In Angola, I believe Luis—how you say—leave me to die in the jungle. The rebels get me, and…" His voice trailed off.

Carla broke in. "They tortured you… again?"

Ramon nodded. "But CIA rescue me. Bring me to U.S., give me money. In return I give information. I tell my contact about the map. He leave agency." He hesitated. "Then I feel bad about what I do. It—how do you say?"

"It haunted you? You felt guilty?" Carla asked.

"*Sí.* Yes. When I hear you come to Miami, and that Michael is dead," he tapped an index finger against his temple, "I know who kill him and why. I find out where you work and go there. To warn you."

Carla reeled back. "You were the one who came to the pharmacy?"

He nodded again.

Blood rushed to her head. Carla felt light-headed. Ramon's visit was what prompted her escape from Miami. She'd thought *he* was the enemy. But if they had met, and she had listened to his story, perhaps she would never have left. Would never have come to Chicago. Or met Francesca. And Luisa would never have been kidnapped. Carla felt like screaming and crying at the same time.

Francesca stepped forward. "You are wasting my time, Suarez. You have exactly ten seconds to tell me who wants the map."

"You do not know?"

Francesca threw a glance towards Gino and the other *soldati*. They started to approach.

Ramon raised his hand. "Ees okay. His name is David Schaffer. He make *electronica*."

"A businessman kidnapped my daughter? A goddammed businessman?" Carla sputtered.

Francesca's cheeks flamed red, and she fisted her hands. Clearly she hadn't wanted Carla to reveal the kidnapping.

Ramon looked shocked. "The little girl?" He gestured to Carla. "Your daughter? They take her?"

Carla nodded, but Francesca answered, apparently deciding to admit the truth. "They shot her boyfriend and kidnapped her. They will kill her unless we give them the map."

"I will help," Ramon said.

Francesca went rigid. "I will never let you get close to my family. Not after the way you made me suffer."

"We have all suffered."

"You turned on us." Francesca drew herself up. "You were a traitor."

But Ramon didn't move. "If I not 'turn' as you say, you would not be same person you are now."

Francesca was speechless, the cords in her neck stretched tight. No one talked to her that way, Carla thought.

"You would still be in Cuba," Ramon went on. "*La esposa* of honored revolutionary. You would have big family. Lots of children *y* grandchildren. Love and happy."

Francesca went still. So did the people around her. The air, too. It seemed to Carla as if time had stopped. And in that instant, Carla realized exactly who Francesca DeLuca was: a pathetic old woman who'd been forbidden to love, and then lost her son, the only tangible product of that forbidden love.

Suddenly Carla pitied her mother-in-law. At least she had had Michael, albeit briefly. And Luisa was still alive. For now. She stole a glance at Francesca. Her mother-in-law's face had gone haggard. As if she finally understood how far she had strayed from her youthful plans. For the first time she looked her age.

Ramon broke the silence. "I want to make right, Miss Pacelli. I want to give them map. Get girl back."

Carla interrupted. "No. They tried to kill you in Florida. They will finish the job here."

Ramon spread his hands. "I do not want the map. Or what comes with it. This is my way to—clean the past."

Francesca didn't reply.

But Carla did. She desperately wanted Luisa back, but there had to be limits. She couldn't send anyone to a certain death. "What if they don't release Luisa? After you give them the map?"

"I have lived my life." Ramon gave her a weak smile, one that reflected an awareness, even a slight embarrassment, at the smallness of his life and how little it mattered. "And if that happens, Miss Pacelli come after them." He turned to Francesca. "*Sí?*"

Francesca stood there.

Carla was uncertain. Her longing to have Luisa back warred with her conviction that Ramon would die. She looked at her mother-in-law.

"Look." Ramon faced Francesca. "They probably already think we partners. They know you have map. Let me do this." He paused. "This is my way to pay back."

CHAPTER FIFTY-THREE

The call came in on Frankie's private line promptly at six, but Frankie moved into action before then, dispatching her people to gather every scrap of intel they could on David Schaffer. She waited in her office, adrenaline fueling her. She was doing something. Engaged. Back in control.

Her *consigliere* reported back first with a D&B on the company, a rundown of Schaffer's personal finances, and a criminal background check, which turned up nothing on the man, not even a speeding ticket. Her lawyers followed with a detailed C.V. Nick's people filled in the blanks with a list of Schaffer's clients as well as an analysis of his relationship with Macedonian Metals. Slowly the pieces began to fit together: how Schaffer had built his company from the ground up; how he nearly lost it when the price of coltan skyrocketed; how he downsized to survive.

Frankie's people even ferreted out the name of the man who had come to work for him from the Agency—the friend of Walters who dealt with Ramon in Angola. The clincher came when one of Frankie's men called Schaffer's house on Beacon Hill, claiming he had to contact him ASAP. His wife told them he was on a quick business trip to Chicago. After the call, Frankie told Gino to call his counterpart in one of the Boston Families and ask him to pay a visit to David Schaffer's wife. Ten minutes later Gino reported that two men were on their way.

So Frankie was prepared when the call came. They'd discussed tracing it, but they knew it would be futile. He would cloak the call through some impenetrable internet labyrinth. He'd also make sure to keep it under a minute so they couldn't triangulate his location.

The voice, probably one of his goons, sounded metallic, altered in some way. Frankie was told to meet them at O'Hare's long-term Parking Lot E at midnight opposite the entrance. She or her deputy should arrive in one car, and only two people inside. It went without saying, the voice added, that no weapons were permitted. Any deviation would scuttle the deal.

The location made Frankie think Schaffer and his people were holed up at one of the hotels near the airport. While she was still on the phone, she motioned Gino into her office.

"What's my guarantee you will give back Luisa?" she asked into the phone.

"She'll be in the car. A clean exchange. The map for the girl." A pause. "But there is one other condition." The voice continued as if reading a script. "After you hand over the map, if we find out you're going after the mine in any way, shape, or form, we will come after you again. And next time we won't be as reasonable."

The call was disconnected.

Frankie looked at the clock. They still had several hours. Gino stood at attention. She hung up and repeated what the voice said.

"O'Hare Long Term Parking? Are you shitting me?" When Frankie didn't answer, Gino blew out a scornful breath. "Fucking amateurs!"

Frankie shrugged, as if to say 'what are you going to do?' Then, "You need to get the word out to the hotels around O'Hare. There aren't that many, and we have connections at almost all of them. Use as many men as you need. We're looking for a man named David Schaffer. He's probably registered under an alias, and he will have paid cash. And he probably has more than one room. He flew here from Boston, if that helps."

Gino scowled. "We can't canvass them all by midnight. There are too many. If we could have narrowed it down, traced the call, it might have been easier."

Frankie's eyes flashed. She and Gino were getting along. Barely. She knew he was still measuring, wondering if a woman was up to the job. But she had promised her father to keep him on. At least for a while. She ignored his objections.

"Like I said, use as many people as you need. Including the other Families, if you have to. We'll settle up later." She paused. "Now, about tonight. He'll be well protected. Probably by paramilitary types. Mercenaries. Maybe ex-Agency men. You need to be prepared."

"Do they know who we are?"

"If they didn't before, they do now. They called me."

The man's eyebrows arched. "How did they find you?"

Frankie thought about it. "That's none of your concern," she said icily. But she *was* curious how they discovered who she was and how she had the map. Later.

"Guy's got to have steel balls to think he can take us on," Gino said.

"That's why you're going to put together a second team. Choose your best men. Position both teams at the hotel by ten." She explained that Schaffer probably would still be at the hotel, and there was an excellent chance they could grab him—and Luisa—before midnight. One team would take Luisa, the other would deal with Schaffer.

"What if they're not there?" Gino said.

"Then you'll find out where they are. Or, if necessary, you'll meet them at O'Hare. I'm not worried, Gino. I have faith in you," she said. She didn't have to spell out the consequences if he failed.

"When do we let him know we have his wife?"

Frankie considered it. "Up to you. But make sure she calls and tells him she's got 'company.'"

Gino nodded.

"Oh," Frankie said, "there's one more thing."

When she finished explaining, her *capo* looked at her with something close to admiration. She even thought she caught the glimmer of a smile. Steel balls indeed.

***

Two hours later, a bellhop at the Intercontinental in Rosemont confirmed to one of Frankie's men that two rooms in the hotel were occupied by a John Smith and a Davy Jones. When asked if a woman was with either man, the bellhop admitted he hadn't seen anyone; then again, it was always possible to sneak in from the parking lot or side door. He also told Frankie's men they hadn't put a credit card on file, but when he described the men and reported how much the front desk man had been tipped, Frankie's guy called it in.

Frankie smiled for the first time in twenty-four hours. She hung up the phone and went into the living room where Carla, Ramon, and a few men waited, including Gino.

"We're in business," she said. "It's time to move." She explained what they'd learned, then looked around. "I don't know about you, but I'm going to take a long bath, and then have dinner. You are all welcome to eat."

Ramon, who had been seated next to Carla on the leather sofa, stood. "I want go with team."

Carla blocked him with her arm. "No."

A twinge of anger twisted Frankie's lips. How dare Carla insinuate herself into Frankie's business again? The first time—well, she was prepared to let it go. She wasn't a monster. She understood how everyone, including Carla, was on edge. But now? Frankie felt her eyes narrow. She was about to reassert her dominance, then remembered Carla wanted Luisa back as desperately as Frankie. She made a mental note to deal with her later. She turned to Ramon. "There's no need."

"Why?" Ramon asked.

"Because there will be no exchange."

Carla's face reflected astonishment. "Why? What are you saying, Francesca?"

Frankie explained she would send two teams to the hotel. "If we have to surrender the map temporarily, for Luisa's sake, once she's safe and on her way home, we will get it back. There will be no one of any rank on the other side to accept it anyway."

Carla's mouth tightened into a grim line.

"All the more reason I go," Ramon said. "I want to make sure."

Carla looked like she might argue, but Frankie studied Ramon. The truth was that he had no importance in her life now. He was merely an annoying gnat she could swat away. Or not. She looked back at Carla, whose expression was both anxious and determined. Finally she waved her hand. "If it is that important to you, go." She glanced around. "The rest of us will regroup in forty-five minutes for supper."

***

While the men and Ramon prepared for their mission, Carla peered out the front window. It was dark, and a light, silent snow began to fall. It was barely more than a mist, but spring in Chicago was like that. Tiny bits of white, caught in the lights from the house, swirled and twisted as they covered the grime, the dirt, and the evil.

Carla remembered how Francesca had taken them in so many years ago. At the time Carla thought she'd done it for all the right reasons. Over the years, though, Carla had come to realize that Frankie's behavior stemmed from her need to control, manage, and manipulate. Frankie's father had crushed her dreams; rather than fight, she had followed in his footsteps. Whatever Luis and Michael once meant to Frankie was now tainted with her need for conquest and revenge. Everything she'd learned in Cuba: the power of love and beauty and equality, had evaporated as surely as the snowflakes dissolved on the hoods of the cars outside.

CHAPTER FIFTY-FOUR

The suburbs in America all looked the same, Ramon thought as he rode in the SUV with Frankie's *soldati*. It didn't matter if you were in Miami, Tampa, or Chicago; it was the same blur of neon signs, chain restaurants, and boxy stores, all of them flanking broad roads that didn't have the grace to wind or bend. The only difference was how flat it was here. The land, the people, the language. The Spanish was dull and monotone, so different from the melodic accents of Cuba.

He glanced away from the window. Four goons were in the car with him, including the driver. The other team, headed up by Gino, was in another SUV half a mile behind. The snow had stopped, but the air was bitter, and the heat in the SUV wasn't the best. Ramon shivered.

When they arrived at the hotel, Ramon was surprised by its elegance. He'd been expecting a seedy space, dark and menacing, not a place with chandeliers, uniformed bellmen, and marble floors. It reminded him of the resort casinos back in Havana, where everything had been big, showy, and brassy.

One of the *soldati* climbed out of the car, presumably to touch base with their contact at the hotel. The others drove around to the back and parked on the street facing the highway. They were quiet, but it was an excited, charged silence that soldiers take on before battle.

Ramon could taste the anticipation. He'd felt that way in Angola with Luis at times. He'd never thought of himself as sentimental, but a hot, achy feeling rose in his throat when he remembered those days. They hadn't seen much action, at least until he was kidnapped, but he remembered drinking Nkiambi's warm beer in the leaky shithole they called a bar just to decompress after a risky patrol.

A few minutes later the goon came back to the SUV with two room numbers. Whoever was in one of the rooms had ordered food a couple of hours ago: burgers with fries and a Caesar salad. Then they ordered an action movie. The person in the other room hadn't ordered anything. The men in the SUV nodded as though there was a significance to the report.

The other SUV arrived, and Gino jumped down to confer with the man who'd gone inside. Then he motioned everyone out of the cars.

"Here's how it's going down," Gino said. "My team will go up to the room that ordered the movie. I'm guessing the girl will be there. We'll get her and deal with the others." He gestured to the men who'd ridden with Ramon. "You will scout the other room. On my command you'll break in and take out Schaffer." Then Gino pointed to Ramon and one as yet unassigned *soldati*. "You two will monitor the lobby, in case Schaffer makes a break for it. If you see him, let me know. *Rapido!*" He made eye contact with everyone, including Ramon. "Understand?"

No one objected. Gino nodded. "All right. We go."

***

Her kidnappers hadn't hurt her, but Luisa wasn't sure how much more she could take. As soon as they'd spirited her out of Ham's apartment, they threw a hood over her eyes and gagged her. Then they loaded her into the back of a car and took off. Without her sight, she tried to rely on what she could hear, feel, and smell. The men didn't talk to each other—someone must have told them not to—and the noises of the car barreling through the night weren't distinct enough for her to figure out where they were headed. As far as smells, Ham's scent was still on her skin, but it was soon overpowered by the body odor of her abductors.

Someone was smoking a cigar in the car, and combined with the car's twists and turns, Luisa felt her throat close up. If they didn't stop, she might throw up.

After driving for what seemed like hours, although she later learned it had only been minutes, they turned right and started driving slightly uphill in elongated circles. A parking garage? A moment later, the engine cut off, and a deep silence unfurled. Then one of the car doors opened. She was yanked out of the back. A man grabbed her shoulders and pushed her forward. When she stumbled, he cursed.

The notion she was in a parking garage persisted; it was cold, but not as bitter as it could have been if they were out in the open. Eventually they led her through a door and into an elevator. As they ascended, more silence caromed. The cheerful ding the elevator made when it stopped startled her.

The scent of furniture polish and astringent permeated the air, and Luisa decided she was either in an apartment building or a hotel. She didn't have the opportunity to figure out which, though. As soon as they exited the elevator, they walked her down halls, winding in what seemed an aimless fashion, probably so she wouldn't know where she was.

Finally they stopped. Luisa heard the catch of a key card, and a lock was released. When they thrust her through a door, the sharp smell of disinfectant and carpet cleaner accosted her. She knew that smell. A hotel room.

She hoped they'd take her hood off, but they didn't. They didn't loosen the gag, either, although she tried to indicate she wouldn't scream. But all that came out were moans and grunts. Someone bound her hands and feet with rope and pushed her down on a bed. At least the mattress was soft. Then a man spoke. He had an unusual accent. "If you needa go to the bathroom, gimme three whimpers. If you're thirsty, ya gimme two. Goddit?"

She nodded, all the while trying to figure out the accent. Was he from New York? Boston? She wasn't sure, but those were the only words spoken. A moment later, a cell phone rang. Someone snapped on a TV loud enough to muffle the conversation.

Luisa knew her kidnapping was connected to the map. They wanted the map as much as Gran. The why wasn't difficult, either. The only questions were who and why they'd shot Ham to get it. When she recalled the crack of the gun, hot tears welled in her eyes. He was probably dead, lying on the marble floor of his condo.

She had no idea how much time passed, but she must have slept, because the noise from the TV, a show with lots of gunfire and explosions, woke her. Then a cell chirped. She tried to concentrate on the conversation, but with the TV blasting, all she could make out were brief cryptic replies.

She must have dozed off again—how, she didn't know—because she came awake suddenly when someone knocked on the door. The men rousted her and shoved her into the bathroom while they answered it. She tried to cry out, but the gag silenced her. Before they let her out she managed to relieve herself.

When they dragged her out, the aroma of burgers, greasy French fries, and coffee saturated the room. Luisa didn't understand: she was miserable, almost in pain, but she was famished. How could she be hungry at a time like this? She wondered how much she'd give for a bite of a burger or a couple of fries. Then she berated herself for even thinking of taking something from these assholes. She had to stay strong. But for how long? Her resolve was starting to crumble. How little it took to render a person helpless. And all because of her grandmother. Luisa didn't understand why Gran hadn't rescued her. Where was she? More important, where was her mother?

Luisa needed her mother, like she did when she had her tonsils removed. The doctor had told them they were as big as golf balls. She couldn't eat or drink for a week and kept spitting out huge gobs of mucus.

Her mother had stayed home with her night and day, trying to relieve the pain, but it was relentless. When nothing else worked, her mother sat on the edge of her bed and stroked her forehead. Knowing she wasn't alone had helped. But this time, there was no one. If she ever got home—no, she mustn't think that way. *When* she got home, she'd have plenty to say to Gran.

***

The end came unexpectedly. Luisa had almost convinced herself that the residual aroma of the burger and fries wasn't bothering her when there was another knock at the door. The men immediately snapped to attention, and she heard the snick of what had to be a slide on a pistol. One of the men went to the door. "Yeah?"

A mild voice came from the hall. "We have a refund on your dinner. We overcharged you."

"Put it on the bill."

"Sorry sir, we need a signature. My boss said so."

Nothing happened, and Luisa imagined her captor checking the peephole to see who was in the hall. When he finally opened the door, the assault was fast, efficient, and thorough. Two shots in quick succession from a gun with a suppressor.

"There she is!" a man cried.

Someone hurried to the bed, while somebody else made a call on their cell. Luisa's gag and blindfold were removed. She blinked like a hibernating animal awakened and thrust into sunshine. When she recognized Gino, she started to cry. She didn't think she'd ever stop.

CHAPTER FIFTY-FIVE

David Schaffer had been dreaming about Christmas Day. He was only about eight years old in the dream, but his parents hadn't bought him any presents. Had they found out he'd been spying on them? Was this his punishment? He was about to ask when his cell trilled. He woke up and groped for it on the bedside table.

"Yeah?"

"David, it's Carol. I—I'm really scared. You have to do something."

"What are you talking about?"

"Two men kicked the door down a little while ago. They won't leave. They want to talk to you."

Schaffer bolted from the bed. "Who are they?"

"I don't know." Her voice was close to hysteria. "But they have guns, David, and they tied me up…"

The phone was snatched away. His wife's voice was replaced by a deep male voice with a thick Boston accent. "How are ya, David?"

"Who the fuck are you?" Fear streaked up his spine. The hand holding the cell grew sweaty.

"You don't need to get nasty. You know who we are."

"Let me speak to my wife."

"Sure, David. In a minute. After you uh—conclude—your business in Chicago."

David looked wildly around the room. How the hell did they find him? As if on cue, there was a thump at his door. David hurried over, hoping it was one of his men. But when he squinted through the peephole, he saw three unfamiliar goons about to break down his door. His stomach lurched.

"I'll get back to you," he rasped into the phone. Then he threw the phone on the bed, grabbed his car keys and wallet, and sprinted to the other door of the suite. He'd studied the hotel's floor plan in advance, then requested this room, congratulating himself for leaving nothing to chance. He cracked the other door, which opened onto an adjacent hallway. Clear. He eased himself through and raced to the stairs.

***

At first Ramon was frustrated to have been assigned such a trivial role. Then he stopped brooding. He was an unknown commodity to the Pacellis. Plus, his wounded leg made him a liability. He looked around the lobby of the hotel. Story of his life. Always unimportant, easy to dispense with. Still, he kept watch on the elevator and stairs. When the stairway door opened and David Schaffer appeared, slinking toward the exit, Ramon yanked his companion's sleeve.

"That's him!" he cried out.

Schaffer spun around, a look of astonishment on his face. When he recognized Ramon, astonishment turned to horror and he rushed to the door, careening into furniture and the few people in the lobby as if he was drunk.

The goon with Ramon took off after him, his cell clamped to his ear. Ramon limped behind. By the time he got to the garage, Schaffer was pinned against the wall by Gino's goons, and Gino was aiming an automatic at him. The acoustics of concrete in the partially open garage made for a clear echo. Schaffer was begging for his life.

"Look. I didn't hurt her! She's fine. All I wanted was the map! But you can keep it. Let me go. And my wife."

Ramon watched Gino hesitate, as if he was considering Schaffer's plea. Then he pulled back the slide on his pistol. Ramon saw the flash of the muzzle. Heard the sharp crack of the bullet. Schaffer crumpled to the ground. Ramon hopped over to gaze at Schaffer's body. A pool of blood oozed out around his head. Ramon squeezed his eyes shut.

Gino spat out orders. "*Vite, Vite!* Get him outta here!"

Ramon turned around. At the curb beyond the parking garage, a pale face framed in black pressed against the window of one of the SUVs. The girl. Although the electric blue light of the parking garage was dim and shadowy, he could tell she was exhausted. And panicked. He thought he saw tears trickle down her cheeks.

"Where should we dump him?" asked one of the men dragging Schaffer's body to the other SUV.

Gino glanced at Ramon, then back at the men. "The regular place." Gino switched to Italian and kept talking, but Ramon didn't understand. He limped over to Luisa. She didn't recognize him and reared back in fear.

He smiled and motioned for her to roll down the window. "I am a friend," he called out. "I know your mother."

She stared at him but refused to lower the glass. She probably thought he was part of the Pacelli Family.

"I knew your grandfather Luis. In Cuba," he added.

She gave him a wary nod.

"I am glad you are safe." He smiled again.

She showed no reaction, but Ramon understood. She was in shock. She'd just survived a kidnapping. He knew what that was like. He would tell her everything after she recovered from the trauma. He would tell her about his friendship with Luis. How they grew up together in Oriente. How they moved to Havana. How Luis was a student of law, history and art. He would tell her about the time he and Luis spent in Angola. What a noble colonel Luis had been. He nodded back to Luisa, about to make his way to the other SUV when Gino called out.

"Suarez!"

Ramon whipped around.

"Stop bothering her! Get away from the car!"

Ramon stepped aside and tried to raise his hands in a "what are you talking about" gesture, but he only made it partway. The bullet struck him in the chest. As it tore through his flesh, he felt a sharp burning sensation, a sensation that cut off his breath. He staggered, then fell to the ground, gasping for air. Although the snow had stopped, he was cold. And getting colder. At the same time, his brain was slowing down. It must be the wind, he thought. It must have picked up.

It was time to go back to Cuba. To the island kissed by warm, tropical breezes, not a frigid wind snaking down the street. Raoul was Presidente now, and reforms had come. Cubans could sell their homes and their cars. They could start businesses. He wanted to die where he was born, not in a strange, lonely city. He knew there were flights from Chicago to Havana. But he should probably find a Santería priestess before he made his plans. She would tell him the best time to travel. The last thing he saw were the eyes of the girl. She shouldn't look so horrified, he thought. As if a nightmare was unspooling. She should smile. This was a happy time. Ramon was going home.

CHAPTER FIFTY-SIX

When Carla saw Luisa come through the door in Barrington, she ran to her, threw her arms around her, and burst into tears. Luisa cried, too. In fact, her return triggered a storm of emotion. Carla hovered, refusing to let her daughter get more than a foot away from her. She immersed herself in the details of heating up soup—no one could do it except her—running a bath—she was the only one who knew the correct temperature. She attended to Luisa's needs as if her daughter had been released from the hospital.

For her part, Luisa couldn't stop shivering, and had difficulty speaking. She refused to take a bath, claiming she didn't want to be separated from the others in the house. Carla promised to stay with her and bring her downstairs afterward, but she still refused. Carla settled her on the couch in the living room with blankets and pillows instead. Someone brought a tray with the soup Carla had heated and a sandwich, but Luisa wasn't hungry.

"It's so strange," she whispered to Carla. "When they had me, I was famished. I kept smelling their burgers and fries. I would have given almost anything for a tiny bite. But now..." Her voice trailed off.

Carla tried not to show her alarm. She figured shock was setting in now that the ordeal was over. She spooned soup into her daughter's mouth. The doctor in her knew her daughter's reactions would be off for days, perhaps weeks. But the mother in her was profoundly worried and could only comfort herself with the fact that Luisa was safe.

Francesca emerged from her office where she'd been closeted with Gino. She smiled benevolently at everyone, then hugged Gino.

"*Grazie mille* again," she cooed. "It is over."

Gino nodded as if this was nothing special, simply a routine day's work. Which made Carla shiver. Then he rounded up his men and left.

Francesca's *consigliere* was still at the house, along with a few others.

Francesca explained that Gino's men had dumped Schaffer's body along with a bag of heroin in an empty lot on the South Side. "When the police come, they'll assume it was a gang shoot-out. A drug deal gone bad." Schaffer's wife was okay, she went on. Their partners in Boston had released her.

Then she went to Luisa and perched on the edge of the sofa. She stroked Luisa's hair. "But all that really matters is that you're home."

Luisa squeezed her eyes shut, allowing her grandmother's ministrations.

Suddenly Carla looked around. "Where's Ramon?"

Her mother in law didn't miss a beat and kept stroking Luisa's hair.

"Francesca," Carla repeated. "What happened to him?"

Francesca hesitated, then licked her lips. "Unfortunately, according to Gino, he tried to attack Luisa. He had to be stopped."

Luisa scowled and propped herself up on her elbows. "Are you talking about the Cuban man?"

Carla nodded and looked over at Francesca. She stopped stroking Luisa's hair.

Luisa twisted around. "He wasn't attacking me, but Gino thought he was and shot him. I saw it happen."

Francesca didn't say anything for a moment. Then, "You must have been mistaken, Luisa. It was dark. You were in shock. Everything happened so fast."

"No, Gran. He was trying to talk to me through the window. He said he knew Granpa Luis."

Francesca looked like she'd stopped breathing, but a muscle in her jaw twitched. And in that instant, Carla understood. Somehow she managed to keep her voice calm.

"Come, Luisa, it's time to go home."

Francesca cut in. "You can't leave. You know better than I she should not be moved."

Carla looked at Frankie. "I can no longer stay in this house. You have betrayed us. And not just Luisa. Michael and Luis as well."

"How dare you talk to me that way? You know nothing about my life."

"I know that everyone who was noble and good and pure is now stained with blood that did not need to be shed."

"I saved your daughter! Would you rather I let her die?"

"There was no need to kill Ramon. He was trying to help."

"He was about to attack Luisa!"

"He was an old man. With a bullet in his leg. He was not going to harm her."

Luisa cut in. "Gran, he was talking to me. I—well, I wasn't sure who he was, so I didn't lower the window." She looked like she was going to cry again. "I should have."

"He was a loose end," Francesca said.

Feeling a boldness she hardly recognized in herself, Carla shot a contemptuous look at Francesca. She straightened up. Her body felt different. Harder. More defined. Perhaps she'd been repressing it over two decades, but oddly, she felt more like herself, more comfortable in her own skin than she had since she'd lived in Chicago.

"He was a loose end only to you," she said. "It has always been about you, Francesca. Your need for revenge. Your need to balance the scales. Your greed. Well, you have won. Now there is no one to stand in your way."

Francesca retaliated. "Tell me, Carla. What is wrong with guaranteeing the security of your family's future? Making sure your daughter will never live in poverty—like you?"

"I would rather live in poverty than be like you," Carla shot back. "You manipulated Ramon. You knew he wanted redemption, and you made sure he paid for it." She blew out a mirthless laugh. "You turned his American dream into a nightmare."

"I saved your daughter. She's home. And her boyfriend is alive."

"Ham is alive?" Luisa's jaw dropped.

"He is. The doctors are operating on him now."

"Mother... we have to go to the hospital."

Frankie cut in. "Not now, Luisa... you are in no shape..."

"Gran," Luisa said. "Shut up." She turned to her mother. "Let's go."

Francesca reddened, her face suffused with rage.

Carla went on as if she hadn't heard her daughter. "You were the one who asked her to research the map, knowing she would do anything to please you. And then you tried to steal what wasn't yours. You have become a monster. Like your father."

"You're right about one thing," Frankie replied evenly. "It wasn't mine. It never was. It belongs to *her*."

Carla turned toward Luisa. "Now the map has not only your father and grandfather's blood on it, but others' as well. Ham's. The man from Toronto. And Ramon's."

Luisa looked up from her seat on the couch, a look of horror on her face. "Is this true, Gran?"

"*Querida*, I had to." She cast an imploring glance at Luisa. "I know you understand."

Luisa gazed at her grandmother in confusion, as if she was trying to sort it all out. Then her eyes narrowed. *She understands*, Carla thought. *Despite her ordeal, she gets it.*

Francesca barreled on. "You're young, but you will learn. You will be taking over the business one day." She smiled. "You've known that."

"But I don't want it," Luisa cried out. "I don't want to be a part of this.

Ever."

There was a moment of stunned silence.

Carla turned to Francesca. "If your son could see you now…"

Francesca cut in. "He would understand. Better than you—you—"

Carla expected the word "whore" to come out of Francesca's mouth. But it didn't.

"I want to see Ham," Luisa said. "Mama, take me to him."

"Luisa Michaela, you are not going anywhere. You need rest," Francesca ordered.

"Mama?" Luisa said. "Please."

"Come." Carla nodded. "We're going."

Carla put her arm around Luisa, and together they made their way out of Francesca's house.

***

Tufts of rose-tinted clouds scudded across a light gray sky. Dawn was imminent. Frankie was alone. Her nerves jangled. For one fleeting, panicky moment, she wondered whether she'd been wrong to investigate the map. To kill Ramon. Argue with Carla and Luisa. Then she suppressed the thoughts. She was no monster. She was on edge. Hadn't she been drinking endless cups of coffee all day?

Luisa simply needed to mature, like Frankie herself had. That's all it was. Once her granddaughter understood the stakes, she would see there could be no alternative. It would be an awkward, perhaps a difficult period, but Luisa would come around. In time.

After all, Luisa was the link to the future. Why else had Frankie endured the loss of both Luis and Michael? For the Family. The next generation. She had made sure of that. With Luisa's brains and talent there was nothing she couldn't do. And if Carla persisted with objections, well, there were ways to deal with her.

Frankie watched the sky lighten. She would go up to rest for a while. Then she'd call Macedonian Metals and tell them about the mine. She would offer them a fair deal. She always did. They wouldn't refuse. Then she'd figure out how to win Luisa back. She smiled, feeling the cold knot in her stomach ease. She turned off the lights and went upstairs.

THE END

ACKNOWLEDGMENTS

Believe it or not, the heart of this book evolved with the help of Twitter and Skype. I was looking for background on the Cuban intervention in Angola so I posed the question on Twitter. Thirty minutes later a British expert on Cuba and Sub-Saharan Africa, Dr. Edward George, replied. Turns out that was the subject of Tedd's PhD thesis, and he'd expanded his dissertation into a book.

I borrowed the book through my library. After reading it, we connected on Skype for a lengthy conversation, which ultimately gave me several essential plot points.   I remain grateful to Tedd for his time and expertise, as well as Twitter and Skype. Sometimes I love technology.

I also want to acknowledge Yane Marquez at Authentic Cuba Travels, and Mario Villa, our Cuban tour guide, for their patience and deep knowledge of Cuban history, landmarks, and customs. Also my friend Jorge Reyes, a Cuban-American aspiring fiction writer, who helped me with my Spanish. Don Whiteman and Mike Green also deserve hearty thanks for sharing their knowledge. As do Susie Levin and Claudia Szewki (Cluny) who helped me come up with the title.

Tania Tirraoro, verbalist extraordinaire, helped sharpen the book description and deserves special mention. As do Mary Ellen Kazimer and Georgette Spelvin who read the manuscript twice... and made this a better book.

As always, my writing group, The Red Herrings, keeps me honest. A reading list follows.

READING LIST:

Edward George
The Cuban Intervention in Angola, 1965-1991: From Che Guevara to Cuito Cuanavale
(Routledge, London, 2012)

Martin Cruz Smith
Havana Bay
(Ballantine, 2008)

Ace Atkins
White Shadow
(Berkley, 2007)

T.J. English
Havana Nocturne: How the Mob Owned Cuba and Then Lost It to the Revolution
(Harper Collins, 2009)

Catherine Moses
Real Life in Castro's Cuba
(Scholarly Resources, 2000)

Eamon Javers
Broker, Trader, Lawyer, Spy
(Harper Collins, 2010)

Carlos Eire
Waiting for Snow in Havana
(Free Press, 2003)

Ramon L. Bonachea, Marta San Martin
The Cuban Insurrection 1952-1959
(Transaction Publishers, 1974)

Faith Morgan, Director
The Power of Community: How Cuba Survived Peak Oil
Documentary, 2006 (DVD)

If you enjoyed this novel, please consider recommending it to your Book Club. Reading Group questions are available, and Libby is happy to appear via telephone, Skype, Google Hang-out, Togather, or possibly in person.

CPSIA information can be obtained at www.ICGtesting.com
Printed in the USA
LVOW11s2132270115

424634LV00005B/357/P